GHOSTS IN THE GARDEN CITY

BY DEE THOMPSON

TO MY SON MICHAEL,
THE LIGHT OF MY LIFE.

CHAPTERS

CHAPTER 1 – THE HURT FOOT

If I close my eyes I can see all of the events of that day with terrible clarity, right up until I can't see any more.

Mama leaves me and my brother playing outside that horrible day. She goes to the grocery store. Our new maid Miss Elaine is inside the house.

It starts off okay. Bubba and I play hide and seek for a while in the back yard. Then we swing on the swing set. We are both barefoot, and we have on shorts and tee shirts. We play hide and seek and I tag Bubba right off and boy is he mad! His face gets red when I tag him and he falls into the dirt. I tell him to zip up his pants and I laugh.

It's real hot, so we stop and get a drink from the hose.

Mama is gone a long time, or so it seems to me. She leaves us with maids a lot and I hate it when she does that. I wish she would kiss us and hug us more but she doesn't like us to mess up her lipstick or her clothes.

I swing real high, up into the sky, while Bubba takes a stick and whacks an anthill.

Tinkling music comes down the street. For a minute I stop swinging and listen. Ice cream truck! Bubba jumps off the swing and goes running down the driveway. He forgets he has no money. Even if it is the ice cream truck we can't buy anything. I feel sad about that 'cause Bubba loves ice cream but Daddy always says don't waste money.

Suddenly Bubba screams. Oh no! He sounds like one of those scary movies.

I drop down hard, dig my feet into the dirt, and hesitate. I can't see Bubba. Then I see him. I jump out of the swing running. My heart pounds. Bubba sounds bad! Bubba is on the ground next to the driveway holding his foot and howling. All I can see is the top of his blonde head. I run over to him and a rusty old nail sticks out of his foot.

Bubba cries hard. He's seven. I have never see him cry. "I'll get help!"

I run back up the driveway and duck through the chain link fence, down the step into the patio area, and lunge for the back door, grabbing the handle even as I push.

The door to our house is locked. I hear our dog, Ranger, barking inside.

Strange.

I shake the door. "HEY!" I holler. "Let me in!"

Silence.

I run around the house to the front door. It's locked, too.

Bubba's sobbing unnerves me.

I stand outside the back door and beat on it. "Bubba hurt his foot let us in!!"

Silence.

I try again. "Bubba hurt his foot we need to come in and call Daddy!!" I scream as loud as I can.

Silence.

Why won't Miss Elaine get the door? Where is mama? Why's she been gone so long?

I know from the long shadows that it's late in the afternoon. Daddy sometimes comes home in the long shadow time. Sometimes he's not home until I am in bed, though.

I can hear Bubba's crying and I am terrified. What if he dies?!?

CHAPTER 2 – TRIGGERED AT MACY'S

"Wait just a minute, Leigh," Dr. Mills says, writing on his legal pad.

Leigh Harrington scowls. She is now thirty-two years old. It's 1996, a blistering August day in Atlanta, Georgia. All the hoopla of the Olympics is past and the city has returned to normal. Leigh was too sunk in grief over her father's cancer and death to care about anything else, even the Olympics.

Leigh looks at her watch. She has carefully dressed for her first appointment with Dr. Mills -- a white cotton blouse, navy blue skirt, and a blue and magenta patterned silk scarf, black pumps with 2 inch heels and small gold hoops in her ears – more dressed-up than her usual daily outfit for selling houses.

Standing just 5'4, Leigh has narrow shoulders and short legs. Dark curly hair frames her oval face and green eyes. She loves it when people say "You sure do look like your daddy!" -- except that he was tall and handsome, and she always felt like a squatty peasant beside him.

Dr. Mills stares at Leigh with his washed out blue eyes. Leigh wishes she were anyplace but this dull office, sitting on his ugly brown couch. It's a nice day outside. *Mills is such a dork*, she thinks. *No wait – that's not fair to dorks. He's a douchebag.*

Mills pulls his wire-rimmed glasses off his jowly face and cleans them with a Kleenex. "I'm going to interrupt you for a moment, Leigh. "You've been having nightmares about that day recently? You said you thought about it the other day at the mall? What triggered you?"

Leigh stares at her lap for a moment, not wanting to recall what happened at the mall. She squeezes her hands together and tries to take a deep breath. Finally, she sighs.

"I smelled the bath oil my mother used to use. I was at Lenox Mall, at Macy's."

"Go on."

Leigh shudders, remembering. "I had run into Macy's to get some new sheets and when I got inside to the house wares department I passed a display of bath products by Caswell & Massey. I stopped to sniff the bottle of Lilac Bath & Shower Gel because the pretty label looked familiar, but I couldn't think why. As soon as I smelled that scent, that terrible day came rushing back to me."

Leigh stops and takes a deep breath. She is getting nervous just thinking about that cloying smell. Her heart races and her armpits feel sickeningly moist.

"What else? Keep going," Mills says in an unemotional voice.

Leigh stares at him in consternation. *Why does he have to act so uncaring? My life isn't dramatic enough?* she thinks.

"My heart started thudding and I started to sweat. I put the bottle back on the table and stood there shaking for a minute. A salesclerk came up to ask me if I was OK and I mumbled something and headed back to my car." Just recalling it makes her want to run out of the office and Leigh takes several more deep breaths to try and calm down.

"Do you want some water, Leigh?" Dr. Mills asks.

Leigh shakes her head. His Mont Blanc pen scratches the yellow legal pad languidly.

"Dr. Mills, why don't I remember the rest of that day?"

Mills finally puts down his pen and clears his throat, as though getting ready to lecture an errant child.

"Small children repress traumatic memories. You were four years old and you couldn't handle what happened, so your brain just buried that memory, repressed it. The brain cut it off, like a light switch. It's a coping mechanism. It's not entirely bad. We just need to be able to fill in the gaps."

Leigh nods her head. *No shit, Sherlock. You look like a big fat smug toad.*

They sit in silence for a moment. "Keep going. Include as many details as you can."

CHAPTER 3 – THE LOCKED DOOR

I finally think to run next door to the Johnson house. Mrs. Johnson answers the door. "Bubba hurt his foot real bad!" I blurt out, starting to cry. She gazes down at me, alarmed.

"Where's your mama, Leigh?" she demands.

"She went to the Piggly Wriggly and left us with the new maid! She won't open the door!" I say breathlessly.

Mrs. Johnson is dressed for church, in a pink dress and pearls and high heels. Her fingernails are painted pink, and she has big white earbobs. She smells like White Shoulders. "All right, show me where Bubba is, Leigh," she fusses. "You are always so overly dramatic child."

"This way!" I tell her as I'm trotting over to our driveway. Bubba stops crying when he sees her. He is curled into a ball of misery, clutching his foot. There's blood on the grass, and I can smell the blood. It smells like pennies.

"Bubba show me your foot Honey," Mrs. Johnson says squatting down. "Oh dear. That's going to need a tetanus shot and maybe some stitches."

"Hurts!" Bubba wails. I want to hug him but I know he won't let me.

"There's not much I can do with your parents gone," she says, standing up and chewing her lip.

"But Daddy – " I start.

"The maid won't let you in, Leigh?" she says.

"No M'am!"

"What on earth is wrong with that girl," she grumbles, marching over to the back door. She tries the handle, then knocks. "Hey, you need to open this door! One of the children is hurt!"

She tries the handle again. It doesn't turn. She knocks again, louder. No answer. She presses her ear to the door. "Sounds like there's water running in there, somewhere," she says. I am right behind her, wanting her to comfort me but she's all business.

Mrs. Johnson steps backwards, almost stumbling over me. "Good gracious, Leigh!" she says. "Shoo! You're gonna make me fall!"

I focus on the word fall. One time Mrs. Johnson fell on top of our dog Ranger and we saw her underwear! Ranger growled at her. The memory makes me smile.

She steps back and hollers again at the door.

"You need to come open this door. This child is hurt!"

Silence.

"Well, Hell. I'm gonna go call your daddy at the bank. Just stay here, Leigh," she says, eyeing my filthy bare feet.

"Is Carol home?" I ask. Carol is her daughter and my friend. "No, she's at Big Mama's house this afternoon," Mrs. Johnson says over her shoulder as she marches back over to her house. "Just stay with Bubba. Your daddy will be here soon."

"Yes M'am," I reply quietly, sinking down on the grass near Bubba.

The shadows are real long now. I hear traffic noises on the street, so I know some of the daddies are coming home.

We sit for what seems like hours. Bubba is curled into a ball, moaning. I can hear Mrs. Johnson on her back porch talking to somebody.

Finally, I hear a car coming. I jump up and look down the long driveway. It's Daddy's blue car. He stops the car and jumps out and runs over to Bubba.

"What on earth happened, Son?!" he says, squatting down beside Bubba.

"I stepped on something Daddy," Bubba says miserably, burrowing his head into Daddy's hand. Daddy is wearing his suit pants and a white shirt and blue tie. We normally aren't allowed to touch him when he wears his good clothes but today everything is different.

"Daddy I'm scared! That bad maid lady won't let us in the house!" I say, sniffling hard. Daddy scoops Bubba up in his arms, and sets him on the picnic table just outside the back door. I hold my arms up and he scoops me up, too. I cling tightly to him, burrowing my face into his neck. He smells like Aqua Velva, Tarryton cigarettes and coffee. He takes out his handkerchief and wraps it around Bubba's foot. "Hold that there, son."

"Y'all stay there a minute. Let me see what's up."

19

CHAPTER 4 – MAMA COMES HOME

Daddy pulls out his keys and opens the back door. I hop down silently and shadow him as he steps into the back hallway. We hear water running in the upstairs bathroom, and the radio is on.

"I told you to stay – damn – okay, but stay here Leigh," he says. I hear the anger in his voice but I know it's not directed at me.

He goes up the stairs two at a time and bangs on the bathroom door at the top of the steps. The radio is really loud, and some negro man is singing a song I've never heard before. I can see up the stairs, straight into the bathroom.

Daddy opens the bathroom door and water pours out the door, along with clouds of steam smelling like mama's expensive lilac bubble bath.

"JESUS CHRIST!" Daddy hollers. "WHAT THE SAM HELL DO YOU THINK YOU'RE DOING?!" He runs in there and I hear the sound of the radio going off and the water getting turned off. "Are you DRUNK girl?!"

I hear the back door bang open.

"Travis!" Mama hollers. "Where are you?"

"Up here Peggy!" he hollers. "Goddamn maid is drunk and passed out in the tub!"

Mama appears, running into the front foyer, high heels in her hand. Her hair is in a fresh bouffant. She must have gone to the beauty parlor and the Piggly Wriggly. I run over and bury my head in her dress and clutch her legs but she shakes me off.

"Leigh! No honey, not now. Stay here! Don't go up those stairs!" she hollers, running up the stairs. "Go keep Bubba company!"

The next few minutes I just stand there, unable to move.

Mama and Daddy are yelling. I hear mama open the bathroom window and holler out and tell Mrs. Johnson to call Uncle Harry and Aunt Martha.

I can hear Daddy cussing. Mama comes out and looks downstairs and sees me. Her face is wild. "Get outside, Leigh!" she hollers.

I creep to the kitchen and squeeze into the space between the fridge and the counter, making myself as small as I can. There's a lot of yelling upstairs. Ranger, who has been barking his head off, comes to see me, and I hug him tightly. He gives my face a reassuring lick. I take a dish towel and suck my thumb, and pinch up a corner of the towel and rub it back and forth with my thumb. I have not done that in a while but I am scared now.

Ranger sits in front of me, as if guarding me. His presence is comforting. I suck my thumb some more and rub the dishtowel frantically, listening to the sounds upstairs. I wish I could have my pink blanket, but I'm too scared to go upstairs and get it out of my room.

I rock back and forth rubbing the dish towel, focusing on Ranger's furry back.

That's all I recall for twenty-eight years.

CHAPTER 5 – TALKING TO THE TOAD

As she told her story, Leigh didn't realize she had fisted a bit of her scarf and was rubbing the corner of it back and forth, exactly as she did that long ago day, willing herself to stay calm.

Dr. Mills is trying to get Leigh to say more about that terrible day but she can think of nothing else to say.

"Come on, Leigh," Mills encourages. "It's okay now. You're safe. What happened? What else do you remember?"

"Look, I don't remember anything else from that day," she says, thinking how bad his breath smells. *Did he eat sauerkraut for lunch? Did he gargle with cat pee?!*

"Well, you remember everything else in great detail. You remember sights, and smells, and what you were wearing."

"You don't understand. I remember clearly because it was terrible, but my brain clicked off at right after Mama came home and I went back downstairs. It's no use. You said I repressed it."

Mills writes. Leigh wishes he would stick that pen in his eye. Feelings of rage are bubbling up.

"Go on."

Leigh looks out the office window, wishing a bird would crash into it. Anything to break the tension. She burps loudly, regretting drinking that Diet Coke.

Mills writes.

You're writing down that I burped?! Or did you finally notice I'm pissed off? Leigh thinks.

Leigh clears her throat and sits up straighter. "The next memory I have that day is sitting in my aunt and uncle's house, being told to eat."

Mills stops writing and looks at her. "How did you get there, to that house?"

"There's a gap in time. I have no memory beyond hiding next to the fridge and hearing yelling, then nothing, then eating dinner."

Mills writes for what seems like a long time. Leigh wonders if he would get mad if she offered him a breath mint.

"Before he died, you never talked to your dad about that day?"

"No. His attitude was if you ignore bad things they go away."

Dr. Mills frowns. "Have you ever asked your mother what else happened that day?"

Leigh shakes her head. "Mom doesn't like to dwell in the past either. She likes everything to be pleasant." Leigh flashes on a mental image of her mother Peggy wearing a linen dress and high heels, so tiny and blonde and petite and perfect – Leigh feels like King Kong next to Fay Wray every time she's near her mother.

"Well you said everything changed after that day. What changed?"

Leigh blinks, then forces herself to answer.

23

"Daddy changed."

"Changed how?"

"He started drinking a lot more." *He got drunk every night,* she thinks, but cannot force the words out of her mouth.

"Why?" Dr. Mills persists.

"I don't know. He stopped singing around the house. He started staying at work more. He and Mom had a lot of fights. Right after I started school, he got a new job and a few years later, he and Mother got divorced."

"Did your father ever talk about that day?"

Leigh shakes her head. "No. In fact, now I remember that I asked him about that day a couple of years later and he said we should just forget what happened, that we should look forward, not back. We never spoke of that day again."

Dr. Mills writes on his legal pad for a few minutes.

"Oh, wait a sec, I do remember something else. He said Miss Elaine had been drinking and didn't know what she was doing that day," Leigh added suddenly

"I know you told me last week, but when did your father pass away, again?"

"A few months ago. Cancer," she says. Even though months have passed since her father died, Leigh hates that word, and it seems unreal. *The pancreatic cancer tore through him like a wildfire,* she recalls hearing a neighbor say. She focuses on breathing, trying not to cry.

"That's right, I've got that noted."

Leigh rolls her eyes. *Way to be sympathetic, asshole.*

"Your parents divorced, you said? How old were you?"

"I was ten." Leigh thought about the terrible days towards the end, a few months after her maternal grandfather's funeral, and what greeted her every day when she got home from school.

CHAPTER 6 – THE NEW MAID

Leigh closes her eyes, remembering the days before her daddy left. The Victorian house was always cold, deep shadows in the corners. The white breakfast dishes were on the Formica table in the kitchen. The house felt empty, but as she crept from room to room she always found her mother, still wearing her nightgown, curled into a ball on the guestroom bed. There was a half-empty bottle of vodka on the floor. A turquoise kidney-shaped ashtray overflowing with Marlboro cigarette butts sat on the walnut night table beside the bed.

"Tell me about that time."

Leigh grimaces. *I've spent years trying to forget that time.*

"Mama was always passed out in the day, and screaming at Daddy at night. The house stank of cigarettes and bourbon and hairspray."

"Do you remember the name of the maid?"

"Elaine was her name."

"Well okay, but what was the last name of Elaine the Maid?" Dr. Mills presses.

"I don't know. I wasn't told that." *Do you not understand how it works, you twit? Maids don't have last names, not in my mother's world anyway.*

"That was the first day she worked for your family?" he asks. "Can you give me any more details about the day? Think hard. Think about before the maid arrived."

Leigh closes her eyes and thinks about that morning. Finally, she speaks:

"I am sitting in the den in my nightgown watching Captain Kangaroo and Daddy has already gone to work, as usual. Mama is drinking a cup of coffee and smoking a cigarette. The doorbell rings and Mama gets up.

I jump up and run to a spot where I can peer out at the front hallway, curious to see what the new maid looks like, wishing Lurline, our former maid, hadn't decided to move to Macon. I loved Lurline.

When I see Miss Elaine, I blink, thinking the early morning sunshine is making me see things. It will be four years later before I get glasses, but all I know is that far away things are always blurry.

The new maid wears a gray dress and white apron, like all the maids, but she isn't old or fat like the other maids I know. She is young, and tall and slender. Her light brown skin is just a shade darker than the color of Daddy's skin in the summer, not the dark brown color of most of the black people I know.

"Leigh, come say Hi to Elaine," Mama says in her formal voice.

For some reason my memory stops there, and picks up again outside that day. Why can't I recall Miss Elaine better? I saw her from the den doorway, without glasses, and I know I walked closer to see her better, but then the memory stops."

Mills has been busily writing on his pad. "Good details. However, I'm afraid our time is up, Leigh."

CHAPTER 7 -- PEGGY AT HOME IN AUGUSTA

Peggy Harrington, Leigh's mother, loathes writer's block. After more than ten years of writing mysteries, she has run out of ideas. She stares at the green words on the computer screen and scowls, then stands up and heads outside to her small garden carrying a cup of oolong tea in a Sevres cup.

Peggy, still a petite blonde, wears white cotton Talbot's shorts and a blue cotton knit blouse. She regards her tranquil garden, and the small oval swimming pool. In the late afternoon Peggy relishes being able to sit and enjoy the peace of the place.

I deserve this beauty, she thinks. *I earned it.* Her childhood was a study in ignoring her mother, Matilda Carruthers Spencer, and pretending to be normal. Matilda appeared to be the perfect Southern lady but in private she liked to drink, and everyone around her suffered for it.

An only child, Peggy grew up with few friends. Peggy decided at age 18 to forget about her childhood, since it couldn't be fixed. She refused to ever look back at that time, except to reflect on the happy times with her friend Jeannie or her father, who was as gentle and sweet as his wife was strident and cold.

Falling in love at 19 with the very handsome Travis Harrington (Leigh's father), dropping out of college, and having two children in four years was the easy part.

Dealing with her beloved father's death and building a life after her divorce from Travis nearly cost Peggy her sanity.

Peggy's current home is on Magnolia Circle, in what many consider the best neighborhood in Augusta, Summerville. Right after her divorce, Peggy had to work as a secretary at a real estate company for two years to make ends meet, but in the evenings, after her children were asleep, Peggy wrote stories.

Then there was the unfortunate - but thankfully brief - marriage to Miller Townsend, a man twice her age. He owned the most prestigious real estate company in Augusta, Townsend Properties. It was not a love match, but Peggy was after security, not love.

When Peggy discovered that Townsend was running a scam selling master's badges at ridiculously inflated prices to TV people, she changed the locks on the doors of the house, put all his belongings in the garage, and informed him coolly that they were going to divorce and he was going to pay her a nice alimony for the rest of his life or she would turn him over to the police.

He grumbled but paid it, until his death 4 years later. By then, Peggy was well launched on her writing career.

Peggy had become restless after Leigh and Bubba became teenagers. After some of her short stories were published, she started writing short mystery novels featuring a petite, feisty woman who runs her own exclusive catering company (Carriage House Catering) in a small southern town famous for a golf tournament. They were all loosely based on gossip she heard around town. Everyone in Augusta, Georgia, read the books to see if they could guess the true identity of all her characters. Each book included a dead body, lots of gossip about the dead body, and the occasional recipe. Now her publisher is demanding book 15.

Naturally, Peggy doesn't use her real name. She writes under the name Anna Matthewson. Nobody in Augusta knows who she really is, and Peggy wants to keep it that way. If anyone found out she wrote the Carriage House mysteries she would be shunned by everyone who mattered in Augusta society – and to Peggy the thought of being a social pariah was simply unthinkable.

Peggy works hard to stay under the Augusta gossip radar. Her author appearances and book signings are never anywhere in Georgia or South Carolina. Peggy checks into hotels under an assumed name and wears a wig and glasses, and keeps to herself. She complains about the subterfuge to her children, but Peggy actually relishes the secrecy.

Peggy looks at her antique rosebush and realizes it needs deadheading. Too many dead blooms – they make her perfect garden look funereal.

She heads into the garage but doesn't see her shears in their usual spot next to the rose food on the shelf. She opens the storage room door looking for her shears, and realizes there is an old brown suitcase she has not seen before. She frowns. Where did the suitcase come from? It's dirty, and has "RCH" engraved in metal letters near the handle. It looks like a feminine suitcase a fashionable woman would have carried in the 1930's.

Peggy pulls it off the shelf and there's a small white envelope taped to the top with the words "to Leigh, Love Dad" written on it in Travis' blocky handwriting.

Peggy stares at the envelope trying to figure out when Travis wrote it, but it's unclear. She grabs the handle, pulls it off the shelf, and takes the suitcase inside, where she puts it on the floor of the laundry room. She stares at it for a minute, frowning, wishing she still smoked.

It must have belonged to Rose, Travis' mother. Rose is a subject Peggy has avoided thinking about for many years. Keep the past in the past so it can't ruin the present, her mother always said.

Peggy doesn't open the envelope. She believes her children deserve their privacy. She was never the type of mother who snooped in her children's rooms or read their letters or diaries. Her own mother had snooped and Peggy had vowed to not be like that.

Travis had eventually built a cordial relationship with Peggy after their bitter divorce. As she stares at the old suitcase she remembers him coming by the house about six months before he died, to discuss his will, and the bequests to Leigh and Bubba. He must have left the old suitcase then. He knew he had cancer.

I really need to go in the storage room more often, Peggy thinks wryly. She goes back inside to call Leigh and tell her she has something from her dad.

CHAPTER 8 – THE SUITCASE

Leigh finishes dusting her light oak coffee table and end tables, and the tall oak bookcase, and puts the Pledge and the old white tee shirt dust rag under the kitchen sink. She turns down the stereo, muting Stevie Wonder's voice.

Leigh's eyes fall on a framed 8x10 photo that sits atop the bookcase. She picks it up and dusts it with her shirttail. It's a black and white photo of her and her father and Bubba. She was seven years old and Bubba was 10. They had been fishing at a small pond and caught 4 small bream. She remembers that autumn day so well because Travis and his brother Harry built a fire on the bank. They roasted hot dogs and drank Coca Colas out of the little green bottles, then fished all afternoon. At dinner time, they cleaned and roasted the fish. It was a warm day, she thinks, not unlike this one. *I played with Bubba and my cousins and we laughed a lot that day. I was dirty, my hair was a frizzy mess, but I didn't care. It was one of the few happy days of my childhood with Dad.* The happy memory of that day is why Leigh went to Wolf Camera and got the little snapshot blown up and framed after her father died.

The phone rings, jolting Leigh from her reverie. It has to be Mother, she thinks. Nobody else would call at 9:30 on a Saturday morning.

"Hello Mother," Leigh says, picking up the phone.

"Hey there Leighbaby," Peggy says brightly, using the childish nickname her daughter despises.

"What's up?" Leigh says with a sigh as she flops down on her couch and starts fiddling with the hem of her tee shirt.

"I found an old suitcase in the storage room that I think your dad brought by here sometime before my last book tour. There's a note to you taped to the outside, so he wanted you to have this old suitcase I guess. Probably belonged to his mother."

"Okay. Where is it now?"

"I wasn't going to bring that dusty old thing in the house. I just had the carpets shampooed. It's out in the laundry room. You can get it next time you come to visit," she says firmly.

Leigh ponders the suitcase. She is very curious about it. She knows almost nothing about her father's mother, Rose, who died before she was born. He didn't talk about his mother.

However, being around Peggy isn't always pleasant. Peggy criticizes Leigh constantly and tries to set her up with the sons of friends.

As if reading her thoughts, Peggy chirps, "Did you ever hear from Steve Andrews, Leigh? Did he ask you out? I know he lives not far from you there in Atlanta."

Leigh's one lunch at the Buckhead Diner with Steve Andrews was tense. Tall and good-looking though he was, his orientation was clear. His immaculate white Brooks Brothers shirt and starched black chinos struck her as a little feminine, but as she drew near him the expensive cologne wafting towards her and the subtle scent of hairspray nailed it. He was trying so hard to act straight, and she felt really sorry for him.

Leigh stifles the urge to laugh. "No, Mother, I told you, he is GAY. Somebody needs to tell his mother because she is living in a world of delusion."

"That's a very ugly thing to say, Leigh. Steve is sensitive, yes –" Peggy starts out.

Leigh can't stand it. She has to interrupt. "Mother, it's not ugly to say someone is gay. It's not a character flaw. Good lord. Drag yourself out of the fifties. Steve's a nice man, very handsome, nice job, etc. but he is gay. I should know, since my uncle Ed is gay! I just hope Steve finds a nice guy to share his life with. He seemed really unhappy."

Leigh had never seen any man look so uncomfortable during their very strained lunch. She didn't even order her usual date meal (a salad) but got a fat hamburger and a beer, not caring about her breath.

There is silence on the other end of the line and Leigh can see her mother as clearly as if she were standing in front of her – the carefully cut and colored blonde hair, pursed mouth, penciled eyebrows, manicured nails with pale pink polish, matching Talbot's outfit, size 4. Peggy sighs dramatically, which means she is choosing not to discuss Steve the Failed Marriage Prospect any more.

"Well, when are you going to come get this old suitcase?" Peggy finally asks. "Or do you just want me to give it to Goodwill?"

Leigh ponders that. Peggy loves to give things to Goodwill.

"I have no house showings this afternoon. How about this. I will drive over there today and spend the night, and leave in the morning. I have an Open House tomorrow afternoon," Leigh says carefully.

"Fine. I'll cancel dinner with Mark and we can have an old-fashioned Girls Night," Peggy says, her voice sounding very falsely chipper.

"Fine."

Mark is Peggy's boyfriend. Leigh can't stand him. He is one of Augusta's leading lawyers, but unlike many lawyers he is a crashing bore. He likes golf, expensive scotch, and Peggy Harrington, on his arm.

"I'll pack an overnight bag and be there by about 4:30. See you then," Leigh says.

"Drive carefully! You always drive too fast," her mother admonishes.

CHAPTER 9 -- GRANDMOTHER MATILDA

Leigh drives 70 on I-20, blasting an Earth Wind and Fire CD on the car stereo, and rolls into Augusta at 4:45. She has her contacts in and wears her favorite sunglasses.

A few minutes later she has left I-20 and she passes her grandparents' house on Walton Way, Augusta's street of lovely old homes and churches. On impulse, she pulls over her Corolla and stares out at the 3 story graceful Greek revival mansion, thinking about her last conversation with her grandmother Matilda, Peggy's mother, in 1974.

The late afternoon sun streams in as Peggy slips in the back door of the huge house, wearing a sleeveless fuchsia cotton dress and matching headband. She walks past a black maid polishing silver in the kitchen, and tells 9 year old Leigh to go sit somewhere and be quiet. Peggy heads off towards the front of the house and Leigh ignores her mother's admonition and follows, heading for the living room where her grandmother sits in a wingback velvet chair, swaddled in a heavy lap robe.

The room is filled with deep shadows, and hot, because there is no air-conditioning.

Despite her 74 years, Matilda's face is heavily powdered and rouged, her dyed blonde hair teased into a high bouffant, shellacked into stiffness. She wears a beige linen dress, stockings, and heels.

As Peggy walks towards her mother, Matilda bellows, "Margaret! Thank God you're here. The girl is stealing from me! That new one you hired."

Peggy closes her eyes for a moment, willing herself to be patient. "Why do you think that, Mother?" She knows "that girl" means the maid.

Matilda, enraged, just stares at her daughter for a moment. "Great godalmighty, why do I have to teach you things over and over Miss College Dropout? Nigras STEAL. They ALL steal. It's bred into 'em."

Peggy sighs. "Mother I really don't think –" she begins, but Matilda's raspy baritone voice cuts her off. "That silver candelabra on the buffet has been stolen and replaced with a cheap imitation. Just look."

Peggy walks over to the dining room doorway and gazes at the heavy silver candelabra on the buffet, where it has always stood.

"Mother that's the antique one that you got for a wedding present, not a replica," she says evenly.

Matilda jerks like she has been electrocuted.

"What? Have you lost your eye, girl?! How can you not see? That's a cheap piece of garbage, not my French Second Empire candelabra!" Matilda bellows.

"Now Mother, calm yourself –" Peggy says.

"You're crazy! I know my things!"

Matilda reaches over and grabs a silver julep cup off the side table and takes a long swig. Out of the corner of her eye she sees the corner of Leigh's dress.

"Get on in here granddaughter!"

Leigh appears in the doorway, ignoring her mother's glare. "Come on over here and let me see you!"

"I'm coming," Leigh says as she walks dutifully towards her grandmother's chair, avoiding Peggy's steely gaze.

"Come over here and gimme some shugah, Leighbaby."

Leigh walks over dutifully and leans over and kisses her grandmother's powdery cheek, ignoring the bourbon fumes coming from the silver cup. Grandmother Matilda occasionally slips dollar bills into her hands, so it's worth listening to her criticisms -- which are really aimed at Peggy.

Matilda pulls back and scrutinizes Leigh carefully. "Good Lord Margaret, this child is growing out of her clothes! That dress is too small! You need to get down to Davison's and buy her some decent school dresses! And those shoes are scuffed. She needs better shoes," Matilda glowers. "She looks like PO WHITE TRASH. Good God."

"Mother – I've been so busy with the library benefit and the Junior League rummage sale –" Peggy starts to say but her mother interrupts.

"Don't give me excuses!" Matilda looks at the unruly black curls framing Leigh's face. "Good god almighty look at this hair! Looks like kinky nigra hair. Maybe we need to get you some relaxer, huh, smooth it down?!" the old lady cackles.

Peggy stiffens. "Go get in the car Leigh," she intones coldly.

Leigh sits in her little Corolla outside the mansion and shakes her head, the memory painful. It was the last time she saw her grandmother alive.

CHAPTER 10 – A NOTE FROM TRAVIS

Two hours later, Leigh wears purple cotton pajamas and sits cross-legged in the middle of the old-fashioned four poster bed in her room at her mother's house. Her thick curly hair is pulled off her face with an elastic. Her glasses are on her face and she snaps her Dentyne gum as she listens to WBBQ from the old radio on her dresser.

Leigh's belly is full of salad. Dinner conversation was, as always, stilted, and focused on Peggy's assessment of Leigh's flaws – her need for a haircut, her need to lose 15 lbs., and why Leigh refuses to join the Daughters of the American Revolution, the Huguenot Society, or the Junior League of Atlanta.

Leigh has long refused to follow her mother's dictates. She refused to play with her dolls and instead played Hot Wheels cars with her brother, or ran around the yard with her shirt off pretending to be a Wild Indian. Leigh refused to take piano lessons, asking instead for a drum set, which was denied. She refused to be a debutante at 17 – resulting in a screaming fight with her mother that lasted for days.

Leigh refused to major in Art History at Georgia, choosing Business instead. She refused to join a sorority and told her mother they were all a bunch of bitchy, pretentious little snobs at the University of Georgia. Peggy bristled and reminded her she was a legacy Chi Omega. Leigh just laughed.

After Leigh graduated from college with a business degree, she refused to get some crappy job and husband-hunt in Augusta.

Instead, she packed her car and headed for Atlanta. In Atlanta, she worked at a Kinko's copy store until she passed her real estate exam, then she chose to live alone and refused to join any church, civic organization or country club – all actions which annoyed her mother.

Despite being an outstanding saleswoman and making good commissions, Leigh feels like in Peggy's eyes she's a washed-up old maid at 32, a total failure.

After dinner, Peggy goes into the family room to watch PBS and Leigh retires to her room, to contemplate the suitcase that her father Travis had left for her. She is vaguely unhappy that Peggy overlooked it for months, but decides to let that go. When Peggy is promoting a new book, she focuses only on that.

The suitcase is grimy with age and dust. Peggy didn't want Leigh to bring it into her room or place it atop the pink and white comforter, but Leigh assured her that she had wiped it off with a paper towel and Lysol.

Leigh didn't do that. She smiles, thinking *I am not a germ freak. I just wanted her to hush.*

Leigh finally takes the note taped to the outside of the suitcase out of the envelope and reads it. Travis's handwriting had become shaky.

April 3, 1996

Dear Leigh –

Your grandmother Rose was a lovely woman, who adored me. I wish you had known her. She sometimes suffered from "bad nerves." I do not know exactly what that means [mental problems?] but I know the summer of my tenth year her "bad nerves" were very bad, and she went to stay with her friend Eugenia Hill in Atlanta all summer. I was as lonely and miserable as a boy could possibly be. She returned with this suitcase and it was put into the attic, behind some boxes. I never saw it again until you were a baby. She died just before you were born, and we had to clean out my parents' house and get it ready to sell.

I've not opened it. I think it has something to do with that missing summer and I've never wanted any sad reminders of that time. At this point in my life I am old and sick and I still do not want to deal with it. I will see her soon enough, on the other side, and then maybe I will get an explanation.

Love,

Dad

Finishing the note causes a flood of tears. Leigh hasn't cried so hard in several weeks. She buries her face in the pillow and sobs for a few minutes before grabbing a box of tissues from her bathroom. As she blows her nose, she remembers the priest at St. Paul's telling her, "Grief is a process, Leigh. It takes a long time. Don't worry. One day you will be able to think of your father without crying."

That day has not come yet, she thinks.

Leigh wishes with all her heart that she could hug her dad and thank him for being there for her, despite everything. Yes, he had, on many occasions gotten drunk and embarrassed her in public, but she could forgive him that because when he wasn't drunk he was a loving and attentive father. He had always held down a job, never gotten a DUI, and was in recovery for years before he died.

41

When Leigh was little, he would get on the floor and wrestle with her and Bubba; tickle their feet, and sing funny songs. Later, after he tucked the children in bed, he would make shadow puppets on the walls of Leigh's room. She loved to see the shadow birds and dogs

cavorting across the wall. Travis would tell his daughter funny stories about the shadow creatures. He had large, expressive hands with long fingers.

Leigh loved the feeling of her father's large hand holding her small one as they walked around Augusta. Everyone knew him, and greeted him warmly. Travis was darkly handsome, with black curly hair and green eyes, like Leigh. He could charm anyone, and he had passed on his salesmanship skills to Leigh.

Tears again.

Leigh finally blows her nose and looks at the old suitcase. *Why did Grandma Rose put it away for twenty years, until her death in 1963?* she wonders.

CHAPTER 11 – ROSE'S SECRET

Leigh stares at the suitcase and wonders about her grandmother.

She calculates the years. *Let's see, if Dad was 10, that "missing" summer would have been the summer of 1942. The family was living on McDowell Street in Augusta. Dad often pointed the beautiful 2 story brick house out to me – I remember it had a huge magnolia tree in the front yard.*

Leigh takes a deep breath and reaches for the small suitcase. She tugs at the rusty clasp for a moment, until it finally gives.

A faint scent wafts out. Coty's L'Origan. Leigh has a keen nose and never forgets a scent. Her dad gave her a bottle of L'Origan for her 16th birthday, saying it always reminded him of his mother. Leigh inhales the scent and smiles. She has always liked it, and wears it sometimes, but never when she would have to hear her mother criticize the scent. Peggy would never wear something as common and inexpensive as L'Origan. She favors only Chanel products.

There are two skirts in the suitcase, and three tops. Leigh unfolds them and holds them out and examines them one by one. The skirts are plain cotton, a blue one and a yellow one. One blouse is white and two of the blouses are patterned with small flowers, one red and blue, the other green and yellow. One has an enormous bow on the front. They are as fresh as new clothes; clearly not worn that much. All of the blouses could be worn with either of the skirts. The clothes seem huge, though – too much fabric.

Leigh never met Grandma Rose, but grew up looking through old photos albums, and occasionally her Dad would tell Leigh something about his mother, such as "You have her laugh, Leigh."

From the photos, Rose was a thin woman, about 5'6, 110 lbs. perhaps. She had masses of dark curly hair, which Leigh inherited from her, a high forehead, an aquiline nose, and a generous mouth. She was always pictured in nice outfits that were probably a size 6. As she examines the clothes, Leigh thinks *These things look like clothes for a fat woman.* She ponders asking her mother to look at the vintage clothes, but then decides she doesn't want Peggy to know what was in the suitcase.

Peggy has never said much about Rose to Leigh, but one of the rare remarks was "She never looked comfortable at the Country Club" – which Leigh felt was a snobby observation about Rose's lack of family connections. In the south, the family tree is far more important than anywhere else, especially in old southern cities like Charleston, Savannah, and Augusta.

Thinking about her thin grandmother in the generously sized clothes, Leigh realizes, with a shock that they must be old maternity clothes. She has never been pregnant but it makes sense. The waistbands are adjustable, the blouses big enough to cover a swollen belly.

But this doesn't make sense to Leigh. *Dad was the youngest of three boys, all born between 1928 and 1933. By 1942, Rose was done having children.*

Clearly this was Rose's suitcase – there's a monogram of her initials on the case – and Travis said it was hers. Yet, the clothes look like maternity clothes.

Leigh quickly looks into the suitcase again. At the bottom, there is an old Bible, the black leather cover cracked with age. She picks it up and flips through the pages, which are as thin as tissue. It looks cheap. She puts it aside.

Nestled in the bottom of the suitcase, Lee spies a brown leather handbag. It looks like it would be carried by someone in an old movie. It appears to be empty. Leigh picks it up and smells the leather. She loves the smell of real leather.

Wait a minute. The purse isn't empty. Leigh opens it up and looks inside; an old lipstick in a metal tube, a small comb, and a crumpled up handkerchief are at the bottom. She sees on the side a tear in the silk lining of the purse, and feels of the lining. A small envelope containing a piece of paper is concealed there. She pulls it out through the small hole, carefully. The envelope is addressed to Rose Harrington, care of Eugenia Hill, but the address is smudged. She can only make out the word "Atlanta." The note inside is a small piece of plain white paper, yellowed with age, and the writing on it is faded. It's dated June 1942.

Rose –

I have enlisted and I am off to Fort Montford for Marine training. I don't know what will happen, but I will get word to you where I am, when possible.

Remember to send word to Millie when the time comes and she and Samuel will come up there.

All My Love -

Nate

Wow. Leigh sits back and ponders the note. It looks like her grandmother was having an affair and she went to Atlanta to give birth to a secret baby in 1942. Rose must have been really unhappy with her husband, Leigh realizes.

Leigh knows her grandfather Horace was an attorney and never home very much. He died before she was born. In photos he always looks very serious and stern, a rail-thin man with a prominent nose and receding hairline.

Leigh puts down the purse and looks again at the Bible. It has a name written on the inside cover, Elizabeth Cunningham. Was she related to Rose? Who was she? Travis had always said his mother was an orphan, and she didn't like to talk about her childhood.

Leigh wonders if Eugenia Hill is still alive. If so, she would have to know what happened to the baby that Rose had in 1942, right? There was no divorce, so the lover, "Nate," might have been killed in the war. Or not.

So many questions.

Leigh briefly ponders calling her brother Bubba, who owns a plumbing supply business in Macon, but then thinks better of it. He doesn't remember Rose, and Bubba is busy with his business, wife Missy, and twin toddler daughters. *He will not want to hear this. He hates messy family things even more than Mom,* she thinks.

Leigh packs everything back into the suitcase and resolves to do some research once she gets back to Atlanta.

CHAPTER 12 -- DREAMS

That night, Leigh dreams she is walking down city streets, turning down side streets, walking and walking, and she can't find her father. She keeps thinking she hears him, but he's not there. It's night, and dark, and she is very tired and scared. She sees flickering shadows on the walls of the buildings, like the shadow puppets from long ago, but when she turns to find the man making the shadow figures, there is nobody there.

She wakes up anxious and sad.

A hundred and twelve miles to the west of where Leigh struggles to sleep, a black woman tosses and turns in her bed also, but her dreams are very different.

She is ten years old and is crouched on the floor of a small clapboard house, frozen in fear, her mother's arms wrapped tightly around her.

White men are outside the house, walking around, laughing and shouting. She hears their heavy footsteps on the porch, and their coughs and grunts. Every so often a barking laugh splits the night.

She also hears, not far away, the crackle of flames.

The front doorknob of the tiny house rattles. "You in there nigger?!" a raspy baritone voice calls out.

She tries to hide herself in her mother's arms, too scared to even pray.

Above her, a large, ugly white man's face appears in the window, distorted from her vantage point. She prays he cannot see her and her mother, pressed against the wall beneath the window, hiding in the shadows, trying to not even breathe audibly.

His fat white face, stubbled with beard, looks ghostly.

Jesus save me from that evil white man, save mama, save us Jesus…

She awakens with tears on her face, wondering why the terrible nightmare had returned. So many years have passed, but the nightmare still pops into her mind occasionally, usually when her life is about to change dramatically.

CHAPTER 13 -- Paperwork

The next day, Leigh is back home in Atlanta. Leigh sits in the dining area of her small Atlanta apartment surrounded by boxes of her father's personal things. His second wife, Sandy, didn't want any of his personal possessions, and she boxed them up and gave them to Leigh right after the funeral.

For months, the boxes have sat beside her small dining table, unopened.

Leigh takes a deep breath and says a prayer, then puts a smallish cardboard box atop the table. It's filled with her father's clothes. She lifts out one of his golf shirts and holds it to her face, but Sandy has laundered it and it doesn't smell like Travis. She decides to keep one or two shirts and give the rest to The Salvation Army.

Her father believed in writing thank-you notes. After his funeral, Leigh asked Sandy and Bubba how they would divide up the funeral thank-you notes and they just stared at her. Bubba declared he was far too busy between his business and his family. Sandy, a cold blonde from Cleveland, Ohio, said she had verbally thanked everyone. Leigh took on the task and wrote a personal note to everyone who sent flowers, food, or came to the funeral. It took her two months, but she knew Travis would have been pleased. She only had to throw away four notes because tears had dripped on them.

Leigh finds a folder marked "Lawyer" and flips through pages of court documents and letters from his lawyer about the long-ago divorce from Peggy. One letter from her father's lawyer, Matt

McElroy, contains the following puzzling sentence: "Travis, let Peggy bring up miscegenation if she wants to. That word shouldn't scare you. She can't prove it. Also, it will reflect back on Leigh and Bubba if it's brought out publicly and I don't think she wants that. It's a scare tactic, nothing more."

Leigh sits there for a minute, feeling puzzled because "miscegenation" is not a word she is familiar with, but she has a very uncomfortable premonition about it. She grabs her college dictionary off the bookshelf in her room and looks it up. Merriam Webster defines it as "sexual relations or marriage between people of two different races (such as a white person and a black person)."

What a nutty thing to say, she thinks, sitting on her bed. *Daddy never had a relationship with anyone black.*

Leigh gets a beer from the fridge and goes outside to sit on her deck for a few minutes, watching the sun set.

When darkness has settled in, she goes back inside and sits back down to go through more boxes, after first turning on the stereo to a classic R&B station that she likes. To motivate herself, every chore involving paperwork is usually done to a musical background of the Temptations, the Four Tops, Diana Ross and the Supremes, The Spinners, and other R&B legends. Leigh knows all the words to every song.

The next box has a photo album. Leigh lifts it out carefully. The photo album has a brown heavy paper cover and black paper pages. There are lots of black and white shots of her dad, his brothers, the dog, the house. Her uncle Edmund loved to take photos. The corners are tucked into little white triangles.

Leigh only finds three shots of Grandma Rose. One is a formal pose with Leigh's grandfather, a studio shot. Rose wears a floral print dress and is smiling. *Grandpa sure wasn't handsome,* Leigh thinks. *I had forgotten that he was years older than Rose. Why did she marry him? Money?*

Leigh remembers what her father said about Grandpa Harrington. An attorney, he worked all the time. He had no hobbies. He demanded a bowl of grits on the dinner table every night of the world, and Grandma complied. Those are the only interesting facts about him that Leigh knows. Her father, Travis, refused to eat grits, perhaps in rebellion against his father's grits obsession.

Another photo shows Rose and another woman, smiling, in front of a small house on a city street. Leigh gently pulls it out of the triangle corners and turns the small snapshot over. On the back it says *Rose and Eugenia, Christmas 1941.* She thinks, *Rose looks transformed, happy, like a woman in love, right?*

Eugenia seems to be about the same age, early to mid thirties, with short dark hair, and a rather large, crooked nose. She is dumpy and not beautiful, but Leigh decides she has kind eyes and a nice smile.

Where was the photo of them made, Leigh wonders? She decides her uncle Harry might know. She heads back to her room and pulls her address book out of the desk. Harry answers on the first ring.

"Hey hey Leighbaby, how are ya' Darlin?" he asks, sounding jovial. Leigh wonders if he has been playing golf all afternoon, his usual Sunday activity.

"I'm fine, Uncle Harry. I just wonder if you could answer a few questions for me. Mom found an old suitcase Dad had left for me, and he left me a note saying it belonged to Grandma Rose. Are you familiar with that?"

"An old suitcase? No. Why would I be?" Harry answers quickly.

"It doesn't have much in it that's interesting, but Dad said she brought it back from staying with her friend Eugenia Hill in the summer of 1942. Do you remember that? I am wondering if Eugenia Hill is still alive."

Leigh waits. Harry exhales heavily, like a man suddenly told something awful. There is a long pause. Harry is a hale-fellow-well-met type of person but Leigh knows he's also very wily, which not everyone knows about him.

He finally clears his throat and talks.

"That was a hard summer. Hard to have my mama gone all summer. I was home from McCallie and I only saw Mama once, all summer. Edmund was busy with his photos and his reading and such, and Daddy was never home. He had some big trial going on. Travis was about 9, I guess, and he just moped all summer and was inconsolable."

"Well, did you ever meet Eugenia Hill?"

Another sigh. "Why you want to bring up all this sad stuff, Leigh? What difference does it make, now?"

Crap- he's fixing to shut me down. Leigh thinks fast. "If my grandmother had "bad nerves" then there's maybe a history of mental illness in the family. I think I should know that. It might explain some things," she says evenly.

"Mama only had "bad nerves" that one summer. Let's see... I remember Miss Eugenia lived somewhere near Piedmont Park, in Atlanta. That's all I know. I only met her once, when we were in Atlanta for a weekend. Dad didn't like her."

"Did he like anyone?" Leigh asks, half jokingly.

Harry chuckles mirthlessly. "Not too many people. He was a good lawyer, though. I think of him every time I eat grits."

"Yeah, Daddy wouldn't touch them. OK, well, thanks for telling me what you know. Love to Aunt Martha."

"All right, Honey. You take care."

Leigh calls her Uncle Edmund next,. He's a very busy photographer for a magazine in New York. After listening to the phone ring six times, a machine picks up, and she just leaves a message. Long distance calls are expensive and Leigh is glad her uncle will incur the charges, not her. Edmund has plenty of money.

Eugenia Hill, where are you? Leigh flips through the photo album another couple of times, but nothing jumps out at her.

Leigh sighs heavily and rubs the hem of her tee shirt for a minute, thinking.

She would be really old, but could Eugenia Hill be in the phone book? Leigh heads into the kitchen where she keeps the three volume Atlanta phone book. After plopping the heavy books on the table, she looks up "Eugenia Hill." There's no-one named Eugenia, but there's an E. Hill. He or she lives in Alpharetta, so likely not Eugenia. People who live in midtown Atlanta tend to stay there forever, unless they leave the in a hearse.

Leigh sits for a moment, thinking and chewing her thumbnail. She fights a battle against biting her nails, with varying degrees of success.

Leigh's friend Amy, had told her over lunch recently that the private investigator used by their law firm could find anyone. Leigh wonders if he would help her, and how much he charges? She decides she will call Amy tomorrow.

CHAPTER 14 – DREAM DIARY

Leigh awakens to tangled sheets, exhausted. She grabs her diary and makes a note:

Every night since Dad died I've had crazy dreams. This dream is a new one, but equally as disturbing. I am back at the university, trying to find my classes, and I don't recognize any of the buildings. I walk and walk, turning down street after street, desperate to find where I need to be. I don't know where anything is, where my class is meeting. It's sunset, and the long shadows make everything look strange. The campus is familiar, yet not.

Up ahead, I see a figure walking. It's Grandma Rose, pushing a huge, old-fashioned baby carriage. I start running, trying to catch up to her. She walks faster than me, though. I run and run but she gets lost in a crowd of students. I run as hard as I can, calling her name, but I cannot find her.

Finally, I sit down on the grass and start to cry .Where is Rose? Why can't I see her?

I woke up wondering why I would dream such a thing. Am I trying to figure out how to reconnect with my grandmother?

CHAPTER 15 – LUST AT THE DENTIST'S OFFICE

"Mr. McDonald? Can you just fill out this New Patient form for us?" the receptionist says, handing a clipboard to Bain McDonald.

"Sure thing, Sweetheart," he drawls, flashing a megawatt smile.

Beneath his dark tailored suit and impeccable white shirt, Bain McDonald is a large, powerful man, 6'4, with incredibly wide shoulders and well-defined muscles. He works out in his home gym every morning for 90 minutes, and plays tennis and golf also. His hair is coal black, thick and wiry, and his brown eyes are dark brown, nearly black.

His face, however, doesn't much appeal to women, with his close-set eyes and an overly large nose and chin. He has always known he wasn't handsome but he found early on that being strong and powerful were some consolation.

He sits down and quickly fills out the form. As he is signing, the door opens and a woman walks in. Peggy Harrington wears a dark green print dress with a white belt and white sandals. McDonald admires her, noting that she is petite and blonde and wears her thick, lustrous hair in a long bob. Her makeup is flawless, accentuating her wide blue eyes, but it doesn't emphasize the lines on her face. She looks, at most, about 45.

Bain recognizes her as an occasional customer of his restaurant. He reflects for a moment on what he knows of her.

Peggy Harrington is a force to be reckoned with in Augusta. Beautiful, from a venerable family, and a pillar of St. Paul's church, Historic Augusta, the Junior League, the DAR (Daughters of the American Revolution), Colonial Dames, and probably a dozen more organizations, he thinks.

While Peggy stands at the window, Bain walks back over and reaches around her to hand the nurse the clipboard. He catches a whiff of her perfume, and recalls a past lover who wore the scent, which makes him smile.

Peggy shifts to the left slightly, then quickly moves away from the window and back to the sofa in the waiting area. Bain is looking forward to observing her but just then the door opens and a nurse calls his name.

Damn, he thinks. *I have to get my teeth cleaned and x-rayed and all I want to do is catch her eye, and perhaps see that beautiful smile... actually it would be great to see her wearing nothing except that smile. Mmmm...*

Peggy notices him noticing her, but she barely glances at him, and her only thought is *what a huge baboon of a man. He's wearing an expensive suit and he has a nice body but wow, he's an unattractive brute.*

As Bain follows the nurse down the short hallway he glances back at Peggy. *I have to figure out how to make you mine one day, Beautiful.*

CHAPTER 16 – MEETING JACK

Leigh sits at a back table in Houston's restaurant in Buckhead, an upscale Atlanta suburb, having a late lunch with her friend Amy and the investigator for her law firm, Jack Briggs.

Jack looks nothing like what Leigh pictured a private eye to be. He is a small man, maybe 5'8, clean shaven, and he wears wire-rimmed glasses. His starched button down blue shirt, khakis, and loafers give him a preppy look. *He looks like a lot of Augusta guys,* thinks Leigh, *except for the badass leather bomber jacket draped over the back of the chair.* She hates to admit it but she finds the jacket sexy.

Amy pushes her salad around on her plate and tries not to look at her watch.

"Do you need to get back to the office?" Leigh asks.

Amy sighs theatrically. "Oh Leigh darlin', Larry is getting ready for a big trial out of town so yes, I'm afraid so." Amy's big brown eyes shine with relief. She stands up and brushes invisible crumbs off her gray silk suit and air kisses Leigh. "Here's my part of the check," she says, slapping a couple of bills on the table.

"Jack, Honey, you chat with Leigh about the questions she has. I've got to run!"

"Okay," Jack says, looking somewhat startled. He is only half finished eating his lunch.

"Bye bye, call me," Leigh calls after Amy.

"Of course!" Amy trills.

Leigh watches Amy walk away from the table, brown curls bouncing. *How does she walk so fast in those spiked heels? Torture devices. Ugh.*

There is an awkward silence. Jack chews thoughtfully.

Leigh wonders what to say.

So far, Jack has said almost nothing. As soon as the meal had started, Jack had ordered a hamburger and spent five minutes adding condiments and arranging it on the bun.

"So how did you and Amy meet?" Jack finally asks, wiping his mouth with a napkin.

Leigh watches his mouth and looks away, willing herself to be calm. "I met her when I sold her a condo in Peachtree Corners three years ago and we've been friends ever since."

"Good market for condos there?" Jack asks politely.

"Oh yes. It's an excellent area," Leigh replies automatically.

They chat for a few more minutes, then Jack finally gets to the point.

"What can I do for you?" he asks.

Not subtle. Just blunt. Clearly he is not in sales, thinks Leigh. Leigh studies him for a moment, wondering how much she should say. Before she can say anything, he speaks.

"I am a licensed private investigator, Leigh. I will keep confidential anything you decide to tell me, even if you don't hire me."

Leigh nods, feeling somewhat relieved.

He produces a legal pad and a ballpoint pen and he scribbles rapidly while Leigh talks.

"Well, I never knew my dad's mother, Rose. She died before I was born. My dad passed months ago. Dad left me an old suitcase of hers but I didn't get it until the other day. Well, um, and I found some maternity clothes, and a bible with the name Elizabeth Cunningham in it. Rose apparently had a baby that wasn't her husband's child, and the baby got adopted." Leigh pauses and looks at Jack. He doesn't looks startled. Leigh takes a breath and keeps going. "Grandmother Rose had two boys besides my dad. Um, so yeah – the baby. I know Rose stayed here in Atlanta in 1942, that summer, to have that baby. I want to find out everything that happened, and see if I can find my aunt," Leigh finishes. "I mean, if it was a girl." She resists the urge to nibble on her pinkie nail, and feels faintly embarrassed that it sounds like her grandmother was some kind of immoral woman.

"What was your grandmother's maiden name?" he asks.

"Uh – I think – well, honestly, I don't know. Wow, this is embarrassing," Leigh stutters, feeling herself blush.

"No need to feel that way," Jack says smoothly. "Ask one of your uncles, or look in the family bible. Hey, you said the name in the bible was Elizabeth Cunningham, right? I bet that was her mother."

"You're not from Augusta," Leigh replies, smiling ruefully. In her hometown, people usually know the names of everyone going back several generations. Leigh has heard her mother meet folks at parties and get to talking about the ancestors and suddenly they realize they are 3rd or 4th cousins.

"No, I grew up mostly here in Atlanta, I'm afraid," Jack replies.

"Well, Dad didn't talk about her much."

"I can probably help you, but I will need you to talk to your uncles and try to find out some more information for me, OK? You can call or email me."

"Um, I don't have an email address. I'm going to get one. How about we meet again in a few days?" Leigh asks. "In fact, why don't you come to the apartment one day soon, and I'll show you the photos? The album is kind of fragile."

"Sounds like a plan," Jack says, signaling the waiter to bring the check. "I work out of my home so I often meet with clients in their homes or businesses. I'll draw up a contract and give you a call. My fee will be forty an hour. That's the friends and family rate because I do a lot of work for Amy's firm."

"Sounds fair. Here's my card. Holler at me," Leigh replies. She hands him one of her business cards. "Maybe I can help you with some of it so you won't have to spend too much time."

"Do you have a cell phone?" Jack asks, reading the card with a puzzled look.

"I've got a phone in my car, in case of emergencies," Leigh explains, feeling lame. "Best way to get me is to leave a message on my home phone. I check it several times a day for messages."

Leigh pulls out her wallet to pay her portion of the check.

"Nope, you're a client now. I've got it," Jack says, grinning as he reaches into his pocket.

Suddenly, Leigh realizes that his plain face and washed out blue eyes are transformed when he smiles. *It's like the sun coming out*, she thinks, marveling at the change in him. *He also has a nice deep baritone voice, which is sexy. I hate high voices.*

Jack counts out exactly the amount of the bill, then stares at it for a moment and adds exactly twenty percent.

Leigh stifles the urge to giggle. "What branch did you serve in?" she asks.

He looks surprised. "Marines. Ten years. How did you know?"

"When Amy and I got here you were already here and you had chosen a table where you could see the door, that wasn't too close to the windows. You sat facing the door. Your posture is perfect. Your hair is very short. You don't make a lot of small talk. Your shoes are highly shined. Your pants and shirt say "preppy" but the leather jacket says differently -- maybe you're a big fan of Top Gun, who knows? Finally, you paid exactly the right amount of the check, plus an exact tip."

His left eyebrow pops up. "Impressive."

"My brother was in the Army for ten years. I know the type." Leigh doesn't tell him that she has also read every Agatha Christie book ever published, plus all the Sherlock Holmes books, Spenser mysteries, PD James, and so on. She likes to solve puzzles and to study people. It also helps her as a saleswoman.

"I see. Well, can I walk you to your car?"

"No thanks. I rode the train from Chamblee so I'll just hop on MARTA and head that way."

It only occurs to Leigh later that Jack likely watched her rear end as she left the restaurant. *Damn, I wish I had worn a skirt. I wish I had let him walk me out! How stupid of me.*

Leigh sits on the train and feels her face and hands tingling – serious tingles always mean serious attraction to a man. Jack is not gorgeous but Leigh senses he's smart and kind, and she loves his voice -- always a serious turn-on for her, a deep voice. For the first time in months Leigh feels almost happy and excited.

CHAPTER 17 – A CHAT WITH ED

When Leigh gets home forty minutes later the light on her answering machine is blinking. She hits PLAY and her uncle Edmund's voice booms. "Leighbaby! I've got a cell phone now and it's just darling. I carry it in my pocket. Call me! Here's the number!"

Uncle Edmund is openly gay with Leigh. They are great friends. On the rare occasion he appears at a family function in Augusta or Atlanta, he dials it back.

Edmund answers on the first ring. "Talk to me," he drawls. "Hey Uncle Ed! How are you?" Leigh asks, happy as always to chat with him. His response is warm, and his Augusta accent as thick as ever, despite his time in the north. "I am fine Miss Leigh! When are you going to come back up here and model for me again?"

Leigh giggles. She had flown up there for a long weekend the previous autumn and had a great time with Edmund and his boyfriend, Greg – the first happiness she had felt since her father had died. Edmund had even gotten her to pose for some photos. "I'm not exactly a model type, but thanks."

"Now Leigh, you are a beautiful girl, Hon. Don't let Peggy get you down," he replies.

"Mom is always nagging me to lose weight, you know. I'm trying."

"Well, I've shown your photos to several friends and they were all very complimentary. You have a lovely face and a cute, curvy figure. Maybe I can find you a husband from up here," Edmund said.

"I seriously doubt it," Leigh deadpans, not wanting to discuss her pathetic love life.

There is a pause and Leigh hears the click as Edmund lights a cigarette with his heavy antique Dunhill lighter.

"Leigh, you still there? I kind of lost you for a moment."

Leigh regroups her thoughts. "Yeah, sorry. Hey listen, I have a weird question. What was Grandma Rose's maiden name? And what do you know about her background?"

There is a pause. Leigh hears Edmund sipping a drink. Finally, he clears his throat.

"I know very little. Before she married, Mama's last name was Cunningham. She didn't like to talk about her childhood. She told me she was raised in an orphanage in Atlanta, and came to Augusta when she was 16 to work at the Bon Air as a waitress. That's really all I know. I wish I had learned more from her before I left home."

Edmund's flight from home at 16 had been caused by a huge fight with his father and nobody except his mother had heard from him for several years afterwards, until his father had had a stroke in 1958.

"Did she ever tell you anything about where she went in the summer of 1942? When she came to Atlanta for her supposedly bad nerves?" Leigh asks.

Another inhale, then Leigh hears him sigh. "I wish I could be more helpful Leigh. That was the summer I figured out that I couldn't stay in Augusta and be gay and happy, so I wasn't thinking too much about Mama and her problems."

Leigh thanks Edmund for his time and hangs up, but senses he is withholding something.

Leigh's dream that night involves her walking around a huge city, likely New York, following behind her Uncle Ed. The tall buildings cast long shadows.

She follows Edmund for miles, through the empty streets, but then, as she writes in her diary the next morning, *"... I lose him and I am running, running around, frantically trying to find anything familiar. I think I see Dad up ahead and I run, but I don't ever catch up to him. I wake up with tears on my face."*

The diary was, ironically, a gift from Edmund, who told her that writing down her feelings might help her deal with them. Leigh writes in it often, admiring the leather cover and heavy paper. She cannot shake the feeling, though, that her dreams are trying to tell her something important, something just out of reach. The Drunk Maid incident, that long-ago day, haunts her.

CHAPTER 18 – THE RIVER TAVERN

In Augusta, the upscale restaurant The River Tavern, is crowded. It's fashionably located on the banks of the Savannah River in the heart of downtown and caters to patrons willing to pay well for excellent service and cuisine.

Hushed conversations provide a low rumble of noise, and periodically a laugh can be heard.

The piano player in the corner plays an understated arrangement of The Look of Love.

The patrons are all well to do, mostly white, people.

Bain McDonald, the owner and manager of the restaurant, stands near the bar drinking a club soda, surveying the room.

His eyes fall on a couple at a table. *The Beautiful Peggy Harrington*, he thinks with glee, *I wonder when she will go back to get her teeth checked again?*

Her date, a bland looking man of roughly her same age is droning on, probably about golf. *She is pretending to look interested*, Bain decides.

Their dinners arrive. She is eating a seafood salad and he is eating a steak.

What a beauty she is, Bain thinks. *What an idiot that guy is to not appreciate her. He's boring her to death with his talk of golf and stock prices. If she were mine I would make her laugh with funny stories and witty gossip, then give her champagne and strawberries – in bed.*

He smiled. Years ago he had read a spicy romance novel his then-girlfriend had finished. He had picked up some tips from it.

Bain genuinely loved women, and had gone to a lot of trouble over the years to study them and learn how to win them over, since his looks alone wouldn't get him anywhere.

He wanted to get to know Peggy much better, he decided.

He had checked on her background and it was just as he had originally heard: wealthy widow, heavily into all the "old money" clubs and organizations, smart and sometimes funny.

Now to strategize. *How can I win her over?*

CHAPTER 19 – DRIFT AWAY

Leigh is in her little Corolla heading home on the interstate. She turns on the radio and flips around, settling on the oldies station. The song "Drift Away" by Dobie Gray comes on.

Memories fill her head. She had listened to him sing it at a bar when she was in 6th grade. *It was our Wednesday night evening together. Bubba was at some kid's birthday party. I wanted to go to Pizza Villa for pizza, a great treat. Dad picked me up in his little red Mustang convertible. We had pepperoni pizza. Somebody played "Drift Away" on the jukebox and Dad sang along. He had a great voice, kind of like Tony Bennett.*

He ordered more beers and played the song 3 more times, to the consternation of the other people in the restaurant. Every time the song was played, Dad sang along, louder and louder. He was a handsome man, and he attracted female attention wherever we went, but as he sang louder and louder, not even women looked at him kindly that night.

"C'mon Leigh, sing with me!" Dad exclaimed jovially, doing a little dance step next to the table. "Gimme the beat boys and free my soul / I want to get lost in your rock and roll and drift away!" Dad sang.

I shook my head and wished I could disappear.

Finally, the manager bustled over, a tall thin man with a bad comb-over. "Sir, please lower your voice and sit down. You're disturbing my other customers," he said nervously, fiddling with his clip-on tie.

"You have a fine eshtablishment here my good man, and singing to these folks while they slurp their beer and gum their pizza is lovely," Dad slurred.

"Look, Buddy, don't make me ask you again."

My face flooded red and I could feel my heart pounding in embarrassment. "Can I use your phone?" I asked, praying Mom would be home.

"In the back, by the restrooms there's a pay phone," the manager said kindly, giving me a sympathetic look. I scrambled out of the booth and headed to the bathrooms. I could hear the manager ask Dad if he would drink a cup of coffee before getting back in the car.

I was mortified with embarrassment. I went to the pay phone and called Mother, crying. Mother appeared at the door of women's bathroom fifteen minutes later and found me in the stall crying. I was afraid to go back out, fearful Dad would make me get in the car with him.

After that, we didn't do Wednesday night dinners any more.

Leigh takes her exit, turns off the radio, and drives the rest of the way home in silence, still feeling the pain and embarrassment of her 12 year old self -- sick with worry for her dad, and embarrassed. It was not the only time something like that happened.

When her dad had gotten sober years later he had asked her for forgiveness for that night, and all the other times he had embarrassed her in public. She had forgiven him readily, so relieved to see him doing better. The sleepless nights worrying about him had stopped for good when he had re-married and his new wife Sandy assured Leigh she would help Travis stay sober.

I miss you so much, Dad, she thinks, blinking back her tears as she parks in front of her apartment.

CHAPTER 20 – THE LIBRARY DATE

When Leigh walks into her apartment she notices the blinking light indicating there's a message on her answering machine. She hits PLAY and Jack's voice fills the room. Her heart lightens immediately.

She calls him back and sits on the sofa cradling the phone. "Hey Leigh, so I was telling a colleague of mine about this mystery of yours and he had a great suggestion. He said the main Atlanta public library downtown has city directories going back to the nineteenth century, when they started being printed. We can go back there and look through the books for Eugenia Hill in 1942 or thereabouts. It will go a lot faster if you go with me. What do you think?"

"What's a city directory?" Leigh asks, smiling to herself.

"Oh, sorry, forgot you're not in the legal profession. A long time ago most large cities printed directories every year, of all the residents – like a phone book but with more information, like job title. You can look up someone every year, see where they went. She may still live at the same house, or perhaps neighbors would know her whereabouts now."

"Cool. When do you want to do this?"

"You free tomorrow afternoon?"

Tomorrow is Sunday.

"Yeah, I don't have any showings, but is the library open?"

"I already talked to the librarian. She said come at 2:00 and we can stay until she leaves at 7, if necessary."

Awesome.

"Hey, what's the nearest MARTA station to there?"

"Forget that. I will pick you up at 1:30," he replies, chuckling.

When she hangs up, she feel ridiculously giddy, like she has a date scheduled with someone special. She feels like a child at Christmas, anticipating opening presents.

As she heads off to the closet to scrutinize her wardrobe choices Leigh feels happy and hopeful – two emotions she has not felt in months.

The next morning, Leigh awakens early, and showers and dresses carefully. Her curly dark hair is held off her face with a headband.

Leigh wears khaki slacks and a deep magenta twin set, remembering how her mother once told her all men appreciate shades of red. She applies light makeup and tries a new shade of lipstick, Strawberry Blush. In the back of her small wooden jewelry box she finds the pearl earrings she got for her 16th birthday, and then dabs on some Joy perfume – a favorite scent, with notes of roses and ylang ylang and sandalwood.

Leigh walks outside with her good summer purse, a small straw bag perfect for summer, and grins when she sees Jack in his big black Toyota truck with the extended cab. He reminds her of a young Marlon Brando in his jeans and a starched white shirt. He is leaning against the truck, grinning.

"Well good afternoon. What a fine day to sit in the library, out of the heat," he says, as he walks around the truck to open the passenger side door for her. *A man who opens the door and offers me his hand to climb up into the truck! I'd like to get used to this.*

"I haven't ridden in a pickup in quite a while, but this one is luxurious," Leigh answers, trying to look graceful as she climbs into the seat.

After she settles in, Leigh opens her purse and shows Jack the photo of Rose and Eugenia.

"Can I keep this for a little while? I think it might be helpful," he explains.

"Sure," Leigh replies. "I got a copy made." He places it carefully in his backpack. *A man who is organized and careful! He didn't just toss them in the backseat! Be still my heart.*

The ride to downtown Atlanta feels like an outing. Leigh likes sitting up high and being able to peer down into other cars.

On the way, Leigh and Jack discuss the Atlanta real estate market, and their research strategy. Leigh explains that she wants to learn everything she can about her beautiful and mysterious grandmother.

The main Fulton County library is a blocky, modern building at the corner of Forsyth Street and Carnegie Way. Jack parks on the street a couple of blocks away and they walk over to the library. On a summer Sunday, downtown Atlanta is quiet, and parking is plentiful.

Leigh steals glances at Jack as they walk. She likes the way Jack walks on the outside of the sidewalk, closer to traffic than she is. Her father had told her years ago that a gentleman always walks like that, protecting a lady. Jack holds the door open for her when they reach the library.

Even though he's just a few inches taller than she, Leigh feels relaxed and safe with Jack.

The special collections are on the fifth floor of the library. They spend a frustrating two hours going through the city directories from 1922 to 1944, searching for Eugenia Hill, by name, and checking all the residential streets around Piedmont Park.

There's no Eugenia Hill in the city directories by name, and nobody named Hill living near the park, that they can find.

Finally, Jack sits back and sighs heavily.

"Leigh, I think we are going to have to try something else. The fact is that it's quite likely Eugenia was renting a house or an apartment from someone and the home would then be in the owner's name, not hers. Or perhaps she was married. Maybe the home was in her husband's name. Women often weren't mentioned. We've found a number of men named Hill in the directories. We could try to write down their names and look them up. However, something else has occurred to me."

He takes off his glasses and rubs them on his shirttail. Leigh realizes immediately that the gesture must be a "tell" – he's really uncomfortable.

"OK, so what is it?" Leigh asks, trying not to sound frustrated.

"Rose grew up in an orphanage, right? How many could there have been that operated between 1908 when she was born, and

1924, when she was 16 and went to Augusta? Maybe the better thing to do is to see if we can find a record of her in one of those places."

Leigh ponders that for a moment, feeling small waves of unease just from the word "orphanage." Her only frame of reference for "orphanage" is the musical Annie, with little girls in tattered dresses singing and dancing – but in real life it feels much more sad. They ask the librarian but she has no idea how to locate that type of information.

"Maybe the census records would show the mother's name? We have the censuses here, on microfilm," the librarian offers.

They spend another hour paging through microfilm for the 1910 census records. No Elizabeth Cunningham shows up, nor Eugenia Hill.

"Do you have the bible?" Jack asks, suddenly.

"Well no, not with me," Leigh replies. "Why?"

He looks thoughtful.

"Family bibles often have records of births, marriages, deaths. They are great resources for genealogists and detectives," Jack explains.

Wow. Leigh had never thought of that. She never saw a bible at home, only in church.

"How about we pick up some dinner and go back to my place and look through the bible?" Leigh suggests.

Jack smiles.

"That works. I need you to sign the contract, too, and we need to discuss how you want to go forward," Jack says, as he stands up and stretches.

Leigh admires his trim body and muscular shoulders as he stretches.

I need to calm down, Leigh tells herself sternly, as they leave the library and head back to the car.

Later, at Leigh's apartment, Jack and Leigh sit at the dining room table, finishing up Chinese takeout food and laughing about old Monty Python sketches. Leigh loved watching that show when she was a child, even though it came on the one channel that was always fuzzy on the TV. *Jack is not the uptight guy he appears to be at all, once he relaxes. Anyone who likes Monty Python's TV show and has seen all the movies is someone I feel really comfortable around. Jack actually owns DVDs of all their movies.*

Finally, they start talking about Leigh's grandmother. Leigh pulls out the bible she found in the old suitcase and passes it to Jack.

"It looks like this bible was published in 1906, and it has no family information in it," Jack notes regretfully. He has examined the bible with the thoroughness of an archaeologist.

"Elizabeth Cunningham was my great grandmother. What about this? She gets pregnant out of wedlock, puts the baby, my grandmother Rose, into the orphanage, but buys a bible and gives it to the orphanage director to give to Rose when she grows up? A memento?"

Jack nods. "Maybe. Wait a minute. Are those the boxes from your father?" He nods at the opened boxes stacked around the table.

"Yep. I don't think they have anything useful, though."

He gets up and walks over to take a closer look, then reaches into one of the clothing boxes and pulls out a large manila envelope and hands it to me. "Saw the corner of this a few minutes ago."

Leigh opens the clasp, which is rusty, and peers inside. She dumps all the photos out on the table, all 25 of them. There are 5x7 school photos for every year Leigh and Bubba were in school, up to their freshman years of college. *My whole childhood is spread out in these photos.*

Jack reaches over and pulls out one of Leigh in 4th grade, with her hair pulled severely back, looking very grave.

"You look so sad here," he says softly.

Leigh looks at her forlorn little 10 year old face and nods. "That was the year my parents got divorced. I remember Mama and I fought and fought over my hair that day. It was a big fight."

Leigh sighs heavily, and looks down. The hem of her shirt is clutched in her right hand and she is rubbing the corner absently.

Jack looks at a photo of Bubba. "This is your brother?"

Leigh nods, and sniffs.

"He doesn't look much like you?"

It's true. Bubba inherited their mother's coloring, her fair porcelain skin and bright blue eyes and straight blonde hair. The only hints of Travis are his squared chin and big hands.

"He looks like Mother," Leigh admits softly.

Jack stares at the boxes for a moment, then turns to Leigh, his eyes soft and kind. "I've noticed over the years that things that are near and dear to folks usually get stored in dresser drawers with their clothes."

Leigh thinks about some mementos in her sock drawer. "True," she agrees, impressed.

"Hey, before I forget. Do you have Rose's birth certificate?"

"Wow. I don't think so. Maybe it's in the boxes with papers?" Leigh replies, nodding at some of the other boxes stacked beside her dining room table.

They spend some time minutes rifling through the boxes with papers. They find Travis's diplomas, old checkbooks, lots of other papers, but no birth certificates.

"Let me give my uncle Harry a call. I bet he knows where that would be. He tends to be very precise about records and such."

Leigh dials Harry's house but he is out. She leaves a message.

Jack ducks into the bathroom while she calls. When he comes out, Leigh is tidying up the table.

"Well, I better get on home. It's been a fun afternoon and evening, not the usual tedious records review I was expecting," Jack says, looking at Leigh. Feeling suddenly self-conscious he nods at her table. "I like things neat, too. Military training, I guess."

Leigh just nods, feeling again the warm glow in her chest, recognizing a kindred soul.

"Hey, call me if you find that birth certificate, okay?" His tone changes to more businesslike. "If not, you can get it from the Georgia Department of Public Health office when you have a chance. It's not far, just over in Brookhaven."

"Yeah, not far," Leigh agrees. Suddenly she wants to tell him how she feels but can only blurt out "Hey, um, I had fun today."

"I did too," Jack replies softly, looking into her eyes and causing major tingles.

They walk to the front door.

"We will get this done, Leigh," Jack says, smiling down at her.

"Oh yeah, I'm sure we'll figure it out – I mean, you'll help me," Leigh responds, opening the door. *I wish he would kiss me!*

Jack just smiles and walks out the door.

Leigh goes to bed thinking about the incident from childhood when Bubba cut his foot. In her mind, she calls it The Drunk Maid Incident. She has the nagging feeling that something about that day holds the key, somehow, to understanding why her grandmother gave up a baby in 1942.

CHAPTER 21 -- JESSICA

Jack calls Leigh to say he has found more information regarding orphanages, but he found no record of her grandmother in either of the two operating in the city in 1908.

"I've got to turn my attention to a big investigation for a firm in Savannah, so I'll be out of town for a couple of weeks but I'll call you when I get back."

"I understand," Leigh says, trying to hide the disappointment in her voice. Jack has filled her thoughts in the week since she last saw him.

A week after Jack's call, Leigh answers the door and her upstairs neighbor and friend, Jessica Birnbaum stands there holding a bottle of wine, a box of Ritz crackers, and three boxes of Girl Scout thin mints. Jessica's long red hair sits precariously atop her head in a topknot and she's wearing sweatpants and an AC/DC tee shirt.

"Hey!" Jessica says in her East Tennessee twang. "I heard you crying last night like your heart was broken. What's up?!"

Leigh opens the door and Jessica comes in. Jessica gives her a hug.

The first time they met was the day Leigh moved into the apartment, and Jessica brought over a pizza and a bottle of wine, "Hey! Jessica Birnbaum! I'm your upstairs neighbor. I thought we should celebrate another single woman in the building!" Covered in grime and sweaty, Leigh could only gape at Jessica, hearing the twangy accent come out of the chunky little woman.

"I'm sorry, did you say Birnbaum?" Leigh asks, thinking she has mis-heard.

"Yep, prob'ly the only East Tennessee raised red-headed Jewish lady in all of Atlanta," Jessica chuckles.

"Well, thanks for coming over. Nice to, um, meet a neighbor."

Jessica barreled in, set down the pizza and wine in the kitchen, and surveyed the mess. "Here, let's get the table cleared off," she said, moving swiftly and decisively, while Leigh just gaped.

Leigh watched, fascinated, as Jessica bustled into the kitchen and grabbed two paper towels off the roll, then poured the wine into two red solo cups.

"What's the matter? Embarrassed? Don't be! Everyone's apartment looks like shit the day they move in! So you're wondering who I am and where I come from -- still, I can see it in

your eyes. And by the way, I have never seen someone with gorgeous black curly hair like yours and green eyes. What a combination! Scarlet O'Hara, reincarnated!"

Leigh laughed and shook her head.

That was six years before.

The two have socialized casually; gone out for a beer, watched a couple of movies together, and for a while were walking together every day. Now Jessica has been out of touch for several months while settling the estate of her mother in Florida, and Leigh realizes how much she has missed her friend.

"Thanks for the hug. I needed it. I'm sorry. If you've been hearing me, I've been way too loud. God that's embarrassing." They walk into the tiny kitchen where Jessica sets everything on the counter. "I think I'm coping really well, but sometimes I just have to cry a while."

"Honey, I brought wine, and I was hoping you would have some cheese for the Ritz. After we've eaten a few – 'cause, hey, cheese and crackers are real food, right -- we can polish off the Thin Mints. To hell with the diets! Tell me what's going on, and I need details. I saw a good looking guy here not long ago so this nightly pity party confuses me."

"Well, you know how much I love cheese," Leigh says with a smile, pulling out a fine Havarti. Everyone who knows her knows her love of cheese -- Camembert, Gouda, salads made with buffalo mozzarella, cheese soufflés, cheesecake.

A few minutes later the two women are sitting on the sofa, noshing on cheese and Ritz crackers and drinking wine from a set of crystal glasses.

Leigh tells her about the suitcase, and the search for more information about Rose.

After two hours, more wine, and many Thin Mints, Jessica is up to speed on Leigh's issues.

"Girl, this is better than a soap opera. Your grandmother had a secret love child and put her up for adoption? That's better than Jerry Springer," Jessica says, burping.

"Yeah, but I just have this bad feeling that there are terrible secrets in my family and I don't know if I want to know or not. For several nights my only dinner has been a pint of Ben & Jerry's ice cream, New York Super Fudge Chunk."

"Oh my God! Isn't that the BEST Ben & Jerry's?! My butt is made of that ice cream!"

Leigh laughs, marveling at how Jessica can lift her spirits.

"Well, yeah, but if I keep eating it like that I will have to buy new pants. I need to get a grip!" moans Leigh.

"So go see the new shrink and let him help you."

Leigh had told her about a new psychologist suggested by a friend.

"I will. I just hope he can help me recall what happened that day."

Jessica rolls her eyes. "I remember nothing before the age of six, except playing doll with my dog Bob. What has your mom said about it?"

Leigh shudders. "I haven't mentioned any of this to her. She would just tell me I was imagining things and I should concentrate on finding a husband."

"So, why don't you?!" Jessica says. "I mean, really. You're a beautiful girl!"

Leigh regards her friend with a bemused smile. "Have you ever watched me walk away? I have so many flaws. I never felt like I looked right for Augusta. I'm not a blonde size 2. I never fit in there."

Jessica lifts her eyebrows and fixes Leigh with a withering look. "I grew up Jewish in East Tennessee! I know all about not fitting in, trust me. But you've made a good life for yourself here. You're a successful real estate agent. You have a hunky possible boyfriend. You're an expert at mysteries, so I know you'll solve this one! Quit kvetching."

Leigh laughs and carries the cheese plate to the kitchen.

"I'm really glad you came over. Thanks for letting me vent," Leigh says, settling back on the couch. "You going back to work soon?!"

Jessica sighs and shakes her head. "Yeah, I have to, unfortunately. Mother's estate had to be divided four ways so I didn't get much. I can just work in my uncle's law office until something better opens up."

"When are you going to quit the office jobs and follow your dream?" Leigh chides her gently.

"Well, I don't know if Atlanta needs a dog spa, but if you can find me a place to locate it, and a backer, we're in business!" Jessica responds. "Speaking of dogs, I need to get back upstairs and check on Bucky." Bucky is her Yorkie Poo, a 7 lb. butterball, much adored – fussed over, bathed, and photographed more than most human babies.

"I don't do commercial real estate, but I'll ask around," Leigh promises. "Thanks for coming over. I needed the company.

"Well we cleaned out my stash of Thin Mints so tomorrow the diet starts anew!" Jessica laughs, hugging her friend gently before she leaves.

CHAPTER 22 – A NEW AGE THERAPIST

Unlike Dr. Mills, Dr. Simerly's office is decorated in soft blues and beiges, with a big soft couch, lots of pastel cushions, crystals, figurines of angels and troll-looking people. The bookshelves have books with strange titles about past life regression, hypnosis, and near death experiences. However, he also has the normal educational diplomas.

His New Patient form is pretty similar to Dr. Mills' form, and then he spends some time talking with Leigh about her goals with therapy and her background.

Leigh tells him about the Drunk Maid incident, and the gaps in her memory of that day.

Dr. Simerly is in his 50's, a tall thin man with a nice head of graying hair, and wire-rimmed glasses. He's wearing khakis and a starched oxford cloth shirt, looking more preppy than New Agey, Leigh decides.

"Do you want to consult your spirit guides and ask if that memory holds a key to something you need to know today?" he asks.

Spirit guides. Hmm… I need to give this some thought. "I don't know."

"Okay. We're almost out of time, so why don't we address that next time, and we can talk some more about hypnosis and past life regression if that's what you'd like to try," he suggests. Leigh nods, suddenly feeling scared and not knowing why. *I feel open to exploring those things but wary, too. I can hear my mother's voice in my head, saying "What nonsense, what a charlatan, Leigh." SHUT UP, Mom..*

Leigh makes an appointment for the following week.

As she walks out of his building and into the sunshine of a warm September morning, Leigh realizes that she actually feels lighter in spirit, freer, and there's some hopefulness, too.

When Leigh gets home she decides to call the Georgia Department of Public Health to see if she can get a copy of the birth certificate of her grandmother. After waiting on Hold for ten minutes, she learns that she can get it, but it will entail proving she has a right to it. She has her birth certificate. It only proves who her parents are. She decides to call her uncle Harry at his office, to see if he has her father's birth certificate.

"Hey Harry, how are you?"

"Fine, fine, Darlin' what's up?" Harry asks.

"Um, you were the executor of Dad's estate. Did you ever go and look in the safe deposit box at the bank?"

There is a long pause. Too long.

"Uncle Harry? You there?"

He clears his throat. "Yep, yep, I cleaned it out. It just had a bunch of papers, Leigh, old life insurance policies, bank books, deeds, stuff you wouldn't be interested in. I also got the stuff from his office, from Sandy. Same deal, nothing interesting."

Leigh tries not to get vexed with him.

"Well, since I am his daughter, don't you think it would be okay for me to see what was in there?" She asks. "Couldn't you just look for Dad's birth certificate and mail it or fax it to me?"

"Why do you want to see it?" he asks warily.

"Look, I don't want to argue about this. Can't you just take a quick look at what was in there? What would it hurt?"

Another pause.

"Well, the boxes are out in the garage somewhere. I don't even know where, exactly. If you want to come look around for it, that would be okay," he gives in.

Leigh ponders this. She has a weekend of house showings, a very busy two days.

"I've got a busy weekend this weekend. Maybe next weekend I can drive down," she says.

"OK, that's fine. Listen, I've got to go into a meeting," Harry says. "You take care now."

Leigh hangs up the phone and stews in her own juices for a few minutes, as her grandmother would say.

Harry, normally the most jovial person she knows, is hiding something. Leigh can feel it. *What is there to hide? My instincts tell me that I am being stonewalled by my own family.*

CHAPTER 23 – A COVERT TRIP

The next day Leigh is up early, to make the 2 and a half hour drive to Augusta before the traffic gets bad. She feels the timing is right. *It's Thursday morning. Harry will be at work. Martha will spend all morning in the beauty parlor and then go out to lunch, like she has for the past thirty years.*

Leigh pulls up to the brick house of her aunt and uncle at 9:30 and sees no cars in the driveway. She parks two doors down, and walks up to the back patio door to knock.

The maid, Ruby, is elderly, and rarely hears any knocking or doorbell. Leigh fishes around in one of the twenty flowerpots on the patio and finds the spare key. She lets herself in the back door. Ruby doesn't see her. Leigh tiptoes through the laundry room and out to the garage. *If Ruby finds me I will just say Harry said I could get my Dad's box of stuff. Ruby has known me all my life and won't question it.*

Harry's garage is an epic mess. Cardboard and plastic boxes are piled haphazardly, everywhere. Boxes of Christmas stuff. Old lamps. Suitcases. Fishing gear is in one corner; a pile of golf clubs, balls, shoes, and other golf stuff is in another corner. There are tools on a workbench, even though Harry rarely does anything with them. No room for a car.

Most of the stuff has been here for years and years and has thick dust on it. Leigh pulls out a flashlight and shines it around, because the overhead light is weak. There's a path to the deep freezer. Leigh looks at various boxes near there and eventually locates one that says "Travis" on the side in black ink. It's a banker's box. There are three other white banker's boxes with lids that surely came from the office.

Leigh hesitates, thoughts racing. *The longer I stay in the garage, the greater the chance I will get caught. Still, if there are no birth certificates and nothing about my grandmother, there's no need to take the boxes.* Glad she wore old shorts and a tee shirt, Leigh settles down on the bottom step from the back door and flips open the lid of the first box.

Harry was right. Lots of boring papers. Bank statements. Dad's will. Then she sees it. *A manila folder marked "Birth Certificates." Thanks for being neat and orderly, Dad.*

Leigh pulls out the two birth certificates and sees one is for Harry and one is for Edmund. She scans them quickly. Nothing interesting. *Where is Dad's?* she wonders. She keeps looking. There's a Marriage Certificate for Horace Harrington and Rose Cunningham. Aha! she wants to shout.

It's dated May 1, 1928. It just says they were married at St. Paul's Episcopal Church. The license might have more information. *Wait a minute.* There are witnesses listed.

Ambrose Pettigrew and Eugenia Davenport. *So Eugenia wasn't married yet and Hill is her married name.*

Leigh tucks the folder under her arm and tiptoes quietly out of the garage and eases out the back door. She replaces the key in the flowerpot. She can hear the TV blaring in the family room, where Ruby is likely watching her soap operas and ironing.

As she walks quickly back to her car, Leigh decides to head to the Richmond County courthouse and see if she can get a copy of their marriage license, if it still exists after almost 70 years. She has never seen a marriage license and has no idea what might be on one, but decides it can't hurt to look.

The courthouse is downtown on Greene Street, but she gets there in less than 15 minutes.

Leigh is directed to the Probate Court clerk. After taking two wrong turns down long hallways, she encounters a middle-aged white lady with bouffant hair and a perky yellow top. Her nametag reads Miss Jenkins.

Leigh explains that she needs to see her grandparents' marriage license from 1928. The clerk has to consult her supervisor. Leigh waits for a while on a hard plastic chair. Finally, Miss Jenkins reappears, frowning.

"Well here's what my supervisor said, honey. Those old licenses are in a separate building where all the pre-1960 licenses are archived."

"Okay, but where is that building?" Leigh asks.

She gets directions and walks over to the nondescript building two blocks down.

This time the clerk is a young black female with very long fingernails painted blue. Leigh fills out a form and waits. The clerk explains in a bored voice that the old marriage licenses are filed away by date, not name, and it will take time to find them.

"That's fine. I can look through all of 1928 if need be."

The clerk looks annoyed. "Just a minute," she says, before walking through a doorway marked EMPLOYEES ONLY.

Leigh waits another 10 minutes. Finally, the clerk reappears and hands her a yellowing folder.

"These are all the licenses issued in April and May of 1928. You can sit right over there and look through them."

Leigh sits at the scarred old wooden table and spends nearly half an hour going through the folder. The pages are old and yellowing. *I bet all these people who got married back then are dead, and in their graves. How sad.*

When she finally finds the license, the spidery handwriting in faded brown ink is hard to read. Rose's address is just listed as "the Bon Air." *Grandaddy's address was his parents' house. It has Race listed. I wonder if that's still done. Seems irrelevant, to me.*

"Can I get a copy of this?" Leigh asks the clerk.

"Copies are a dollar a page. I will make it for you," the clerk answers.

While Leigh is waiting, she studies another license.

When Leigh gets back the copy, it's a poor copy. She studies the original and goes over some of the writing on the copied page with a black pen, then folds up the copy and sticks it in her purse.

Leigh is walking back down Greene Street to her car, which is parked next to a meter, when a man walks around a corner and calls out to her. It's Hugh Brannon, a neighbor of Peggy's. Hugh sells insurance. Hugh is about Leigh's mom's age and wears a blue suit, white shirt, and yellow tie. He greets Leigh warmly.

Leigh has to stop and chat. The two face each other next to an old brick building.

"Hey there Leigh! What are you doing in our fair city on a week day?"

"I just came over to search for some old records in the courthouse. How's Margie?" Leigh asks, quickly wanting to steer the conversation away from herself.

"Oh she's fine, fine. She loves that garden club with your mama. They have the best time."

"Well that's awesome. I don't have much time left on the parking meter. I need to get back to Atlanta for a house showing. Great to see you, Hugh! Give my love to Margie!" Leigh calls as she heads towards her car.

Once back in the car, she sighs heavily. The marriage license had no information about Rose's mother or background. Still, it's interesting to read.

I wonder where Grandma Rose is buried? Hillcrest? No, no – Magnolia Cemetery. That's right. She and Grandaddy are there. I remember going once with Daddy. I'll swing in there and see if I can find the grave.

Leigh heads down 3rd Street and turns into Magnolia. There's an office right near the entrance. She pulls her car into a space and walks inside. A few minutes later she is walking past rows of graves, searching.

Magnolia Cemetery is one of the oldest in the state, dating back to 1818. The lush green grass and old-growth trees are soothing to Leigh's nerves. After twenty minutes of searching, she finds the graves.

Rose Angela Cunningham Harrington

1908 - 1963

Beloved mother forever in our hearts.

There is an angel carved above her name. Leigh wonders if her uncle Ed designed the gravestone. The lettering is beautiful and graceful. Her grandfather's stone is similar in size and shape, but only has his birth and death years, no sentiment.

As she looks at the stone, Leigh wishes she could have known her grandmother. *Rose, Grandmother, I feel you here. I am going to solve this mystery. I am going to honor you.*

Leigh bows her head and says the 23rd Psalm, the only one she knows by heart:

The LORD is my shepherd; I shall not want. He maketh me to lie down in green pastures: he leadeth me beside the still waters. He restoreth my soul: he leadeth me in the paths of righteousness for his name's sake. Yea, though I walk through the valley of the shadow of death, I will fear no evil: for thou art with me; thy rod and thy staff they comfort me. Thou preparest a table before me in the presence of mine enemies: thou anointest my head with oil; my cup runneth over. Surely goodness and mercy shall follow me all the days of my life: and I will dwell in the house of the LORD for ever.

Leigh crosses herself, and walks back to the car.

CHAPTER 24 – JACK COMES BACK

When Leigh gets home it's clear word has already reached her mother that Leigh went to Augusta and didn't go by Peggy's. The message on Leigh's machine is curt. "Well, I had to hear from Hugh Brannon that my daughter was in town and didn't even call me. What on earth?! Call me. Today."

Leigh flops down on the sofa to eat her Wendy's burger. *I am not in the mood to call you.*

The phone rings.

Leigh will not answer it. Then she hears Jack's voice on her machine and she quickly grabs the receiver.

"Hey, how are you?" she asks, trying to quickly swallow a bite of burger.

"Good. Good. It occurred to me that maybe we need to have a chat. Are you home tomorrow night?"

"Um, sure. I was going to call you anyway. I went to Augusta and got my grandparents' marriage certificate today."

"Great. I look forward to seeing that," Jack replies, sounding distracted and totally uninterested in it.

"Listen, why don't I bring some food when I come tomorrow night? Sort of a working dinner?" he asks.

"Sounds good."

"Great. I will see you at 7 tomorrow, then."

"Cool. See you then."

When Leigh hangs up she ponders the conversation, for a moment. There was an undertone of something she can't identify, in his voice. Excitement? Uncertainty? She is not sure.

CHAPTER 25 – THE NEW HAT

Peggy calls Leigh's apartment again. The phone rings 5 times, and then the machine picks up. Peggy slams down the phone.

She pours herself a glass of Chardonnay and goes into her back yard, to sit on the side of the pool with her lower legs in the water.

To be told by her neighbor that her own daughter came into town and didn't even bother to call her, much less come by the house, was embarrassing. *Leigh has no idea what it's like to be mortified with embarrassment*, she thinks, *to live one's life trying to look normal and act normal and avoid public embarrassment.*

Peggy closes her eyes trying to block out the memory but it rushes in, unbidden and unwelcome.

Easter Sunday, 1952. Peggy is 11 years old. She is eating lunch with her parents at The Partridge Inn. Peggy is proud to be wearing a lovely pink dress and a new hat.

At the next table, Bobby Mills sits with his family. Peggy has a crush on him.

Peggy's mother Matilda pulls a flask out of her purse and pours a huge tot of bourbon into her coffee cup, not bothering to hide what she's doing.

Matilda talks non-stop for the next fifteen minutes, laughing too loud and waving at other tables. Peggy tries to pretend she is invisible, praying nobody will notice her loud mother.

A few minutes later, Matilda says to Peggy "Come on, let's go to the ladies room."

"I don't need to go, Mama," Peggy says, knowing what will come next.

"You come on with me, little lady, and let me hold on to you!" Matilda barks.

With a sigh, Peggy wipes her mouth and puts her napkin on the table. Her mother stands up and puts her hand heavily on Peggy's shoulder, leaning on her as she walks awkwardly towards the bathroom.

Peggy feels eyes on them, seeing her mother weaving slightly, leaning heavily on her. Suddenly, Matilda steps on a wet spot on the tile floor and her high heels betray her. She falls with a thud.

Peggy draws away from the heap on the floor that is her mother, horrified as Matilda starts laughing hysterically. Her father rushes over to try and get his wife off the floor. A small man, he struggles.

"Hahahahaha! I think I peed myself!" Matilda cackles. A dark stain on her linen dress proves that, and Peggy smells the sour urine.

Peggy turns and runs out of the restaurant, down the stairs, and out to the parking lot, shaking with embarrassment.

CHAPTER 26 – BROWN EYES

It's after 5 the next day, and Leigh gets back from a showing on a house to a young married couple in Dunwoody, and dashes up to her apartment door.

Leigh stops, to stare in astonishment at her uncle Edmund standing in front of her front door, talking on his cell phone and smoking as he paces. He sees Leigh and quickly ends the conversation, pushing down the long antenna on his phone and slipping it into his pocket.

"Leigh! I am so glad to see you! I hope you have a cold beer in the fridge," he says jovially, but his eyes betray him. Leigh sees worry there. Edmund wears jeans and a golf shirt that look brand new.

"You know I always have beer. It's great to see you. Come on in. Why are you here?!" Leigh asks, giving him a quick hug.

"Let me cool off and I'll tell you."

They sit down on Leigh's small back deck a few minutes later.

Edmund explains he's staying at a friend's house in midtown, not with his niece. "I came into town for my friend Mark's birthday this weekend."

Leigh doesn't believe him. His voice sounds rehearsed.

"Are you hungry?" she asks. "I have some cheese in the fridge. Gouda, I think."

"Um, no, not really, I had a snack at the airport."

They make small talk for about ten minutes while sipping their beer and watching cars roll by. Edmund is fidgety and ill at ease. Finally, there's a lull in the conversation and after a few minutes he says, "Let's head into the living room, okay?

"Sure."

Leigh gets another beer from the fridge for herself and one for him and joins him in the living room.

"OK, well, you've never just dropped in on me in my entire life, Ed, and New York is pretty far away, so let's cut to the chase, okay? I want to know what's going on. What's REALLY going on," Leigh says, fixing him with her best Perry Mason stare.

He flicks an imaginary piece of lint off of his shirt and clears his throat.

"Your mother called Harry. Harry called me. We actually got on a conference call, all of us, last night. We know you went to Harry's yesterday and snooped around. One of the neighbors saw you and called your mother."

Leigh sighs.

"I wanted to see some of my father's papers that Harry had in his garage. So what? Harry said it was fine. So they appointed you to fly all the way down here from New York and lecture me? Just for looking through some old boxes without informing him first? That's bizarre."

"Something like that," he mumbles into his beer. "I was planning a visit anyway, like I said.."

Leigh stands up and starts pacing. "Good godalmighty! Why all the secrecy? Why is it so important I not learn anything about my own grandmother? Why does nobody ever talk about her? Based on her photos, apparently I am the only grandchild who looks like her. Daddy always said I laughed like her. I have her love of houses and mysteries. He said she loved Agatha Christie and Perry Mason. I have green eyes like hers – "

Edmund is shaking his head. "She had brown eyes, Leigh."

Leigh stops pacing and glares at her uncle.

"Okay. So what? So Grandaddy had green eyes I guess? What difference does it make? Y'all have stories about him. I've heard them. He was a jerk, right? A stereotypical asshole lawyer?"

"Yes, Leigh. My father was not a nice man. A very effective litigator, yes. Not a nice man. He hated everything about me.. Mother was a saint to put up with him. She needs to rest in peace, though. There's nothing important about her you don't know."

For a moment, all Leigh can do is take deep breaths, and try not to lose her temper. She tries to tell herself that even though he's her favorite uncle, *Edmund IS a different generation, and we think very differently.*

She tries to speak calmly, but fails. "I'm very confused. I'm wondering why you are suddenly aligned with my mother, a woman you've never liked, and your brother Harry, whom you rarely see, against me. I've always thought we were allies, Ed. I've always adored you. It really hurts me to see you acting like this," she says, as calmly and evenly as possible.

Edmund looks at Leigh, startled. He lights a cigarette and sighs heavily. "You know I adore you, like you were my own daughter. Why will you not let the past stay in the past? Bringing up all that serves no purpose."

Leigh stares down at her uncle, trying not to hyperventilate.

"No purpose?! Well I am grieving hard for my father and I am not holding it together all that well. I like to eat Ben & Jerry's for dinner at night and I'm on my third therapist in a year. Some days I barely function. Then, I get a suitcase filled with things that belonged to Grandma Rose, a suitcase that leaves me with a lot of questions, and no answers."

"What was in the suitcase?" Edmund asks.

"Like you don't know?" Leigh says, irritated.

"I don't understand."

"Clearly not."

They continue to argue for the next few minutes, getting nowhere. Leigh goes over to the kitchen and suddenly freezes when she looks out the window and sees Jack's truck pulling up. Edmund sees her looking out the window. "I think you've got a visitor, Leigh," he says evenly.

Crap. *Why did I have to move into a ground floor apartment?!* Leigh thinks.

A knock on the door sounds too loud. *Oh shit*, Leigh thinks, *I totally forgot about Jack coming over.*

Leigh swiftly opens the front door, wishing she had gotten a shower and changed clothes, but seeing Jack's face makes her heart sing with gratitude. He's holding a large pizza box and a plastic grocery bag which looks like it contains a bottle of wine.

"Hey Leigh, sorry to be early – I went by DaVinci's and thought they'd be crowded and they weren't, and the traffic wasn't so bad, so here I am –" he begins, stopping when he looks past Leigh and sees her uncle.

"Come on in," she says, grabbing his arm. Jack looks hesitant.

"I don't want to interrupt –"

"No, you're not interrupting. He's my uncle. Just put the food in the kitchen and come join us," she says, a bit too forcefully.

Edmund's face has changed from extremely agitated to a bit bemused. "You didn't tell me you had a date, Leigh."

"Jack is not a date. Jack is a private investigator I hired to find out the truth about MY OWN GRANDMOTHER," Leigh says, trying not to raise her voice and failing. "Since my own family won't tell me anything."

Edmund looks startled for a moment, then shakes his head and stares at the floor. Jack, in the tiny kitchen, hears everything.

Wait a minute. Hold the phone. Why have I been just verbally sparring? I have proof! Leigh pulls the little suitcase off the floor of the dining area and plops it onto the dining room table and opens it. She grabs the skirt and blouse with the big bow and holds them up to herself.

"Why exactly was Grandma wearing maternity clothes in 1942, when her last child – that I knew of – Dad - was born in 1933?" Leigh practically shouts at Edmund.

He looks horrified, for a moment. A heavy silence fills the small apartment.

Jack comes into the living room area and clears his throat. "Can I get anyone a glass of wine? It's a nice red, according to the guy at World of Wines…"

"I'll take a glass" – Leigh realizes she and her uncle have spoken simultaneously. The tension breaks, and they both chuckle.

"Edmund Harrington, uncle to Leigh," Edmund says, sticking out his hand.

"Jack Briggs. Private investigator. Nice to meet you."

The two men shake hands. Leigh heads into the kitchen to get out the wine glasses.

A few minutes later Jack hands Ed a glass of wine, then pours one for Leigh. They all sit in the dining room.

Edmund takes a big sip of wine and then looks at Jack.

"Not too many years ago I went to the Methodist Children's Home to see what I could find out about Mama, but the lady said there was no record of a Rose Cunningham ever being there. Ditto for the state home for children. That puzzled me."

Jack is nodding. "That actually squares with what I had to share with Leigh tonight." He turns to her. "Can I tell you in front of your uncle what I learned yesterday?"

"Sure. I want to know everything you learned about MY grandmother."

Jack looks thoughtful.

"Your grandmother was raised at the Carrie Steele-Pitts home, which is the black orphanage in town."

"What? That doesn't make sense –" Leigh begins. Then she realizes what he is saying.

Jack glances at Edmund, who doesn't look surprised.

"There's more. I found a death certificate for Rose's mother, Elizabeth Cunningham. She died in the flu epidemic of 1918. She was listed as "Mulatto," which means mixed race in the parlance of 1908."

Leigh sits in silence for a moment, the words *the black orphanage* echoing in her mind. Then she looks at Edmund, who has his father's fair skin and brown hair, but surprisingly deep brown eyes. "You knew about this?"

Edmund nods, fiddling with the heavy gold bracelet on his right wrist.

"Yes, I've known it for many years. It only made sense – there were only three orphanages in Atlanta back then, so she had to have been in the Carrie Steele Pitts home. It doesn't matter to me. My mother was lovely and kind, and funny – a delightful person. I don't care if she was mixed race, but to some folks in the family it's something to hide," he says sadly.

"Like my mother? She found out and was upset, I take it?" Leigh says, not bothering to disguise the bitterness in her voice.

Edmund just nodded. "You know what she's like."

There is a long silence, while Leigh tries to absorb this information. Finally, Edmund speaks again, his voice lighter.

"I'm starved. Can I have a piece of that pizza, Jack?"

"Absolutely," Jack replies. They get up and go to the kitchen, leaving Leigh to sit and think for a minute. *Maybe they thought I was going to cry or throw a fit. Men seldom stick around for things like that. I'm not upset, though.*

"Hey, come back in here, guys, I have questions," she calls into the tiny kitchen area, hearing Jack and Edmund talking softly. "And bring me a piece of pizza."

Jack comes back in carrying a plate for her, and they settle down to eat around the table.

"Are you sure the Elizabeth Cunningham you found was the right person, Jack?" Leigh asks, taking a bite of the large pizza slice, which seems to be covered with everything you can put on a pizza. She wipes her mouth and chews, happy to be doing something normal during a very weird moment.

Jack nods, swallows a bite and wipes his mouth with a napkin.

"I wasn't sure, for a while, but then I got lucky. I have an acquaintance who works in the records department at Grady Hospital and she was able to find the same Elizabeth Cunningham, and the record of her giving birth in the colored hospital in 1908, to a girl named Rose. Then I found a record of Elizabeth dying from flu in 1918."

106

"Did the birth certificate for my mother list a father's name?" Edmund asks.

Jack gets up and grabs his backpack, then sits back down and pulls out a piece of paper and hands it over. "No, unfortunately the father's name is left blank. My guess is that he was white, so she had to leave it blank."

Leigh frowns, puzzled but uneasy. "Why? What difference would it make?"

Edmund wipes his mouth with a napkin, and explains, "In 1908 it was illegal for two people of different races to marry, or even to have sex. Children would obviously be evidence of sex, and thus both parties could have been arrested. It's called the crime of miscegenation."

"Wow." Leigh takes another bite of pizza. *Where have I seen that word, "miscegenation"? It's a weird word. Oh yeah, the divorce papers.*

"Hang on a minute," Leigh says, reaching behind her to grab the box with the divorce papers. She finds the letter from her father's lawyer and shows it to Edmund. "Did you know about this?" she asks.

He reads the letter, a pained look on his face.

"What Peggy was saying was that she didn't want to be married to Travis because he is partly black," he says after a minute of reading. He puts the page down, looking disgusted.

"What?!" Leigh laughs, mirthlessly. "That's ridiculous. Dad never looked black, or even mixed. He could only have been maybe what, one eighth black?!"

Jack, who was now reading the letter, looked up. "It's the one drop rule, Leigh. According to the law in the 19th century if you had one drop of negro blood, you were negro. However, after several generations with a lot of Caucasian mixed in genetically, sometimes people could "pass" – go into the white world and hide their black ancestry. I suspect that Rose figured out sometime early in life that she could pass. Elizabeth couldn't obviously, since she gave birth in the Colored section of Grady."

Leigh looked at Edmund. "How old were you when you figured it out?"

"A teenager." He got up and took a long final swallow of wine. "I need to get to my friend's house, Leigh. He's expecting me. I will come back soon and we can talk some more," he says, picking up his bag and giving Leigh a quick kiss on the cheek. "Nice to meet you, Jack," he says, shaking his hand.

Leigh watches him get into his rental car, frowning. *All these years he knew this huge secret and didn't tell me. Not one word. Dad didn't tell me either.*

Jack clears away the pizza plates and Leigh walks into the kitchen a minute later, where he is wiping the counter.

"Thanks. You don't have to clean up when you're here."

Jack chuckles, then tosses the paper towel in the trash. "Are you feeling all right, Leigh? This is a lot to have to deal with," he says, looking at her tenderly .

"I'm fine. Do I look black?!" Leigh asks, staring at Jack.

Jack throws his head back and laughs. "Are you kidding, Miss green eyes?! You look maybe… slightly Hispanic, or Greek? Possibly? Not black. Not that I would care."

"I don't care either. I mean, I'm not a racist. It's just that I'm sort of in shock."

"Well, of course you are. It's unusual news and your mother thought it was a problem."

Jack walks over and wraps his arms around Leigh. She rests her head on his shoulder for a moment. He rubs her back, then kisses the top of her head and pulls away, looking searchingly at her face.

"Should I stay? Do you want to talk? Or would you prefer that I go and leave you alone now?"

Leigh thinks for a moment. "I appreciate you coming over and bringing the pizza, and the wine. You are truly a thoughtful man. I think I'd like to be alone now, but I will call you in a day or two, okay?"

"Sounds like a plan, beautiful."

Leigh chuckles. "I don't feel beautiful."

"But you ARE beautiful, Leigh. I don't care if your grandmother was mixed race or your great-grandmother was called a mulatto. Everyone I know is a mixture of things genetically."

"Thanks," she says softly.

After Jack leaves, Leigh puts on an old bathrobe, then spends a good thirty minutes just sitting on the sofa thinking, reviewing her life and what it feels like to be not totally white, which she has never done before. Thoughts roiling, she knows sleep will be elusive, so she writes in her diary.

I went to private schools where there were almost no black children. I went to a 98% white church growing up. I saw few black students when I went to the University of Georgia. I am around many more black people and people of all races in Atlanta now, in 1996 but I live in a white area.

Aside from listening to Stevie Wonder and Aretha Franklin albums, and other black artists, and struggling with hair issues, I can think of nothing I might have in common with a black person. Yet that is as much a part of my heritage as my mother's people who came over from England and France before the American Revolution.

Leigh ponders the fact that Clarice, a black maid, took care of her and her brother, and ran their house, for years. Clarice was more of a mother figure than Peggy was, and Leigh adored her. Still, after Leigh grew up, Clarice quit. Leigh grieved, but didn't do more than exchange Christmas cards with Clarice for a few years.

I've no idea how it really feels to be a black person. How should I live my life differently, now that I know the truth? That's a question I will struggle with for a long time, I am sure.

Leigh sits and stares at her grandmother's maternity clothes, and reads her great grandmother's death certificate, over and over, until she finally falls asleep on the couch.

CHAPTER 27 -- GOSSIP

Edmund paces back and forth in the guest room of his friend's apartment, looking agitated.

"You are going to wear a hole in my carpet. Sit down," Mark says.

With a sigh, Edmund drops into a chair and lights up a Marlboro. "I just feel terrible. I love Leigh like my own daughter, and I told her to stop asking questions about her own grandmother. I sided with Harry and Peggy. I hate myself for doing that."

Mark hands him a fresh Scotch and soda. "What would horrify Peggy more than anything? Really make her upset?"

Edmund looks at Mark, and sips his drink. "Well, she has always been way too concerned with people's opinions of her."

"Well, why not start some gossip that will embarrass her?" Mark suggests. "Don't you stay in touch with a friend there in Augusta?"

Edmund smiles. "Why yes. Yes I do. Brilliant idea."

The next night, Peggy is drinking Scotch, neat. She sits on her back patio in the dark, wishing she still smoked. So many questions are bubbling in her head.

Did Edmund do his job yesterday and get Leigh to back off her insane quest to learn more about Rose? What the hell was in that old suitcase? Why didn't I just look in there? She bitterly regrets not looking.

Then, there is the even more troubling question of who knows what about her.

Peggy had eaten lunch at the Country Club after her regular Saturday morning tennis lesson, and everyone in the Grill seemed to be looking at her and whispering. Someone else wouldn't have noticed, but Peggy has lived in Augusta all her life, and she knows her town and her people.

The Grill is the informal dining area of the Augusta Country Club. Nobody dresses up to eat in the Grill. Peggy had walked in and greeted folks and sat at her usual table to wait for Susan Wells, her longtime friend and tennis partner. Peggy was wearing the same tennis dress she had worn for a couple of years. Same pearl earrings. Same lesson.

Peggy was keenly aware that heads were swiveling ever so slightly to look at her. Whispers were audible. In the inimitable way of old monied folks, nobody was confrontational, but there was definitely a buzz in the chilled air.

In all the years she had been writing her books, Peggy had been exquisitely careful that no-one should associate her with the pen name Anna Matthewson. Now, people were talking, and she had to know why.

Susan had said she had no idea why anyone would be talking. Peggy suspected she was lying.

Peggy picks up her phone and calls her ex brother-in-law Harry. He knows everyone and everything. He is one of only two people in Augusta who knows she is Anna Matthewson, because he manages her investments. *Time to pick his gossipy brain, if it isn't too pickled in bourbon...*

CHAPTER 28 – A PAIR OF EARRINGS

Sunday morning, 10:30. Leigh still hasn't fully processed the information she learned on Friday night about her mixed-race family.

Leigh didn't hear from Edmund Saturday, which hurt and surprised her. She showed houses all day, but called and checked her home voice messages four times during the day.

She stretches, throws back her vintage pink chenille bedspread, and showers. Twenty minutes later, she heads to the kitchen.

Tea in front of her, along with a piece of toast and an apple, Leigh sits outside on the deck, noting the brilliant blue sky, a deep blue seemingly washed clean after last night's rain.

The one thing Leigh knows with utter certainty is that she wants to know more about her grandmother Rose. What must it have felt like to give up a child and stay married to a cold, work-obsessed jerk? How did she reconcile that? Would having an obviously black child have forced her to stop "passing"? Would she have had to then live in the black section of Augusta? Would her husband have taken revenge on her for infidelity? Exactly how big of a jerk was he?

What happened to "Nate" – her baby's father? Was he black? Did Rose ever see him again? Were the adoptive parents related to him in some way?

So many questions. So few answers.

Leigh heads back inside and calls her office to say she is taking a couple of personal days.

As she ponders her earring collection, Leigh wishes that she could be close to her brother, Bubba, but he's closed off, focused totally on his business and his family, and golf. Like a lot of boys raised in Augusta, he's a golf addict.

Last year for her birthday, he sent her a pair of earrings, tiny golf balls.

My poor sister-in-law. I will NEVER marry anyone who spends the entire weekend playing golf. I cannot imagine why golf widows put up with that crap, Leigh thinks.

She realizes she still hasn't finished reading the divorce papers found in her father's things, and she heads back to the dining room table. A few minutes later Leigh's phone rings. It's Edmund. He says he will be at her apartment in an hour.

Leigh's tea grows cold as she reads, frowning. The divorce file is as ugly as Leigh had feared. Peggy took Travis to task over everything from the children's educations to who would

pay for braces and sports activities, the exact day and hour the kids would be returned to her, and where Travis could vacation with his own children.

Peggy had family money behind her, and her divorce attorney was such a powerhouse in Augusta even Leigh knew his name, Miller Thackston. Her father's attorney was a one man show, and not very effective.

Allegations were made that Travis had married Peggy under false pretenses because she had no idea he was the son of "a mixed race woman." Leigh noted that nothing was said about that in publicly-filed pleadings, just in letters.

What a consummate snob you are, Mother.

Leigh also thinks to herself, *my grandfather Harrington was from an old Augusta family, and that's likely what attracted Mother as much as Dad's handsome face.*

Leigh reads the Final Decree with her brows furrowed, scowling. The divorce terms were cut and dried, with Travis bearing the brunt of Peggy's post-divorce fury. Travis had to protect Peggy's reputation in the community. Travis had to swear never to discuss his mother's family publicly. Travis had to pay Peggy's country club membership for 5 years. Travis had to not drink around his children.

Ah, and the all-important master's badges. Leigh read a 2 page letter about that, and the reply, with great interest. Badges for the Master's Tournament, played every April in Augusta, are a hot ticket in the sports world. Normally, after the death of a badge-holder the badge can only be transferred to a surviving spouse, but Travis had managed to circumvent that rule. His father had helped Bobby Jones obtain the original land on which the Augusta National was built, and the Harrington heirs were guaranteed badges by a special waiver. A prized possession of Travis' was a photo of his father with Bobby Jones, taken in 1933, the year of the first tournament at the National. Along with the badges, the photo had passed to Bubba when Travis died, the only male heir carrying on the line.

Peggy wanted the use of Travis's family's badges but there his attorney held firm. The badges would never go to Peggy, but would pass to Bubba on his father's death, since he was carrying on the Harrington name. That hearkened back to Grandpa's 1952 will.

116

Good for you, Dad, for sticking to your guns on that one. Mother has her own family's master's badges!

CHAPTER 29 -- WHISPERS

Leigh puts the kettle on for more tea and thinks sadly about her father.

Her father struggled with alcohol until Leigh was fifteen and then he married Sandy. She insisted he "dry out" at a rehabilitation place before she would marry him, although they had been living together for two years. His realization that he had to get sober was good and bad. Good for his health, but bad for his relationship with his children. Instead of being a slave to alcohol he became a slave to his beautiful, cold-hearted wife.

Leigh reflects on the fact that her father chose two very beautiful but cold, calculating women to marry, both very blonde and fair-skinned. The big difference was that Sandy didn't want children, thank God.

The phone rings. Leigh heads back to the living room and picks it up only to hear her mother's clipped "I am furious" voice, one she knows too well.

"Leigh? I need to ask you a very important question."

"Yeah, okay, what is it, Mother?" she says, sighing.

"Who else did you see when you were here stealing from your uncle?"

"Well first of all, I didn't steal anything. If Harry had been there he would have let me in. I have just as much right to the papers belonging to my father as he did. Secondly, I didn't see anyone when I was in town last week, except that guy I ran into downtown, Brannon. Why are you so riled up?"

Silence. Leigh grabs the hem of her shirt and twists it.

"People at the country club were whispering about me yesterday."

Leigh stifles a laugh.

"Why? Did you have too many Bloody Marys and belch loudly?!"

"What an ugly thing to say. Unlike your father, I never get drunk and embarrass myself in public."

"No, you get drunk in private and make everyone around you miserable," Leigh retorts. *I hate that she always provokes me to say ugly things, but she does. She knows all the buttons to push.*

"I didn't raise you to talk like that, Leigh, and I don't deserve that attitude."

"Hey, maybe they were just talking about the fact that you're the only woman in your age group that hasn't gotten a face lift from that doctor in Alabama that everyone goes to, what's his name? Dr. Frozenface?"

Leigh hates the country club atmosphere. She has never felt comfortable there among the beautiful people. Peggy knows that.

Peggy loves the Augusta Country Club. It's her element. Her people.

"That's not remotely funny, Leigh."

"Well what do you want me to say, Mother? I'm sorry? I have no clue why people were acting weird around you. Maybe someone has discovered that you write ruthlessly about all the pompous assholes in that snobby little town you love so much? Did THAT ever occur to you?"

There is a momentary silence on the other end of the line.

"HOW DARE YOU! THOSE BOOKS PAID FOR YOUR COLLEGE EDUCATION!!" Peggy screams, then slams down the phone.

Leigh winces, and puts down her phone, wishing she drank hard liquor. Since her father was an alcoholic and her mother is a borderline alcoholic, at times, Leigh vowed at a young age to never touch a drop of anything hard, just to stick to one or two glasses of wine or one beer. She has kept that vow.

Leigh puts her head in her hands and cries for a few minutes, wishing she had a mother who didn't care so much about appearances.

CHAPTER 30 – THE PSYCHIC

Liz Williams closes and locks her front door, and shuts off the light in the living room, walking to the back of the small frame house to the kitchen, ready to fix lunch.

Liz's mother Millie lives with her, and since arthritis limits her mobility, Liz takes care of her mother.

"You all right Mom?" she calls out, as she passes the open doorway of her mother's room.

"Just fine. Hungry," Millie answers. Millie can still hear pretty well at the age of 76.

Liz ducks into her own room and changes out of her "work" clothes and into sweatpants and a tee shirt. When seeing clients she always dresses as though she's going to church.

Liz is a psychic and a medium, and a retired teacher. She lives in Benton, a little town outside of Athens, an hour east of Atlanta.

Liz Williams doesn't advertise, but people in the black community all know her, and they come from as far away as Birmingham and Memphis sometimes, to consult her. She charges only $20 per session.

Liz puts on a saucepan of water to boil, to make a pot of spaghetti. She opens the lid of the crock pot and smells the aroma of tomatoes, basil, ground beef, Italian sausage, seasonings, olives, and onions. Her mother loves spaghetti so they eat it once or twice a week.

A pile of mail catches her eye. Liz had grabbed the mail earlier in the day and put it on the kitchen counter. While the pasta water boils she flips through it. Bills, junk mail, the usual. Wait. A letter.

She puts the pasta in the water and sets the timer for 15 minutes, then pours a glass of red wine and sits down at the wooden kitchen table to read.

Travis died last August. This letter is from Harry. He states succinctly that he will continue the prior arrangement, as he agreed to do when Travis died, sending the money regularly, but now there is a condition.

"If you are contacted by Travis' daughter Leigh Harrington you are not to reveal your identity. To do so will mean the termination of our agreement and no more checks will arrive."

Liz sits back in her chair, thinking. So Harry has now realized that Leigh is close to connecting the dots and understanding what happened.

Liz wishes for the millionth time that she hadn't gone along with the coverup of that long-ago day, that she had somehow resisted, but she was 24, and naïve, and didn't realize that by agreeing to not press charges in exchange for a monthly check she would feel the shame and guilt for years to come, and it would delay her inner healing.

She puts down the letter and prays for guidance and peace, for herself and for Leigh.

CHAPTER 31 – HER RED VELVET CAKE

Late Sunday morning. There's a knock at the door. Leigh wipes her eyes and lets her uncle Edmund into the apartment.

He looks terrible, his face drawn and pale. He nods at Leigh and walks in past her, and puts down a large coffee on Leigh's kitchen counter, then a small bag

Edmund finally turns to his niece. He is wearing the same outfit he had on two days before, and he clearly hasn't shaven.

"Are you okay?" she asks.

"I am okay Leigh, just old and tired of subterfuge. I was up half the night, thinking. I've never really looked hard enough into my mother's past. I think I was afraid of what I would find. I did do some investigation, years ago, but I want to know more. I should never have taken Harry and Peggy's side. I'm sorry, Honey."

Leigh walks over and hugs him, smelling his familiar scent of Polo cologne and Marlboros.

"It's okay. They can be horribly persuasive at times."

"No, it's not okay. I met with your friend Jack earlier this morning. I paid his bill up to today and told him to send future bills to me. I want him to find out as much as he can about my mother's life and my grandmother, Elizabeth Cunningham. I want to know who I really am."

Leigh pulls back and looks at him. "Wow. You didn't have to pay him. I hired him. Thank you, though. Are you okay?"

Edmund sits on the sofa and buries his face in his hands. Leigh sits down next to him on the sofa and pats his back, then hands him his coffee and the big box of Kleenex she keeps on the end table.

"I buy these at Sam's, 3 boxes at a time."

He chuckles softly, and blows his nose. "I tend to forget you've been through so much Leigh. I'm too self-absorbed, as Greg says. I've spent more than 10 years watching my friends die of AIDS. Then I lost Travis. I forget sometimes it hasn't been easy for you either."

"Losing your friends is terrible, but family is maybe worse," Leigh notes sadly. "I miss my father so much. I think about him all the time."

"I miss him too."

"Want some water?"

"No thanks, Darling girl. You forget I brought my Dunkin Donuts coffee, the elixir of life. You've been crying. I'm sorry, Baby. I just noticed. What's up?"

"Mother called a few minutes ago. People in the country club were whispering about her. Of course, in her mind that's my fault. It's always my fault. She screamed at me, and then banged the phone down."

Edmund looks stricken. He opens his arms and gathers Leigh into them. Leigh thinks, *He has always been a great hugger and cuddler.*

Finally Leigh pulls away, sighs and blows her nose. Edmund heads to the bathroom. Leigh walks over to the window and looks out on the late morning and sips her second, now cold, cup of tea, trying to think of happy things.

"Well, it's not all bad. You are the daughter of a famous woman who is going to leave you a nice inheritance," Edmund reminds her, coming back into the living room and patting her back. He is sipping his coffee.

"Yeah, if she can maintain her subterfuge and keep writing about Augusta's elite without their knowing."

He smiles. "How does she do it? I read every one of her books and I'm always amazed at her audacity."

"You know Peggy. She knows everyone who is anyone. You do know all the groups she's in, right? The Daughters of the Revolution. The Daughters of the Confederacy. The Huguenot Society. The Vestry at St. Paul's. The Junior League. Three different garden clubs. The Augusta Country Club. Historic Augusta."

"So true," he smiles, sipping on his coffee.

"That's how she gets away with her little mysteries. I think she loves being a spy on all those privileged people with skeletons in their closet. I just noticed something. You didn't bring me any doughnuts?"

"Yes, of course I did. I'm not a monster! Grab that bag from the kitchen."

Leigh walks into the kitchen and greedily checks the bag – two French crullers from Krispy Kreme. He knows her well.

"So you go to Dunkin Donuts for coffee, then head to Krispy Kreme for doughnuts?!" Leigh asks with a smile.

"Well of course. I was raised right," Edmund replies, eyes twinkling. "Why do you think I was so late getting here?!"

"So true. Most folks are eating lunch now."

"Hand me that jelly donut, there's a dear. You know, Leigh, Peggy just loves secrets, right? She would have been right at home dating Machiavelli, a few hundred years ago."

Leigh sips her tea and finishes her doughnut. Edmund polishes off his jelly then eats two glazed doughnuts in about ten seconds.

"I have a question for you," Leigh says, returning to the couch to look at him intensely. "Did Grandma Rose ever talk to you about her race?"

He looks pained. "No. We never had that conversation. I figured since she could pass for white, she would be upset if she knew that I knew her secret."

"Why? Why would she be upset?" Leigh asks, truly puzzled.

Edmund sighs and wipes his mouth with a paper napkin. "It was a different time, Leigh. People didn't talk openly about such things as bastard children and Negroes passing for white, or gay sons. It wasn't until the late 1960's and later that those things were really brought out into the open."

"Great godalmighty! How stupid. So I'm assuming you don't know anything about the baby she had in 1942?"

He glances at the suitcase. "Well, yes and no. I found that suitcase in the attic when I was a teenager, just before I left home. I assumed she had just stuck the clothes in the old suitcase because she didn't need them any more. Never occurred to me they were from the 1940's, not the early 1930's. I'm not sure I knew they were maternity clothes, either."

Leigh stares at him. "Really?!"

Edmund shrugs. "Why would I know about vintage women's clothing?"

"Okay, fair enough."

"Jack told me about the letter when we spoke this morning. I hope he can find out more, discover what happened to the child. He would be my younger brother."

"What makes you so sure the child was a boy?" Leigh asks, arching her eyebrow.

"Wishful thinking?! I bet he's handsome!"

"But wait a minute. Did you tell Dad what you found about Rose coming from the black orphanage?"

"Yes. He wasn't surprised. We were never real close, but Travis was always far more understanding of me and my orientation than Harry was. We were always friendly."

"There's something missing here. There's something we don't know."

Leigh goes to the table and picks up the divorce file. "I read through this once already but maybe you could take a look, see if you see anything more about race. I just found a few ugly things in letters."

Edmund reads through the file quickly. They pass papers back and forth as Leigh re-reads. He finds the letter with "miscegenation" in it, and a couple of other references, but nothing new.

"Leigh I know you and Peggy aren't close but why don't you just ask her what she knows about my mother?"

Leigh shoots him an incredulous look. "Are you nuts? She would shut me down in a New York second. Nothing ugly or controversial is allowed to intrude upon her serene highness. I'm amazed she called you."

He snorts. "It was not a long conversation."

"I just have to think if Eugenia Hill is still alive she could fill in the missing information, don't you? Jack and I hit dead ends in searching, though."

Edmund sits quietly for a moment, then snaps his fingers. "Wait a minute. I have an idea. My friend Eric lives in a building right next door to a little house and the lady in it has lived there since the 1920's. She knows everyone in the 10th Street area. I bet she would know if Eugenia Hill lived in the area during the war years. I can call Eric and see if he could arrange for us to go see her. I love her name - Miss Maudie Cheney."

Edmund gets on the phone and chats, walking outside to light up a Marlboro while he talks. When he comes back in, his face is animated. "Eric said to come on down and he will take us over there. He goes in and out all the time. They're great friends."

Ten minutes later they are on the way to midtown in Ed's rented Mustang, listening to an oldies station. The radio is playing "Tainted Love," a song Leigh listened to in college, a song the deejay had referred to as "a real oldie."

"Hey, Ed, how did my mom and dad meet? I have no idea. Do you know?"

Edmund smiles.

"Funny you should ask. I do happen to know. Travis got drunk at his bachelor party and regaled everyone with the story. He was a grad student at UGA and your mother was a Freshman. He was giving standardized tests to the Freshmen and he noticed her. He said she was gorgeous. She was. I remember. She did poorly on the math portion of the test and he offered to tutor her. Two years later, Bubba was born, after the biggest wedding Augusta has ever seen."

Leigh is silent, thinking about a terrible memory.

"What are you thinking?" Edmund asks, noticing Leigh's pained expression.

"Mom and Dad had been fighting. I was ten. They were both drunk. Mom had been going through the wedding photo album, pulling out each photo and saying something ugly about it – "Look at that bitch, your old girlfriend, and her too tight fake Chanel!" or "Who the hell is that guy? Some old drinking buddy?" and Dad would say something like "I never dated her!" or "That's one of YOUR asshole relatives!" The shouting is etched in my mind. I sat in the hallway listening, in my nightgown, hugging Shep, our Pomeranian, for hours. Years later I saw the movie, "Who's Afraid of Virginia Wolf?," on TV and was only able to watch about 10 minutes of it before turning the channel. Liz Taylor and Richard Burton's vicious fighting was all too familiar."

Edmund shakes his head sadly. There's an awkward pause.

Finally, Edmund asks "Say, whatever happened to all those wedding photos I took of your parents? That was my first wedding. Got me a lot of business."

"They're all gone, Ed. Mother made a bonfire in the back yard and burned them, every one of them. It was the biggest fight I ever saw. Dad moved out right afterwards."

"You saw the fight?"

"Well, I heard it. I'm sure everyone that lived near us heard the shouting."

They are both silent for a moment, reflecting on the ugly past.

"Somebody said something to me not long ago that was very appropriate. I can't recall the exact quote but it was something along the lines of "It's okay to visit the past sometimes, but don't unpack your bags and move in," Ed said quietly.

"Easier said than done."

Ed turns the car onto 10th Street and in a moment the cars pulls up in front of a tidy little craftsman bungalow. "Is there any parking around this place?" Leigh asks.

"I'm sure we can find a place on the street," Ed says, a little too cheerfully. Leigh is glad he changed the subject.

Twelve minutes later, Edmund and Leigh are seated in white wicker chairs on the cheery enclosed sun porch of the bungalow, balancing cups of Lipton tea in Sevres cups on their laps.

Miss Maudie, as everyone calls her, is a tiny, wizened woman in her 90's, sitting in front of the window in a wheelchair. She is resplendent in a coral pink dress with a sky-blue afghan around her shoulders. Her cap of gray Mamie Eisenhower curls, mottled skin and stooped posture proclaim her age, but her light blue eyes are sharp and inquisitive.

"Who did you say your daddy was, Child?" she asks Leigh.

Leigh speaks louder than normal but tries not to shout. "Travis Harrington, a banker in Augusta. He died last year."

"Harrington, Harrington… Old Augusta name. Prominent family. Yes. I used to go see my cousin who lived there, go to that golf tournament sometimes. Who was your mother?"

Leigh smiles. *Only in the South would such a question be routine.*

"Mama was a Spencer, Margaret Spencer – Peggy is her nickname. Her mama was Matilda Spencer, maiden name Carruthers, from Savannah. Her daddy was Ward Spencer, and he was an accountant."

Leigh thinks of the huge Greek revival mansion on Walton Way where her mother had grown up. It was a world of teas, country club parties, European vacations, and debutante balls. Leigh had always felt like an outsider in her grandparents' elegant house. Her grandfather's second wife, Annabelle, had always been gracious and kind to her, though.

Leigh snaps out of her reverie when the tip of Miss Maudie's cane pokes her foot. "Wake up, child!"

"I'm sorry Miss Maudie, I was just lost in thought," Leigh says apologetically, ignoring Edmund's look of annoyance.

Eric, a slender man in his 50's, clears his throat diplomatically. "Miss Maudie, Leigh wanted to know if you ever saw her paternal grandmother here in Atlanta, around 1942, just after the second world war started. Show her the photo, dear."

Maudie looks at Eric like he's an imbecile. "I know when the war started, boy. I'm not stupid or senile. Land's sakes."

Edmund puts his hand over his mouth to hide a smile, and he tries not to chuckle. Leigh pulls the photo of Rose and Eugenia out of her purse and hands it to Miss Maudie, who takes it in her claw-like hands and brings it up to her face.

"The dark-haired lady is my grandmother, Rose Harrington."

After peering for a moment, Miss Maudie straightens up in her chair. "Claudelle! Bring me my magnifier!" she bellows with surprising force.

A huge black woman wearing a white polyester pants suit appears seconds later holding the biggest magnifying glass Leigh has ever seen. It's the size of a small paperback book. She places it gently onto a pillow and puts the pillow on Miss Maudie's lap, then slips the photo under it. "There you go dear," she says kindly.

Leigh smiles at Claudelle, and thinks *we could be related*.

Miss Maudie studies the photo intently, then closes her eyes. After a few minutes, everyone is afraid Miss Maudie has fallen asleep, but then Miss Maudie opens her eyes and starts talking.

"I've lived on this earth for 94 years but I never forget a face, particularly not a beautiful face. This one here (she points to Rose) lived around here in the summer of 1942, in a rental house over on Argonne. The Phillips family had moved to Macon and rented out their house to this ugly woman and her husband," she says, pointing to the homely Eugenia.

Leigh catches her breath, hope flooding her heart. "Did you know them? Did y'all socialize? See each other at church?" she asks.

Miss Maudie sighs heavily, a look of sadness coming over her face. "My mama was sick from 1938 until 1944 when she died. She lived here with me and my husband and I nursed her. I didn't get out much during those years, even to church, although we went to First Baptist. I do recall seeing the ugly one sometimes, working outside in the yard of that house, like a field hand, no hat, no gloves, nothing. Ruins the skin, staying out in the sun that way."

Edmund smiles. "Miss Maudie, the pretty lady in the photo was my mother Rose Cunningham Harrington. Do you ever recall seeing her pregnant?"

She looks up at Edmund and frowns. "In my day, nobody used such words. We said 'in a family way,' or 'expecting.' I don't like crude talk, young man. Let me think some more." She closes her eyes.

Another silence, for almost a full minute.

Leigh takes a sip of the tea, and gratefully accepts a shortbread cookie from Claudelle. Finally, Miss Maudie clears her throat and speaks again, turning her face toward Edmund.

"There was a Chinese laundry on Tenth Street. I recall going by there one day and seeing your mama in there, talking to the owner. She was expecting. Tall lady, so she carried it well, but she was definitely in a family way. Why do you want to know? Was that you she was carrying?" she asks, fixing Edmund with an unflinching stare.

He uncrosses his legs, then re-crosses them, jiggling his cordovan loafer impatiently. Leigh senses he is wishing for a cigarette.

"No, M'am, that was not me, but I'm flattered. I was born in 1928."

Leigh interrupts. "Miss Maudie, do you have any idea if the other lady, Eugenia Hill, still lives around here, or is still even alive?"

She shakes her head. "She and her husband never had any children. Her husband was a salesman, I think. They left right after the war. I think somebody told me they moved up to Acworth but I could be mistaken."

Edmund frowns. "Did you ever see my mother carrying a baby, like out walking with a baby carriage?"

Maude fixes Edmund with a frank stare. "No. I take it this baby is the reason you're here, quizzing me? I'm thinking that baby would be a half sibling you've never met?"

"Uh... yes," Edmund mumbles.

Wow, sharp old lady, Leigh thinks.

Maudie sits up straighter and motions for Claudelle to take away the magnifying glass and give her back the photo. "I'm sorry your granny died before you were born, Leigh. It's so important for us to know our people, know who we come from."

They sit in silence for a moment. Leigh glances at Edmund. He is struggling to compose his face, because there are tears in his eyes.

Maudie looks at Leigh. "I take it you've checked the records for Crawford Long? The birth records from August and September 1942? That's likely where she had the baby. It's the closest hospital."

Leigh looks at Edmund and his eyebrows are arched almost to his hairline.

"No, but thanks for that tip, Miss Maudie. We will check," Edmund replies, setting his cup and saucer on the wicker coffee table.

Claudelle picks up the cup and clears her throat diplomatically. "It's about time for your lunch Miss Maudie."

Everyone rises.

"We'll head on out," Eric says diplomatically. He leans over to kiss Miss Maudie's papery cheek and pats her hand. "You have a good lunch, dear. I'll come see you again soon."

Miss Maudie looks annoyed. "Well, fine, go on off then. But come on over and watch Jeopardy with me one night soon. And next time don't wear so much cologne! Land sakes, my whole porch smells like that Yankee Ralph Lauren!" She pronounces his name "low rent."

"Thanks for your help, Miss Maudie," Leigh says, reaching out to her gratefully.

To Leigh's shock, Miss Maudie grabs her hand and looks at her intently. "You look a lot like your grandmother, Leigh. Now I'm going to tell you something I've learned in my long life. Listen up, Honey. I may be dead before you see me again. Every woman holds secrets, deep in her heart. We have to take care of everybody, all our lives. It's the burden of Eve, it sure is. But we also have the blessing of being able to love more than any man can even comprehend. We love true and for always. Your grandmother was a loving person, a gentle person. It shone out of her like a light. That's why I remember her so well, even though we didn't really know one another. Whoever that little baby belonged to, trust that your grandmother did right by her. I know she did."

Leigh is too choked up to speak. She just nods and mouths the words thank you, and they leave.

Outside on the sidewalk, after saying goodbye to Eric, Leigh stops suddenly. "Crawford Long is just up Peachtree Street, not really that far, and it's a weekday. Let's head up there and see if they have records back that far, ok?"

"You think they might still have them?" Ed asks, incredulous.

Leigh shrugs. "Who knows? It's worth a try. Besides, I feel like walking."

They set off, and in twenty-two minutes they've covered the city blocks and are standing outside Crawford Long.

The medical records clerk is unimpressed by Edmund's relationship to Rose Harrington, and she explains even if it were possible to hand over the records, she can't, because they don't have anything back to 1942.

Leigh and Edmund leave and head back to the car. The drive north is mostly silent, each lost in their own thoughts.

"Hey, how about we swing by the Varsity and get some chili dogs and onion rings? There's one on Jimmy Carter Boulevard, not far from you, right?" Edmund asks.

"Sure. It's close to the apartment," Leigh replies. "What'll ya have? What'll ya have?!" Leigh hollers, just like the clerks at the famous fast food chain.

Edmund smiles.

Over lunch, and throughout the remainder of the afternoon, as they wander around the antique shops of Chamblee, a suburb near Leigh's apartment, Leigh asks Edmund questions she has never asked before. What was Rose like as a mother? What were her favorite colors? Favorite songs? What were her hobbies?

He shares his memories of her, and builds a picture in Leigh's head of a person she wishes she had known.

Rose was an attentive and loving mother who always made a big deal out of birthdays, taught her boys good manners, and gave them extra attention because their father was so uninterested in parenting.

Edmund points out a lamp in a shop, its purple/pink shade very 1920's. "She loved blue and pink, and flowers. She loved gardenias and camellias."

As they look through old 78 rpm records in a bin, he says "Bing Crosby was her favorite singer."

Back at the apartment, as they relax on the deck with beers, he continues. "Mama liked to work in her garden, and read. She was a good cook, but she couldn't cook when she got married. She used to say that her mother-in-law taught her, but it wasn't exactly true – she learned to cook from Loretta, her mother-in-law's housekeeper."

"She couldn't cook?" Leigh asks.

"She was raised in an orphanage, remember?!" Edmund reminds her gently, taking another swig of beer and lighting a Marlboro.

Leigh thinks about that.

In Augusta Georgia, no matter how wealthy a woman is, she is expected to be a great cook, and have several "specialty" dishes that she is known for. "What dishes was she known for?" Leigh asks her uncle with some excitement, wondering if they are things she loves to eat.

"Mama was known for her red velvet cake and her green beans. Her green beans were cooked all day, with fatback, and they were heavenly. I've tried to make them myself but it's hard to find fatback in New York City," he says, smiling wistfully.

"We need to go down and eat at Mary Mac's next time you come visit," Leigh says with a smile. Mary Mac's, a venerable landmark in Atlanta, serves traditional Southern cooking.

"I'd like that. Let's see, what else? Mama loved to listen to Jack Benny on the radio, and to watch Milton Berle on TV," Edmund says.

"Did she drink?" Leigh asks, wondering where her father got his drinking habits.

"No, not really. She once drank a small glass of sherry – which was all she ever drank – and taught me to do the Charleston. It's my happiest memory of her. She looked like a young girl, that day."

"You need to teach me," Leigh says, trying to dispel the look of sadness on her uncle's face.

"One day. You know, she was excited about your birth. She told me she hoped for a girl, and she thought you'd be a girl. Travis told her if the baby was a girl they would name her Leigh."

"What did she die of?" Leigh asks.

"Brain aneurysm. One minute she was fine, out in her garden, and the next minute she was gone. Her yard man, Winston, found her and called the ambulance, but it was too late. At least she didn't suffer," Edmund says wistfully, wiping his eyes.

Leigh hugs him. "I wish I had met her."

They sit quietly for a moment, then Edmund clears his throat.

"Hey, let me go out to the car. I almost forgot to give you something."

140

Edmund hurries out to his rental car and reappears a few minutes later, carrying a leather briefcase. "I was going through my oldest photo files and I found some prints I had forgotten about, that I made when I came back from being away, the first time. You know, when I left home as a teenager I lived in Atlanta for more than ten years before coming home, and in that time I worked at a camera shop and learned a lot about being a professional photographer. When Dad got sick I came home and I took a lot of shots, just for practice."

He pulls a stack of 8x10 photos from his briefcase and lays them out on the dining room table. Leigh gasps in delight. They are color prints of the family.

"Oh, these are wonderful! I've never seen color prints of everyone!"

"Black and white was the preferred thing back then but I wanted to learn color, so I took some money from savings and bought some color film and practiced on the family. This is one of my favorites."

Edmund pulls out a shot and hands it to her. It's Rose, sitting on the sofa, with Travis beside her. "She was in her fifties, but she was so lovely, wearing that blue dress. She was always proud of her beautiful hair, and wore it down around her shoulders in soft curls, always. That was her signature red lipstick. Look at your dad, so handsome and sporting a crew cut. He had to be sitting right beside her."

Leigh notes Travis is grinning and holding a glass of something she suspects was bourbon.

"I come from very attractive people," she remarks softly.

"Absolutely. See, Sweetheart, you really do look like her," Ed says. "You can keep these prints. I have duplicates."

Leigh nods, tears choking her throat and obscuring her vision. Edmund wraps her in a hug and kisses the top of her head.

After her uncle leaves, Leigh sits and looks at the photos for a long time. After washing her face and brushing her teeth, Leigh records her thoughts in her diary.

There is something very familiar about them, something I can't put my finger on. In one photo, Rose wears a long strand of pearls and a blue dress, and looks like she's going somewhere, like a night on the town, or a fashion show. Cool and elegant. The dress and pearls look so familiar to me but I can't think why.

Despite Ed's wonderful gift of the photos, I feel bereft. What have I really learned recently, aside from the fact that I am part black? I know a little bit about Rose, but it made my uncle sad to talk about her.

I have learned that my grandmother married a man she didn't love, to "pass" in the white world, and she was so ashamed of her background, or maybe just fearful, that she lived her life ignoring what must have been a very difficult childhood.

My own childhood was painful. I recall the sad times all the time, triggered by a smell or a sight, or a sound. Did she endure that too? Did she ever look at her lovely house in the upscale area of Augusta and her white sons and wonder what life would be like if she could be with the man she loved, and raise the child from that love?

How did she endure such a life, such sadness? I have a therapist. Who could she talk to? Eugenia?

I have decided to remember the words of Miss Maudie. "Your grandmother was a loving person, a gentle person. It shone out of her like a light." Maybe the love she had for her sons sustained her. Maybe if even just one person loves you with their whole heart, you can build a life around that.

Leigh's dreams that night are filled with the voices of Bing Crosby and Jack Benny, and the smell of gardenias. She sees Rose in her garden, young and beautiful, and laughing and talking to someone just out of sight. Leigh wants to join them, but no matter how fast she runs, she can't ever reach the garden.

Maybe that's a metaphor for life, she thinks, as soon as she opens her eyes.

Liz walks outside to the tidy garden behind her house in Benton, Georgia, and surveys the rich earth. She planted okra, tomatoes, squash, cantaloupe, string beans, eggplant, and cucumbers. The earth rested all winter, enriched with coffee grounds, eggshells, peelings from vegetables, and the occasional overripe banana. Now the plants are producing record amounts of vegetables, in earth that teems with worms.

A fat red cardinal lands on the old rose bush at the back of the yard and surveys Liz, head cocked.

Liz looks at the cardinal, silently, and knows it is a messenger from her mother. The bird flies off, encircles the yard, and lands again on the rose bush.

Liz knows what is being conveyed. "Find her. It's time." The bird looks at her and cocks its head, and flies away again.

Liz closes her eyes and smells L'Origan, and wishes she could hold her mother in her arms, but it cannot be. She loves her adoptive mother with all her heart, but Liz misses her biological mother very much, an old ache.

She turns and heads back to the porch, where there are some votive candles. She lights one and stares into the flames, asking God to lead her niece to her.

CHAPTER 32 -- HAPPY

Leigh finishes up at a house closing in Buckhead at 3:46 and gets in her white Toyota Corolla and turns on the air conditioner. On the dash of the car under the windshield wiper is a folded note, a piece of yellow legal pad paper. Annoyed, Leigh steps out for a second and grabs the note, sliding back gingerly onto the hot driver's seat to open it.

Saw your car parked here and wondered why. Call me. I need to tell you something. - Jack

Whoa. That's weird. Leigh looks around. She is outside of an office building. She doesn't see Jack's truck, though. *Maybe he was here earlier. But how did he know it was MY white Corolla? There must be thousands of them in Atlanta.*

Leigh decides to use her car phone. She opens the glove compartment and plugs it into the cigarette lighter.

He answers on the first ring.

"Hey, it's Leigh. Are you in the car?"

"Yep, you are too I bet. I can hear the traffic. You driving?"

"No no, I'm not crazy. I'm sitting in the parking lot at Century Center. Your note freaked me out."

"Sorry about that. Look, I'm on Peachtree. Hang on a sec, let me pull over. I agree, talking on the phone while driving is dangerous."

Leigh waits a moment. "Where are you?"

"I'm not too far from the Borders near Lenox. Want to come meet me there for a cup of coffee?"

"Sure. See you in the little café area in about ten minutes." Borders is her favorite store in the world. Whenever she is bored, Leigh swings by Borders to lose herself in books, music, and videos.

When she gets there, Leigh parks the car and walks into Borders, surveying the large store with happiness. She takes the escalator up to the coffee area but Jack isn't there yet. Mysteries are upstairs, alphabetical by author, so she heads over to check out the latest Anna Matthewson (her mother's pen name) book.

Creamed Corpse is her mother's usual "cozy" book, replete with a dead body in the country club pool, a scandalized garden club where everyone suspects everyone else, and so on. The books follow a standard formula but the details are always interesting. The biographical section is a couple of sentences, and says the author lives in Savannah with her husband and three children. *Ha. What a load of crap. She wants everyone to think she's still got kids at home and is in her thirties.*

Leigh is sipping a cup of tea and reading the first chapter of the book when Jack walks up.

She feels a shiver of excitement just seeing him. She is glad she is wearing her typical "closing clothes" – a flowered skirt from Talbott's that's knee length, a violet blazer, and white silk blouse. Her hair is tamed into a chignon, and her makeup is warm and exotic, enhancing the cool tones in her green eyes. She even re-applied a deep plum lip gloss just before leaving the car.

"Hello Beautiful," Jack says, grinning that grin that transforms his face.

"Hey yourself," she beams.

"Been here long?" he asks.

"Nope. Just got here 5 minutes ago. I got you a coffee," she replies, nodding towards the small cup already on the table.

"Thanks," he says, grabbing some packets and stirring the sugar into the coffee. He has on a blue button down shirt and black Chinos and loafers. So very preppy.

"Hey, I have a question. How did you know my car?!" Leigh asks, really curious.

He chuckles. "I remembered that the last time I saw your car you had a James Patterson novel on the back dash, easily visible in the window, a bumper sticker that says Myrtle Beach, and flip flops on the floor of the passenger side."

"Ah, okay. I need to clean it out."

"Not necessarily. It wasn't dirty, just a little cluttered."

"My apartment is always neater than my car."

Jack sips his coffee. "If you had to pick one to be neat, I'd say you made the right choice."

"You said in the note you wanted to tell me something. She sips her tea and tries to look nonchalant.

Jack takes a sip of coffee and looks down at the table, suddenly self-conscious. This is a new side of him that Leigh hasn't seen before. She wonders if he has learned something awful about her grandmother or great-grandmother.

147

"Well, this is a bit awkward, but here goes," he says quietly. "Now that your uncle is paying my bills, you aren't technically a client of mine. I have rules about dating clients. It's not a good idea. I was feeling very conflicted about my attraction to you the other night. However, since you aren't a client any more, now I feel free to ask you out."

Leigh closes her book, just wanting to listen to his voice, and finally takes a deep breath.

"Okay."

Jack looks a bit worried now. "You don't have to say yes."

"Oh no – no – you don't understand. I'm tickled to death you're asking me out."

She stops, feeling ridiculous, but also excited and relieved they can finally date -- officially.

Jack studies Leigh's face as though memorizing it, and smiles.

"What do you think about going out to eat, and then to a movie? Say, this Friday night?"

"Sounds like fun." In her head, Leigh hears her mother's voice saying *Wear something low cut. You're not getting any younger.*

CHAPTER 33 – THE FIRST DATE

Friday afternoon. Leigh dresses for that date with far more care than any job interview. After reviewing all her clothes, she finally settles on a crimson cotton dress, strappy sandals, and a white cotton sweater thrown over her shoulders. She wears her hair off her face, held back by barrettes, and adds a little makeup and lipstick. She mists on a spicy floral perfume around her neck and smiles at herself in the mirror. *Whoa aren't you a lucky guy, Jack?!* She thinks.

Jack arrives to pick her up, wearing jeans and a white polo shirt, smelling faintly of some citrus cologne, and smiles that smile she loves, the one that makes his face light up.

"Hello beautiful! You should wear that color more often. You look radiant."

Leigh and Jack head to Phipps Plaza, a very upscale mall, before the traffic gets terrible, and watch the movie Twister, which is exciting and, Leigh thinks, very unrealistic – *what kind of crazy people want to chase after tornadoes? Yikes.*

Afterwards, they walk. Leigh likes walking around Phipps because of stores like Neiman Marcus, Saks Fifth Avenue, and Lord & Taylor. She doesn't shop there but admits that she likes to "window shop."

They settle in for dinner at a small restaurant called The Bistro. Leigh orders a chicken club sandwich and Jack orders a burger.

"You're a burger guy all the way, aren't you?" she asks, smiling.

Jack grins. "Guilty. Most places don't use high quality meat, or they don't cook them properly, or they're greasy. I am always in search of a great burger." Leigh reaches to move the salt a bit and touches his hand briefly.

"You know, I was thinking as I was getting ready, Jack knows a lot about me and my family and I know nothing about him."

He takes a sip of beer and shrugs. "Not much to know. I grew up all over. My dad was a Marine. I have a brother and sister, both younger. We moved all the time until finally settling in Atlanta for Dad to head up the recruiting station here when I was in middle school. I got a degree in political science from UGA then didn't know what to do with myself, and went into the Marines. When I got out, one of my friends had started doing investigations and it sounded like fun so I went into business with him. Then he left to go out to California and I carried on by myself."

Leigh nods, thinking *we have almost nothing in common at all, so why do I feel so comfortable around this man?*

"What do you like to do for fun? I mean, besides search Atlanta for the perfect burger?"

The waiter brings their food and they dig in. Jack takes a bite and chews thoughtfully. Finally, he wipes his mouth with his napkin and takes a sip of beer. "I like to go hiking in the mountains. I play tennis twice a week with a friend. I like reading mysteries and thrillers. Love Tom Clancy books. Lee Child. Love action movies. I'm a pretty fair cook because I like to eat well and I'm budget-conscious so eating out isn't an everyday occurrence. I am trying to learn Spanish. I listen to language CDs while I walk on the treadmill every morning."

Okay, now I feel self-conscious. I am not trying to stay fit or improve my mind like he is, and although I was forced to learn French for 8 years at the Day School I've forgotten most of it.

"Wow. I'm a slacker in comparison to you."

"I wouldn't say that," Jack says gently.

"Well, I went to UGA and majored in business, but I spent a fair amount of time just hanging out with friends. I wasn't a great student. I loved Athens. I only graduated because my parents threatened to cut off my funding if I didn't finish up. I had too much fun."

Jack grins. "Nothing wrong with that. I've been known to drink a few beers and cut the fool, as my grandmother used to say."

Leigh takes a bite of her sandwich and chews, trying to picture Jack acting silly. They eat in comfortable silence for a few minutes. Finally, she wipes her mouth and takes a sip of water.

"I need to tell you something. You may hear it and think, that woman is nutso. That's okay. If you want to know me, though, the real me, you need to understand this about me."

Jack sits up straighter in his chair and looks thoughtful. "Okay. Let's hear it."

Leigh tells him about the Drunk Maid incident. She tries to tell it drily and unemotionally, but when she gets to the part about smelling the Caswell and Massey scent and getting upset a couple of months ago, he looks at Leigh with eyes shining with sympathy.

"Maybe it was just that on top of still mourning for my dad, but I've been having a hard time for months. I'm seeing a therapist."

Jack nods.

"I totally understand what you're saying. I was in Iraq during the Gulf War. It took me months to calm down when I came back. I have seen therapists, too. I am a "borderline" sufferer

of Post Traumatic Stress Disorder, PTSD. Loud cracks don't freak me out as bad as they used to, but I still get anxious when I hear firecrackers, or a car backfiring. I know all about triggers. Triggers are jolting. You were just a little girl."

Leigh's eyes fill with tears. She doesn't want to sob and make a scene. Relief washes over her, though. *He doesn't think I'm a nutcase.*

Jack grabs a clean napkin off another table and hands it to her. "Give me a minute to pay the bill and then let's head back to the car, okay?" he says gently.

Leigh just nods, feeling emotional and trying to not think about it.

Ten minutes later they are in Jack's truck. Leigh feels an enormous sense of relief. She was taught that one must simply never cry in public, ever.

They get back to Leigh's apartment before 10, and just sit on the sofa and talk. Jack drops the cautious military guy and relaxes, and Leigh confides in him. She feels like she can say anything, and he will not judge – a far cry from most of the guys she has dated.

Jack leans in for a kiss and Leigh closes her eyes and surrenders. His arms feel very right, and his kiss is sweet but not too urgent. Leigh loves the feel of his shirt under her hands, and the scent of him.

"I don't want to rush things, Leigh," Jack says, pulling back. "I am not looking for someone to just date. This feels right, and real, and I want to take things slowly and carefully. Are you onboard with that?"

Leigh almost wants to giggle. "Yes! I've been through so much emotional stuff in the last year that I don't really want to get too serious too fast, but I want you in my life. I want to take things slow and careful, too."

Jack kisses her again, tenderly, then heads out.

Leigh writes in her diary later, *I know my life has turned a very important corner. For the first time since my father died, I am starting to really feel safe and hopeful that I can find someone to love.*

That night she dreams of a house by the beach with a wide porch. Her father is there, and they walk along the shore, laughing and talking. She awakens feeling peaceful for the first time in a long time.

CHAPTER 34 – THE SNUB

After two weeks in the Bahamas with her boyfriend Mark, Peggy Harrington needs to refill her pantry. She breezes into the Fresh Market on Saturday morning to get her favorite seafood salad, and to check out the wine that is on sale. Like most wealthy people, she still relishes a bargain.

Peggy grabs a tiny cup of coffee and heads back to the cheese section. After a few minutes, she has picked out a buttery, expensive French brie. *Mark loves that brie*, she thinks. She mentally pats herself on the back for buying cheese even though she can't eat it.

Peggy loads up her basket adding some saffron, two éclairs, and some fresh asparagus. For Mark, she will cook, although normally she doesn't. As she studies the prepared meats in the case, she becomes aware of a figure to her right, a small elegant woman wearing khakis and a white oxford cloth shirt with a periwinkle blue cardigan thrown over her shoulders.

Peggy turns her head slightly to see who it is.

It's Louise Perkins, whose husband is the president of the Augusta Historical Society.

"Well, Hi, Louise, how are you?" Peggy asks, turning to look and smile, trying to sound upbeat and chipper. Louise is a bigger social butterfly than Peggy and a force to be reckoned with in Augusta society.

Louise turns her head very slightly and coolly nods, a barely perceptible nod, but says nothing. She turns and walks over to the coffee section of the store, not quickly but not slowly either.

Peggy feels the blood rush to her face and her heart starts pounding. She has known Louise for more than thirty years, and although they aren't friends they are always cordial. The cool nod and walk away was not an outright snub, but it was close.

Peggy had decided, in her own mind, that the incident at the Country Club was just her imagination, and she was just being paranoid.

Now, with a feeling of horror, she realizes she had been right to feel odd at the Country Club before she left town. She *was* being snubbed, and there was a good reason. Why?! She thinks wildly *I have lived my entire life so carefully, so impeccably, how can anyone be snubbing ME?!*

Peggy hurries to the checkout line and gets flustered trying to write a check, finally just handing the clerk her credit card.

"Would you like some help –" the clerk starts, but Peggy cuts her off. "NO! I am in a hurry!" she squawks, grabbing all the bags and practically running out of the store.

When Peggy gets home twenty minutes later she grabs a bottle of Brandy from the cabinet, pours a tot and swallows the fiery drink, trying to stop her hands from shaking.

Godalmighty damn! What the hell! She cannot reconcile her impeccable reputation with the way Louise Perkins had treated her. It makes no sense.

She grabs her phone and calls her ex-brother-in-law, Harry. She relates the snub story about Louise.

"Okay, okay, I hear you Darlin.' We'll get to the bottom of this. I'll put Martha on the trail of discovering whatever bullshit gossip is causing this crazy snubbing. Don't fret about it."

Harry's wife Martha is plugged in to all the gossip in town. She practically runs the Sunday School program at First Baptist and her sister is a longtime member at First Methodist so between them, they can find out anything in Augusta.

Harry knows this is serious. Time to circle the family wagons. Tongues had to stop wagging. Repairs had to be made, and possibly retaliation.

In his studio in New York, Edmund smiles as he puts down the phone. Phase one of his plan was executed beautifully.

Wylene Drummond and Edmund have been best friends for years, and she keeps him plugged in to the Augusta gossip, with weekly phone calls where they both drink too much and smoke too many cigarettes.

Wylene collects information the way an antique dealer collects old furniture from the attic. She takes what she finds, polishes it up, and sells it at a markup. In such a way, she learned that William Drummond was in the very early stages of Alzheimers, and fifteen years before, Wylene had swooped in and married him before anyone could say a thing.

When he died five years later, Wylene was a rich woman. She quit her teaching job and insinuated herself into Augusta society, quickly becoming a sought-after hostess of parties and chairwoman of many committees. She also ran the Sunday School Department at First Presbyterian, and she knew who showed up on Sunday morning and who didn't, and why.

After carefully talking it over with Edmund, Wylene had told two ladies who were the biggest gossips in Augusta that she had had it on good authority that Peggy Harrington was sleeping with Bain McDonald.

Within 24 hours everyone in Augusta knew.

That gossip was incendiary.

For years, everyone had wondered if Peggy was faithful to her dull and boring boyfriend. Now they knew the truth, they thought. Bain had a reputation as a man who loved to charm women into his bed, and usually succeeded. It was his defining characteristic, like some men were known as great golfers or good shots. Bain was a modern day Rhett Butler.

Nobody could understand why he scored with women so easily, but there were rumors about his stamina, his equipment, his kinky tastes.

It was generally believed that he was not the sort of man Peggy Harrington would ever in a million years sleep with, which is why the gossip was so delicious.

Edmund had a good reason for encouraging Wylene to spread this fiction.

He loved Leigh. He also knew there might be very valuable information in his brother Harry's garage, but Harry wouldn't give it up unless he had to, and Peggy could make him do it.

Edmund had decided to let Peggy experience the shunning for a while before calling her and offering her a truce. After the way she had treated his brother Travis, it was fun to get some payback.

"Okay darlin' sounds like we've done enough damage for the moment. Keep me posted, alright?" Edmund purred.

"You know I will Brother!" Wylene responded. "Nighty night. Give Greg a kiss for me."

Edmund didn't say what almost caused him to guffaw – that his boyfriend would rather be stung by a wasp than let Wylene kiss him. She wore fire-engine red lipstick and always reeked of Jungle Gardenia. The thought makes him chuckle as he hangs up the phone and heads back to the bedroom.

CHAPTER 35 – JACK AND LEIGH

Two weeks later, it's a sunny Monday morning and Leigh sits in the home office of Jack's house in Decatur, drinking a cup of hot tea with honey from a chunky white mug and going through the phone book.

She was amused to see Jack's kitchen with all its matching white plates, bowls and cups. "My mom got it all at some discount home goods place," he had explained. "I told her paper plates and plastic forks were fine, and she brought me dishes and cutlery the next day."

Leigh smiled. "She sounds like my mom – except nicer, of course. My mother gave me a set of Limoges and a silver chafing dish for my last birthday, even though I tried to explain that I don't entertain like she does."

"Well, what are we gonna do? Mamas," Jack grinned.

Leigh is making a list of all the nursing homes in or near Acworth. She and Jack have decided to call them all and see if they can locate Eugenia Hill that way.

Leigh loves Jack's house. It's a bungalow in an old section of Decatur, near Agnes Scott College. The yard is small, but the trees are old and big, and the house has a large front porch with a swing.

The house is furnished simply with solid looking old furniture ("Most of it was my grandparents," Jack had explained) and some family photos and maps adorning the walls. Jack loves old maps, Leigh has learned.

Each photo and map on the wall is perfectly aligned. Leigh is tempted to tilt each one, just a bit, to see what he would do. She restrains herself.

Jack and Leigh have had fun getting to know one another, and Leigh now feels like they are truly a couple.

As she had told Jessica on the phone after the second date, "I don't feel self-conscious around him. He loves The Far Side, just like me. He likes action movies and/or comedies. He loved the original Mel Brooks movie of The Producers, which is my litmus test – any guy who doesn't love that movie doesn't get another date with me. Jack can quote lines from it. He doesn't mind previewing houses I want to show clients – we looked at two on Saturday. He thinks my musical burps are funny."

"He's a keeper!" Jessica had laughed. "Ask him if his brother is single."

"Okay, will do," Leigh had replied, smiling.

Most important of all, Leigh can relax with Jack, and not feel on display. Jack hasn't put any pressure on Leigh to sleep over, which is a relief.

Jack is practically perfect, which is a bit scary to Leigh. She has dated several guys who appeared perfect and then turned into nightmares after a short time, like the guy who tried to get her to move in with him on the second date.

She keeps waiting for him to reveal something negative about himself, but so far he hasn't, aside from the fact that he's obsessive about being on time, and he prefers beef over any other kind of meat. She can live with both of those.

160

While Jack does some work, Leigh finishes her list and surveys her handiwork. The yellow legal pad has the names and phone numbers of 26 nursing homes in and around Acworth. It seems like a lot, but they have all afternoon.

"Very nice handwriting," Jack notes, coming in and sitting next to Leigh.

"Thank you. My mother used to review all my schoolwork and make me re-copy it if the writing wasn't neat. I thought a list was easier than flipping through the book."

"You know, one day we won't even use phone books," Jack says.

"What? How will you find someone, or find a business?" Leigh asks.

"You'll plug in the computer, open up a browser, put in the name of the business or person, and it will all be on there. The directories, all the paper records, all those will go away. Every business will have a website and there will be search engines to help you find everything -- people, businesses, information."

Leigh rolls her eyes and shakes her head. "The computer is a fun toy and it makes word processing easier, but I don't see that ever happening."

Two hours later they have called every nursing home on the list. They have found that Jack didn't fare as well as Leigh, because she could say, truthfully, "I want to visit a lady named Eugenia Hill, who was a close friend of my grandmother, who has died." Leigh got more sympathy because of the personal connection. She doesn't mention that her grandmother died in 1963.

"Could Miss Maudie have gotten confused? Maybe she meant Alpharetta?" Jack asks. He is sprawled on his sofa rubbing his eyes.

"I don't think so. She seemed really sharp, to me," Leigh responds.

They sit silently for a moment, each contemplating the dead end.

"There's only one thing we can do now," Jack says, his eyes twinkling.

"What?"

"We can go to lunch. I'm starving."

"Sounds like a plan!" Leigh responds enthusiastically.

That night, Leigh has a vivid dream. She is a little girl, wearing her pajamas, and her father is doing shadow pictures on the wall for her. Usually, he made lots of different animals – birds, dogs, crocodiles. In the dream, though, Leigh is sitting in his lap and he is singing to her.

By the light, of the silvery moo-oo-oo-oon – I will sit with LeighBaby and croon this tune…

His hands somehow show her the shape of the moon on the wall, while he sings the tune softly. He tickles Leigh and she giggles. Next, he holds up his hands and there is a big bird outlined on the wall, in shadow.

He never made a bird like that in real life. What does that mean? Leigh writes in her diary the next morning.

Unfortunately, when she calls Jack the next morning he informs her he has to turn his attention back to his regular business. He is doing surveillance for a big client and he may not be able to see her for a week or so.

Leigh is disappointed, of course, but then again she needs to sell some houses, too. They agree to check in by phone every day.

Before hanging up, Jack speaks to her sternly. "Leigh, go ahead and call Mindspring and get an internet account. I will help you get your laptop running this weekend."

Leigh writes down the number of Mindspring and follows his instructions as to how to power up the laptop. An hour later she has an email address. She calls Jessica to come see her email account.

Jessica walks downstairs and appears at Leigh's door holding a plate of homemade knishes. Leigh eats three in one minute

"So good! I love your food," she gushes.

Jessica laughs. "Next time I will bring matzoh ball soup!"

"My favorite!" Leigh says enthusiastically.

Leigh shows Jessica the Gateway computer. "Wow, how nice of your mom to buy you one of those! They are super cool!" Jessica gushes, admiring the large monitor on the computer.

"Well, I think it was actually because she wanted me to email her every day and report on my husband hunting assignment, but so be it," Leigh chuckles, ruefully.

They sit and chat about the internet and email accounts, and finish up the knishes. Leigh feels so grown up with her very own computer...

CHAPTER 36 – FINDING EUGENIA

Leigh fixes herself a tuna salad sandwich and sits on her deck eating lunch and scanning the Creative Loafing magazine, a local newspaper that covers Atlanta's thriving cultural and arts scenes. The newsprint reminds her of the phone books she had pored over.

Wait a minute. There was an E. Hill in the phone book not long ago. Why not call?

A few minutes later Leigh sits at her dining room table with the phone, having unplugged it from the back of the computer.

She calls the E. Hill in the phone book. The phone is answered by a kid, which is unexpected.

"Hullow" says a bored male voice, about ten years old.

"Um, hi, my name is Leigh and I'm looking for a lady named Eugenia Hill. I wonder if this is her home?" she asks, keenly aware of trying not to sound like a telemarketer.

"MOM!" he bellows, "Some lady on the phone about Aunt Jeannie!"

Aunt Jeannie? Leigh thinks *oh my god maybe this is it*! She holds for a moment, then the phone is picked up by an adult, presumably his mother.

"Hello?!" a nasal female voice says, sounding tired.

"Hi, my name is Leigh Harrington and my grandmother Rose Harrington was friends with a lady named Eugenia Hill? I am trying to locate Mrs. Hill, to ask her some questions about some things I inherited from my grandmother? Are you Mrs. Hill's niece?"

"I am the wife of her great nephew John. My name is Alice. She's in a nursing home over in Marietta, on Moon Street, right near the Big Chicken. What did you say your name was again?"

"My name is Leigh Harrington."

Startled, Leigh recalls her dream - *Moon Street, Big Chicken. That's what Dad was trying to tell me in the dream..*

"Harrington sounds familiar. You from Augusta?"

"Yes, m'am," Leigh responds, wondering how she knew that.

"Well then. That's the connection. Your father was a lawyer?"

"No, no. My grandfather was, though, Horace Harrington. He was married to Rose, who was a friend of Eugenia Hill."

"Yes, yes. Now I get it. Well my goodness. Aunt Jeannie has talked about him some, over the years, about what a terrible man he was. I'm sorry, but I'm just being honest here."

Leigh shrugs, even though the woman can't see it. *Grandpa was an asshole. That ain't news, lady.*

"Yeah, that's what I understand. He died before I was born, you see, as did Rose. She left me a suitcase and it contained some things I'd like to ask Mrs. Hill about, since they were friends. Could you give me the name of the nursing home?"

"It's Pinetree Gardens, on Moon Street, just off Highway 41, about 2 miles past the Big Chicken. She had a stroke about a year ago, so she can't talk too well, and she can't hear well enough to use the phone. You're welcome to go see her. She's 96 now, so she doesn't get too many visitors. Hang on a second. I've got the number right here near the phone."

Everyone in north Atlanta knows the landmark in Marietta known as the Big Chicken. It marks one of the first Kentucky Fried Chicken restaurants in the area and features a 56 foot tall metal structure designed to look like a chicken rising up out of the restaurant. Locals often give directions like "Turn left about a mile past the big chicken."

The two women chat a few more minutes and Alice gives Leigh the number of the nursing home. Leigh thanks her for her help.

I didn't call Pinetree Gardens yesterday. It's not far from Acworth, but it's definitely Marietta. Why didn't I call there? Who knows. It doesn't matter.

Leigh sits a few minutes pondering what to do. She is itching to go see Eugenia Hill, and find out what she recalls about Rose. Leigh wants Jack to go, too, though. She gives him a call.

"Can you take a lunch hour and run up there and meet me?" she asks, hating to sound needy.

Jack sighs audibly. "Leigh, I would like nothing more than to go see a 96 year old lady in a nursing home in Marietta but unfortunately I am tailing the wife of a rich guy who thinks she's cheating on him. I hate these kinds of cases but I need the money. Just call me later and tell me what happened."

"Okay, or hey – I can email you!" she remembers, smiling. "Check your email, ok?!"

"Awesome! Proud of you, Sweetheart!"

Leigh dresses in blue cotton slacks and a white cotton sweater set, and puts on some face powder and lipstick. The day is humid so her hair is a frizzy mess but she pulls it back from her face in clips. Within 30 minutes she is on I-285 heading towards Marietta, directions to the Pinetree Gardens nursing home taped to the dashboard of her car.

When she turns in to the parking lot of Pinetree Gardens, she refreshes her lipstick. Old ladies always think young women should wear lipstick.

Leigh has never been to a nursing home, but the modest, one story brick building is not what she expected. It looks more like a house than a hospital, and there are boxwoods and azaleas out front, and only about twenty parking spaces. Leigh checks her purse again for the photo of Rose and Eugenia. She has also brought the letter from the suitcase.

There's a tiny reception area done in beige and rose colors, with comfortable chairs covered in faux leather, a few occasional tables and a tired looking tall plant. Leigh gives the lady at the desk her name and in a few minutes she is walking down a short hallway behind a tall nurse named Loretta, according to her nametag.

Leigh can feel her heart pounding with excitement.

The tiny room holds only a bed, a tiny table, and a wooden straight chair. Eugenia Hill sits in a wheelchair by the window, a tiny, wizened lady who likely weighs no more than eighty lbs. Short white hair sticks out in wisps, her face sagging on one side. She wears a shapeless gray cotton dress and a gray sweater. *I don't know what I expected – I guess just an older version of the tall lady in the photo – but Eugenia Hill looks nothing like what I thought she would.*

"Miz Eugenia there's a young lady here to see you, name of Leigh Harrington, says you knew her grandmama," Loretta says loudly but kindly.

"Hi, Mrs. Hill – " Leigh begins, but Loretta is shaking her head before the words leave her mouth. "Honey, she's real hard of hearing and don't wear that hearing aid. You gonna have to talk louder. Here's a chair."

Loretta brings over the wooden chair, places it by the wheelchair and nods at Leigh. She sits down, acutely aware of the smells of disinfectant and other things she doesn't want to identify.

Before leaving, Loretta gently puts a pair of thick glasses on Eugenia's face, and Eugenia sits up straighter and stares at Leigh.

"Call if you need anything," Loretta says before she bustles out.

Leigh smiles, unsure quite how to open this very odd conversation. "HOW ARE YOU THIS MORNING?" she finally asks. Eugenia's eyes widen and Leigh realizes she is probably speaking too loudly.

"My name is Leigh. I am Rose Harrington's granddaughter," she continues, softer.

Eugenia Hill sits up and leans in closer to study Leigh's face. "Rose?" she asks, except it sounds like "Roghuh?" Leigh realizes the stroke has left her with a speech impediment.

"Yes, M'am, she was my grandmother," Leigh continues, reaching into her purse to pull out the photo. She places it in Eugenia's age-spotted, claw-like hands. Eugenia holds it close to her face, hands trembling, and stares at it for a full minute.

When she looks up at Leigh again, her eyes are filled with tears. "My sweet friend," Eugenia says slowly, and with great effort. "You look so much like her," she says, patting Leigh's hand. "So lovely."

"Thank you, Mrs. Hill. I wish I had known her," Leigh says, her own eyes filling with tears. *I have a weakness, an inability to not cry when I see someone else cry. It's like I feel their hurting and I can't help it. The tears always come.*

Leigh sniffles, and reaches again into her purse and pulls out the old letter, the one from Nate to Rose. "I'm going to read you a letter and I want to ask you about it, okay?"

Eugenia nods slightly.

Leigh clears her throat and reads:

Rose –

I have enlisted and I am off to Fort Montford for Marine training. I don't know what will happen, but I will get word to you where I am, when possible.

Remember to write to Millie when the time comes and she and Samuel will come up there.

All My Love -

Nate

"I have a suitcase of hers and it has maternity clothes and things. I don't know what happened to the baby, though, who would have been my aunt or uncle. Do you know? Can you tell me?" Leigh asks, trying to sound calm.

Eugenia Hill holds out her hand and Leigh gives her the letter. Eugenia stares at it, reading it silently, her lips moving.

"Hard to talk," she says finally. She motions to a small chest of drawers by the bed, and makes a writing gesture. Leigh realizes she wants her to look in the drawer. Leigh gets up and walks over to the chest and gingerly opens the top drawer. There's a small pad and a ballpoint pen. Leigh brings them over to Eugenia and puts them in front of her, on top of a small lap desk she finds next to the wall.

With some difficulty, Eugenia opens the pad, and writes. She labors over the letters. Leigh sits there for a full 15 minutes, waiting. Finally, with a great sigh, Eugenia puts down the pen and pushes the pad of paper towards Leigh.

Rose had a girl, named her Liz. Could not raise her because the baby looked negro, like Nate. Nate killed in the war. Millie and Samuel friends of Nate's in Augusta. Took the baby to raise.

Rose wanted divorce but husband said no.

Yr granddaddy caught Rose sneaking off to see Liz. Rose saw her every week until Liz was ten years old. Then Samuel was lynched. Millie took Liz and ran away.

Leigh finishes reading the words and then reads them again.

"Why was Samuel lynched?" she asks, cringing at the thought. Eugenia just shakes her head slowly, then shrugs, deep sadness in her eyes.

"What was Samuel's last name?" Leigh asks, handing the pad and pen back to Eugenia. She writes *Washington.*

Leigh sits for a moment staring at the paper. *I know the name of my aunt. I know her whole name.*

"May I keep this?" Leigh asks. Eugenia nods. Leigh carefully tears the paper out of the pad, folds it, and puts it in her purse. Leigh then reaches for Eugenia's hand and sits and holds it.

Leigh closes her eyes for a moment, flooded with gratitude, trying not to cry. *Thank you, Lord, thank you for bringing me to see this lady. I feel so close to learning the truth, now.*

Loretta opens the door. "How you doin' Miss Jeannie?" she asks, looking at her carefully. Eugenia's eyes are half closed and she looks like she is going to fall asleep.

Leigh realizes it's time to go, and withdraws her hand.

"Mrs. Hill, may I come again to see you?" Leigh asks. Eugenia doesn't open her eyes but reaches out and squeezes Leigh's hand, "Thank you for coming to see me," she says, her words very slurred.

Loretta nods her head. "You can come again but the visits have to be brief. She gets tired real easy since she had the stroke."

Leigh digs around in her purse and fishes out a business card and hands it to Loretta. "Would you call me and let me know if anything... happens, with her? I know I'm not family but I'd be grateful."

Loretta nods again, looking thoughtful. "I've never seen her so lively. She usually won't talk at all, just sits and looks out the window. Don't write unless somebody's here. She was happy to see you. It was a blessing, you coming today."

Leigh's eyes fill up with tears again and she can only nod.

Leigh looks over at Eugenia Hill, who is leaning to the side, eyes closed. She leans over and kisses Eugenia's papery cheek. "Thank you, Mrs. Hill. Thank you so much for your help," she says softly. Eugenia opens her eyes and looks up at Leigh, and half smiles.

The rest of the afternoon and evening are like swimming underwater for Leigh. Over and over, the words *I know the name of my aunt* resound in her head. Leigh can feel herself getting close to something critical to understanding the mysteries of her family.

Business has to be handled, however.

Leigh previews a house in Buckhead that one of her clients wants to see, walking through the rooms like a sleepwalker, mentally ticking off the selling points – crown molding, lots of natural light, small yard easy to maintain. Inside, though, on another track, her mind keeps fantasizing about what it must have been like for Rose, to only be able to visit her child weekly, to not be able to divorce, to be yoked to an older man who was a jerk. How did she survive that, emotionally? Did her daughter Liz know that Rose was her mother? Where did Liz go when her dad was killed and she left Augusta? So many questions.

After calling and getting his answering machine, Leigh painstakingly types everything into an email to Jack later. She is a slow typist. Then she calls him again and leaves him a message telling him to check his email.

That night her dreams are non-specific and non-memorable, until just before she awakens.

Leigh wakes up and goes into the living room to drink a glass of water.

She writes in her diary. *I dreamed I was back in the old house, and Bubba is hurt, and Mom and Dad are upstairs screaming at the drunk maid. Rose comes into the room, though, in*

my dream, and sits on the floor and pulls me into her lap, singing softly to me "You are my sunshine, my only sunshine / you make me happy, when skies are gray." I relax in her arms and snuggle in, feeling loved and safe. I wish it had really happened that way. My dream was so real, though. I woke up smelling L'Origan.

Leigh returns to bed hoping she will dream of Rose again.

CHAPTER 37 – TARRED AND FEATHERED

Peggy Harrington is furious. Everywhere she goes in Augusta, she is shunned. Nobody will speak to her in the French Market Grill or Le Café Du Teau or Calverts.

Her garden club meeting is canceled by the president citing ill health, the first ever cancellation in more than twenty years.

Peggy sits on the back patio at the home of her ex-brother-in-law Harry and sips her glass of Chardonnay, trying to be calm. Her carefully-constructed public persona is in peril, and she feels utterly vulnerable again, like she felt as a child when her mother would embarrass her.

Harry has discovered the gossip that Peggy is sleeping with Bain McDonald and told her.

He has never seen someone turn so white before, a shade of white he had never seen except on a corpse. He hurried to refresh her drink.

Peggy's cell phone rings, and she glances at the number. New York area code. Must be Edmund. She answers grumpily.

"Hello, old girl, it's your New York ex-relative," Edmund trills. "Where are you?"

Peggy scowls. "I'm actually sitting on the back patio of Harry's house, watching him incinerate steaks."

"Oh good. Put me on speaker. You do have that feature on your phone, right?"

"Yes, of course," Peggy grumps, signaling Harry to come sit beside her. She presses the speakerphone button and puts the phone on the table between them.

"I am sure by now you are in a very foul humor, Peggy, because everyone in Augusta thinks you are sleeping with Bain McDonald."

Peggy's mouth drops open and she stares at the phone in astonishment. "How the hell?!" she sputters.

"Now Pegasus, I am Augusta bred and Augusta born. I still know everything that goes on in that wicked little town, and I can create gossip even up here in Yankeeland, darling."

Harry's face has purpled. "What the hell, Ed!"

"Ask me why," Edmund says evenly.

"Why?" Peggy sputters.

"Pegleg, you have chosen to try to keep Leigh ignorant about her very own grandmother. When I was in Atlanta recently I realized that I am sick and tired of all the lies and subterfuge. I am sick to death of it. I will no longer be party to the family conspiracy to keep Bubba and Leigh and even your girls, Harry, in the dark, so to speak. I have news for you. Leigh now knows her grandmother was mulatto. She wasn't at all upset about it. She wants to know everything she can about Rose and her great-grandmother, and even her aunt."

There is a full minute of silence. Edmund chuckles and lights another cigarette.

Peggy wishes she still smoked.

Finally, Peggy speaks, and her voice is icy. "Okay, so we know you can create gossip, but can you quash it? Can you un-ring that bell, you old fairy?!"

Ed sighs. "I really don't like your tone, Pegboard. Yes, I can un-ring it, quite easily, in fact. Never mind how. But before I do that, y'all are going to have to do what I ask. So listen up. Here's the deal. Harry, you are going to get every single thing that belonged to our brother Travis, those boxes that you're hoarding in that nasty garage, and ship them to Leigh in Atlanta. EVERYTHING. Peggy, you are going to give Leigh the letter that's in the safe deposit box at the bank. Once Leigh calls me and tells me she has it, I will make sure the gossip-fest disappears."

Harry sneers at the phone. "And if I choose not to do that?"

"Well, it's quite simple. I will make sure everyone in Augusta knows about your relationship with Mimi Sloan."

Peggy looks at Harry and stifles the urge to giggle. She knows that Harry has been having an affair with Mimi for over a year, but he swore her to secrecy. Mimi is an upstart Yankee intruder, a multiple divorcee with a lot of money and no brains. Nobody likes her. She has huge breasts, though, and Harry is a breast man. Right now Harry looks like he's getting ready to have a heart attack. If his affair with Mimi becomes known his wife will divorce him and all his old moneyed clients will decamp. His life will be ruined.

"You wouldn't, you old faggot," Harry sneers with false bravado.

"Ah, there's the real Harry, the brother of my childhood, who used to taunt me and beat me up," Edmund replies, sighing.

There's an awkward silence.

"Wait just a damn minute," Peggy says. "What letter are you talking about?"

"Oh puh-leeze, Pegleg, don't play stupid with me. The letter Rose wrote to Leigh before she was born. I know you were instructed to save it for Leigh and give it to her when she turned 18. You didn't do it. She deserves the letter. It was written to her."

Peggy thinks wildly for a moment. She has only the vaguest memory of her mother-in-law giving her a letter for Leigh when she was about 8 months pregnant. Suffering through an Augusta summer, her feet swollen, nauseated, Peggy's temperament had been horrible.

"Ed, I have no idea what happened to that letter, I swear. I really don't know what happened to it." *Did I put it in the baby book?* she wonders.

"Well, I suggest you find it, my dear, or else I will not rescind the gossip about you and Mr. Ugly."

"Who cares? I could care less. Lots of women in Augusta have slept with that coarse man."

Edmund chuckles and Peggy hears him light another Marlboro. "Oh Pegboard, never play poker dear. You'd lose everything. Well let's see, what else can I use against you… I know. I may actually go so far as to reveal your nom de plume to certain key figures in town if you don't produce that letter. You think you're shunned now? Wait until everyone knows you're the author of the Carriage House mysteries. You'll be tarred and feathered."

178

"You would not dare –" she splutters, feeling her heart start to pound and her mouth go dry.

"Oh, wouldn't I? You drove my brother to drink and scarred your own children emotionally for life. You're always cutting down your own daughter, treating her like dirt, and I'm sick of it. SICK of it! Leigh is a lovely, sensitive, smart young woman. I want her to know the truth, finally. Get everything I've asked to Leigh, asap. You both have one week. After that, the gloves come off and I promise you, you will both face social ruin."

Edmund hangs up. He lights another cigarette and looks at Greg, his boyfriend. "Well that felt GOOD!" he cackles.

Liz struggles to sleep.

She wakes up and turns on the bedside lamp, and drinks some water from the glass by her bed. She looks at the photo on her bedside table, made ten years before when her son TJ graduated from college.

Liz puts on her bathrobe and her reading glasses and goes to her desk, opening the drawer and pulling out a photo of her with Travis, a photo she rarely shows anyone because she would then have to explain their odd relationship.

Okay Travis, I need your help. I sense that Leigh needs answers. What do you want me to do? Do you want me to just seek her out and tell her everything? Give me a sign.

She waits, looking at the photo and humming, "You Are My Sunshine," a song her mother used to sing to her. No signs are forthcoming.

179

She hears her mother snoring in the other room, and decides to try sleeping again.

CHAPTER 38 – A CAUTION

Bain's secretary, Eileen, comes into his office and sits down opposite his desk. A middle-aged woman with a brown bouffant hairstyle and a no-nonsense attitude, she loves Bain like a son and handles his business matters with ease, but she is clearly irked.

"Well, just have a seat then, dear. You've got a bee in your bonnet, clearly," Bain says with a grin.

She plops into the chair and fixes him with a steely glare.

"You know what people are saying, right?" Eileen asks, her voice raspy from years of smoking.

'You mean the gossip about me and Peggy Harrington? Sure. So what? People love to gossip about me. If I did half the stuff they gossip about I'd never have time to run the restaurant," he laughs.

"Yes, but Peggy Harrington is a force to be reckoned with, in this town. She's the ultimate blue blooded clubwoman. I don't like her, but I hate to see her reputation sullied. It's not true, is it?"

Bain now laughs. "No! Good god, Eileen, have you ever seen me with her, heard me talk about her, anything?" he says, shaking his head.

"No, but you can be pretty wily."

"Listen, the irony of all this talk is that I have admired Peggy Harrington for a long time. I've seen her here a few times, and I ran into her not long ago. We have the same dentist. She's not only beautiful, but she's smart. I asked my aunt about her. She's really something. I would love to go out with her."

181

Eileen looks at him with concern. "I can understand that, Bain, but I want to point out a couple of things. One, she's older than you are, by at least 7 years. I think that's too much. Two, she has been married twice and both marriages were disasters. I know you're looking to get married and settle down, but Peggy Harrington is not the way to go. She will make you miserable."

"Why do you think I want to get married?" Bain asks, frowning.

Eileen sits up straighter in the chair and leans forward slightly, speaking as though to a child. "I know you. I've watched you go home alone many nights. I've seen you laughing and playing with the kids that come in here, seen how your face lights up around them. I've seen you

quietly slipping into the back of Good Shepherd on Sunday morning. You like this reputation you have as a playboy but that's not the real you."

Silence descends on the office.

The phone rings. Bain shrugs, looks at the phone and hits the button. "Bain McDonald. Hey there Ben, how are you?"

Eileen gets up and quietly goes back to her office. She decides to call Bain's aunt and fill her in on the gossip.

CHAPTER 39 – ANYTHING AND NOTHING

The day after her visit to Eugenia Hill, Leigh spends the morning in a frustrating quest, on the phone.

After eating a two egg omelet with artichoke hearts, feta cheese and mushrooms, plus drinking two cups of tea, Leigh is ready to turn off the "Today Show" and get to work.

She calls Directory Assistance for Augusta and asks the operator for numbers for Millie Washington and Liz Washington. There are no listings for either. She then calls other major towns in Georgia – Macon, Albany, Columbus, even Valdosta. Nothing.

She decides to fire up her computer and see what happens. She uses a search engine called AltaVista and carefully types in the names Elizabeth Washington and Millie Washington.

Nothing.

Could they have moved to Atlanta? It made sense. More jobs, bigger city, so easier to be invisible. Leigh gets out her two heavy Atlanta phone books and looks for those names. Nothing.

Of course, both women could have married, and had phones listed in their husband's names. Or they could have stayed with friends. They could have come to Atlanta but moved away. Anything could have happened.

Leigh finally gives up. She has to get dressed and show a house to a couple from Michigan who want to live in East Cobb. She plods back to her closet and pulls out a black skirt and black cotton top, feeling like mourning.

CHAPTER 40 – THE SPECIAL BATH

Three days later, and Leigh is lying on the sofa in Dr. Simerly's office wearing jeans and a tee shirt, trying to be as relaxed and comfortable as possible. She's breathing deeply and evenly.

She cannot relax enough. She is being hypnotized to try to recall the Drunk Maid incident.

After her dream where Rose came to her – which felt incredibly real, she tells Dr. Simerly – she has the overwhelming feeling that getting her memory back of that day is the key to many things.

Unlike in the movies and on TV, hypnosis doesn't mean one doesn't remember what goes on. For Leigh, it's simply a guided exercise in trying to recall a traumatic day in her early life. Dr. Simerly had explained that he would try to help her remember, but no guarantees.

"If it's not safe for you to remember, you won't be able to, I'm afraid," he had warned her.

He talks Leigh through the hypnosis steps – she is walking down a long hallway with many doors, seeing each door, and behind each one is a memory, and at the end of the hallway is a beautiful room -- but the gap in her memory of the Drunk Maid day remains, stubbornly denying her what she wants to know.

Leigh finally sits up on the sofa and drinks some water, trying to calm down, although she wants to cry in frustration.

"You cannot force these things, Leigh, I'm sorry."

Leigh feels herself getting angry at his measured tone. "I just have this feeling that if I can get back those memories it will explain everything. Can't you tell me the way to do that? You're not like other psychologists I've seen. You understand there is an unseen world all around us that we can tap into, which I've felt to be true all my life. I just need you to tell my spirit guides that I need to know where my aunt is, NOW."

Dr. Simerly had spoken about Spirit Guides to Leigh and she agreed that perhaps such beings existed, although she was privately skeptical. She decided that when he said "spirit guides" she would just think "guardian angels" and that would sound better.

Dr. Simerly sighs, pulls a tube of Chapstick out of his pockets and runs it around his mouth, and clears his throat. Leigh watches the gesture with resignation. *Whenever he pulls out the Chapstick, he's nervous. It's one of his "tells" – and it means he isn't sure what to say to me.*

"I'm sorry, Leigh, but our time today is up. Look, there is no magic formula. Perhaps you can ask your spirit guides to share those memories with you when you're at home, perhaps when you're more relaxed."

"You mean, hypnotize myself?" Leigh asks, not disguising the skepticism in her voice. Her hands are nervously twisting the hem of her shirt.

"Sure. People do it all the time. I've done it. When I'm asking my brain or my guides to share something with me, I want it to meet at least four criteria, that the only information that comes into conscious awareness will be safe, timely, useful and constructive. Ask that, and listen for an answer."

185

"I don't think it will work," she mumbles.

"Maybe not, but you won't know until you try, will you?" Dr. Simerly says gently.

Leigh leaves his office feeling really frustrated, but as she pulls her car out of the parking lot, she has an idea. She heads south on Peachtree Street, to Lenox Mall. She parks in front of Macy's. She has time to run in before meeting with some home buyers.

Back at her apartment, Leigh runs a hot bath and strips off her clothes. She piles her hair on top of her head and secures it with bobby pins.

Next, she pulls out the bottle of Caswell & Massey Lilac Bath and Shower Gel she had purchased earlier, and pours a few drops into the water gushing out of the tap. Immediately, the lilac scent fills the steamy bathroom, and Leigh takes a deep breath and cuts the water off.

Leigh has always loved bubble baths. She figures if she smells the triggering lilac smell while relaxing in the bath maybe her guardian angels will let her have her memories back. Theoretically.

The lilac scent permeates the air in the small bathroom, though, and makes her nervous. Her heart starts to pound. Before she can chicken out, she says a prayer for help and asks her angels to ensure that the only information that comes into conscious awareness will be safe, timely, useful and constructive.

Leigh sinks into the tub of warm bubbles and concentrates on breathing slowly and deliberately, in through the nose and out slowly through her mouth.

Without thinking about it, she pulls her knees up to her chest and hugs her knees, starting to rock slightly. Her eyes close. She thinks back to the day when she was 4 years old, the day everything changed. She sees herself watching television, eating, playing with Bubba. Then the locking out, the frantic beating on the door. The sweat rolling down her face. The feelings of panic. Daddy coming home.

Screaming.

She later writes in her diary: *I feel like I'm back in the kitchen of the old house. I wish I could cuddle our dog, Ranger, who always comforted me.*

I tried to recall what happened that day, what my parents were yelling about, but nothing came through after the screaming. It was just darkness, and quiet. I sat rocking for a few minutes. Nothing was going to magically come through. I don't know if that's good or bad.

At least I don't have to fear the smell of Caswell & Massey Lilac Bath and Shower Gel. I can handle it now.

The loud ring of the telephone breaks the spell. Leigh had left the door of the bathroom cracked so she could hear the phone. It rings persistently. She imagines it's a client calling.

Leigh stands up in the tub and grabs her huge fluffy pink towel and throws it around herself, then zips out to the bedroom to grab the phone.

"Leigh? Are you all right?" Jack's voice sounds nervous.

"Yes, I'm fine. Why?"

"I don't know. I just had the sense something was wrong, and you needed me. I thought I should call and check on you," he says tenderly.

"Well, I was in the bathtub, so can I dry off and call you back in a few minutes?" Leigh asks, trying to hug the towel closer and prevent dripping.

"Whoa. Hold on. I am picturing you…" Jack says teasingly.

Leigh laughs. "Get your mind out of the gutter."

"Why?! I can't help it. I haven't seen you in a while. I miss you," Jack replies.

"Well, why don't you come over and eat dinner with me? I can cook, you know. You always bring food, but I'm actually a good cook. I want to tell you more about my meeting with Eugenia Hill."

Leigh wanted to tell him more than was in the email, and get his thoughts about what to do next.

"Okay. I think I can take a break and do that. What can I bring?"

"Just yourself. See you at 7, okay?"

"Sounds like a plan."

Jack arrives on time, carrying a bouquet of daisies, and hands them to Leigh.

"I love daisies! Thank you, Sweetie!"

Jack looks more relaxed than she's seen him, in khaki cargo shorts and a short-sleeved white cotton button down shirt worn over a purple Adidas tee shirt.

Leigh has prepared poached salmon steaks, a salad, and Jasmine rice with herbs. She sets out some fresh goat cheese and club crackers to munch on while the salmon finishes cooking.

Jack leans on the counter, watching her cook. He carefully places some cheese on a cracker and drinks a beer while Leigh adds some chopped carrots and cherry tomatoes to the salad and tosses it.

"Sorry about not having beef. I doubt I could find good enough beef to satisfy your sophisticated palate," Leigh teases him.

"I will be fine. I like salmon. I want to hear more about your trip up to Marietta."

Leigh describes the meeting with Eugenia Hill in as much detail as she can, and shows him the piece of paper. He reads.

Rose had a girl, named her Liz. Could not raise her because the baby negro. Nate killed in the war. Millie and Samuel friends of Nate's in Augusta. Took the baby to raise.

Rose wanted divorce but husband said no.

Yr granddaddy caught Rose sneaking off to see Liz. Rose saw her every week until Liz was ten years old. Then Samuel was lynched. Millie took Liz and ran away.

Jack reads the paper, shaking his head.

"What?" Leigh asks, studying Jack's troubled face.

"Well… Ever since you told me about meeting Eugenia Hill, I've been thinking about this, about the lynching. I have a theory about what happened but it's just a theory. Do you want to hear it?"

"Of course."

"Well, I contacted a friend with the Augusta police department after you sent me the email about this. He ran a search on Samuel Washington. Nothing came up. Normally there should have been some sort of incident report. However, it's possible that the Klan lynchings were not reported during those years because there were men on the police force who were part of the Klan. It might have been kept out of the papers too, for the same reason. They operated in secrecy."

"Oh my God."

"Yeah. A horrible thing nobody wants to think about, but it happened. Could your grandfather have been in the Klan?"

Leigh closes her eyes for a moment. She has never heard anything nice about her grandfather so it's possible. *Could that be why Rose stayed with him? Was she afraid? Then again why would he have stayed with her if he knew she was part black?*

Leigh opens her eyes and takes a swig of beer before answering.

"I suppose he could have been, sure. I've never heard anything good about him, to be honest," Leigh reluctantly replies. "Anything is possible. He drove away his own son, my uncle Edmund, just for being gay."

Jack nods.

"He probably saw Rose sneaking off to see Liz in the black neighborhood and just went berserk. He might have thought she was having an affair with Samuel. Who knows?" Leigh guesses.

Silence descends on the little kitchen. Leigh takes out two plates, forks and knives, and hands them to Jack, who sets the table for her.

After dinner, after Jack has helped her rinse the dishes and put them in the dishwasher, they sit on the deck, in the darkness, and talk.

"That was an excellent dinner, Leigh. Thank you."

"Sorry about dessert. I'm trying to not eat sweets," Leigh says, apologetic.

"No big deal. I don't need sweets either. Once I became a civilian I had to watch it. I don't run 5 miles a day now," Jack responds.

"I have never in my life run 5 miles," Leigh chuckles. "Hiking is okay."

"I like to do some hiking. Would you go with me sometime? We could hike around Stone Mountain, maybe climb it."

"Sure. I will enjoy hiking a lot more if I'm with you."

Jack gazes at Leigh and she moves over to his lap and into his arms. He nuzzles her neck.

The phone rings. Leigh tries to ignore it but it keeps ringing. "It might be a client. I'm sorry. I'm going to grab it," she says, reluctantly getting up.

"No problem."

Jack sips his beer and looks at the full moon, thinking about how nice it feels to be with Leigh.

She reappears a moment later, looking stricken.

"What's wrong, Honey?!" Jack asks, getting up to hug her. Leigh wraps her arms around Jack and buries her face in the space between his cheek and neck.

"That was the nursing home. Eugenia Hill died this afternoon. The nurse thought I'd want to know. Oh Jack, I wanted to go talk to her some more. I finally felt hopeful, felt like we might get somewhere with this."

He holds her and rubs her back wordlessly as she cries.

CHAPTER 41 – A SPECIAL PAINTING

Peggy Harrington takes another sip of her Vodka martini and tries to calm herself. She cannot locate the letter that Rose had written to unborn Leigh.

She has to find that letter. Edmund has already damaged her reputation, but it is salvageable. However, if he doesn't stop the rumors about her and Bain McDonald, she will be socially ruined. It isn't just that he is a cad. He's a social nobody. McDonald isn't from a good family. He moved to Augusta from somewhere else. How he had managed to get the loan to open his restaurant, nobody knew. The place is elegant and has terrific food, but Bain is a nobody as far as old Augusta is concerned.

The problem is, Peggy has a terrible feeling she might have burned the letter. She could admit to herself that her drinking had gotten out of hand there for a while, during the last days of her marriage. The drunken rage that had resulted in a bonfire of wedding pictures was not the only such incident.

Perhaps the letter was put in the safety deposit box at the bank? Or perhaps she gave it to Travis? It might still be in the banker's boxes in Harry's garage. Maybe she should just go over there and look through the boxes.

Peggy picks up the phone and dials Harry's number. She knows it by heart.

"Hey there darlin'" Harry drawls. "What's shakin' pretty lady?"

Wow, it's not even 8 p.m. and he's already sloshed, Peggy thinks.

"Hey, how you doing, brother-in-law?"

"Oh just dandy. You find that letter yet?" he asks.

Peggy picks up on the edge in his voice. She knows him too well.

"Funny you should ask. I can't find it. You know that time just before the divorce was… really awful. I've tried to forget it, to be honest. Anyway, the letter isn't in Leigh's baby book, or any photo albums or scrapbooks I've got around here. I'm betting Travis put it in the safe deposit box. You got all that stuff, right? And his office stuff?"

"Well, yes, that's what was in my garage, but I sent that stuff to Leigh already. I didn't even look through the stuff, just sealed up the boxes and sent them on. Cost a pretty penny to ship the boxes, but so be it."

Peggy's heart sinks.

"Okay, well, I'll keep looking. Time's almost up."

"Good luck with that, darlin'."

Peggy hangs up the phone and ponders the situation. She keeps worrying it around in her mind, like a child wriggles a loose tooth.

Without thinking why, feeling somehow propelled, Peggy goes into her den and pulls a photo album out of the bookcase. This one contains black and white photos from the time of her marriage to Travis.

Peggy sinks down into a club chair and slowly flips through the pages. She has not seen the album in many years because she has never wanted to remember that time. Leigh had put in the photos, a bit sloppily, after finding them in an old shoebox. The album is cheap and the plastic sheets over the photos are yellowing. Peggy hadn't wanted anything to do with the project and made Leigh spend her own money on the photo album.

Peggy again feels a familiar jolt of irritation that she has a daughter who won't let go of the past.

The old shots bring memories flooding back. There is Bubba, chocolate cake all over his face at his first birthday party. Peggy and Travis are dressed up for a Christmas party in 1960's finery. There's Leigh in a cowboy outfit and no shoes, her hair a wild tangle, at her third birthday party. She wore wax lips all day, and shot everyone with a water pistol. In the next shot, Travis grins and holds up a fish he caught while camping with the kids, an activity that never involved Peggy.

There are shots from Christmas 1962, with baby Bubba, and Ranger as a puppy. Peggy stares at the photo, frowning. *Why is Rose's face in there, behind the tree?*

Peggy grabs her glasses and peers at the old photo, puzzled. Finally, she realizes that what she is seeing is the portrait of Rose that Travis commissioned after his mother's death. Edmund had taken a whole series of beautiful color portraits of Rose, and a painter friend of his had used one to create an elegant formal portrait of Rose. That large painting had hung in the living room of their home for several years. What had happened to it?

Peggy sits lost in thought for a few minutes, forcing herself to remember those terrible years leading up to their divorce. She vaguely remembers a screaming fight where she and Travis were both drunk, several years after the Drunk Maid Incident.

"And why in hell do we have to have that enormous painting of your mother in our goddamn living room?!" Peggy screamed, an iced tea glass full of Scotch in her hand. She was pointing out the painting with her long red fingernail, accusingly.

Peggy and Travis had been to an anniversary dinner at the Country Club, and the strain of appearing to be a happy couple had unnerved them both. They had come home and started drinking seriously.

Travis faced her, pale and shaking, "Because she was my mother, and I like to be reminded of the one woman in my life who ever really loved me," he said quietly, trying not to slur his words.

"Well I am sick of it. You take that goddamn monstrosity and stick it in the garage!" Peggy had screamed, trying to pull down the heavy painting.

"Keep your hands off of it!" Travis warned her. He pushed her roughly aside and took the painting down from the wall, and headed towards the door to the garage.

"How dare you manhandle me! I'll call the police on you!" Peggy had screamed.

"No.You.Won't. You don't want the neighbors to see the police here at our lovely home," Travis sneered.

Peggy shuddered. He was right. She never wanted to see police cars outside their home. Ever.

The next morning, after taking four aspirins and telling the children to get their own breakfast, Peggy had found Travis carefully wrapping the painting in heavy paper.

"I'm going to send this up to Edmund, in New York, because I know he will take proper care of it," Travis had said.

"Good. Just get it out of my house. And stop screaming. My head is killing me," Peggy had mumbled.

Travis turned to look at her, noting the stained and torn nightgown and the unlit Marlboro at the corner of her mouth. "Where is the letter Mother wrote to Leigh?" He asked.

"What? How should I know? Probably her baby book."

Coming out of her disturbing reverie, Peggy realizes that Travis must have gotten the letter and sent it up to Edmund with the painting. He had to have done it. The letter was never seen again, by Peggy, and she had turned her house upside down looking for it. Peggy reaches for the phone. *That old queer has the thing himself. Ha.*

CHAPTER 42 – THE BLUE SKY

Edmund stares at the painting in its crate, in his living room. Edmund had been startled when Peggy called him. He wasn't sure she was being truthful but she insisted that Travis had sent the painting sometime in the late 1960's or early 1970's.

He had totally forgotten about Travis shipping him the painting. He had probably not paid any attention to the crate, as his apartment had been a study in 60's kitschy mod furniture in those days. People were always sending him things. Somehow the crated painting got stuck in the storage unit and forgotten.

After prying open the heavy crate lid and getting his partner Greg involved, the two men together lift the heavy painting out and prop it against the wall. "I need a drink," Greg says, heading towards the kitchen. Edmund stares at the painting. "Fixing one for you too, dear," Greg calls out.

Edmund carefully tears off the brown paper, away from the canvas. Rose had looked regal and beautiful when he photographed her, like a queen, in a blue brocade dress, with diamond earrings in her ears, long pearls draped around her neck, and her hair in an upswept style. *She was really a lovely woman*, he thinks as he admires the portrait, *even in her 50's*.

Edmund doesn't see any envelope in the crate. Finally, he looks at the back of the painting. *Aha.*

The letter is taped to the back of the painting. How fitting. The heavy cream stationary with the embossed monogram was what his mother always used for her correspondence. The envelope isn't sealed.

Greg comes in with the drinks and the two men sit on the sofa and read the letter together. Greg looks carefully at Edmund, knowing he might cry. He pats Edmund's back.

Dearest Darling Leigh,

If you are reading this, I am in heaven with Jesus, which is the best place to be. My only regret is not being able to give you hugs and kisses and watch you grow up.

I know you are a girl but I can't explain how. I just know. I can picture you in my mind. I hope the beautiful little girl I see bears some resemblance to me. Maybe it's selfish, but Harry's girls look like their mother. I so hope you look something like me, and like your handsome daddy.

I will always be with you, dear Leigh, in spirit if not in person.

My mother died when I was small. I have felt my mother's spirit around me many times in my life, and I know spirits can be around those they love. Sometimes I even smell her perfume, and I know she is near. I will make every effort to be around you, as you grow up.

You may not know this but your other grandmother, Matilda, was a terrible alcoholic. She raised your mama in a home filled with strict rules and harsh punishments. I think that's why Peggy has a hard time being a loving mother, because she got so little growing up. Try to forgive her.

The most important thing I can give to you is this piece of advice that I was given as a child: We all go through life paddling our little boats through seas of trouble. Heartache, mistakes, weariness, cold unloving people – so many bad things are everywhere. Everyone has heartache all around them. The way to steer your little boat safely through those dangerous waters is to always keep looking up. Look towards the horizon. Look at the blue sky and know it is filled with blessings. Focus on those blessings and thank the Lord for them, every day. That's the best way to steer your boat through the bad times.

I used to think on that a lot, during the hard times in my life.

Love well, Leigh. Remember that God's greatest gift to us is love, and the magic of it is, the more you give away, the more you get back. Love even people who are not loveable, because they often need it the most.

My love will be all around you as you grow, Leigh. I will always be nearby, cheering you on. Always be proud of yourself, and proud of your family. Never let anyone tell you that you are anything less than wonderful.

Much love,

Grandma Rose

Edmund finishes reading the letter and realizes tears are sliding down his face. Greg gathers him in his arms.

"I could hear her voice as I read this," Edmund finally says, sniffling. "It's like she's right here with us. God, how I miss my Mama."

"You have me. You are loved," Greg says, rubbing Edmund's back.

"Thank God. I'm so lucky," Edmund says, sighing. "And Leigh loves me. She's like the daughter I never had," he muses.

"Let's get Leigh her letter tomorrow, Honey," Greg whispers. "Right now, let's go out to dinner."

"Good plan."

CHAPTER 43 – BLAME IT ON WANDA

Edmund keeps an old Polaroid camera in his studio because sometimes he wants to see what something looks like right away, instead of waiting for the negatives or for proof sheets. He takes a Polaroid of the painting of Rose and includes it in the envelope with the letter.

His scrawled note to Leigh reads in part "Do you remember this portrait? It was in your house for several years before your dad sent it up to me. The letter to you was taped to the back of it."

After the letter goes off to Leigh he gets on the phone with Wylene. He's reluctant to quash the rumors about Peggy and Bain McDonald, but Peggy did try to comply with his wishes. It's not her fault he didn't realize he had the letter he asked her to find.

Wylene agrees with him that the easiest fix is to put out the rumor that the woman seen coming out of the motel with McDonald looked a lot like Peggy Harrington but was not, in fact, her. It was, in fact, a hairdresser named Wanda Plunkett, from Pensacola, who was in town for a convention. Peggy was faithful to her boring boyfriend. Wylene and Edmund laugh while filling in the details of the naughty and very fictional Wanda.

Edmund and Wylene chat a while, then he asks her a question that he had long wanted to know the answer to.

"Did you use a service called Reliable Maids back in the 60's?" Edmund asks, lighting a Marlboro and trying to sound casual.

"No, I didn't. I was still teaching school back then, don't you remember?" Wylene retorts, an edge to her voice.

Crap. Ed realizes he has made a serious misstep. Wylene hates to be reminded of her days as a nobody, before she married money.

"Now Darlin' don't upset yourself. I just forgot. I need more coffee! Well let me tell you why I asked. I need you to look into the whereabouts of a maid named Liz Washington who worked for that agency in 1966."

Wylene sighs theatrically and takes another sip of her Bloody Mary. "Now, Ed, you know as well as I do that finding one little gal from all those years ago will be next to impossible, right?"

"I know it won't be easy, but I also know your housekeeper Marylou has been with you for thirty-five years and the black community in Augusta is a tight-knit one."

"Hmmm... Well, Marylou might know. Then again, she might not want to tell me. She can be peculiar," Wylene pouts.

"Well why don't you buy her a nice hat? Say you bought it for you but then changed your mind. Ask her if she wants it. That way it doesn't seem like a bribe."

Wylene smiles, pondering this. Marylou loves hats. She's very religious and goes to church three times a week but hats are her one indulgence. "I'll give it a try, but no promises. Why don't you buy the hat and send it to me? If it's from New York City she will be beyond excited."

Edmund rolls his eyes. Fine. "Good plan. Look for it in the mail soon!"

"All right then," Wylene drawls, lighting another Virginia Slims menthol.

"All right, you stay sweet, Sister," Edmund drawls, lighting a Marlboro.

"You be good up there, Brother," Wylene replies.

The fact they are not related doesn't stop Edmund and Wylene from using those very southern endearments.

CHAPTER 44 – THE CHRISTMAS CARD

Leigh gets a call at her office from the manager of her apartment complex, Sharon, at 2 p.m. She is almost out the door to a house showing when the receptionist, calls her back inside. "Leigh! Hang on a minute!" she calls. "It's Sharon at the apartment office on the phone for you, line 2."

Irritated, Leigh bustles into the empty cubicle near the door and punches line 2. "Sharon? What's going on?"

"Leigh, honey, there's a delivery here for you of 4 banker's boxes from Augusta! Are you expecting this?" Sharon asks, gazing warily at the Fed-X driver.

"Um, no, but that's great. Would you mind signing for them, and getting one of the maintenance guys to put the boxes in my apartment?" Leigh asks, hope surging in her.

"OK, but look this is just because I like you. Don't make a habit of it, okay?" Sharon says.

"Don't worry! I have no idea where the boxes are from. I rarely get any kind of package."

Leigh smiles, wondering if Edmund had been able to talk Harry into giving up those boxes or if Harry was being nice.

After work, Leigh speeds home. Leigh parks her car at the apartment door and gets inside in 2 seconds flat. The banker's boxes are stacked just inside her door. She throws down her keys and decides to look through the boxes right then, knowing they are from Harry.

An hour later, Leigh sits on the floor, the boxes all around her, their contents spilling out. Leigh wants to scream in frustration. Old canceled checks, old insurance policies, papers, papers, papers. No birth certificate.

Suddenly it hits her. DUH. *What an idiot I am! I can just go down and get a copy of Dad's birth certificate and that will lead me to Rose's birth certificate. Why on earth didn't I think of that weeks ago?!*

She glances at her watch: nearly 3:00. She changes out of her work clothes, grabs a bottle of water and a Snickers bar and heads back to the car.

The Georgia Department of Public Health Vital Records Office, an old brick building that might once have been a school, is a busy place. Leigh walks into a small room with neon green

tile on the floor and ghastly fluorescent lights overhead, crowded with cheap plastic chairs. She walks over to the window. The clerks behind the windows all wear the same sour expression. Leigh tells a clerk what she needs, and is informed she will have to wait.

Leigh takes a number and waits. Her stomach growls repeatedly, in protest against the lone Snickers bar lunch.

Finally, Leigh is called up to the window, and explains to a bored middle-aged black clerk named Miss Wood what she needs. She waits another ten minutes, until Miss Wood saunters back to the window with a piece of paper.

"That will be $15, $25 if you want it certified."

After paying the $15, Leigh finally holds a copy of her father's birth certificate, showing that Rose Cunningham Harrington is his mother.

"Okay, now I need a birth certificate for my grandmother, Rose Cunningham Harrington," Leigh asks, trying not to sound excited. 'See, she had my father, and here's my birth certificate showing he's my father, so I have a right to see Rose Harrington's certificate."

Leigh hands the clerk both birth certificates and waits, trying not to seem impatient.

"What is it you want to see, again?" the clerk intones.

"The birth certificate of Rose Cunningham, my paternal grandmother."

The clerk examines both birth certificates and purses her lips as though eating a lemon.

"I will look. Just a minute," the clerk replies, looking bored. She is back in a minute, while Leigh impatiently tries not to bite her nails.

"We don't have one for anyone named Rose Cunningham."

Leigh's heart sinks. "Can you look again? There must be one. It's from 1908."

"A lot of those old records are not on the computer. I'm sorry. It's also possible, that far back, that she was born at home and a birth certificate didn't get filed. That happened a lot, especially out in the country."

207

Leigh is devastated. She stands there for a moment, lost in thought.

"Miss, what else do you need?" Miss Wood asks. "I got more people to help."

"Um, can you search on the computer and tell me if Rose Harrington is listed as a mother on any other birth certificates? I think she had another baby, who I never knew, but she would be my aunt, Elizabeth."

"Year of birth?"

"I think 1942?" Leigh replies.

"Have a seat. This might take a few minutes. Was the birth here in Atlanta?"

"I think so."

Leigh sits back in one of the plastic chairs and wishes she had brought a book to read. The small room is hot and stuffy. A young mother comforts a crying toddler with juice stains on her tee shirt. Four small black children sit in silence next to their mother, who looks exhausted. Even in her jeans and button down shirt and Keds, Leigh feels overdressed and overly white.

Wait a minute, idiot. I am not lily white! Leigh almost smiles at the thought. *I have to rearrange my thinking. I am mixed race, not white. Not that these people would care.*

After sitting for what seems like an eternity -- but was actually twenty-two minutes -- the clerk calls Leigh back to the window.

"This is what I found," she says, showing Leigh the copy of a birth certificate. "She gave birth at Grady, in the colored hospital," Miss Wood says, looking puzzled.

Leigh glances at it to make sure Rose is listed as the mother.

"Yes, that's it, thanks!" Leigh almost squeals with joy, ignoring the clerk's confusion.

"I need another $15 for the copy," the clerk intones. Leigh pays her the money and heads back to her car, not hearing the screaming toddler in the waiting room.

She can hear Miss Woods behind her saying "She says her grandmother gave birth at Grady to a black child, but look at her, she's white."

Sitting in her car, running the air conditioning to get the car cooled down, Leigh looks at the second birth certificate. The baby was born at Grady Hospital on August 4, 1942, a female, 7 lbs. 4 oz. The father is listed as Nathan Dudley of Augusta, and his race is listed as "Colored." The mother's race is listed as "Mulatto."

The baby girl was named Elizabeth Elaine Harrington.

Wow. I am holding in my hand actual proof that I had an aunt. I know her full name and her exact date of birth, so that will make it easier to track her down. Where is she now? She would be 54 years old.

Leigh sits there staring at the certificate for perhaps 5 minutes. It occurs to her that the adoptive parents who gave the baby the last name of Washington might have further changed the name, but she decided it was unlikely. Elizabeth Washington would be much easier to find. Hopefully.

Back at the apartment, Leigh is searching through one of the banker's boxes for a small card she had just glanced at, earlier. It's a Christmas card postmarked 1970. It's addressed to Travis only, at their home address. There's no return address.

The small card depicts a snowman and a small cottage, and inside it simply says Happy Holidays! It's signed "Laney."

Who is that? Leigh thinks. She cannot recall anyone with that name among her parents' circle of friends.

CHAPTER 45 – THE PHOTO ALBUM

Two hours later, Leigh has eaten a late lunch or early dinner consisting of a peanut butter and jelly sandwich and a Diet Coke. She sits with her childhood friend Carol at the small oak kitchen table of her comfortable house in Lilburn, chatting about Carol's life as a housewife and mom to baby Zack. Carol is a tall brunette with very blue eyes who had once thought she might be a model, but now she has gained "baby weight." She is still lovely, although not svelte any more.

"Isn't it funny, I'm a stay at home mom and you're the big career lady?" Carol chuckles. "When we were kids it was always me who wanted to see the world."

Leigh took a sip of Diet Coke and shook her head slightly. "Hey, don't knock it. Every month I worry about selling enough houses and getting commissions. It's nerve-wracking being a real estate agent. At least you have somebody to support you and pay the bills, and a beautiful baby."

"Yeah, but I bet you get to sleep all night."

They are interrupted by Carol's mother coming in the back door. At sixty, Amelia Johnson is still trim, and she wears blue jeans and a white tee shirt and sandals.

"Hey there honey, how are you?" Amelia smiles warmly at Leigh, and accepts a hug.

They chat for a moment about Leigh's job and career. Amelia Johnson moved into the condo near Carol a year before and they chat about her leaving Augusta.

"How's your mama, Leigh?" she asks.

"Oh, you know Peggy. Feisty as ever. Always busy."

There is a strained silence. "How's your mama" is a ritual question in the south, but it doesn't always mean someone really wants to know about your mama. It's politeness.

Leigh doesn't want to talk about her mother, especially since Carol had told her a while back how Peggy made snide remarks about Amelia Johnson one day in garden club. Peggy had noticed fake flowers in Amelia's foyer at a party a few months before Amelia moved to Atlanta. After years of friendship, Amelia was upset, although she defended her use of silk flowers, pointing out they were cheaper than real and looked lovely. The friendship cooled noticeably after that incident, and Amelia was glad to leave Augusta.

Now, Amelia sits at her daughter's round kitchen table, drinks a small glass of Chablis and notes that Leigh has turned into a lovely woman, losing the girlishness of youth but gaining a more mature beauty.

They talk about beauty and skincare routines for a few minutes, then Leigh switches the topic to her search for information about her grandmother and the aunt she wants to find. Amelia and Carol are fascinated.

Leigh pulls the little Christmas card out of her purse and hands it to Amelia.

"I found this in a box of Dad's things and the name is unfamiliar to me. I wonder if you know who "Laney" might be."

Amelia looks at the signature on the small card and shakes her head. "I'm sorry Leigh, I don't know any of your parents' friends with that name. Of course, I didn't see Travis much in those last years, once he'd married Sandy. I would run into him on Broad Street sometimes, and we would chat for a minute."

Leigh sighs and accepts the card back. Often, when couples divorce, friends choose a side. Amelia chose Peggy's side.

"Okay, I understand. Just thought it was worth asking about. There's something else, too," Leigh says, taking a deep breath.

"Do you remember an incident when I was about 4 years old when we had a maid get drunk and lock me and Bubba out of the house? Bubba cut his foot? You came over and tried to help, and called Daddy to come home from work since Mom was out?"

Amelia's face changes from amiable to guarded. She recalls the incident very well. The screaming that had erupted from the house was blood-curdling. She had called Harry, who thankfully lived just 5 minutes away. She clears her throat and sits up straighter in her chair.

"Leigh, I remember that day, but I never found out exactly what happened. All I did was call your dad and Harry. I'm sorry."

There's an uncomfortable silence for a moment.

Carol speaks next. "Well, seems to me that if a drunk maid locked you and Bubba out of the house, it would be some kind of crime right? Maybe you can track down the police report, Leigh?"

Leigh stares at Carol. *Of course. A police report. Duh.*

Amelia interrupts Leigh's thoughts. "Nobody called the police."

Carol and Leigh both stare at her.

"Mama, are you sure? Wouldn't you have called the police in that situation? I would call the police if a drunk maid locked my kids out of the house and my little boy hurt his foot."

"Peggy would never have wanted anyone to see police cars at her house, for any reason. I guess that's why they weren't called," Amelia explains.

Carol looks puzzled.

"Why bring up all that mess, Leigh? What difference could it possibly make, all these years later?"

Leigh ponders what she should say, and how. Finally, she clears her throat and talks.

"After Daddy died I started seeing a therapist, to cope. I realized a few weeks ago that the Drunk Maid incident is still haunting me, somehow. I remember some of the day, but not all of it. I was in Macy's recently and I smelled Caswell and Massey Lilac bath products –which is what Mother used and what the maid had put in the bathtub that day. I felt like I was going to pass out. I mean, it brought back feelings of fear and anger, and… I don't know what else to say. My therapist thinks I have repressed memories of that incident because they were too terrible. So I am trying desperately to find out what actually happened that day. What would be so scary that my 4 year old self blanked out the memories?!"

Almost without realizing it, Leigh's voice breaks on the word "memories" and she feels herself in the grip of sadness and fear once again.

Amelia's small hands rub Leigh's back, and she makes soothing noises.

A red cardinal appears on the patio just outside the window. It cocks its head and looks right at Carol. Carol stands up abruptly. "I'll be right back," she says.

"Oh Leigh, I am so sorry, dear. So sorry," Amelia croons.

Carol reappears with a photo album. "Remember that time we had the kitchen fire and my birthday party had to get moved from our house to your house?"

Leigh thinks for a moment. "Um, vaguely? I was about five years old, right? You were turning six? That it?"

Carol nods. She sits beside Leigh at the table and flips pages in the photo album. "Here we go. See these photos from the party? Daddy had a new camera and he took tons of photos. Take a look."

Leigh is puzzled by Carol's attention to the photos but she gamely flips through the photo pages. Kids at the party, cake, balloons, presents – all the standard stuff. Leigh isn't sure what Carol is trying to show her. "Um, okay? I'm not sure what's significant here?"

Carol points at one of the photos. "See here? What's that in the background?"

Leigh peers at the small black and white photo. Her grandmother's portrait stares back at her. "Oh my God! Good lord! I remember that portrait now!" Leigh says, feeling her heart pounding wildly.

Amelia looks over Leigh's shoulder at the photo.

"Exactly. The portrait was there and then it wasn't. I think your mom made your dad take it down and ship it off to your Uncle Edmund," Amelia says. "I think I remember Peggy telling me about it like it was so wonderful, that she had forced Travis to get rid of it. I thought she was being mean."

"Well that's what Mother does; she manipulates the world to suit herself," Leigh replies bitterly.

"I remember admiring that portrait when I was a kid," Carol says quietly. "I honestly don't know why, but it seems significant." She looks at her mother but Amelia remains silent, looking down at her hands. Carol knows her mother feels very conflicted.

"Grandma Rose had on a blue dress and pearls in this. I remember thinking she was a queen. She was beautiful. I was never told what happened to the portrait," Leigh says quietly. "I haven't even thought about it in years."

The back door opens and Carol's husband Ronny comes in carrying baby Zack. "Hey Honey, he needs a diaper change so I cut short our walk. Hi Leigh!" Ronny says. "Good to see you."

Leigh's face brightens as she regards the chubby blonde baby. "He looks just like you, Ronny! Adorable!"

"Give me that boy. Gramma will change that diaper," Amelia says, holding out her arms. She trundles off with the baby.

Ronny grew up in the same neighborhood as Carol and Leigh. "Hey, so sorry to hear about your dad."

"Thanks, Ronny."

They chat for a few minutes and Leigh heads home.

After she gets to her apartment, Leigh is surprised again. There's a note taped to the door from Jessica that says to come see her, that she accepted a letter for Leigh, special delivery.

Leigh runs up the stairs to Jessica's apartment and knocks on the door. Jessica answers. Her makeup-free face brightens, seeing Leigh, and she throws the door open.

"Git in here! I can't wait to know what you got!" she says, thrusting the manila envelope into Leigh's hands. "It's from your uncle in New York City!"

Jessica's apartment, unlike Leigh's, looks like a yard sale staged by a chimp. Clothes and dishes are everywhere, and magazines. Jessica collects frog figurines and dolls and they are perched on every flat surface.

Leigh sits on a hassock in front of a chair that looks like it time-traveled from 1955 to Jessica's apartment. She opens the envelope and reads the letter from Edmund, then the letter from Rose to her. She looks at the little Polaroid of the portrait and starts shaking.

She puts down the package and buries her face in her hands.

"Can I read it?!" Jessica asks gently.

Lee nods.

Jessica reads both letters and gazes at the photo before hugging Leigh.

"This is wonderful! What a treasure! Aren't you excited?!" she trills. "I say this calls for a celebration. I'm opening a bottle of wine – the good kind, with a cork!"

Leigh is too overwhelmed to speak for a few minutes. Finally, she picks up Rose's letter and reads it again.

Jessica comes back from the kitchen and hands Leigh a glass of wine. "I'm so thrilled to see the letter, yes. I'm also more determined than ever to find my aunt. Let me catch you up."

Leigh tells Jessica about the recent events, particularly about Eugenia Hill.

"Well, there's only one thing we can do," Jessica says.

"What's that?"

"It's two for one Margarita night at El Tapatio."

"No, sorry, I'm not much of a drinker. My dad was an alcoholic. I have always tried hard to be different from that. I think I'm going to just walk. Walking helps me think things through."

Jessica is crestfallen, but she shrugs. "I understand. Call me if you want to talk, okay?"

"Okay. Thanks for accepting the letter."

The two friends hug, and Leigh leaves.

Leigh puts the letter and her purse in her apartment, and starts walking. She stays within the apartment complex, which is fenced. She walks fast, at first, thoughts roiling.

The thought that keeps returning to her brain is that Rose knew her, knew she was soon to enter the world, wanted to be there for her, wanted to hug her and love her and watch over her. Yet a brain aneurysm had ended her life before Leigh took her first breath. How cruel was that?!

Maybe she was there for me, though. Maybe she was always near, unseen, but there, as she said.

These lines from the letter keep echoing in her ears, as though Rose herself is speaking.

"My love will be all around you as you grow, Leigh. I will always be nearby, cheering you on. Always be proud of yourself, and proud of your family. Never let anyone tell you that you are anything less than wonderful."

Leigh walks up to the apartment pool and sinks into a chair. Nobody is at the pool. It is almost 8:30 and there is a bit of a chill in the air, and the sun is setting rapidly. It's September and the weather is finally switching gears and becoming more fall-like.

Leigh vaguely recalls that the pool is heated, and she takes her Keds off and sticks a toe in the water. It is delightfully warm.

Without thinking, Leigh takes her keys and jams them down into the toe of one of her shoes, then dives into the warm water.

She swims a few laps, lazily, loving the feel of the water on her tense body. The exertion and the warm water help her relax.

Leigh turns over and floats on her back, feeling herself lightened and buoyant. She thinks of a Cat Stevens tune she loves, "*The Wind*," and hums it.

A voice cuts through her reverie and she is jolted back to reality.

"Leigh! Are you nuts?! You'll catch a cold!" Her eyes fly open, and Leigh rights herself and stands up in the water. Jack stands there by the pool looking worried and, holding a towel. "Good thing I had a clean towel in my gym bag!"

"Hey," Leigh says lamely, feeling annoyed.

She swims over to the ladder and gets out. Jack wraps her in the towel. "Let's get you back to the apartment. You don't want to catch cold," Jack says.

Jack reads the letter from Rose while Leigh dries off.

Leigh comes out of the bathroom a few minutes later wearing shorts and a tee shirt. She looks at the cartons of Chinese food on the kitchen counter, chooses Kung Pao chicken and fixes herself a plate. "Thanks for bringing the food. Did you eat already?"

"Nope. Waiting for you," he replied. "I called you and called you and you didn't answer your phone so I came on over."

"Thanks for checking on me," she says, walking over to give him a quick hug. "Well I'm starving. Swimming always makes me hungry," she says. "Sorry about being out of touch. The letter from Rose just rocked me."

Leigh pours herself a glass of water from her Brita pitcher and sits down and starts eating.

"Yeah, I wondered what made you want to start swimming laps. I know it's still pretty warm for September and everything but it's starting to get a bit cool in the evenings now," Jack notes as he spoons food from the small takeout containers onto his plate and sits down.

"The pool has become my refuge in recent years, although it hasn't always been that," Leigh says, adding some soy sauce to her food.

"Why not?" Jack responds.

"I was a competitive swimmer until I was 18," Leigh says with a sigh.

Jack digs into his beef with peppers. "What made you stop?" he asks, then chews his food thoroughly.

Leigh sits quietly for a moment, also chewing, somewhat distracted by Jack's methodical way of arranging food on the plate. Even Chinese takeout has to be precise and ordered in his world.

"My mother couldn't get me to take social, or be a debutante, or do anything like that. Girls in Augusta who came from families that belonged to the Country Club did all those things. I didn't want to."

"Why not? And what's social?"

"It's learning ballroom dancing, basically. Refusing to do all that was my way of rebelling – not that I ever felt comfortable in that world anyway."

"But that was all you knew. What made you want to go against everyone?" Jack asks, wiping his mouth with a napkin.

"I never felt like I fit in. I was, in fact, from a privileged family and I went to private schools but I always felt weird. My best friend was actually Asian. Her family owned a restaurant. They didn't belong to the Country Club. So anyway, when I was 14, Mother decided to push me to be an Olympic swimmer. Put in a pool at the house. Hired a coach and everything. Demanded I swim four hours a day."

"Did you want to go to the Olympics?" Jack asks, taking a sip of beer.

"I thought I did. For a while. I worked hard. I just wasn't fast enough. Plus, most swimmers are tall and have long muscles. I'm short. I have boobs and a butt. I don't look like a swimmer. The tall girls started beating me right and left after a couple of years. I worked harder and harder. I think I really just wanted my mother to love me, and she was nice to me when I was in training."

"She wasn't nice to you normally?" Jack asks, looking puzzled. "Your mother?"

"No. I mean, she just ignored me, mostly. Most of the time when she spoke to me she sounded annoyed. My brother looks like her, acts like her, is the favored child. He took social, loved playing golf and tennis, embraced the whole country club thing. I guess every time she looked at me she saw Rose. In Bubba, she saw herself. I realize now what she must have thought about me – there's my kid who looks like a colored woman ," Leigh says bitterly, putting down her fork and covering her face with her hands.

"Don't be silly, Leigh –" Jack starts to say but Leigh cuts him off, and angrily glares at him.

"You don't know her, okay? You don't know Peggy. You know why I'm a nice person? A fairly normal person? One reason: Clarice Jones. She was our housekeeper from the time I was five until I was in college. She was black. She was always there for me. She loved me. Peggy was too busy going to meetings and shopping and whatever the hell else she did. Clarice packed my lunches for school, and took me to piano lessons, and taught me how to sew on a button. She loved me like I was her own."

Jack just shakes his head slightly, perplexed.

"I'm sorry. I shouldn't have snapped at you," Leigh says, thinking *Oh lord, I finally find a great guy and I act like a bitch because he asks a simple question. Have to get a grip.*

"So you quit swimming when you went off to college?" Jack asks.

"Well, I told Mother on my 18th birthday I was through with her and her crap, and I left. I moved in with Dad and Sandy. Worked as a waitress for a year and then went to college. I didn't see or speak to my mother for a solid year, and that was wonderful. As soon as I moved out, Clarice left and moved away to North Carolina. I got Christmas cards from her for a couple of years, but then she died."

Jack is silent, not knowing what to say. Leigh goes in the kitchen and gets a beer from the fridge. Jack comes in and leans against the counter after throwing away his paper plate.

"Something occurred to me. What about calling your stepmother about that Christmas card? Maybe she has an address."

Leigh looks puzzled for a moment, then grins at him. "You know, I had to think for a moment who you were talking about when you said 'stepmother.' Sandy was my Dad's wife but I never thought of her as a stepmother. I'll give her a call but I doubt she will know. She and Dad led pretty separate lives. I never did understand why he married her, except that she was beautiful, in a glacial sort of way."

"You have photos?" Jack asks.

Leigh nods towards her bookcase in the nearby living room, where family photos are displayed.

Jack picks up a color 8x10 photo of Travis and Sandy and looks at it while Leigh gets her address book, then presses buttons on her phone.

Leigh stands there looking at the phone, for a moment, then hangs up. "That's weird. There's a recording saying the number is no longer in service. Hang on a minute. Maybe Bubba will have a number for her."

Leigh sits on the sofa and dials her brother's number, and speaks for a few minutes.

Jack looks at her expectantly. Leigh sits on the sofa, phone in her hand, winding the coiled cord around her hand. She looks upset. Jack sits down beside her and rubs her back.

"Bubba said Sandy moved back to Ohio and is already engaged to somebody else. He doesn't know her number there. Wow."

Jack pulls back, startled. "Damn. You're right. She sounds cold. Your dad's been dead what, ten months?"

"Yep."

"Wow."

"Yep, Sandy makes Mother seem warm and fuzzy."

They both chuckle.

"Say, does everyone call your brother Bubba?"

Leigh smiles. "No, just family. To everyone else he is Ward Harrington, named after Mom's father."

"Does he know he is mixed race? Did you tell him?"

Leigh's smile disappears. She turns away from Jack and goes into the bathroom.

Jack is puzzled by her total lack of a response, but he sits on the couch and waits for her.

Leigh finally comes out and sits down opposite him. She hands Jack a color 5x7 of herself and Bubba, clearly made at his wedding.

"I'm sorry I didn't answer your question. I didn't mean to be rude. It just caught me unaware. I realized that I have not really begun to scratch the surface of what it means to be mixed race. I guess I am waiting to find my aunt, postponing it until I can talk to her."

Jack looks at the photo and just waits for her to continue.

225

"Bubba would be… probably horrified to know that he is not entirely white. Or maybe not. I don't see him much. He tends to spend holidays with his wife's family now they have the babies. He doesn't look anything but white, you know? The light brown hair and blue eyes? We do look like siblings, though our coloring is different. I just don't know how I feel about everything, to be honest. I'm still processing all of it."

"Okay. I'd still like to meet him one day."

"I'm sure you will." She stretches and yawns. "I have a house showing early in the morning," Leigh says gently. "Thank you so much for coming over, though, and worrying about me." They kiss, and Jack says "I need to get up early too."

Leigh has a hard time going to sleep. When she finally does, she dreams she is back on the porch of the home where she lived with her parents, and Rose and Travis are sitting in the porch swing, drinking sweet tea, and laughing. Leigh keeps trying to walk over to the swing but she can't. It's like quicksand is pulling at her legs, and the more she tries to run, the further away the porch recedes.

She wakes up in a tangle of covers, frustrated and wondering what the dream means, if anything.

CHAPTER 46 -- CAUGHT

Peggy is in Aiken, having driven over to Beatrice Arbuthnot's house for a DAR meeting. Beatrice has more money than anyone and lives on a horse farm that has been in her family for almost a hundred years. It's only a 45 minute drive from Peggy's house but it might as well be on the moon, the way Peggy curses under her breath as she drives her Lexus down long country roads.

The program (Eighteenth Century Agriculture and Its Impact on the Revolution, by Professor Arnold West from Augusta College) is deadly dull, but at least Peggy is not being shunned any more. Everyone is nice to her.

She dressed very conservatively for the evening in a navy cotton skirt and sky blue button down shirt, with only small gold hoop earrings.

The group of eleven ladies, all over age fifty, harbor no illusions about the refreshments. Beatrice prides herself on being a gourmet cook but she is either indifferent (Saltine crackers with the crab dip) or too oddly adventurous. The ladies pretend to like the deviled eggs that taste like cheap mayonnaise and have diced up sardines in them. They positively gush over the cheese straws, knowing they were bought at Harris Teeter and are therefore delicious. Nobody can identify what is sitting on a tray surrounded by Ritz crackers but it looks like purple vomit. One lady adventurously digs into the strange dip and chews for a moment, then grimaces and runs for the bathroom; returning only to report the purple stuff tasted like eggplant and peanuts.

Beatrice is rich enough to be called "eccentric" instead of nutty.

After the lecture, Peggy gets a paper cup of Chablis and listens with rapt attention to Susie Watkins go on and on about her granddaughter Missy, who at three is the most brilliant ballet dancer in her class and will doubtless one day dance in New York. While Peggy listens, she smiles and mentally composes her grocery list for the next day.

Peggy then listens to Winnie Mapleton gush about her daughter's new boyfriend, a golf pro down in Florida who will one day win the Masters.

As everyone admires the antiques, the Persian rugs, and the portrait of Beatrice's ancestor who fought with General Washington, they slowly start drifting out and getting in their Cadillacs and Beamers for the long drive back to Augusta.

When almost everyone is gone, Peggy comes out of the guest bath off the kitchen and sees a man petting Beatrice's ancient Cocker Spaniel, Buttercup. He looks up, and she gasps, startled. It's Bain McDonald. He's wearing khakis and a blue Polo sports shirt and Docksiders

with no socks. She thinks for the thousandth time, *how on earth did such an ugly man become so successful?*

"Well hey there Peggy Harrington, how you doin' darlin'?" Bain asks smoothly, straightening up.

"We've never been formally introduced. What are you doing here?" Peggy blurts out. *Oh my God, he may be ugly but look at*

228

those muscles. He looks like he could power lift a telephone pole.
And he has a lovely speaking voice, ironically, deep and sexy.

"We have the same dentist so we are practically cousins," he drawls. "Beatrice is my aunt. I told her I'd run by and make sure everything was cleaned up and locked up after the meeting. She tends to drink too much sherry and things don't get wrapped up properly after she entertains," he says, smiling and looking admiringly down Peggy's blouse, which she realizes has one too many buttons undone.

This information doesn't square with what Peggy has heard about Bain, so for a moment she is flustered.

"It's a long drive for you to come out from Augusta," is all she can think of to say.

"I don't mind the drive. I usually spend the night here and have a visit with Beatrice in the morning before I go back," he responds.

Buttercup woofs, and Bain picks her up carefully and cuddles her. "She's got some arthritis, but she still has some spunk. I bought her for my aunt fifteen years ago."

"She has a sweet face," Peggy responds automatically.

"Do you like dogs? I love them. I just don't have one right now because I'm not at home much. The restaurant keeps me really busy," Bain says, carefully putting Buttercup in her doggie bed.

"Well, I love dogs too but I stay so busy I'd never have time to walk one, so I don't have one.. If you'll excuse me, I need to get on back to Augusta!" Peggy trills, heading out the door before even finishing her sentence. She marches out as quickly as her high heels

229

can carry her across the pea gravel. Her Lexus is parked in the driveway but there's a Mercedes Benz right behind it, blocking her.

"Oh sorry, didn't realize I had blocked you in, Peggy," Bain says smoothly, coming up behind her, crossing the gravel in three strides.

Peggy opens her car door and throws her purse and sweater into the passenger seat before turning to face Bain, who at 6'3 towers over her.

"I have to be up early, so I would appreciate it if you could go ahead and move your car," she smiles, praying no-one sees her talking to him. The gossips would reignite the stupid story about them.

"Oh sure, but first, you have something in your hair, I believe," Bain says, suddenly invading her personal space and pretending to pluck something from her hair.

Peggy starts breathing hard.

He smells like a combination of some spicy men's cologne and Scotch, and suddenly his hands are on her waist.

Before she can think, he bends over and kisses her, delicately at first, then harder, while his hands expertly pull her towards him.

Peggy knows she should scream and slap him, but her hormones are buzzing and she can't think straight. His tongue in her mouth is attacking her tongue, and her hips strain toward him as her hands claw his back. His hands are pushing her skirt up when suddenly car lights blind them both.

Bain pulls away and shields his eyes, "What the fuck?!" he curses.

Peggy lurches away from him, adjusting her clothes.

"Oh dear, I put it in drive instead of reverse!" a cheery voice calls through the car window. Peggy realizes with horror the voice belongs to Delores Wright, one of the biggest gossips in Augusta.

"Buh bye y'all!" she calls out again, throwing the car into reverse and backing down the drive.

Bain has backed away from the car and stands in the shadows, shaking his head.

Peggy can only stand there in shock, for a moment.

"She was the last one to leave," Bain says, chuckling. "Ah, what luck."

"You have no idea," Peggy says icily. She turns and watches the Lincoln head down the road.

"Well, by tomorrow morning everyone in Augusta will know about it, so why not just enjoy ourselves?" he says, suddenly behind Peggy, nuzzling her neck.

"Good god, you upstart –" she starts to argue, but then his mouth finds hers again and she is lost. She is feeling things she hasn't felt in years. He picks her up easily, and heads to the house's back porch where there is a door that leads to a small den with a large sofa..

CHAPTER 47 – CALL THE BEAUTY PARLOR

The call from Marylou Anderson is unexpected to Millie, but not to Liz.

Millie takes the receiver and says "Hello?!" and listens.

Liz closes the dishwasher door, wipes out the cast-iron black skillet, rubs some peanut oil in it, and sets it back on the stove, hearing her mother's voice on the phone.

She joins her mother in the den, reaches down and hits a button on the phone, turning on the speakerphone feature, then gently takes the receiver and replaces it.

Marylou's rich alto voice fills the small room.

"Edmund Harrington, live up in New York City, talks to Wylene all the time, he asking about Liz," Marylou says.

"Harrington? Then he's her other son," Millie says, her voice anxious. "Lord, lord…"

"Well, do you want me to keep quiet or not? I won't tell Wylene anything unless you say so," Marylou says.

"Hang on a minute," Millie says, then looks at her daughter. "Liz's right here."

"Hey Liz," Marylou says.

Millie looks at her daughter and says "Marylou Anderson, old friend of mine from Augusta, says Mr. Edmund Harrington,

Travis' brother, wants to talk to you about his niece, Leigh, Travis' daughter."

Liz had known when she heard the phone ring a few minutes before that the call would be about Leigh. "Right," she says, taking a deep breath and sinking down to sit on the other chair next to her mother's recliner.

"Mrs. Anderson, this is Liz. I remember meeting you once when I was a little girl. You always wore beautiful hats."

"Yes, I am known for my hats. How you doin' honey?"

"I'm just fine. I've retired from teaching. I appreciate you calling before giving out any information to Wylene."

"Well, of course. I'm not going to tell that old gossip anything without your say so."

"Go ahead and give her this phone number. I've known for a while that a meeting with my niece was inevitable." She looks at her mother's worried face and pats her hand.

"If you say so, I'll do it. Maybe God is looking to help you know your white family, at last. God Bless you, Child."

"You too. Thanks for calling," Liz says, smiling as she hits a button to end the call. Nobody calls her "child" except very old ladies.

"You sure about this?" Millie asks, anxiety in her voice.

"Yes, I am sure. I know Harry will stop sending the checks if he finds out, but I don't care. We don't really need that money since TJ finished pharmacy school. I am getting plenty of customers wanting readings."

"It's not the money I was thinking about."

Liz sits down opposite her mother.

"I want to know Leigh. She's got a wound inside of her from that day, a wound only I can heal. I want to help."

"She her mama's child, and you know what that Peggy Harrington is like," Millie says anxiously.

Liz nods but replies "Mama, Leigh is not like her mother, not at all."

"You sure on that? That come from one of your feelings, or is it just wishful thinking?" Millie asks, fearful. She doesn't want to see her daughter hurt again.

"Leigh is a good person. I talked to Travis about her before he died. He said she lives in Atlanta, sells real estate. She doesn't get along with her mother."

"Well, all right then. You drivin' to Atlanta?"

"No. I will tell them to come here," Liz says, smiling. "You get to meet them, too."

"I better call the beauty parlor, then."

CHAPTER 48 – LIKE AN OLD MARRIED COUPLE

Jack comes over for dinner and Leigh grills hamburgers on a hibachi on her deck.

"You would not believe the day I had. Yikes," she says as Jack kisses her on the cheek and puts a six pack of Jamaican beer in the fridge.

"Oh, I don't know. I had to spend the morning searching utility records for a guy who has the last name Smith, first name Ed. You know how many Ed Smiths there are in Atlanta?!"

They eat casually, digging into the burgers and potato salad, and discussing their days. Leigh thinks happily, *We feel like an old married couple, sharing stories of our days with each other. I love this.*

After dinner they sit on the couch to watch a movie. Leigh is startled when the phone rings right after she hits Play on the VCR.

"I'll let the machine pick up," Leigh says, snuggling into Jack's side. He pauses the VCR tape. "No, go ahead and take it. It might be important," Jack replies, gently reaching over to put the phone in Leigh's lap.

"Hi Uncle Ed! How are you?" Leigh says when she hears his voice.

Jack gets up and cleans the kitchen while she talks. Then he wipes off the table where they ate dinner. Finally, he bags up the trash and walks outside and down to the dumpster. When he returns,

Leigh sits on the sofa chewing her thumbnail and looking thoughtful.

"What's up, beautiful?" he asks, settling down beside her.

"He thinks he might have found my aunt. We are going to a little town near Athens tomorrow after I pick him up at the airport."

"Excellent! Mind if I tag along?" Jack asks, eyes twinkling.

"Can you come with us?! That would be wonderful!" Leigh exclaims, throwing her arms around his neck.

"Wouldn't miss this for anything. I just feel bad it wasn't my skills that found her."

Leigh pulls back and looks at him. "I know you did everything you could."

When Jack kisses her goodnight Leigh resists the urge to invite him to spend the night. Although she is attracted to him, she decides it needs to wait until life settles back down a bit.

That night, she dreams she is in a car driving through a town that looks sort of familiar, but isn't really. She needs to get home to Atlanta, but she can't find the right highway. It looks like Athens in places, and like Augusta in places. The traffic is terrible.

Suddenly Rose is there in the car with her. "Just drive, Leigh. Don't worry about where we're going. Just drive." Then they are on a highway with mountains up ahead and beautiful fields and trees on either side of the highway. Rose turns on the radio and Bing Crosby's voice fills the car, singing, "Don't Fence Me In."

Leigh feels cherished and loved.

CHAPTER 49 -- SMUDGED MAKEUP

Peggy awakens on a foldout sofa in a small den in Beatrice Arbuthnot's Aiken home, staring into the eyes of an orange cat. Her head pounds from a hangover, and there are other sore places on her body, places that haven't been sore in years.

As she struggles to sit up, Peggy realizes she is completely naked, and the tall, hairy body stretched out next to her and softly snoring is Bain McDonald.

She looks at him in horror, remembering the night before. After the initial shock and shame, she studies him. Somehow in sleep, he is not quite so ugly.

Plus, he has the heavy musculature of a powerful weightlifter. His beautiful body almost makes up for his face.

A shaft of sunlight pierces the room, and Peggy winces at the hangover pain in her head, from the bottle of wine they drank last night. She groans softly as she thinks about the waves of gossip that are undoubtedly lighting up the phone lines of Augusta. Damage control. She has to think in terms of damage control.

How could I give in to his touch? How could I act like such a slut! Now everyone in Augusta will think I'm a horrible person. Damage control. Focus on the future, not the past.

She struggles into her clothes, trying not to move her aching head. After surveying the shreds of pantyhose, she throws them away.

Fully dressed, Peggy grabs her purse, and tiptoes out, praying Beatrice won't see her. The cat jumps off the sofa bed and stalks off. The small den had been added on to the old mansion and it only opens into the kitchen.

Peggy stops at the kitchen door, looking for signs of life. A coffee maker gurgles, and coffee is pouring out into the carafe. A newspaper sits on the old wooden table, but otherwise there is nobody around. Peggy has to pee but she decides against trying to get to the powder room down a short hallway.

Good thing Beatrice is 76, going deaf, and likes to sleep late, she thinks, as she eases out the back door, holding her high heels in her hand.

Ten minutes later Peggy is in the bathroom of a Shell station, trying to fix her hair and wipe off yesterday's smudged makeup. She puts on her sunglasses and goes back into the light of a hot May morning wishing she had two aspirins to go with her crappy fast food coffee, then gasps.

"Morning my dear. You're looking lovely," Bain says, appearing to her left. "I saw your car and thought well that's where she ran off to. I want to buy you breakfast."

"Go away." *How in hell can he be wearing the same clothes he had on last night but look clean and refreshed?! Damn.*

"Oh c'mon now Margaret, don't be a killjoy. We had some fun last night, but I'm not going to ask you to marry me," Bain says teasingly.

"Good godalmighty! Perish the thought!" she hisses, quickly covering the remaining 5 feet to her car door.

He follows.

Peggy wheels around and looks at McDonald, cursing the fact that he looks totally calm, and clean, his hair still wet from a quick shower.

"How did you know where to find me?"

He chuckles. "I knew the road you'd take back to Augusta, and I know the Shell station has a reasonably clean bathroom. You drive a silver Lexus. It wasn't difficult. We do need to talk, however, so I suggest you follow me to the café just down the road."

"And why exactly would I do that?!"

"Because I know who you are, Ms. Matthewson."

Peggy inhales sharply and whips off her sunglasses, staring daggers into McDonald's dark brown eyes. "I don't know why you called me that."

"Of course you do. Now get in your car and follow me," McDonald says curtly, heading off to his own car, a new black Mercedes.

Peggy's heart flutters with major anxiety. She starts shaking.

Ten minutes later they are sitting opposite one another in a tiny café on the outskirts of Aiken, the Tick Tock, studying the limited menu while their bored waitress stands there snapping her gum

Bain speaks first. "Black coffee, two fried eggs, grits."

The waitress, a taciturn older white woman whose name tag identifies her as Margie, looks pointedly at Peggy.

"Black coffee, scrambled eggs, no toast. By any chance does your establishment sell aspirin?"

Margie grins and walks off. Twenty seconds later she is back with an enormous bottle of generic aspirin, which she hands to Peggy while she pours coffee for them.

"Thank you, you're a lifesaver," Peggy mumbles, shaking three pills out of the bottle.

Bain studies her face while he sips his coffee.

"You know, a few weeks ago I noticed you at my place eating, Margaret."

"Nobody calls me that. Please stop."

"You rarely come into my restaurant, but I know you are a major force in the upper echelons of our fair city. I also know your boyfriend isn't rocking your world in bed. He's one of the most dull guys I've ever seen. I bet he's on and off in 2 minutes, right?!"

"How rude and crass of you to say a thing like that."

Bain grins. "I was surprised, however, to learn recently that the Augusta gossip mill was lit up with rumors of us having an affair."

"I had nothing to do with that."

"I have no doubt of it. I know how important breeding and family are to you, and you would never pick me to be your royal consort, despite my connection to Beatrice. After all, I am an uncouth outsider, rich but outside your social whirl, and eight years younger than you."

Peggy puts down her coffee and glares at him. "There's no need to be rude."

Bain laughs, and yawns. "It's not rude. You're still a beautiful woman, Margaret. I decided to trace the source of the rumors. It took some time, but I found out. The rumors were started by Wylene Drummond, who is a close friend of your ex-brother-in-law, Edmund Harrington."

So that's who keeps Edmund informed, Peggy thinks. *Hmm.*

"I also wondered how you support a pretty lavish lifestyle when you are a divorcee with no visible source of income. I hired an investigator to figure it out but he got nowhere."

"Of course not." Peggy studies her fingernails as though they are works of art.

"I bided my time. Finally, I happened to be reading an in-house publication of Barnes & Noble and there was a photo of well-known author Anna Matthewson, signing autographs in Los Angeles, and despite the brown wig and glasses, she looked like you, with her beautifully pointed little nose. She was also wearing a lovely antique emerald ring. It was clearly visible in the photo. I sat there wondering where I had seen that ring before. I finally remembered it. You

were eating lunch at the French Market one Monday and when I passed your table I noticed the ring because it's a large stone, actually rather large and vulgar for a woman with small hands."

Peggy frowns and knits her brows, struggling to remember.

"You didn't see me. I notice antique jewelry because my brother has a very successful business dealing in fine antiques, in

Atlanta, and he wants me to go into a partnership with him so he can expand. I've been learning as much as I can for the past couple of years."

The food arrives, and Peggy silently blesses the aspirin for doing its work and the eggs and grits for filling Bain's mouth so he cannot keep talking. She needs time to think.

After seven minutes, their silent meal is over. Peggy wipes her mouth and stares at McDonald. "So what is it exactly that you want from me in exchange for keeping quiet about my writing?"

Bain's large black eyebrows knit for a moment as he ponders her statement. "Your reputation is shot."

"Don't be ridiculous."

"You really think after last night you have a good reputation now? Now that you've been caught practically having sex beside your car? Those books are the least of your worries, Margaret. Good thing you don't play chess."

"I don't – how dare you –" Peggy splutters. The check appears and Bain reaches for his wallet and pulls out a twenty dollar bill.

"I am going to make you an offer that I suggest you not refuse. Listen carefully. I just bought two gorgeous townhouses in Buckhead. I am turning over the running of my business in Augusta to my partner, Bob Adler, and I am going to be spending a lot of time in Atlanta. I will rent you the other townhouse."

Peggy is furious and in no mood to entertain the notion of leaving the city where she has lived all of her life.

"I would never rent a house. I'm only interested in equity. Besides, what would I do in Atlanta? I know nobody there."

"I thought your daughter lived in Atlanta?" McDonald asks, puzzled.

"Well, yes, but we aren't close."

Bain studies Peggy as she re-applies her lipstick, then blots it with her napkin.

"You could help me in my antiques business, and be my girlfriend. You could also continue to write your little mysteries, because I know a ton of Augusta gossip, enough for 5 books."

"You seriously overestimate my discomfiture regarding what that crazy old bat Delores Wright says about me. She's old as the hills and she shouldn't even be driving."

Bain sighs, then shrugs. He stands up and starts for the door, then turns around. "Call me when you're ready to discuss my idea."

The tiny restaurant is empty except for the two of them -- *thank GOD*, Peggy thinks wildly.

"Don't hold your breath. Oh – and if you tell anyone about my books, I'll tell them you are a homosexual."

Peggy is annoyed as Bain throws back his head and laughs loudly, but with genuine delight, before walking out the door.

She ponders his insolence. *How dare he suggest my life is not in Augusta. Why on earth would I leave Augusta? The city of my birth? The most beautiful, gracious town in the South? To deal with huge, vulgar Atlanta, with its horrible traffic and social nobodies? I should think not.*

Peggy heads for the ladies room shaking her head.

Bain pops in a CD of Stevie Ray Vaughn as he speeds back to his aunt's house. *She'll come around,* he thinks. *She has no idea what awaits her,* he chuckles.

CHAPTER 50 -- FAMILY

Leigh waits impatiently by her phone the next morning. She reviews the letter from Rose four times.

Leigh picks up the Polaroid of the portrait of Rose and puts it in her purse, along with the letter found in the suitcase.

Finally, Jack calls her, clearly on the cell phone judging by the traffic noises in the background. "I got Ed. We are going to stop by the rental car place and will be there in about an hour."

An hour and ten minutes later they are on their way, in a rented Camry which holds three people comfortably, unlike Jack's truck or Leigh's compact car. Ed is sipping on Dunkin Donuts coffee while he drives, and he and Jack are eating Krispy Kremes and laughing about some TV show.

How could two such very different men find anything in common? Leigh wonders. *The macho private eye, ex-Marine, and the gay photographer old enough to be his father.* Leigh drifts off to sleep around Madison and doesn't wake up again until they are almost to Benton.

"We made good time. Let's pull over and take a break," Edmund says. "We aren't expected until 12:30."

They pull over at a gas station and use the bathroom, and then get back on the road. When they get close to Benton, Jack reads from a note with directions on it. They travel miles down a country road before coming to a long gravel driveway that disappears into some woods. A wooden mailbox is beside it.

"You're sure this is it?" Jack asks.

"Yep, see the cardinal painted on the mailbox?" Edmund asks. "That's the one."

There is a red cardinal painted on the black mailbox beside the numbers.

"Yep, I see it. But where's the house?" Jack asks, feeling uneasy.

"She said to head down the driveway and the house would be at the end," Edmund says.

Edmund turns down the narrow gravel driveway, and the car creeps along as it winds around through pine trees. Leigh tries to stop the anxious thoughts in her head. Finally, they get

to a clearing. In the clearing stands a small white wooden farm house with a wraparound porch. An older model Buick sits in the driveway, next to a Volvo, on the side of the house.

Jack gets out first, followed by Leigh, then Edmund.

The front door opens and a small, chubby black woman in her 70's comes onto the porch, walking slowly, leaning on a cane. She has tight gray curls and wears heavy glasses. Her pink cotton flowered dress is starched and crisp. She welcomes them with a smile.

"You must be the Harringtons. So nice to finally meet you," she says, smiling. "Come on up and set with me on the porch for a few minutes." She sits in a small rocker and indicates the other chairs on the porch.

Leigh wonders why she can't just meet her aunt, but she walks up the stairs to the porch with Edmund and Jack.

Edmund shakes her hand. "So nice to meet you Mrs. Washington. Edmund Harrington. This is my niece Leigh and this is her boyfriend Jack Briggs."

Leigh and Jack sit on the porch swing. Edmund stands. "I've been sitting all morning so I'd like to stand a bit if you don't mind."

"Of course. Can I get anyone anything to drink?" Millie asks. They all shake their heads.

"Well, the reason why I am delaying taking you in the house is simple. My daughter has had a vision of how the meeting with Leigh should go, and she needs your help. She feels it will be traumatic for Leigh, so she asks for your patience in setting things up so as to cause the least amount of stress."

Jack looks at Edmund, who looks thoughtful. "I think I understand. What would you like us to do?" Edmund asks.

Millie looks at Leigh. "You look like your grandmamma, Child, you surely do. What a blessing. So does Lizzy. Y'all should have met long ago, but I will leave it to her to explain why you didn't. I'd like you to go on in alone and sit down on the sofa in the front room there, the blue one, and close your eyes."

"Okay," Leigh answers hesitantly. She looks at Jack. He has looked behind him, into the window, where he can clearly see the blue sofa. He nods at Leigh almost imperceptibly.

Leigh stands up and goes into the small living room. She isn't really sure why, but she is glad that Edmund and Jack can see into the room from the porch. It's a small room with soft blue-gray walls, a small wooden coffee table, and the overstuffed sofa, upholstered in dark blue fabric. A small curio cabinet with glass figurines stands in the corner. The walls are bare except

for a framed diploma and a photo of a tall young black man in a graduation robe, holding a diploma and grinning at the camera. It's clearly the "company" room.

Arranged in front of the window and opposite the sofa are two upholstered chairs, with a small table between them.

Leigh settles herself on the sofa. "I'm here," she calls out to Millie.

"Close your eyes, Child, and don't open them until you are told to," Millie says.

Leigh takes a deep breath and closes her eyes. She hears footsteps come into the room, then the sofa gives way as someone sits beside her.

The presence smells of Coty's L'Origan. Leigh instantly feels comforted.

"Hello Leigh. I am your Aunt Liz. I am so happy to see you again."

"Again?"

"Yes, we have met before. The first meeting was when you were 4 years old but you don't remember it. I am going to talk you through that time, and you are going to remember, but not feel

248

scared or worried. It's a form of hypnosis. You will be on the outside, looking in. There is nothing to be afraid of. Are you ready?"

Leigh feels a woman's hand take her own hand.

"Yes M'am. I am ready," Leigh says quietly.

"Good. Now I want you to relax and travel back, in your mind, back down the driveway, then down the road, then down the highway, then on the interstate, to Augusta. I want you to travel back down Walton Way and back down Grand Street, to the first house you remember, the big brick Victorian. As you travel, you go back in time. Back to being in your twenties, then your teens, then your childhood. It's a hot June day in 1968 and you are four years old. Do you see the den with the TV?"

Leigh nods. "I see it. I am watching "Captain Kangaroo"."

"Exactly. You hear the doorbell. Tell me what else you recall."

Leigh sighs heavily.

"It's okay. These memories will not hurt you. You are safe. It's safe to remember," Liz says softly.

Leigh next speaks in a voice higher than her normal adult voice. It's more like her childhood voice.

"I am sitting in the den watching "Captain Kangaroo" and Daddy has already gone to work. Mama is drinking a cup of coffee and smoking a cigarette in the kitchen. The doorbell rings and Mama gets up.

I jump up and run into a spot where I can peer out at the front hallway, curious to see what the new maid looks like, wishing

Lurline, our former maid, hadn't decided to move to Macon. I loved Lurline.

When I see the new maid, I blink, thinking the early morning sunshine is making me see things. Far away things are always blurry.

Miss Elaine wears a gray dress and white apron, like all the maids, but she isn't old or fat like the other maids I know. She is young. Mama tells me to come say, "Hi."

Leigh's face twists into a pained contortion.

"What happens then?" Liz asks softly. "It's okay to remember."

Leigh takes deep breaths and finally speaks. "This new maid, this lady, looks like my Grandmother, in the painting in the living room. As soon as I get close I see it. She has darker skin, but the same eyes, and forehead. She wears red lipstick like Grandma Rose, in the portrait. She also looks like my daddy. I don't know why we would have such a lady in our house. Why doesn't Mama see it?"

"Do you think your mother looked at the maid's face?" Liz asks softly.

Leigh thinks for a minute.

"No. She doesn't look black people in the face. Ever. She looks past them or through them. So she didn't notice, which is so weird."

Leigh's right hand grabs the hem of her blouse and twists it. Liz holds her left hand.

"Tell me about the rest of the day," Liz says.

Leigh talks through her memories.

Jack and Edmund are staring at the scene, through the window. Millie speaks softly to them. "I'm going to go around to the back door and go in the kitchen. You all can go in the living room real quietly and sit on those chairs. Don't disturb them, though."

Edmund helps Millie to her feet and she heads around the corner of the wraparound porch.

Edmund and Jack very quietly slip through the door and into the living room and sit in the chairs in front of the window.

Edmund studies his half sister in the light pouring in through the windows. She is tall and slender, and wears her hair relaxed but in a short bob. Her skin is darker than Rose's skin, but it's a medium brown, still light. Her features are very similar to Rose's except that she is taller and her face is a bit larger. The mouth is also a bit smaller, he decides.

Jack looks at her too and feels a startled recognition. Liz looks very similar to the portrait of Rose he had seen in the Polaroid Edmund sent to Leigh. She is wearing a simple blue cotton dress with small white flowers on it, and no jewelry. Her face is unlined despite her age, and she has very kind eyes.

Liz looks at the two men and nods slightly, but they sense it's important not to disturb Leigh.

Leigh is still talking about the day, but as she gets to the part about where her father comes home, her voice rises in pitch and she twists the hem of her blouse in her hand even more. Her head, which had been drooping down, comes up.

251

To everyone's astonishment except Liz, Leigh's eyes open but they are unfocused and Jack senses she is not seeing the room, or the furniture, or her aunt beside her. The notes of panic in her voice concern Jack but Liz looks directly at him and almost imperceptibly shakes her head.

Liz puts her arm around Leigh and holds her tight, speaking in a soothing singsong.

"It's okay, baby, it's okay now. You are not alone. You are safe. What do you smell?"

Leigh closes her eyes again, squeezing them shut as if to deny the images.

"I am going up the steps and I smell Mama's bath stuff, and I see the bathroom door open. Oh no."

Liz talks softly and gently. "What else baby? What happens then?"

"I hear the screaming," Leigh says, her voice very high.

"Tell me about the screaming. Remember, you are not part of it."

"It's terrible. Daddy's screaming at Mama. The water is splashing. I hear a choking sound –"

Leigh clutches her throat and whimpers. Liz gently takes her hand away.

"Go on."

"I run up the steps and I see them then. I SEE THEM!"

"Remember, you are okay and you are safe, and there is nothing bad to see, just old data, just film to see, without judgment. What do you see?"

"The maid is half out of the tub and she's naked! The water is going everywhere! Mama has her hands around the maid's throat and Daddy is trying to pull Mama away because she's choking the maid! Mama's screaming at her! She's screaming, "NO! NO! BLACK BITCH, YOU DON'T BELONG HERE!"

Edmund and Jack exchange a look. Edmund has long suspected the truth, though he was never told the details. He shakes his head sadly.

"What was your mama trying to do, Leigh?" Liz says gently, sadness heavy in her voice.

Leigh's breathing becomes labored and she finally howls.

"I think she was trying to kill Miss Elaine! My mama was trying to kill her!"

Liz's hand rubs Leigh's back. "You're okay. These memories can't hurt you."

"I'm scared.."

"What happened then?"

Leigh sighs heavily and pulls away from Liz, pulling her knees up to her chest.

"I ran back down the stairs, and I grabbed Ranger and scrunched down next to the fridge on the floor and hugged Ranger. He kept me safe. The screaming kept going. I could hear water splashing and everything. Ranger stayed with me, though. Then

253

Uncle Harry came in and ran up the stairs, and Aunt Martha grabbed me and put me in the car and we sat there a long time."

"OK, that's great Leigh. Good job recalling details. Now, you are going to come back from that, out of that house, back down that road, back down I-20, and back here to us. You are now 32 years old and you are safe here. The memories can't scare you or hurt you anymore because you've faced them. They will stay in your memory but it's okay. You've seen what happened and you are okay now."

Leigh gasps and opens her eyes, draws back and looks into Liz's face. For a moment, she just stares, then a sob catches in her throat. "Oh, my God, I am so sorry!"

Tears roll down her face. Liz pulls Leigh back into her lap like a child, while Leigh sobs.

"It's okay Baby, it's okay. You are safe. I am safe. Everything is fine. Let it go."

Leigh sobs.

"Let it go, honey. It's the past. It's done. We are all fine now. You remembered, and now you will never be fearful of those memories again. They have no power over you."

Liz rocks for a few minutes, rubbing Leigh's back while she cries. Liz hums softly "You Are My Sunshine."

The two men look at each other. Jack's face registers sorrowful shock, and he softly shakes his head.

The three of them sit for another few minutes while Leigh cries, then Jack notices a box of Kleenex on a small table beside the sofa, and he hands it to Liz, who nods gratefully and pulls several out for Leigh.

Leigh looks up and notices the two men as she blows her nose. Millie appears and hands Liz a wet washcloth. Liz gently wipes off Leigh's face. Leigh gazes at her aunt in wonder.

"But your name is Liz?"

"When I took the maid's job I used my middle name, Elaine."

"How did you know? How could you know how that day haunted me?"

Liz smiles a bit sadly. "I know because I was there. I've never forgotten your face. You were so terrified. I also know because Travis told me you sometimes had bad dreams after that, and you woke up crying, screaming Mama, no, in your dreams. Finally, I know it haunts you still because I am a psychic and a medium."

Silence descends on the room.

Edmund clears his throat and stands up. "I cannot tell you how sorry I am that my sister-in-law acted that way, Liz. I was in New York. I knew something bad happened but I had no idea of what."

Liz rises and faces her brother. "I know you didn't, Edmund. You didn't know."

Edmund reaches out his arms to her and she walks into them. They hug.

Jack interjects "I'm sorry too, but I am also curious about something. Why were you working as a maid?"

Liz pulls out of Edmund's arms and looks at Jack, smiling sadly. "I had a degree from Spellman, but I couldn't find a teaching job. I wanted to live in Augusta near where my husband was stationed, at Fort Gordon. I took the maid job just to tide us over."

"Well, forgive me for asking Liz, but what happened that day? I mean, why did you...?" Edmund asks, puzzled.

Liz looks sad, and shakes her head slightly. "I had no idea when I walked in that house that I would see a portrait of my mother, whom I had not seen in years. It made me cry. I poured myself a brandy, to calm my nerves, and since I never drank, I got drunk fast. I knew no better. Then I just got scared. I thought I'd get a quick bath because I was dirty and sweaty from cleaning, and I wanted to meet my brother, see if he looked like me. I just didn't realize the doors were locked. I always lock doors when I'm alone in a house, because of a trauma that happened to me as a child. I simply forgot about Leigh and her brother. Next thing I know, Travis and Peggy found me. I was so embarrassed -- and still drunk."

"It was also 1966, a bad time to be black in the South," Edmund says thoughtfully. "Why didn't you have Peggy arrested for attempted murder?"

"She didn't have me arrested for drinking her liquor and locking her kids out. That's what the police would have focused on."

"Yeah, but she overreacted, didn't she?!" Edmund says, smiling ruefully.

Liz chuckles, ignoring the shocked look on Leigh's face. "I have to laugh. It's better than crying."

"What a terrible thing to go through!" Leigh interjects. "God, this explains so much to me. Maybe Mother has been so cold to me all these years because she was afraid I would remember and confront her."

Liz explains, "She and Travis and Harry were afraid you would one day remember. They weren't sure but they were fearful. I should probably tell you that Travis and Harry have been paying me for years to keep quiet, to not bring charges against Peggy for attempted murder, and – though it was never said it was always understood – to keep quiet about my mother being black. Travis and I became friends, despite the incident, a friendship I treasured. Harry and I are not friends. Over the years I saved the money and used it to pay for my son's education. Harry contacted me recently and told me specifically not to see you, Leigh. I thought it was time you knew the truth, however."

Leigh cannot remember the last time she felt such anger.

Leigh blurts out, "So are you going to bring charges against my mother? There's no statute of limitations is there? She needs to pay for what she did!"

Liz shakes her head. "No, Leigh, I'm not going to bring charges. What happened cost Peggy her marriage to Travis, and alienated her from you. She has suffered, and I think Peggy is suffering some more, right now, socially."

Edmund frowns and looks at Elaine. "What are you talking about?"

Liz chuckles. "I am a seer, Edmund. Let's go eat some lunch and I will tell you what I see."

"I'm Jack Briggs, Leigh's boyfriend," Jack says, stepping forward to shake Liz's hand.

"Of course, you are her boyfriend. I could tell the moment I saw you. I'm so happy to meet you, Jack," Liz says, shaking his hand warmly.

There is no dining room, but they walk back to the spacious kitchen in the back of the house, where the table holds a gracious display of food. There is a platter of fried chicken, hot biscuits, deviled eggs, green beans, and a pitcher of iced tea awaiting them.

"Wow, what a feast!" Edmund exclaims. "I was going to suggest going out to lunch. Y'all must have been cooking all morning. You shouldn't have."

Liz laughs. "I love to cook, Edmund. So does Mother. We rarely get to meet new family members so it's a privilege to cook for y'all."

When everyone is seated and the tea is poured, Millie asks everyone to join hands.

"We thank you, oh Lord, for all your many gifts, but especially this gift, family. Thank you for the healing that has taken place. Thank you for the coming together of Liz with her brother and her niece. Thank you for letting me live long enough to see this happy day."

She stops praying and looks around the table. "*Oh happy day. Oh happy day. When Jesus walks. Oh when he walks…*" Millie sings. Liz joins in with her strong alto and the then Leigh joins in.

258

She knows the song because Clarice used to sing it around the house.

After a few minutes of singing, the women stop. "That was awesome!" Jack says.

"My heart is filled with happiness. I just had to let it out," Millie chuckles.

As Leigh tucks into her food, she looks around and realizes *These people are my family. Every one of them. They love me. They claim me. Thank you, God. It really is a happy day.*

CHAPTER 51 -- FORGIVENESS

Liz hugs Jack and Leigh and Edmund goodbye, after an afternoon spent talking and getting to know each other.

Millie is in her room napping, snoring away.

Liz waves as the car heads down the driveway, then turns back and goes in the house, her thoughts whirling. She cannot remember being so tired in recent years. Emotions were bubbling on high, all day. Recalling the incident from 1966 took more out of her than she cared to let on. It was such a relief to help Leigh get past the old trauma, though. It healed something inside Liz herself, something she hadn't known needed healing until today.

Liz puts on a loose old cotton housedress, pours herself a glass of wine and sits on the porch as the sun sets, rocking and thinking. She closes her eyes and allows the memories to come back.

Peggy doesn't look at me when she opens the door. She is cool and polite. There's little Leigh, peeping around the corner, so adorable in her little pajamas. The work is exhausting, scrubbing floors, washing sheets, scrubbing the four bathrooms in the old Victorian. Dust is everywhere. Toys are scattered everywhere. I forget totally about eating lunch. Peggy leaves out the back door and I lock it, out of habit, because being in a big house alone scares me. The kids are playing next door, I think. Didn't Peggy say that? The kids are next door?

I save the living room for last. It's a big room with lots of stuff to dust but no toys to pick up, thank God. I enter the room and flip on the lights and survey it, the cream colored matching sofas, the bookcase, the mantle. I suddenly notice there is a large portrait of a beautiful dark-haired white woman with black eyes, hanging above the mantle. I go closer and stare at it, almost not breathing. Oh dear Jesus. I realize it is a portrait of Rose, my birthmother. I sink to my knees. Oh my God, help me. This is my brother's house. There are family photos on the mantel, proving this. As my eyes roam over the photos I panic and think that I should never have taken this job! Oh my God. Now it's almost done and my brother will be home from work soon. I see a decanter filled with amber liquid and small crystal glasses around it. I have never touched liquor in my life, but I decide it's time to get some liquid courage and I drink a full glass with trembling hands. Instantly, I feel nauseated. I give the room a quick dusting and look down at my dirty dress. He can't see me like this. I have to look clean and nice. I have to get a bath.

Liz rocks, her eyes closed, willing to let the memories come, one last time, so she can finally be rid of them, finally free.

I'm in the tub scrubbing myself with the lilac stuff, wishing I could wash my dress. What's that noise? Was that a door? No, couldn't be. I have time. Why didn't I lock the bathroom door? I close my eyes and sink further into the tub. Footsteps on the stairs! I freeze in horror. Before I can think what to do, the bathroom door is thrown wide open. Travis stands there. I take one look at his face and I just know he is my brother. "What the hell are you doing!" he barks. I cannot speak. His eyes are filled with anger. "Why did you lock the children outside?!" "I, I, didn't know they were outside? I thought they were next door?" Before I can think what else to say, more footsteps. Peggy appears in the doorway. "GET THE HELL OUT OF THAT TUB YOU BLACK BITCH!"

I start to rise, to grab for the towel. Peggy's eyes are like laser beams of hate. I can explain – but then I see little Leigh. Oh baby no, no – "STOP STARING AT HER!" Peggy screams at Travis. "GODDAMN IT I SAID GET OUT NIGGER!" Suddenly her hands are at my throat and I fall back into the water, my screams choked off by her hands -

Liz stops rocking and opens her eyes. The spirit of her mother Rose stands in front of her. Liz hears her voice in her head, clearly. *"Those memories have no power any more. None. Forgive yourself for what happened to Leigh. Help her to forgive Peggy. Forgiveness is key to everything, daughter. Forgive, and the memories will have no power over you. Forgiveness means healing."*

Oh Mama, I wish I could hug you! Liz thinks.

"Forgive," her mother says again, without words, before her image fades, gone in the last rays of the sun.

CHAPTER 52 – JACK AND EDMUND

The trip back to Atlanta is a down time for Leigh. She curls up in the back seat of the rented car and falls asleep, the emotionally exhausting day finally catching up to her.

In the front of the car, Edmund and Jack hold a quiet conversation, once they are sure Leigh is asleep.

"So you had no idea, I mean Travis never told you, that Leigh's mom had choked Liz?" Jack asks, still having a hard time processing something so gothic and bizarre. Jack comes from a family where feelings are kept under wraps, and even on holidays there is minimal drama.

Jack looks out the car window at the warm Georgia night, the dark blurs of pine trees, the sliver of moon dipping in and out in the clouds.

Edmund sighs, wishing he could light a Marlboro, but he has run out. "Well, I knew something had happened that drove a wedge between Travis and Peggy, but not what it was. I mean, they had a pretty good marriage up until 1966, and then things fell apart. You have to understand, though, I rarely visited my brothers in the 1960's. Mother had died in 1964, which was devastating to me. I was in San Francisco part of the time being a hippie, then I moved to New York City. I hung out with Warhol and went to a lot of parties and, to be honest, dabbled in drugs. The whole decade is sort of a big blur to me."

"Okay," Jack says, unsure how to react. He has a hard time picturing the elegant Edmund as a hippie.

An uncomfortable silence descends on the car, then Jack breaks it.

"Were you surprised that Liz is a psychic medium? Do you believe that stuff?"

Edmund thinks for a minute before answering. "I don't disbelieve it, let's put it that way."

"You don't think it sounds nuts?"

"Liz is a retired school teacher, caring for her mother. In my experience that doesn't usually indicate mental instability. I am looking forward to getting to know my sister better, actually."

"Yeah, I am thinking Leigh would benefit from spending a lot more time with Liz since she isn't close to Peggy," says Jack.

Edmund is thoughtful for a moment. "Didn't Liz say something about Peggy suffering socially? I meant to ask her for an explanation of that but then I forgot about it."

"Yeah, now that you mention it, I vaguely recall that. I wish she had explained it."

"Me too."

There is a brief silence. Jack still has more questions.

"Leigh told me recently she needs to figure out how to deal with being mixed race. What do you think of that?"

Edmund grins. "Unlike me and my brothers, Leigh embraces that part of herself. All the love she ever got growing up was from housekeepers Peggy had hired, all of whom were black, of course."

Jack glances in the back seat to satisfy himself that Leigh is still asleep, then turns around, sighing heavily.

"Can I tell you something in confidence?"

"Sure."

"I am in love with Leigh. I've never met anyone like her. I'm thinking of asking her to move in with me. I'm not sure I want to take on a lot of family drama, though."

Edmund looks at Jack. "I respect that. You've only been seeing her for a couple of months, though. Give it some time. Before the divorce, Leigh was a bright, cute little girl, full of life, smart as a whip. The divorce, when she was ten, really did a number on her. I think once she gets past the newness of her relationship with Liz and stops caring about Peggy's opinion of her, she will be fine."

"You think she cares about Peggy's opinion?"

"Oh yes. She probably doesn't even know it, but she does. Oh, and by the way – go ahead and send me a final bill for your services and I will get it paid."

"There's no need. I haven't really done anything since I sent the last bill. You and Leigh have done the heavy lifting recently. I'm sorry. I've had big clients keeping me really busy."

"It's okay. We found my sister, so I don't think there's anything else to do."

The two men drive in silence the rest of the way to Leigh's apartment, each lost in his own thoughts.

CHAPTER 53 – DELORES TALKS

After he drops off Jack and Leigh, Edmund heads down the road to the Hilton.

As soon as he gets in the room, Wylene calls Edmund on his cell and says, "Call me back on a real phone!" He is tired and wants only to sleep in his hotel room, but he calls her immediately on the hotel phone.

"Brother, you will not believe what Peggy is up to now."

"What is it Wylene? I'm really tired."

He lights a Marlboro and pours himself a tot of Scotch.

"Well, after the DAR meeting last night Delores Wright saw Peggy and Bain McDonald having sex outside, next to her car!"

For a moment, all Edmund can do is frown. He has questions. "Honey the DAR ladies are usually pretty elderly. Is Delores sure of what she saw?! Has she had her eyes checked recently?"

"Yes! She even stuck her head out of the window to get a better look! It was them! Gossip also is saying Bain is leaving Augusta and moving to Atlanta and taking Peggy with him!"

Edmund laughs.

"Well, shoot. I cannot wait to hear more about this. All that work we did erasing the rumor about those two, and now Peggy can't keep her panties on around that vulgar man! Lordy mercy. I love it!"

They both laugh, for nearly a full minute.

"I knew you'd want to hear this!" Wylene crows. "Well, night night!"

"Night darlin'!" Edmund responds, hanging up the hotel phone.

He gets his small camera from the bag and checks, but he knows he has taken up an entire roll of film. He and Liz spoke privately about spending some more time together and especially about visiting the Carrie Steele Pitts home to learn what else they can about Rose's background. Problem is, Edmund has to fly back to New York for a shoot so the visit will have to wait.

He calls Greg just before going to sleep and shares the events of the long and tiring day, thankful to have someone waiting for him.

Jack kisses Leigh carefully, on her forehead, at the door of her apartment. "Honey, I've got to go out of town tomorrow, and I'll be in Miami about a week, but I will call when I get back."

Leigh struggled to wake up when Edmund pulled into her apartment complex, but now she is fully awake.

"Wait a minute, I don't understand. Miami?! I wanted to talk to you?"

"We can talk when I get back. I'm sorry I didn't mention this before. It's a new assignment from a big law firm, and I couldn't turn down the work. My flight leaves at 8 in the morning. I'll call you!" he calls, stepping out the door and closing it.

"Well, okay, I guess." Leigh feels bereft. As she watches his truck drive away she wonders if it will always be like this, not seeing him very much. It's a familiar ache because she spent the last part of her childhood missing her father.

After she has her pajamas on, she pours a glass of wine and gets out her journal.

This whole day was like a crazy thrill ride of emotions and I was seriously thinking it might be time to invite Jack to stay the night, now this defection to Miami!

She listens to some Simon and Garfunkel and eats some Ritz crackers with a nice Camembert cheese, and finally realizes sleep is long overdue.

That night, though, for the first time in a long time, there are no bad dreams.

CHAPTER 54 – THE END OF THERAPY

Dr. Simerly looks at Leigh after she finishes telling the tale of her remembering the Drunk Maid Incident at Liz's house. A week has passed since Leigh got back from Benton.

"So you witnessed your mother trying to kill your aunt? That's what you had repressed all these years?"

"Yes. My aunt who looks very similar to my grandmother, whose portrait I saw every day."

"Well that would be quite traumatic for a small child. Have you talked to your mother about what happened?"

Leigh stared at him. *Is this guy dense or what?*

"Dr. Simerly, I don't ever want to see or speak to my mother again. I've always suspected she was a terrible racist. Now I know for certain. She was trying to kill Liz because she was suddenly confronted with knowing her mother-in-law was, in fact, part NEGRO so her husband was part negro and her children, of course, had to be part negro – and I'm only using that word because it's the word she would use."

"You don't think she was angry because Miss Elaine – I mean, Liz -- had locked you and Bubba out of the house, gotten drunk and messed up the bathroom?"

Now Leigh was furious. "I just said what caused Mother to snap. She is a racist. Pure and simple. Plus, she didn't want the police at her home."

Dr. Simerly scribbles notes on his legal pad.

"Leigh, cutting off contact with your mother doesn't resolve the issues between you two. I think it would be really helpful if your mother would come to see me, so I could counsel you both."

Leigh laughs. "She would sooner walk down Broad Street stark naked than go to a psychologist."

"I really think it would be beneficial –"

Leigh gets up, purse in hand.

"I don't think I need to see you any more, Doctor. I feel like the weight of the world is off my shoulders now and I am going to be just fine. Thanks for your time. Send me a final bill."

"Leigh, I really think –" he starts, but Leigh is out the door before he can finish his sentence.

CHAPTER 55 -- Mismatched

Peggy is furious. She stands in the office of her brother in law Harry, unloading.

"Nobody will talk to me at the Country Club! Susan canceled lunch with me! Nobody in the DAR or the Huguenot Society will return my calls! My friends at St. Paul's are barely civil! It's like I've got AIDS or something!"

Harry notes that Peggy is wearing one blue sandal and one black sandal. He has never seen her in flats, much less mis-matched sandals. One of her eyebrows is drawn crookedly and her flowered cotton blouse is buttoned wrong. Her khaki pants are wrinkled and look like they have been at the bottom of the dirty clothes hamper. If she had not said one word, Harry would have known something was terribly wrong.

"Now, Peggy, you know how people love to gossip. It will blow over," Harry says soothingly, using the same voice he uses with clients whose investments have tanked.

"It isn't just gossip, though, Harry. It's true," Peggy moans, sinking into a chair. "I was tipsy. He caught me in a weak moment. Goddamn him to hell."

Harry pours Peggy a glass of sherry and hands it to her. She accepts it gratefully and takes a swallow. Harry picks a note up from his desk.

"Well, hey, I do have some good news. I got a note this morning from my sister Liz, sending back the check, and she said the monthly payoff is over."

Peggy sits up straighter in her chair and gasps. "Why is that good news, Harry?! Is she fixing to go to the police after nearly thirty years?!" Peggy hisses, horrified.

Harry frowns. "No, no you misunderstand. Here, I'll read you the letter."

He sits down in the client chair opposite Peggy and puts on his reading glasses. He reads:

Harry, I have decided to end the financial arrangement we came to many years ago, for several reasons.

One, I am quite secure financially and it's not necessary.

Two, I met with Edmund and Leigh recently. Leigh and I discussed the incident and she was able to recover the memories previously blocked out. Talking about what happened was a healing experience for us both. I like Leigh very much and I look forward to getting to know her better.

My final reason for ending the arrangement is quite simple: I no longer want to dwell in the past. Seeing the monthly check reminds me of that sad day all those years ago, and I want no more reminders. I have retired from the teaching profession, and my son is finished with school and a successful pharmacist. Aside from the need to care for my mother Millie, I am very content with my life. No regrets.

Oh, and I suppose now it is okay to tell you something important. I am a psychic medium. As a gesture of goodwill, I want to give you two pieces of advice. One, do not invest in anything to do with dotcoms. Two, pass this along to Peggy: it's time for her to leave Augusta and move to Atlanta.

In case you have any doubts of my abilities, let me mention this to you, Harry: your daughter Angela is soon going to leave her husband and announce she is pregnant, and Angela and her lesbian lover will leave Virginia and move to Florida.

Harry chuckles and puts down the letter. "Imagine saying that about my baby girl! She has no idea how much Angela is in love with Barry. She has no idea what she's talking about."

He glances at Peggy's face as he is speaking. She has turned a corpse-like shade of white. "Peggy? Are you all right?"

"Mark told me last night at dinner we're through. Bain McDonald wants me to move to Atlanta and go into the antiques business with him. I haven't mentioned that to ANYONE, though. Not a soul."

They both stare at each other, profoundly uncomfortable. Although neither one would admit it, they both have a sneaking suspicion that there is some truth to the idea that there is an unseen world, and that spirits exist. What if everything Liz says is true?!

The day Peggy tried to choke her sister-in-law to death with her bare hands, she didn't feel in control of her own voice or her own body. She had felt possessed by an other-worldly rage, a rage that felt like it belonged to someone else but was being channeled and manifested through her. Specifically, Peggy had felt possessed by the evil spirit of her mother, a terrible racist and snob. She had never shared that with anyone.

That rage would wash over her at other times, too, especially during fights with Travis. At times, she could hear her mother's raspy voice in her ear, and feel completely vulnerable to fits of unreasonable anger, especially at the thought that she had married a mixed-race man.

The drinking didn't help. In fact, Peggy had gone to a great deal of trouble to conceal a two-week stint at a Swiss clinic in 1973, just after the divorce. The drinking had gotten under control and the clinic had helped her restore her physical and mental equilibrium.

Now, all of it was being threatened again -- her personal reputation, her ability to move easily in and out of all the influential social groups in Augusta and thus get material for her books, her personal relationships.

Peggy looks down and realizes she has on two differently colored sandals. *Good Lord, I can't let anybody see me like this! I look crazy.* She stands up suddenly. "Harry, I think I need to get home."

"I understand, Honey. Let me walk you out."

They walk over to the closed door of Harry's office and Harry opens it.

The phone on Harry's desk rings. His secretary calls out, "Harry, that's Angela on line one."

Peggy stops in her tracks and looks at Harry. He looks back. The phone rings insistently. Harry walks over to the phone like a sleepwalker and picks it up. "Hey there, Butterbean!" he says jovially. He listens for a few moments. "You are leaving him? No, you –"

Peggy stands at the door and watches as Harry drops into his chair and puts his face into his hands.

"How far along are you?!" he asks, his voice shaking.

CHAPTER 56 – DURING THE WAR

It's a sunny Thursday and Leigh has taken a personal day off from work.

Millie and Liz sit in Leigh's apartment eating ham sandwiches and drinking iced tea. Leigh has invited them to come over so she can learn more about her aunt's life. They have talked all morning.

They finish their lunches and Leigh hands around the homemade brownies she has prepared.

"Oh my, these are so moist and delicious. You are a talented cook, Leigh," Millie exclaims, after thoroughly chewing the moist chocolate brownie.

"Thanks. Our housekeeper when I was growing up was an incredible cook, and she taught me how to make them. I include almond flavoring and a teaspoon of brewed coffee. That's why they taste a bit different."

Liz finishes her brownie and looks at Leigh. "So what are your questions for Mom?"

Leigh shows Millie the note she found inside the suitcase.

"I'm really curious as to how you and your husband came to adopt Liz, how that all came about."

Millie reads over the note and shakes her head slightly.

"Poor Nate. He died in Italy in 1944, without ever seeing his baby girl."

"Wow, how sad. The story is just fascinating to me. I wonder how Rose met him?"

Millie sighs deeply, and takes a sip of tea. "You sure you want to hear all this?"

Leigh nods. "Absolutely. I want to know more."

Millie tells the story.

"After Pearl Harbor, America changed quickly. We were suddenly in the war, not just standing on the sidelines.

My husband Samuel and I had been married for 5 years. Samuel had a good job working at the Castleberry Foods plant. I did seamstress work. We wanted children so bad, but we just weren't blessed.

To make a little extra money, I decided to rent out our spare room to Nate, because he worked with Samuel, and we knew he was a good man and would be a good boarder. Nate came from down in Cordele, from a sharecropping family that had all passed away by the time he was 18, so he had come to Augusta to work.

Nate was a good looking man, over 6 foot tall, with a beautiful smile. He had been married and his wife had died, so he stayed single after that, not wanting to get hurt again.

The story Nate told us about how he met Rose, is he was walking down Broad Street one day and she was standing at her car all upset because the car had a flat tire.

Nate was good with cars and he got the tire changed and the spare on there and drove the car over to a filling station where his friend worked.

He told me later he had never seen anyone so beautiful. She was, Leigh. Rose was just a lovely woman, and her beauty was enhanced by her kindness. She had a gentle spirit, and people were drawn to her.

I don't really know how they managed to have a love affair, because your granddaddy was a mighty strict, joyless man. He expected his dinner on time, every night, and his house had to be spotless and his children had to behave. Rose had help, of course, but being a mother to three rambunctious boys is a full-time job in itself.

When Rose found out she was pregnant she was in a tizzy. Rose was able to hide her belly for months, but finally she came to see me one day and said Millie, I just don't know what to do. That's when we hatched the plan for her to go to Atlanta, away from the small town atmosphere, and then Sam and I would get the baby and keep her with us, and raise her."

Millie looks at her daughter and smiles.

She continues. "From the moment I saw Liz I knew she was gonna be a little sweetheart, and she has been. Rose gave us money to help with expenses, and paid for the adoption, but she stayed in Liz's life as long as she could."

Leigh senses what is coming next, but she feels compelled to ask, anyway.

"Why did Rose stop seeing Liz?"

278

Millie stares down at her lap, and shakes her head slightly, the weight of the memories clearly making her sad.

"Rose came to see Liz every Tuesday afternoon, like clockwork. As far as Horace knew, she was volunteering at the hospital that afternoon. One day, though, he happens to be out in his car and he sees her in her car, heading down the street, away from St. Joseph's, towards the area of town where black folks live. He follows her and sees her go into our house.

That night after dinner, he confronts Rose. She says we are just friends of hers, but he knows that's a lie. Black folks and white folks don't socialize with each other in 1941, in Augusta. As far as Horace knows, Rose is white. Also, like most lawyers he can tell when someone is lying.

Rose had a maid named Sallie, and Sallie was cleaning up the supper dishes and heard the fight. She knew something bad was going down because she had never seen Mr. Horace so furious. She told me she was afraid for Rose.

Horace tore out of the house around 9, like demons was chasing him. He had taken Rose's car keys and threatened her. Rose told Sallie to get on over to our place and warn us. She suspected Horace was going to do something bad.

I don't know how Sallie got to our house so fast. We didn't really know her, but she warned us to get out of the house, and we were packing up to leave when the Klan showed up. I grabbed Liz and ran and hid in the neighbor's house, but I saw them drag out poor Samuel and string him up. I like to died, I was so scared."

Leigh looks at Liz, shocked. Hearing about it was far worse than seeing scribbled words on a piece of paper.

Liz looks at Leigh and nods. "Yes, I saw the lynching. I will never forget it as long as I live. It was 1952. I was ten years old. I didn't know things like that still happened, but they did. The police never did anything about it, either."

Millie resumes the story. "After they killed Samuel they set fire to the house. Liz and I hid out with neighbors for a few days, then we went to Philadelphia. I heard there was a hotel up there needing housekeepers and we could stay with my mother's sister who lived up there. I started calling Liz Elaine, just to be safe. I wrote a note to Sallie saying we were okay and she passed it along to Rose, but we didn't hear from Rose again. I think Rose was just afraid of her husband, scared of what he might do if he found us. It was too dangerous to even write to us, and I really think Rose feared for her life."

"Do you think he knew that Liz was Rose's child?" Leigh asks.

"I think he suspected it," Millie replies. "We will never know, though. "

The three women are silent for a few minutes.

"What made you want to come back to Georgia?" Leigh asks.

Liz speaks next. "I finished high school and got a scholarship to Spelman College, and so I lived in Atlanta and went to college. I moved back to Augusta in 1966 when my husband was at Fort Gordon. Mother moved here to Benton because her cousin was a widow and wanted to share a house, and it was a way for her to stay not far from me."

"So you never saw Rose again after 1952?" Leigh asks Liz.

Liz looks thoughtful. "Actually, I did see her, one time. It was after her husband died. I was at Spelman in 1963, and I decided to try and call Rose in Augusta. I had a feeling her husband had died. I got her number from directory assistance, called and spoke to her. That weekend, she came to Atlanta on the train and we spent two wonderful days together, staying at a hotel and just getting to know each other again."

Liz looks at her mother Millie. "I never told you that, Mama. I didn't want you to be upset."

Millie looks stunned, but not surprised. "I would not have been upset, Baby. It's okay."

Leigh is excited to hear about this but tries not to sound overly eager. "Did you take any photos that weekend?"

"No, neither of us had a camera. I wish we had. We were walking down the street that Saturday afternoon and men were trying to pick us up, flirting and laughing, calling out. Rose was still beautiful. I felt beautiful beside her. We looked like sisters. It's a happy memory."

"Did she talk about passing for white?" Leigh asked.

"We never spoke of it. She did tell me she had married Horace way too young, just looking for security and a stable family. He had changed after they married, though. Right after your dad was born they stopped sharing a bed, she said."

"Why didn't she just divorce him?" Leigh asked.

Millie was ready for that one. "Leigh, in those days, a divorced woman had no social status and no power. Horace would've taken her children, she told me once. She had asked him once what he would do if they divorced, and he threatened her. She was scared of that. He was a powerful lawyer. So she stayed for them, for her boys. Then after Samuel was killed I imagine she stayed out of fear."

"I wish I could have known her," Leigh said softly.

"She knew you were on the way, Leigh. We talked about it, that weekend in Atlanta. She was excited. She knew you would be a girl, and Travis had told her the name they'd picked out," Liz said.

The three women sit silently for a moment. Leigh feels a spasm of longing and sadness, wishing she could have known Rose.

"Leigh, have you spoken to your mother since you met me last week?" Liz asks, speaking softly and carefully.

Leigh stands up and begins clearing the table.

"No. I don't ever want to speak to her again. We've never had a good relationship and now I hate her. I wish she were dead. I'm embarrassed to be her child."

There's an awkward silence. Millie and Liz exchange a look.

"Mama, Leigh and I have an appointment at the Carrie Steele Pitts home in forty minutes. You'll be okay here. Maybe you would like to take a nap?" Liz asked.

Millie's face brightened. "I am not tired, but I want to watch my stories. Leigh, can you show me how to work your TV?"

"Sure," Leigh says, coming out of the kitchen area.

Fifteen minutes later, Leigh and Liz are on their way in Leigh's car.

CHAPTER 57 – SO ALIVE

Peggy sits alone in her swimming pool, a glass of wine in her hand, miserable. Nobody at the Country Club will speak to her. Her phone isn't ringing. She is shunned from Augusta society, and trying to figure out a way out of her situation is giving her a headache.

Just as she is contemplating getting up and putting on sunscreen, a cheery "Hello there beautiful!" drifts across the patio.

Peggy looks up, squinting in the bright sunlight, and watches in horror as a large, hairy arm reaches over and unlatches her fence gate.

"Who's there?!" she calls, although she has a pretty good idea who the arm attaches to.

Bain McDonald steps through the gate and latches it behind him. "I knocked on the front door, but when you didn't answer I figured you might be back here in your heated pool."

Bain strides over to the pool, grinning.

"Well you've destroyed my reputation so what the hell do you want now?!" Peggy barks, aware that the alcohol is affecting her manners but not caring. She pushes her sunglasses up to look at his face.

"I want to talk. Plus, it's a hot day, so I think swimming is an excellent idea. I didn't bring my trunks, but who cares?" Bain says, grinning as he shucks off his khaki pants and blue sports shirt.

"What the hell are you doing?!" Peggy stutters.

Before she can say more, Bain is naked and he dives in her pool and swims expertly across the water to where Peggy sits on the steps.

About 5 feet from her he rights himself, throwing back his head and splattering her with water droplets.

"I did NOT invite you here!" Peggy says, although it's far less snarky than usual because her brain is fighting with her hormones.

Peggy admires his body once again. Bain McDonald is like a creature hewn from rock, muscle upon muscle, but not freakishly bulging with muscles like a professional bodybuilder. He lifts weights and plays tennis and golf, and his body is sculpted into Greek god perfection. His excessive black hair doesn't mar the effect at all, but rather gives him the appearance of an ancient warrior.

"You may not have invited me but you want me here," Bain grins. "And I want to know when you are going to go with me to Atlanta and start your new life."

Peggy's knee-jerk reaction -- "Never! Why would I go live with you in Atlanta and be your mistress?! The idea." She takes a quick gulp of her drink and starts coughing, which makes Bain chuckle.

He swims nearer to her and looks up at her, grinning.

"I only offered you a rental on a townhouse and a partnership in the antiques business, but if you want to be my girlfriend that would be awesome. I don't believe I've heard the word 'mistress' used in normal conversation in my entire life?! Must be a word only writers use, Ms. Matthewson." He swims a few lazy strokes around Peggy, circling her.

"Oh! How rude of you to bring that up," she splutters, taking off her sunglasses which have now been splattered with water from his swimming. "Surely you aren't thinking of blackmailing me." She puts her sunglasses beside the pool and slips under the water, walking out further into the cool water.

"Well no, not really. I don't want you to go unwillingly. I want you to go because you realize there's nothing left for you in this stale old town with all its rules and prejudices. In Atlanta you can be whoever you want to be."

Peggy starts to retort but thinks better of it. Perhaps he's right. She realizes that he is very close to her now, but she doesn't care.

He pulls her into his arms. She doesn't resist. She can't, because of the surge of passionate feelings welling up inside her. He covers her mouth with his own, a kiss so deep and passionate that Peggy forgets everything, and loses herself again, lost in sensations that arouse her so thoroughly she cannot control anything, and she doesn't care.

She has never contemplated having sex in a swimming pool, but before she knows it her one piece bathing suit is off and his head is on her breast. A few minutes later they are on the steps, and she is in his arms, sitting astride him, breathing hard and rhythmically.

Just as Bain lets out a loud groan and Peggy shrieks with a powerful orgasm she can feel down to her toes, she realizes that the sound of a lawn mower has started up and the back gate is opening. It's lawn service day!

"Aaaaargh!" she manages to get out, before pulling away from Bain and diving under the water to get her suit off the bottom of the pool.

"Hey there, can you give us a few minutes?" Bain says casually, getting out and walking over to the chair where Peggy left a towel.

The small brown man with the leaf blower grins and goes back out through the gate.

A few minutes later they are inside the house, drying off, and laughing. Despite her embarrassment, Peggy hasn't felt so alive in years.

Bain admires her trim body as he dries his own.

"Want to go again?!"

"Not at the moment. I need to rest these old bones," Peggy chuckles. She realizes she is relaxed and happy in a way she hasn't been in a long time.

Bain has brought in sandwiches from a deli, plus potato salad and fruit, and he and Peggy sit in her kitchen eating. Peggy ponders the fact that mark never brought food over, always left that up to her.

Bain also clear the remains of their meal away after they eat, something Mark never did.

They spend the rest of the afternoon sitting in the family room of Peggy's home talking, about everything. Augusta. The Masters. Families. Food. Children.

Peggy cannot remember the last time she talked so freely to anyone, and Bain is a good listener, rarely interrupting except to ask a question.

They find they both love mysteries, antiques, swimming in the ocean, old movies, and Australian wines.

As Peggy contemplates how much she would like to be kissed again, the doorbell rings. Peggy makes her way to the front door wearing only a bathrobe.

She peers through the peep hole, aghast to see her son Bubba standing there. "Mother? You gonna let me in?" he calls through the door.

Bubba wears jeans and a sport shirt and sneakers, not his typical work outfit. His blonde hair is cut short, and his sunglasses and keys dangle in his hand.

She opens the door quickly and pulls him inside.

"Hey there, sweetie, what a nice surprise!" she says with false charm. "I just got out of the shower. You're not working?"

Bubba looks at her in the bathrobe and one eyebrow shoots towards his receding hairline. "I had to come in town but my meeting isn't until tomorrow. Do I hear a man's voice?"

Bain is whistling as he buttons his shirt and steps into view.

"Well, yes, I have a friend visiting – " she starts, then notices Bubba's eyes widening as he takes in the sight of a Bain McDonald striding towards them, barefoot, hair damp. Peggy turns around.

"Hey there, Bain McDonald, nice to meet you. You must be Peggy's son," Bain says genially, sticking out his hand.

Bubba shakes the huge hand tentatively, looking from his mother to Bain, puzzled.

"I'm just going to excuse myself for a minute and throw on some clothes. Be right back," Peggy says, heading towards her bedroom.

Bubba looks at Bain."I'm starving. I wonder if Mom has anything to eat."

"Let's see. I bet we can find something," Bain chuckles as he and Bubba walk back to the kitchen, which is just down a short hallway off the front foyer. Bain ponders the fact that there is no food left from their lunch.

Bubba thinks *Mom rarely has anything to eat besides takeout salads*, but follows the huge man back to the kitchen. His mother diets religiously and rarely buys more than salads to keep in the fridge. Bubba opens a cabinet door and finds an old box of Carr's water crackers, likely left over from a party, and munches loudly while talking at the same time.

Bain watches, bemused. "What's your real name? I know it's not Bubba."

"Well, no, that's the nickname my sister gave me. My actual name is Ward Harrington. I'm in plumbing supplies, down in Macon."

"Is that right?" Bain says, amazed a woman as fascinating as Peggy could have such a bland and boring son. "You think there's any cheese around here?"

"I doubt it. Mother is lactose intolerant, and never keeps it. I think that's why my sister is a cheese expert and eats it all the time."

Bubba opens the fridge and pulls out a jar of olives. "Want an olive?"

"Sure," Bain says, selecting a black olive and popping it in his mouth.

"So how long have you and Mom been dating?" Bubba asks, trying not to betray that he already knows the gossip, and that is actually why he drove to Augusta to see his mother.

"Oh, not long," Bain says casually.

Peggy comes back in the kitchen, looking cool and collected despite the damp hair, which she has pulled back in a ponytail.

Bain looks at her face, scrubbed free of makeup, and thinks *my God, even without makeup, what a beauty you are, and how the hell am I going to keep you for myself?*

Peggy hugs her son and cannot meet Bain's eye.

"Well, I didn't mean to interrupt," Bubba says, looking pointedly at his mother.

"I need to be going. I'll let you two catch up," Bain says, reading the look that passes between mother and son expertly.

"I'll be right back, Hon," Peggy says, grabbing Bain's arm and walking him to the back door.

"Look, I don't know what to do about seeing you," Peggy says. "I'm totally conflicted."

He chuckles. Softly, he looks down at her and says "Oh yes, we will see each other again, and again, and soon you will realize just how much we are supposed to be together."

Equally softly, she says, "Whoa, Tiger, it's early days."

"Maybe, but you know we've started something important here," he says softly. He kisses her lightly on the lips before heading through the back door and back out to his car.

Peggy walks back in the kitchen and Bubba throws an envelope down on the kitchen table in front of his mother. "New photos of the girls. They are walking all over the place now. We can hardly keep up."

His twin daughters are eleven months old, blonde and blue-eyed just like their mother and maternal grandmother.

"Oh how precious," Peggy exclaims, quickly looking through the printed photos. "Did the little dresses I mailed last week fit them?"

"Yes, thanks. Missy took some photos of them in the dresses. Mom, why haven't you answered your phone in two days? I've been trying to call. Your answering machine wasn't on either."

Peggy doesn't want to answer that question. "Hey, I have an idea. It's almost 6. Why don't we go to the Chinese restaurant over on Wrightsboro Road?"

Bubba frowns. "You rarely eat Chinese food, Mother. Why not the Country Club?"

Peggy swallows hard and wishes she had two aspirins. "Well, I'm tired of that place and all those stuffy people."

"Are you ill?! Good God Almighty Mother! What is going on?"

Peggy straightens up and glares at her son. "I don't like that tone."

"Well I'm sorry, but I don't like my oldest friend calling and telling me my mother is the talk of the town because she was seen screwing some huge baboon in a parking lot!"

Bubba had thought surely Clay was joking, or drunk, when he called, but then his father in law had called and confirmed the horrible news.

"It's all just a big misunderstanding!" Peggy says indignantly, standing up and walking over to the liquor cabinet.

"Really? McDonald said you two are dating. How's Mark taking that news?!"

"We broke up. It just wasn't working. Nobody's fault. Listen, though, I'm glad you're here. Guess what? I'm thinking about moving to Atlanta. I'm going to get Leigh to find me a great house in Buckhead, somewhere close to the mall."

Before the words left her mouth, Peggy didn't know they were going to come out. The moment she has said them, though, she realizes with utter shock that they are true.

"What?!" Bubba can't disguise the shock in his voice. "Have you lost your mind? You've never lived anywhere but Augusta, except for college. What the hell are you going to do in Atlanta?"

Peggy sits down hard at the kitchen table, and feels like a great weight has been lifted off her shoulders. She closes her eyes and thinks, *I can go to Atlanta and make new friends, friends who have no idea who my Augusta friends are, or my family, or anything. Friends who don't care who I am or who my daddy was, or what church I go to or how many antiques I have. Friends who just like me for myself.*

Feelings of fear struggle with feelings of relief, and even hope. What a relief to not care about one's place in society.

There is life after social disgrace.

She realizes Bubba is staring at her, waiting for an answer.

"I am re-inventing myself, Son. Fasten your seatbelt."

CHAPTER 58 – TO THE ORPHANAGE

Liz and Leigh settle into Leigh's Corolla and fasten their seat belts.

"Okay, so we're going to go 285 and be on it for, what, maybe 30-40 minutes?"

"Yeah, at least that," Leigh replies, turning left out of the apartment complex. "We could take 85 south into town but I heard there was an accident on the Grady curve so I think 285 will be a bit faster right now."

Liz settles sunglasses on her face. "Well, that's good, actually that we have some time, because there's something I want to tell you -- a story."

"Awesome. I love family stories."

"How did you know it was a family story?" Liz asks, smiling.

"Well, you're a long-lost family member, and I am still learning about you so it was logical to deduce it would be a family story," Leigh shoots back.

"Fair enough. Deduce, huh?! You do read a lot of mysteries. I would have loved to have you as one of my American Literature students."

"I would have loved to have been in your class!" Leigh says, with a grin, as she eases the car into the traffic of I-285, the 8 lane freeway that encircles Atlanta.

"Well, this story is about me and my life." Liz looks out of the car and sees the trees whizzing by in a blur, and remembers picking peaches as a child.

"My earliest memory is Mama putting up peach preserves in the kitchen, and the whole kitchen smelling like peaches. I loved to help her cook, and putting up peaches was always my favorite week of the year.

I also loved for Daddy to come home in the summer and we would get outside in the garden and work on the tomatoes, okra, beans, squash, carrots, peas – we grew everything, and mama canned it for the winter. I loved to be outside with him.

We didn't have a lot of money, but I never felt the lack of it.

Every Tuesday afternoon a lady I always called Miss Rose came by to see us. She usually brought me a little present of some kind – some flowers, a paper doll book, a bottle of Yoo Hoo. We would sit and chat. Sometimes we would swing on the swing set in the back yard. I felt a special bond with Rose as a child, but I didn't wonder why she came to see me. I sensed her care

and attention were more family than mere friendship, but I simply looked forward to her visits, and enjoyed spending time with her.

She was a kind lady, but I was not told that she was my mother until after we left Augusta. Mama worried that it would upset me, that it would be confusing since I was so much darker skinned than Rose. You may not know this, but in the world of black folks, light-skinned colored folks are higher up on the social scale."

Leigh frowns. "How ridiculous! It's just melanin."

295

Liz nods. "You are so right, but the world will never be as we want it to be. Anyway, where was I? Ah, childhood. I made good grades in school, and I got piano lessons, which was unusual in my neighborhood. I felt very special, but I wasn't spoiled. I still had chores to do at home, and I was expected to get good grades.

One day, when I was 10 years old, on my birthday, Miss Rose took me to the Woolworths and we got milkshakes, and then we went home in her big car. She rarely took me anywhere in the car so I felt really special.

That night after 9 o'clock – I know because I was getting ready for bed -- a lady knocked on our door that I didn't know. Mama and Daddy talked to her for a few minutes, then they talked to each other for a while. I was supposed to be in bed, but I heard them. I sensed there was something bad going on by the worry I heard in their voices, but I didn't know what.

Mama told me to get dressed and put my clothes in a grocery bag, and she started packing a suitcase for her and Daddy.

Now, packing clothes was something strange to me. We had never been on a real vacation except once, when I was 5, and we went to Atlanta on the train to see Daddy's father in the hospital.

About 8:30, there was a lot of noise outside the house – angry shouts, talking, laughing – and then loud knocking on our front door. I could hear men's voices, lots of men, and they sounded angry.

Mama grabbed me and we went out the back door, and slipped next door to the neighbor's house.

I was supposed to be in the spare room of their house lying down but I snuck in the front room and looked out the window. Mama came up beside me and held me, because I couldn't be pulled away from the window.

There were several men on our front porch, and they were wearing white robes, like ghosts. They were angry and shouting. After a few minutes, they tied Daddy's hands behind him and dragged him to the big magnolia tree in our front yard."

"Oh my God," Leigh says, remembering Millie's account. Now, hearing it from her aunt, it has become even more personal and a horrifying picture forms in her mind.

Liz continues in a soft voice, still anguished. "I will never forget that sight, as long as I live, Daddy with a gag in his mouth and his hands tied behind him, kicking and struggling as they threw the rope over the branch, then kicked the chair out from under him.

Mama had her hand over my mouth so nobody could hear me scream, and she sat there with me all night, on the floor of the neighbor's house. When Daddy was still struggling, then they set our house on fire. We hid in the shadows, praying and crying.

The fire department came out, but by then the Klansmen were long gone.

I couldn't speak for a week after that. I literally just couldn't speak. I kept seeing Daddy's body swaying from that tree.

Mama had grabbed the coffee can with her saved money before we left the house, and it was enough money for two train tickets to Philadelphia. Our neighbor drove us to Columbia to catch the train, and we didn't tell anyone where we were going because

Mama was so frightened. I don't know how she did it, got us both to Philadelphia and built new lives for us. She was only 34 years old and had been married since the age of 16. She had never had a real job, just done some sewing, altering clothes for folks, to make extra money.

My name changed to Elaine, during that time. Mama felt it would be safer, in case anyone was looking for us. I used that name when I signed up with the maid agency years later. I don't know why. Just sensed something bad, I think.

I went to school in Philadelphia, and we lived with my aunt for two years in her small apartment. Finally, Mama had saved enough money so she could quit her housekeeping job and get a decent job. She had put herself through business school so she got a secretarial position, and, finally, we were able to get our own little apartment.

For about a year after we left Augusta, I had nightmares all the time about what I saw that night. The smell of a fire, that smoky smell, would trigger me and I would re-experience the horror of seeing our house burn, and Daddy's swaying body and start crying. It took me a long time to process those feelings, and of course I felt bad when I upset Mama. I still have nightmares once in a while, actually. Childhood trauma is a terrible thing to process. So I understand your trials over the years, very well.

When I was 11 years old, I met a lady named Miz Lottie, and she changed my life. She was about 70 years old and she was the midwife in the community where we lived. Lots of poor folks couldn't afford a doctor, even in the 1950's, so Miz Lottie helped them out.

Mama realized one day that I had the gift when I predicted the outcome of a pregnancy."

Liz pauses in her storytelling, wondering what details to share.

"I really want to hear more about your gift," Leigh says quietly. "I think it's awesome you can see and know things like that."

"Okay, well, I was just 11, and I was in the grocery store and I looked at Mrs. Wainwright and saw she was just about 3 months along. I said "You're gonna have two big boys, over 8 lbs. each one of them. You'll need to go to the hospital." She already had 4 children so it wasn't exactly welcome news, you understand. She was so upset, she told Mama to make me keep my mouth shut, and then she told Miz Lottie.

Next day, Miz Lottie paid me and Mama a visit, and asked why I had said such a thing. Mrs. Wainwright wasn't showing yet. I said because I just know. Don't you know? Isn't it obvious?

I was not speaking disrespectfully. I was sincere. I was also puzzled as to why Miz Lottie and Mama looked at each other.

You see, I thought everyone just knew things, the way I did. A child only understands the world the way it is presented to them."

Leigh glances at her aunt, somewhat puzzled, but says nothing.

"Before you got glasses, I bet you thought everyone saw blurry objects, right? Same with my gifts. I thought everyone had them, until I was told differently. I could look at an envelope and know what was inside, in the letter. I could look at a piece of clothing in the store and picture the person who would wear it. I thought everyone could do that, see inside things, see inside people, just like I saw those tiny infants in Mrs. Wainwright.

So anyway, about six months later, Mrs. Wainwright had twin baby boys, just like I said, and Miz Lottie took me to see her mother to get instruction in how to be a psychic and a medium. Miz Lottie's mama was almost 90 years old, but she had *the sight*, and she schooled me in how to make the most of my gifts."

"Why didn't you do that for a profession, then? Be a psychic medium?" Leigh asks. "Why be a teacher?"

Liz sighs heavily and finally speaks, "I wanted to go to school and get an education, and have a normal job. Rose had talked to me many times about the importance of getting an education, and having choices. She wasn't educated, and that's why she had to marry your grandfather, she thought, to have a man to take care of her. She wanted me to have options. Being a seer is financially risky, because black folks don't always have money to support a seer, and I don't always make contact with the spirits."

"Why not have white clients?" Leigh asks, puzzled.

Liz looks out the window at the city of Atlanta going by in a blur.

"Leigh, I have to be honest. I was afraid of white folks for a long time. After the Klan killed my father all white folks seemed evil and scary to me. In Philadelphia I went to black schools, lived in black neighborhoods, had black friends. I didn't want to be around white folks. It took years, but I got over the fear, eventually."

"Did you think Rose was white, or black? She always looks white to me, in photos."

Liz looks thoughtful for a moment. "That's a good question, Leigh. I knew she was a very fair-skinned black lady, as I recall. My sight told me that. I don't remember thinking much about it, to be honest. As a child I was mostly impressed that she always wore nice clothes, and that she always smelled wonderful, and drove a nice car. I probably knew that white folks would think she was white, but it never mattered to me."

"And then you grow up and a white woman tries to kill you!" Leigh says, regretting her words as soon as they have left her mouth. *Why did I just blurt that out! How insensitive.*

Liz smiles ruefully. "Well, not all white women are like your mama, Leigh."

"No, not all are homicidal bitches, just Peggy and a few others."

Liz composes her face again.

"I don't like to hear any woman described with that word, Leigh. It's disrespectful."

"I'm sorry, but she is horrible and I hate her," Leigh says forcefully, her hands gripping the steering wheel tightly.

Liz sighs. "I need to explain something to you, Leigh. Listen up. The only way to live is to forgive people who wrong you. You need to forgive your mother."

"Are you nuts? What she did was terrible. I will never forgive her! She doesn't deserve it!"

301

Liz shakes her head. "It's not about what she deserves or doesn't deserve. For one thing, your mother is a product of a time and place, and all her prejudices relate to that. But this is what you really need to understand: forgiveness is about letting go of the resentment, letting go of the anger, the mistrust, all of it. If you don't, it poisons you, not them. I know this for a fact."

The two women ride in silence for a few minutes.

"I understand what you're saying, but I don't know if I can forgive her," Leigh says.

"Well, I think you can. I forgave your grandfather, and I forgave the Klansmen. I forgave your mother, too."

"Good Godalmighty! How?!" Leigh exclaims.

"I asked the Lord to help me, and he did. You have to ask the Lord for help. Hey, I think our exit is coming up. Fairburn Road, right?"

"I think so."

"Right," Liz says, squinting at the paper in her hands. "God taught me how to forgive, Leigh, but Rose talked to me about it, too. Rose knew all about forgiveness. That weekend we spent in Atlanta, the main thing she wanted me to know was the importance of forgiveness. That's when I finally lost most of my fear of white people."

"We're almost there. I want to continue this discussion, but maybe in the car when we head back?" Leigh asks, turning right.

"Sure. Let's see. Make another right at the next intersection," Liz says, reading.

The Carrie Steele Pitts home is not what Leigh expects. She had pictured in her mind a large Victorian building with iron bars, something like an awful, forbidding place. The small brick cottages and quiet, landscaped grounds are surprising.

"You know this isn't where Rose lived, right?" Liz remarks. "They moved to this location in the 1950's."

"I didn't know that, but it makes sense. I hope they moved the records here." Leigh remarks.

They park the car and find the administration building, a simple one story brick building. When they enter, they are in a small foyer and there is an office door on the left. A tall black woman dressed in a gray suit and black pumps stands by the door.

Althea Whitman smiles and greets them. "You must be Mrs. Williams," she says with a smile, extending her hand to Liz, who shakes it warmly.

"Ms. Whitman, thank you for taking the time to see us this afternoon," Liz says.

"Not at all."

"This is my niece, Leigh Harrington." Althea shakes Leigh's hand. "So nice to meet you."

"Nice to meet you," Leigh replies. "I am so looking forward to learning more about my grandmother's life."

"Well, I'm afraid there's not much I can tell you, but we always welcome back alumni and the descendants of alumni," Althea replies. "Right this way."

"Can you tell us a little bit about this place?" Liz asks.

"Well, it was founded by Carrie Logan because in the late 19th century there were many orphaned black children on the streets of Atlanta. Carrie Logan had been born a slave, but she worked for the railroad and she took in abandoned children. She started off keeping them in a boxcar during the day, and taking them home at night. Eventually, she founded the orphanage in 1888, with financial help from the county, and it grew from there. She died in 1900. When your mother arrived in 1908, the director was a lady named Clara Maxwell Pitts, who served for more than 40 years."

"Wow, that's a long time for a non-profit to be in existence," Leigh says.

"I'm sure your facility has made a huge difference in many children's lives," Liz notes.

"Yes. Okay, so I pulled the file on Rose Cunningham after we spoke the other day, and, frankly, I am amazed there is still a file in existence going back that far. The pages are brittle and yellowing. I made you a copy of what I could find about your mother, but I'm afraid there isn't much here," Althea says, handing over a small sheaf of papers to Liz.

"Do you mind if we take a few minutes to read these?" Liz asks.

"Not at all. Take your time. I will be back in ten minutes. Can I get you all anything to drink?"

"No, thank you," Liz murmurs, her eyes scanning the pages. As she finishes reading, she hands each page to Leigh.

The records are of Rose's health and grades in school, and there are notes from some of the workers that she was "an alert, active child" and "smart for her age." The first page about her simply says that she was born to Elizabeth Cunningham, age 15, a domestic servant. She was left at the orphanage at two days old.

"I was hoping there would be photos," Leigh says wistfully.

"Well, they probably didn't have extra money to photograph the children back then. "

Althea comes back into the room. "Do you have any questions?"

Liz takes off her reading glasses and puts down the sheaf of papers."There is nothing in here about my grandmother, Elizabeth Cunningham. By any chance, is there anyone you know of who was around between 1908 and 1918? Mother said her mother would come visit her here, until her death in the 1918 flu epidemic."

"I doubt we have anything in our records. I will ask around, see if we have contact information for anyone who might have been here that long ago, who is still alive, but I doubt it."

"I understand. Thank you for taking the time to meet with us, and copy the records," Liz says. "I would like to leave you with a contribution." She reaches into her purse and pulls out a check.

"That would be very kind," Althea says with a smile, accepting the proffered check.

In the car on the way back, Leigh is quiet, but then she asks, "You know, something occurred to me when you mentioned on the phone the other day about visiting the orphanage, but I was hesitant to say anything," Leigh says quietly.

"What's that?"

"Well, I have never met a psychic medium before but if you can contact the dead, why don't you just have a talk with Rose and Elizabeth, ask them questions?"

Liz chuckles quietly. "Oh Leigh, I wish it were that simple. Spirits don't always make themselves known, and they don't speak to me in the way you and I are speaking. I see images of things, like echoes of past events or shadows of future events. Sometimes the images are obvious, the meaning is clear, and sometimes not."

"Well, can you ask the spirits to come to you, I mean, say you want a visit?"

"I can ask. They don't always appear, though. They don't always answer my questions, either. That's why it's not an easy thing to do, give readings. Sometimes I get answers, sometimes not."

"What happens if you don't get answers or make contact?" Leigh asks.

"I don't charge anything. I don't think it's right. Some people pay a few dollars anyway. That's probably why I will never make a huge amount of money from what I do, but it's okay. I don't advertise. I just rely on word of mouth, and I try to help people who are grieving. It's more like a call to ministry than a money-making endeavor, as I see it."

"What happened to your husband?" Leigh asks. "I hope you don't mind my asking."

"Not at all. My husband Jamie was killed in Vietnam in 1969. I had been teaching for a couple of years by then, and I left

Augusta and moved in with Mother, so she could help me raise my son. He grew up in Benton."

"Wow, you were so young to be widowed."

"It was a difficult time. There was a lot of racial tension in Augusta so Benton suited me better. I taught in Athens, which is only a 20 minute drive."

"You couldn't find work in Benton?"

"Well, no. It's just a tiny farm community. Mother and I both worked in Athens. I taught high school English and she was a secretary for a real estate company."

"What does your son do?"

"He is a pharmacist, and he lives in Athens now. He's engaged to be married."

"Cool. Does he know anything about Rose?" Leigh couldn't help herself.

"You mean does he know she spent most of her life passing for white? Yes, I've told him. I had no photos, unfortunately. However, Edmund sent me some lovely photos last week and I'm going to have them copied for TJ."

"I'd like to meet him."

"I hope we can arrange that one day soon."

"Did he inherit your gifts?" Liz shakes her head, smiling slightly. "No, and he is actually very skeptical of my gifts. He is a man of science, so it's not surprising."

"Does that make it hard to have a good relationship, the fact that you disagree about something so important?" Leigh asks.

Liz is thoughtful for a moment before speaking. "We had quite a few lively arguments when he was younger, but now that he is not really a kid any more, we have been able to talk a lot more easily. We can agree on one very important thing: we love each other and we want to

continue to have a good relationship. So we accept that we will not agree, and we go on. Our bond is far more important than any disagreement, even about something important. Make sense?"

"Yes. I wish…" Leigh starts, and then stops.

"You wish you could have such a relationship with your mother, now that your father is gone. You can, Leigh, but it will not be easy."

Leigh looks out at the Atlanta landscape whizzing by and feels only anger and resentment towards her mother, but just behind that feeling is a longing for a connection, a longing that she does not want to acknowledge.

She decides to change the subject.

"When we get back to my apartment, would you try to contact Rose and Elizabeth?" Leigh asks, hesitantly.

"Sure."

However, when they get back to the apartment and open the door, they find Millie is dozing on the couch, and somewhat disoriented when she awakens.

"Laney? Where am I? What's going on?" Millie says anxiously, sitting up and looking around at the small apartment with alarm.

"Now, Mama, we are in Leigh's apartment, remember? Leigh, my niece?" Liz says, holding her hand.

"I don't know this place. I want to go to the bathroom, and then, I want to go home," Millie says loudly.

"I'm sorry, Leigh. I need to get her home. She gets like this sometimes when she is away from our home," Liz apologizes, helping her off the couch and steering Millie towards the bathroom.

A few minutes later, belongings have been gathered, and Millie is in the car. Leigh has given Liz the suitcase that belonged to Rose, which she accepted. "She was your mother, and she wore these when you were still inside her. It's only right you have these things," Leigh says, only keeping the note from Travis.

In front of the apartment building, Leigh and Liz embrace, and as they pull apart, Liz gazes intently at the space behind Leigh's right shoulder. "I am seeing my brother Travis behind

you, Leigh," she says softly. "He says he will visit you soon and give you some messages. You have vivid dreams of him sometimes, right?" she asks, looking searchingly into Leigh's eyes.

Leigh turns to look behind her and immediately feels foolish.

"You can't see him, Honey, but he is there," Liz says softly, smiling. "You have dreams of him sometimes?"

"Well, yes, but they are just dreams." Leigh asks. "Right?"

"Spirits contact us in whatever way they can, and dreams are a powerful way. Keep your heart open to communication, and your dad will come to you in dreams. Write down the dreams, because even sometimes powerful dreams get forgotten in the light of day."

"Wow, I never thought about it like that, Thanks!"

The two women hug again.

"I want to discuss your gifts sometime, Leigh. You definitely have some abilities. You just need to learn how to use them," Liz says warmly.

"I would like that very much. I love you Aunt Liz," Leigh says.

"Love you too, baby girl."

Leigh later writes in her journal: *Although the trip to the orphanage wasn't very productive, I got to know my aunt a lot better, and I feel a close bond with her. She has been more motherly and concerned than my mother, and I want to spend a lot more time with her.*

Leigh goes to bed and feels peaceful and relaxed, but her dreams tell a different story.

Leigh doesn't dream of her grandmother or great-grandmother that night, however. In her dream, she sees her mother wandering around the Country Club in Augusta, looking lost. Nobody can see her but Leigh. Everyone looks at Leigh, walking beside Peggy, like she's a foreigner, and they turn to each other and make mean remarks, right in front of her. Then Peggy takes off and

Leigh keeps running after Peggy, trying to get her attention, but Peggy just hurries away, around the corner, over the hill, sometimes near the pool, sometimes on the golf course, but always out of reach. No matter how hard Leigh runs she cannot catch up.

Finally, Leigh sees a large man with black hair striding towards Peggy. He has a huge body, like a weightlifter, but his face is turned away from Leigh. Peggy turns around and sees him and stops. Leigh thinks she can finally catch up to her mother, but before she reaches her the

man has scooped Peggy into his arms like a baby. He lifts up, and flies away with her. Leigh feels frustrated but the beautiful smile on her mother's face is a revelation.

Leigh awakens the next morning and writes down the dream, but wonders about the meaning of it.

CHAPTER 59 – THE BLENDER

Jack is in Miami, at the airport, waiting to board his flight back to Atlanta, and thinking, as usual, about Leigh.

The timing of the trip to Miami had been serendipitous because he was starting to feel like maybe there was just too much drama surrounding Leigh. He was afraid maybe he had been too rash in saying he was falling in love with her.

Jack is the type of person who studies a problem from every angle, weighing all options, researching and studying, before taking a step. He feels this gives him a huge advantage over most people, who are prisoners to their desires and whims.

Leigh is different.

That is why she fascinates him.

He thinks about the awkward conversation they had recently. They were sitting on the deck at Leigh's apartment, having been swimming and eaten a pizza. They were listening to music and watching the stars come out.

He asked Leigh if she was going to buy a new blender, because hers had broken one night when they made daiquiris. "I already bought the blender," she said.

"Already?" he asked. The blender had been out of commission only a week.

"You want to see it? I can't wait to try it out."

Jack stared at her, thinking *hmmm… she just went out and bought it?!*

"Did you research blenders, to figure out the best kind? Did you check out which stores offered the best price for the best brand?" he asked her, staring in puzzlement.

Now it was Leigh's turn to stare. "No. I went to Sears, found the blenders, and bought the one that was on sale."

Jack was stunned that Leigh would do such a thing. Jack had a rule of thumb that any purchase over $20 was researched and carefully thought-out before it was made. He had a 5 year subscription to *Consumer Reports*.

He didn't want to start an argument so he kept quiet but her rash, impulsive purchase seemed foolish to him.

The obsession with finding out about her grandmother's mysterious life and secret child, he understands, but she is awfully emotional, at times. Like a lot of men, Jack is highly uncomfortable around a crying woman, although he hides it well.

Then again, he is strongly attracted to Leigh and he loves a lot of things about her.

Her apartment is usually neat and tidy. She dresses conservatively and well, without a lot of jewelry. She always smells good, but not overly perfumed.

Leigh is a good cook. Jack is a fairly decent cook, after years of living alone, but Leigh has a flare for cooking that he does not. She has more spices in her cabinet than he has ever seen, for instance. He has salt, pepper, ketchup, Tabasco, and garlic salt in his kitchen.

Most importantly, Leigh is funny and smart, and he knows his family will like her.

He smiles to himself, wishing his flight could be called sooner so he could get back to Atlanta.

Despite her foolish purchase of the blender, Leigh is nearly perfect for him. He resolves to see if she will agree to moving in with him, sort of a trial run for marriage, once they have dated another month or so. Three months of dating seems about right to broach that subject.

Jack smiles, thinking about the joyful reunion with Leigh planned for that evening.

CHAPTER 60 – A GLIMPSE OF ELIZABETH

Liz is making cherry pies for the church bake sale on Saturday.

Millie has already made three gift baskets containing cookies, corn muffins, homemade pickles, and a set of cute potholders. The gift baskets will be raffled off to raise money. Now, Millie is napping.

Liz works quickly to get the pies in the oven to bake. She sets the kitchen timer, then goes out on the back porch to shell peas for supper.

As she sits on the porch shelling peas and listening to the late afternoon sounds, particularly the birds, she becomes aware that she is not alone.

Liz stops her shelling and looks slowly to her right.

A shimmering form stands there on the porch, about 6 feet away. She is smiling at Liz. By her upswept hairdo and long dress, Liz wonders if it is her grandmother Elizabeth. The woman nods.

"Hello," Liz says softly. "Thank you for coming to see me. I wish I knew more about you."

The figure smiles sadly, and motions for Liz to close her eyes.

Liz closes her eyes.

An image of a young light-skinned black girl appears. The girl is wearing a long calico dress and has her hair in pigtails. She looks to be about 13 or 14. She is carrying a bucket and she starts picking blackberries in the meadow. Liz senses that the girl must be Elizabeth.

Liz thinks, *she looks so young…*

A thunderstorm comes up, and Elizabeth starts picking faster and faster, but finally takes the bucket and runs, across the field, to an old dilapidated barn.

She runs inside just as the fat drops of rain start.

A boy appears behind her, a dirty, unkempt white boy. He is tall, with white blonde hair. Elizabeth doesn't see him, as he grabs her from behind.

Elizabeth screams and drops the bucket of berries. The boy is too large and strong, and he throws her on the ground and pushes up her skirts to rape her. Elizabeth fights him hard, fists flailing, screaming.

Oh my god… thinks Liz, horrified. *I don't want to see this.* The boy roars in anger and grabs Elizabeth's head and slams it to the ground. She passes out.

That scene mercifully ends.

The next scene shows Elizabeth in the hospital, giving birth. The baby is placed in her arms. *This must be Rose, Elaine thinks.*

Elizabeth's parents are there, dressed modestly in clean but threadbare clothes. They are talking and shaking their heads.

Liz jolts awake and stares. The ghostly Elizabeth has left.

The tears in her eyes are real. Her mother was the product of a brutal rape. Who was that white boy? Why would he do such a terrible thing? What happened to him? Knowing the racial climate during that time, Liz assumes he was never prosecuted. What a terrible thing to go through for a little girl, that brutal rape. Liz bows her head and starts to pray, asking God to help her accept that terrible vision, since it cannot be changed.

CHAPTER 61 – THE RUMOR MILL

Leigh spends the morning with her uncle's friend Eric, who wants to buy a condominium in midtown.

After the last listing Leigh has arranged for Eric to see they go for coffee at a Starbucks.

As they chat about the condo's great features – the fireplace, the coffered ceilings, the proximity to the gallery where Eric works, Leigh has the strangest feeling that she should call home and check her messages. She ignores it.

"And you know, I may want a house one day, but for now I think that condo would really be the best thing –" Eric says, then notices Leigh's faraway look. "Are you okay?"

"Sure, why do you ask?" Leigh says, startled.

"You just look like you've seen a ghost or something."

"Eric do you have one of those cell phones you can carry around and use anywhere? I can only use mine in the car," Leigh says, apologetically. "I have a strange feeling I need to check messages."

"Sure, here you go," Eric says, handing her his phone.

Leigh calls her home phone. There's a message from Carol that startles Leigh. "Oh my god! You have to call me! It's about your mother!" Carol practically shrieks.

Leigh looks so alarmed that Eric is worried. "Leigh, what's wrong Honey?"

"There's something going on with my mother. I need to go to my car and call my friend Carol. It's long distance," Leigh says, feeling slightly queasy.

"Just go ahead and call. Use my phone," Eric encourages her.

"You sure?" Leigh asks, aware how expensive cell minutes are.

"Go right ahead. I'll be back in a few," Eric says, heading for the restroom.

Leigh dials Carol's number.

"Oh my God! You know what everyone in Augusta is saying, right? About your mama and Bain McDonald?"

Leigh grimaces. "No. I haven't talked to her in a while. I'm really angry at her. What's she doing with McDonald? He owns that restaurant down on river walk, right?"

"Leigh, she was seen having sex with him outside a DAR meeting!"

"What? No, that can't be right. She wouldn't do that." Leigh starts tearing a napkin into small pieces.

"Well, she did. Then, they were seen having sex in the pool behind her house!"

"Seen by whom?!" Leigh starts shredding her empty paper tea cup.

"The lawn service!"

"What?? Oh my god!"

Now Leigh is up and pacing, as she heads outside.

"Nobody in Augusta is talking to her. In fact, nobody has seen her at church, or garden club, or anywhere, in days. Mama heard it from her friend Susan Miles, and Susan doesn't gossip, but this is too much!"

Leigh looks at Eric as he walks outside and finds her. "Listen, I was worried she might be ill or dead. That's not the case. So look, can I call you later, after the baby is asleep?"

"Yes! Talk to you after 8:30!"

Eric looks worried. "Honey, you okay? You are pale!"

"My mother has become Augusta's geriatric town slut. I am NOT okay!"

When Leigh gets home she calls her uncle Harry because she can't call her mother yet. Harry answers and they chat for a few minutes. Peggy is alive and well. Harry saw her the day before at Winn Dixie.

"What do you think about the gossip about her and Bain McDonald?" Leigh asks.

There is a pause.

"Honestly, Leigh, I think it's true, but I don't think it's a bad thing. McDonald isn't a jerk, like you might have heard. He's actually an okay guy. Don't worry about your mama," Harry says.

"Thanks. I'm glad to know she isn't in a mental hospital. Physically, she's okay," Leigh says.

"I know you have a hard time getting along with Peggy, but you know she loves you, right kiddo?" Harry says. "She's not good at showing it, but she does."

Leigh wants to scream at her uncle *you have no idea what she is*, but she closes her eyes and wills herself to be calm.

"Uh, well. We may have to agree to disagree on that. Thanks Uncle Harry. See you later."

When Leigh hangs up she wonders why Harry said such a thing. He never talks about emotions. Finally, she just shrugs and goes into the kitchen to start dinner.

CHAPTER 62 -- BEATRICE

Peggy sits at her kitchen table, her laptop open before her, busily typing away at her new novel. She has 102 pages already and she can't write fast enough. She didn't even do her usual meticulous outline, just sat down and started writing.

She has a full glass of iced tea beside her, and her hands are flying over the keyboard. This new book contains not just a cozy little mystery, but a romance. In fact, the romance is key to the story and it includes a lot of sex. The words are tumbling out of her, and she rejoices that her writer's block is gone.

She jumps when the deep chime of her doorbell rings.

"Screw it, I'm not stopping now," she says aloud, annoyed.

There's a pause of perhaps thirty seconds, and the bell rings again. Then there's knocking.

"SHIT!" Peggy fumes, standing up and striding through the kitchen and foyer, aware that she wears a pair of Bubba's old gym shorts, a black tee shirt with a rip in it and no makeup. No shoes or even flip flops. She had started writing at 6:30 a.m., right after an erotic dream that involved Bain McDonald.

She peers through the peephole and gasps.

Beatrice Arbuthnot stands there, looking irritated. "I know you're in there Margaret, so open the door," Beatrice says loudly.

Beatrice is famous for rarely leaving her beautiful country home in Aiken, except for occasional trips to Augusta for lunch with her sorority sisters twice a year. Most of them are now dead, however. Beatrice is 76 years old.

Peggy opens the door. "Well, hello Beatrice, um, won't you come in?"

"Finally," Beatrice huffs, plodding inside and looking around.

"Nice house. Too new for my taste and too much beige and green, but there's no accounting for taste," Beatrice remarks as she walks into the living room which is adjacent to the foyer and sits down in a green upholstered chair.

"You may bring me a small glass of sherry," she instructs Peggy.

Peggy doesn't say a word, but heads back to the kitchen.

Beatrice is a doyenne of Augusta society, despite living in Aiken. Her grandfather had come down from up north around the turn of the century and built the house where Beatrice now lives, but it was his summer home. His second wife was a Butts, an old Augusta family, so he was instantly accepted into society. The Georgian mansion on Walton Way where Bain now lives was the main family home.

Beatrice is 5'1 and weighs almost 200 lbs. She wears only dresses and heels when away from home. Her hair is dyed blonde and teased into a semi-bouffant. She decided on that hairstyle in 1965 and never saw any reason to update it.

She wears clothes that look like they came from Talbot's but in fact did not, since Talbot's does not make clothes in her size. Her dresses are all handmade and tailored for her.

A widow with no children, Beatrice is proud of her lineage and spends a fair amount of time paying researchers to dig up famous people in her background. So far she has uncovered 5 presidents, 18 senators, and a connection to P.T. Barnum which she does not discuss.

"Can you crank up the air conditioning in here? It's nearly eighty outside," she remarks, taking the glass of sherry from Peggy. Peggy walks into the back hall and puts the thermostat on 70, thinking *Maybe that will freeze the old cow and she will go away...*

"How are you?" Peggy says, trying to think of something to say.

"I am the same as always. The pertinent question is, how are YOU, missy?!" Beatrice says, fixing Peggy with a stare that would wilt most people.

Peggy sits on the maroon and cream loveseat and ponders the large arrangement of silk flower on the coffee table, and the back issues of *Town and Country* beside the flowers.

"I'm just fine."

"Really? With your reputation in ruins? I doubt it."

Beatrice is known for her bluntness, but that remark borders on cruelty.

"Well, I don't know –" Peggy starts, but she is interrupted.

"I didn't come here to argue, Margaret. Your reputation is ruined and you know that as well as I do. However, all is not lost. I came here not to condemn, but to instruct and encourage," Beatrice says, then takes a sip of her sherry. Harvey's Bristol Cream. *Well at least she had the good sense to buy decent sherry*, Beatrice thinks.

"That's very nice of you but –" Peggy starts, but Beatrice cuts her off.

"I remember your parents, Margaret. Your father was one of the finest men I've ever known, kind to everyone, a pillar of the Episcopal church, president of Kiwanis, on the board of University Hospital, a Mason. A fine man. Beloved. Your mother, however, was a vicious drunk, thoroughly disliked."

Peggy gawks at Beatrice, annoyed and a bit scared.

"Why would you say that about my mother?"

"Why not? It's the truth. I'm too old for pretense. Besides, your mother is long dead. I've decided in my old age I'm going to tell the truth more and to hell with anyone who criticizes me for it. I'm tired of pretentiousness. Nobody in Augusta liked your mother. When you married Travis I thought well good for her, a love match, and a fine man, despite his mean, skinflint father."

Beatrice takes another sip of sherry and puts the cordial glass on the side table, on the coaster of course.

"However, then you divorced Travis and drove him to drink. You became an alcoholic, too."

"How dare you –" Peggy says, but is again cut off.

"You never lived in the country Margaret. You lived in the city. Do you think the neighbors didn't hear all the drunken fights? Did you think that time you built a bonfire in the backyard and burned all your wedding photos that nobody knew about it? Good

325

heavens. You were the talk of the town there for several years. We all just felt sorry for you though so we kept quiet and hoped you would just get a divorce and quit the foolishness, for your children's sake if for no other reason."

Peggy opens her mouth to say something, but finds she cannot think what to say. Her mind is filled with shame, because Beatrice is right. She was on the verge of total alcoholism, just like her horrible mother. In the late 1960's a divorced woman was frowned upon in Augusta society, but it was better than being married to a negro man, she had decided. However, with her leadership of many social clubs in Augusta, Peggy felt like she had built her reputation back, and nothing would ever tarnish it again – until recently.

"Would you like some more sherry?" Peggy finally asks Beatrice, realizing the old lady is waiting for her to say something.

"No, one is my limit, in the afternoon. I have not finished what I wanted to say to you. Bain McDonald is not, in fact, my nephew, although that's what we tell people. He is my son."

Peggy just stares at Beatrice. "Your son?"

"Yes, my son. My husband William, you may recall, was a fine man, a good man from a nice family in Charleston. However, he was sterile. He had had mumps as a child. Ten years after we married, we went to a Greek island and vacationed. It was a fantastic trip. I became infatuated with our guide and translator, a man named George Mikonos. I became pregnant by George. A few months before Bain was born, I went to Jacksonville to stay with my sister, and ended up staying long enough to give birth. I stayed in seclusion for weeks, seemingly ill with mononucleosis. She told everyone she had adopted the child. We decided not to tell Bain until he was old enough to handle the information.

Bain had a fine upbringing and made me proud. When he was 15 he started asking questions. He noticed he didn't look like his brother. We decided he was old enough to know the truth. Everyone in our family is small, fine-boned and fair-haired. Bain looked like his father, of course. He has always been very dear to me, but when he came to Augusta to open the restaurant fifteen years ago, we decided to keep his origins secret and invented a fictional farming family. When I die, though, he inherits everything I have."

"Wow," is all Peggy can think to say.

"I know you set a great store by breeding, so I wanted you to understand about Bain. I also wanted you to know that the original gossip about you and Bain was not solely due to Edmund spreading it. Wylene Drummond is a friend of mine. We had ascertained, a while back, that Bain was infatuated with you from afar so she invented the story, hoping it might somehow help things along. I encouraged it. I also encouraged him to come over after the recent DAR meeting, so he could run into you accidentally on purpose."

"Oh my god," is all Peggy can think to say.

Beatrice looks very pleased with herself.

"Bain is wealthy now, and he will be much more wealthy soon, when his new antiques business takes off, which I'm sure it will. He has a degree in business from Wharton and a master's in business from Yale. He has a genius level IQ, and many friends. After I die, it will become known that he is my son. I suspect in the near future people will care far less about illegitimate family connections. Whether you realize it or not, he is a smart, good man, and he adores you, despite the age difference. You would be an idiot not to take him up on his offer to go with him to Atlanta."

"That's a lot to digest at one time."

Beatrice chuckles. "I thought that would be your reaction. Look, once you and Bain get married and the gossip dies down, you can come back to Augusta and see old friends, but for right now, I urge you to go to Atlanta and make a new life for yourself. Get out of this small town and live a little."

"Married?! We've only had six dates!"

Beatrice sits up straighter and fixes a stare that nails Peggy. "Bain told me it's tough to talk to you at times because you are so worried about what people think. You won't be seen with him in public."

Peggy winces and looks away. After a moment of thought, she says "But I don't know that I ever want to get married again. I've been married and divorced twice. That makes me gun shy."

"Look, I see you doing exactly what I did, for so many years. I played the game. I worried about what everyone thought of me. I went to the right church, wore the right clothes, associated with the right people. I gave up my rights to raise my own son, to watch him grow up every day because I was worried about people's opinion of me. Let me tell you how that plays out. You end up old and bitter and the young ones run the show. The old ladies don't run anything. We are shelved. The only thing I do now is DAR. I don't even fool with church any more. I like to watch that show on CBS on Sunday mornings while I have a bloody Mary so I don't go to church. I'm sure the Lord doesn't care. I don't worry about entertaining anyone.

I'm even thinking of just letting my hair go completely gray. Who cares?!"

Peggy stares at Beatrice, her head cocked, trying to digest this information. "You're still a force to be reckoned with, you know."

Beatrice smiles. "Not like I was. I'm not president of the Women's Club. I'm not in the Opera Guild. Who cares? I read trashy novels and eat what I want, and most importantly, I please myself. You need to learn to please yourself. Quit worrying about other people's opinions so much. Do what you want to do. Get out of this town, for a start."

Beatrice had gotten what Peggy would think of later as a "wild" look in her eye, as she spoke. She was clearly passionate about the subject of conformity. Peggy realizes suddenly that the more she thinks about Bain, the less she cares about Augusta society. She hasn't worn makeup in days. She ate an entire bag of popcorn for dinner the night before. She canceled her tennis lesson.

"Atlanta might be just the thing for me. I've been seriously thinking about it, to be honest with you. I think it's time for a change. There are lots of eligible men in Atlanta, too," Peggy replies with a smile, thinking *your son is not the only fish in the sea, lady!*

Beatrice stands up and stares down at Peggy, frowning. "Humph. Eligible men in your age bracket? I doubt it. Listen, Bain loves you, and the two of you would be a good match."

Peggy starts to argue but is cut off.

"Margaret, I love that boy dearly. I can tell you this for a fact: if you hurt him, if you break his heart by rejecting him, I will

329

tell everyone in Augusta that you write those gossipy Carriage House books. The rejection then will be absolute, and final. You will be lucky not to be tarred and feathered and ridden out of town on a rail. Literally. I will spearhead the effort myself. Do not mess with me, child, or I will be your worst nightmare."

Beatrice marches to the front door and lets herself out, while Peggy just sits there staring at the door.

That night, Bain comes over for dinner at Peggy's request.

In dressing for the evening, Peggy decides to be very casual. She wears khaki pants that are a bit loose, and a plain white tee shirt. Her only jewelry, small gold and pearl earrings.

Peggy decided the menu should be steaks, a big salad, and baked potatoes. An unimaginative cook, and long out of practice, she figures that's a meal even she can manage.

Bain rings the doorbell precisely at 6, and Peggy smiles as she welcomes him inside her home. He wears jeans and a dark green golf shirt with Augusta Country Club embroidered on the sleeve.

"Well hello there. Don't you look cool on this hot day," Peggy says with a smile. "Come on in."

"I wasn't sure of the menu so I brought a nice Australian Chardonnay which goes with everything, or so I'm told."

She chuckles. "I know very little about wine, but thank you. I've got steaks ready to go on the grill, the potatoes are nearly done, and the salad is ready, if you're hungry now."

"I can wait. I'm pretty good with a grill, if you want me to take over the steaks."

"Terrific. I like mine just pink in the middle," Peggy says, leading him back to the kitchen.

After dinner, they sit by the pool and talk. She tells him about his mother's visit.

He shakes his head. "Wow. She has never done anything like that before. She must approve of you. That's quite something."

Peggy chuckles. "I hope so."

"She loves me, but she feels bad about not acknowledging me. I told her not to worry about it," but she does still care what people think, despite what she told you."

Peggy nods, but says abruptly "Look, it's easy to say you're going to quit caring about your reputation but much harder to do. I should know."

They continue to talk.

At 10 p.m. he helps her clear the dishes. "I need to go by the restaurant and see how things are going. Thanks for dinner. I truly enjoyed it," he says.

"I'm glad you could come over, and we could really talk," Peggy says, truthfully.

He leans over and gives her a light kiss on the mouth.

"We still need to talk about Atlanta, you know."

331

"I am thinking you are right. I want to go and look at places, and see how I feel about living there. I've never really thought about it," Peggy admits.

"Good night. I will call you tomorrow," he says.

As Peggy watches him get into his BMW and back down her driveway she realizes that she feels a great lightness of heart she hasn't felt in a long time. *I don't really care what old Augusta thinks of me. I truly don't care.* She looks up at the starry night sky. "Screw you, Mother, you old witch. You don't control me anymore. That man makes me happy."

She chuckles as she turns and goes back inside her house.

CHAPTER 63 – THE BIG FIGHT

Jack awakens at 10:32 on that October Saturday morning, hearing a persistent knocking on the door of Leigh's apartment. Leigh sleeps heavily next to him, not hearing the knocking. Jack smiles at her, remembering their night together, and eases out of bed to put on his shorts and see who is at the door.

The knocking has increased and Jack is glad there is no doorbell to ring and wake up Leigh. He grabs his glasses and puts them on, then carefully shuts the bedroom door and pads over to open the apartment door, after first looking through the peephole.

"Yes?" Jack says, opening the door. *Who on earth is this woman? She looks like a Hollywood actress,* he thinks. *She looks familiar, and yet strange. Hmm..*

Peggy stands there wearing a yellow cotton dress that clings a bit to her small frame, and flats. Her makeup is impeccable, and her blonde hair hangs loose and frames her face in a long bob. She removes her sunglasses and looks carefully at the shirtless young man in front of her. He is small, but well-muscled and he has lovely eyes.

"I am here to see Leigh. I am her mother. And you are?" she says, with a small smile.

"Ah, yes, I see the resemblance now," Jack says with a smile, moving aside to let Peggy in the apartment. The remark is made out of politeness, as there is very little resemblance between Leigh and her mother, but they both have low melodious voices.

"I'm Jack Briggs, Leigh's boyfriend." It occurs to him that despite seeing many family photos from Leigh's family he has never seen but a few of Peggy, and there are none displayed in the apartment. Peggy looks a good ten years younger than her 53 years, except up close where the fine lines around her mouth and eyes are more obvious.

Well la de dah, my daughter got herself laid last night. Now I understand why she has been so uncommunicative lately, Peggy thinks. She knows she should be stern and disapproving but she isn't. She's glad Leigh has someone, and Jack Briggs looks like a good guy.

"Um, Leigh is asleep," Jack says.

Jack tries not to stare at Peggy. She is staring at the banker's boxes stacked inside the open dining room area of the neat little apartment when the bedroom door opens. Leigh comes out wearing her glasses. Her hair is a wild mess, and she is wearing only a long tee shirt and panties.

"What do you want Mother?" Leigh says coldly, making no move to approach Peggy.

Alarm bells go off in Jack's head. He thinks, d*anger, danger, female drama up ahead. Here we go.*

Peggy smiles and tries to keep her voice casual and neutral."Well, hello to you too. I wish you would return calls. I have been calling you for two days, but all I get is that machine," Peggy says evenly. "Big news. I want to find a house here in Atlanta, and I thought you could help me. Why don't you hop in the shower and get dressed, and we can all go out to breakfast, my treat?"

Leigh stares at her mother with the accumulated fury and frustration of more than thirty years of resentment.

"Get out. Get out and don't ever come near me again. I want nothing to do with you," Leigh says, in a very low voice, trying not to lose her temper in front of Jack.

Jack is putting on his shirt, thinking *Shit I was right, so right, I do not want to be here. Shit.*

Peggy stares for a moment at her daughter, then takes a deep breath. "So this is how you repay my kindness?"

"Kindness?! What kindness?! Are you insane? You have always been a BITCH to me, Mother. Get OUT."

Peggy stares at her daughter. "I have always done everything possible to help you reach your full potential, to have a good life."

"Really? Trying to force me into being some stupid phony size 2 debutante MORON? Trying to make me an Olympic swimmer? Trying to force me to straighten my hair and stay out of the sun so I wouldn't look so different from lily-white YOU?!"

"Don't be ridiculous. You need to drink some tea and calm down."

"Worse than that, though, now I know that you tried to kill my aunt. I went to see her a couple of weeks ago. I know the family paid her to stay silent for almost thirty years. I KNOW EVERYTHING NOW. So of COURSE I want nothing to do with you."

Peggy's eyes narrow. She can feel her mother Matilda inside her, fighting to get out and spew venom.

335

"I must correct you. I recall that day very well. I found an intruder in my home and my child hurt. I lost my temper, yes. But to my credit, I should have had that girl arrested. I didn't. She has benefitted financially from that little encounter for years. I thought paying her was ridiculous, but your father and Harry insisted. The one thing I did not want was for you to remember and go seeking her out."

"Why not? Because you didn't want me to know I am black?!" Leigh spits out the words, glaring at her mother.

Peggy recoils, visibly. "You are not black! Don't be ridiculous. I just didn't see how it would be beneficial to you to know your grandmother had committed adultery and had an illegitimate child."

"Bullshit."

"Nice way to talk to your mother."

Leigh thinks, *You aren't going to play innocent with me, you witch.* "You've tried to run my life as long as I can remember, but I don't need you anymore."

"I don't care for your tone, and I don't deserve this attack," Peggy said quietly. "How dare you question anything I did when you were growing up?! I always did what I thought best for you. You were an incredibly difficult child to raise."

Peggy moves to go out the door but Leigh moves swiftly around her, and with her back to the door, leaning in, she hurls her words at Peggy.

"Oh no, you need to hear this, now, because I don't ever plan to see you again, Peggy. You let me SUFFER from repressed memories and nightmares, for nearly thirty YEARS! You treated Daddy like dirt after that incident, just because you found out you had married someone not purely white! You actually LOVED someone NOT WHITE! How does that feel, huh? You have children who are NOT WHITE! I don't care how blonde Bubba's girls are, their great-grandmother was born a negro and they are mixed race too!"

Peggy pulls back, breathing hard, still trying not to yell.

"It's entirely unfair of you to paint me as a racist. My issues with your father had nothing to do with that."

Leigh points to the banker's boxes. "Oh no you don't. I have seen all the papers about the divorce, Mother. You used the word miscegenation. You were HORRIFIED that Rose had been raised in a black orphanage, that she had concealed her race from Grandpa, that she had never told her sons her secret. You used that against Daddy. Your rejection of him is WHY he became an alcoholic. He wasn't one before all that nastiness came out of you."

Leigh glares daggers at her mother, shaking from emotion.

Peggy's head held high, her back straight, she says quietly, "I don't have to stand here and listen to this. Everything I've ever done was to protect you from the shame –"

Leigh won't listen. She moves away from the door and gets close to her mother now, hissing and spitting out her words. "THAT is what you will NEVER UNDERSTAND! I am NOT ashamed of being part black! I'm not ashamed of being Rose's granddaughter! I embrace it! The only thing I am ashamed of is being YOUR DAUGHTER!"

Jack has been watching this verbal sparring match with shock. "Leigh, I think you need to calm down –" he starts. Leigh cuts him off.

"No, Jack, I've held all this inside for too long. It's not bad enough she is a racist, now I hear she has been having sex in public with a man in Augusta! Screwing him on top of a CAR?!"

Peggy gasps, now truly horrified to know Leigh knows that information. "Wait a minute, you don't know the real story –"

"I have no interest in your side of it. Before you leave, I want you to know this, Mother. You are a WHORE and an EVIL MURDERING BITCH and I want NOTHING to do with you EVER AGAIN! FUCK OFF!"

The last two words are delivered in a scream, as Leigh throws open the apartment door and points outside.

Shocked, Peggy walks rapidly out the door.

She walks stiffly down the four steps to the parking lot, gets into her Lexus, shaking, and can barely get the key in the ignition. As she backs out, she narrowly misses hitting another car.

Blinded by tears, Peggy doesn't see the chubby little red-haired figure of Jessica fly down the stairs to Leigh's door.

Jessica doesn't even knock on the door, but seeing it still open, she steps inside.

"JESUS Leigh, why are you down here screaming? You want to get the cops called? What on earth?!" Jessica bellows, then stops when she sees Jack, who is rapidly putting on his shoes. "Oh, I'm so sorry –"

"Don't be." Jack snaps as he brushes past Jessica, shirt and keys in hand. "I'm out of here." He brushes past her and heads out the door, quickly gets into his truck and drives off.

Jessica, who has watched Jack, turns back, astonished to see Leigh on the sofa, curled into a ball, shaking and crying.

Peggy's car phone rings but she doesn't answer it.

She drives to the diner off North Druid Hills Road and walks in, seeing Bain sitting in a booth, as they had arranged earlier. He stands up as she walks over.

"Hey, tried to call you but you didn't pick up. Good morning, Sweetheart –" Bain begins, then stops when he sees her tear-streaked face.

"I need to fix my face. Order me a cup of coffee," Peggy mumbles, turning to head towards the ladies' room.

Bain sits back down and motions to the waitress. "A cup of coffee and another menu, please."

He assumes that Leigh heard about the rumors flying around Augusta. He now regrets his style of wooing Peggy, realizing that collateral damage has been done. He will have to work hard to win the trust and respect of the children, considering what they have heard.

He reads the Atlanta Constitution for a few minutes, and then Peggy reappears. Her eye makeup is gone, and her lipstick, and she looks haggard, defeated.

"What happened at Leigh's place?" Bain asks softly, as Peggy picks up her coffee mug with both hands and sips.

"We have always had a difficult relationship, but now she outright hates me. She actually screamed at me to Fuck off."

"What?! Why?" Bain asks. "She heard the rumors about us?!"

"Yes, but it's much more than that," Peggy says wearily. "I have a lot to tell you about the family. I was thinking this morning how much fun it would be to move here, to start over, to be your girlfriend because I really do like you. But now I realize I have a lot to atone for with my daughter. I want to have a good relationship with her, but I keep messing it up. I've done a lot of stupid things in my life."

The waitress appears and takes their food orders.

For the next hour and a half, Peggy tells Bain the story of her life, the real story, not omitting any of the ugliness.

Jessica goes over to the sofa and sits down and starts rubbing Leigh's back.

"Honey what on earth is going on? Talk to me?"

"Oh my God! I am SO STUPID! I just unloaded on my mother and told her off, and in the process I drove Jack away! Aaaargh! I realized when I finished my rant and saw his face that he had never seen me really lose it. I actually told my mother to fuck off."

"Great godalmighty!"

"It was horrible. I have never been that angry. Things with Jack were going so well. I had a fantastic, romantic night with Jack – our first time making love – and then Mother shows up, telling me she is moving here to Atlanta!"

Jessica rolls her eyes and shakes her head.

"After the way you've described your mother, I can see how that would be upsetting, but Leigh you were screaming like a madwoman," Jessica says, kindly. "You scared me, and I'm not easily scared. I totally understand family drama."

Leigh sits up and blows her nose. "Where have you been lately? I haven't seen you."

"I started a new job! The hours have been crazy but tell me what's been going on with you."

Leigh tells her friend about meeting Liz and regaining the painful childhood memories from long ago, and about the gossip she heard about her mother and Bain McDonald.

"Wow. Just WOW. That's some drama. Wow."

"And now Jack has seen me act like a teetotal bitch from hell, and he thinks I'm awful. Mother is petite and blonde and beautiful, and men always take her side."

"Oh, now you sound just paranoid," Jessica says, hoping it doesn't sound lame.

"No. You don't understand. She can flirt with and charm just about any man she wants."

"Really? At her age?" Jessica says, puzzled.

In response, Lee gets off the sofa and goes to the bookcase where she grabs a photo album. She flips to the back and pulls out a professional studio photo Peggy sent to her a couple of years before. Jessica's eyes widen when she sees it.

"Wow. Okay, I totally understand your inferiority complex now. What a nightmare. What is she, a size 4?!"

"Smaller. It's horrifying. There's never any food in her house. Her idea of pigging out is eating one roll at a nice restaurant. I'm a size 8 and I feel like an elephant near her. "

"Listen, you haven't eaten and I need food too so let's go get brunch at our favorite place, and figure out a strategy to get Jack back."

"I don't know," Leigh mumbles, miserable.

"Can you smell the waffles?" Jessica says with a smile.

"Let me see if I have some cash," Leigh says, finally brightening a bit.

Twenty minutes later the two friends are sitting at Waffle House. They eat waffles with syrup and drink Lipton tea and chat about the scene with Peggy, because Leigh cannot bear to discuss Jack. Finally, she pushes her plate away.

"I have to face it. He saw me at my worst. He saw me just melt down."

"Considering what your mother did, I don't blame you," Jessica says sympathetically.

"Yeah, but Jack is buttoned down. Ex-military. My brother was in the military. I know the type. They hate drama. Jack really

342

hates it. And that's good, because he's the opposite of me. I tend to get way too worked up and overly emotional about things. He's calm and cool."

Jessica regards her friend with concern. "What does Liz say about all this? Have you talked to her? She sounds like a really smart lady."

"Waitress? Can we get our check, please?" Leigh digs around in her purse looking for tip money.

Jessica pulls some money out of her wallet and puts it on the table. "There's my share. You didn't answer my question."

The waitress appears and takes the money. "Keep it," Leigh said, sliding out of the booth. "Let's waddle on back."

In Leigh's car, she finally sighs heavily and looks at Jessica. "Liz says I should forgive Mother. She said it's the only way I will ever find peace."

"Wow. That's not what I would want to do, but I see her point. Holding grudges doesn't hurt her, really, but it hurts you, right? What does it accomplish?"

"So you agree? Forgive the woman who ruined my life?!"

Leigh angrily starts the car and pulls out of the space.

Jessica looks in the side mirror with some alarm. "Calm down, Leigh. I don't want to die in a car accident before I can even find a husband. My family would be so upset."

"That you were dead or that you hadn't yet found a husband?!" Leigh asks, eyes twinkling.

"It would be a tossup, I'm telling you."

"Okay, but you have no idea."

"No but really, Leigh, think about this. You're only what, 32 years old? Your life isn't over. It isn't ruined unless you let it be ruined. In fact, I'd say here recently you've made a lot of progress at getting rid of your old demons. Your dad is at peace. Your repressed memories are gone. You are a great real estate saleswoman. Maybe if your mother moves here, she will relax and not be so critical of you."

Leigh is silent, mulling over her friend's words.

"I find it hard to believe she would leave Augusta. She's lived there her whole life, except for two years of college. If people are really shunning her, though, I can see why she might leave.."

"Well why would she stay where she had no social life, right?"

As Leigh pulls into the apartment complex, she looks at Jessica. "Thank you for helping me calm down. I really owe you. You're a good friend, and I really appreciate it."

Leigh parks the car and the two friends get out. Jessica hugs Leigh.

"I'm always here if you need me, kiddo," Jessica says.

"Next time, I want to hear all about your new job," Leigh says, smiling.

"You got it!" Jessica calls as she heads up the stairs.

When Leigh gets back inside her apartment the light on her answering machine is blinking and there's a message on the phone from Edmund. She presses Play Messages and Edmund's voice trills. "Call me pronto, Leigh-baby!"

Leigh sits on the sofa and unbuttons the top button of her jeans before she dials the phone, eager to pour out her tale of woe to her uncle.

Edmund picks up the phone on the first ring. "I knew it was you Babygirl! I've been sooooo busy for the past week I didn't answer the phone or do anything except shoot supermodels, and what a tiresome job that was. So I get home and check my messages and wow. You will not believe what gossip I have heard from Golftown!"

"Mother is having a torrid affair, and, in fact, was seen having sex with some guy named McDonald outside a DAR meeting," Leigh says drily.

Edmund inhales his cigarette deeply and sighs. "Well, hell. You just took away my fun," he says throwing himself on his couch and arranging his cat in his lap. "Ow, Banana Mae watch those claws, dear. So how did you find out?"

"My friend Carol called me the other day. I have news for you, though. I've screwed up my entire life. Mother came to see me this morning and I told her off. Really let her have it. Told her actually to fuck off."

Edmund chuckles. "Well good for you. How do you feel? Triumphant?"

"Noooo! You don't understand. Jack came in from his trip last night and took me out to dinner and we had a wonderful evening, and then, he –um – well, he spent the night. I went to sleep dreaming of what kind of wedding we will have. First thing this morning, about 10:30, Mother comes to the door and Jack answers it –"

"Was he naked?!" Edmund asks, laughing. "I bet she would have enjoyed that."

"No! He had on shorts, but you know how grumpy I am when I first wake up. I just lost it, Uncle Ed. I just had this flashback to Mother trying to choke Liz to death, and then all the hell she put me through all my life, and I just verbally ripped her a new one. Problem is, Jack is so quiet and polite and laid back, he now thinks I'm horrible. He couldn't get out of here fast enough."

Edmund shakes his head, and says softly "Oh dear oh dear. He hates drama. I get it. I surely do. You know, I am not really good at advising anyone in this type of situation but you know who is? Greg. He should be home any minute. He's out buying groceries. Let me talk to him and see what thoughts he has, and I'll call you back, okay?"

"That would be nice. Oh, and I almost forgot to mention something. Mother said something about moving here, to Atlanta. Everyone in Augusta must be giving her the cold shoulder, I guess. I would almost feel sorry for her, except she puts entirely too much stock in what people think."

"Oh my stars. Now that is news. Let me call you back in a little bit, Sweetheart."

"Okay, thanks Uncle Ed."

346

Peggy finishes her tale, and finally looks at Bain. Breakfast is long over and they are lingering over coffee.

"So you see, I am not a very nice person, and now both my children despise me."

Bain shrugs. "You are like a lot of women I know. You run in certain circles. You see life in a very specific way. You were raised with a lot of ideas about society and wealth and the importance of bloodlines and ancestors, and all those ideas have always informed your life and your decisions. Everyone is a product of their environment, Margaret."

His words surprise her. He is being gentlemanly and kind. She looks at the huge man, with his designer clothes and expensive haircut and manicure, yet rather homely face, and comes to a startling realization. She doesn't care if he is illegitimate. She doesn't care if old Augustans sneer at him behind his back. She doesn't care that he's considered very promiscuous and bad – those rumors mean nothing. He's fun to be around, she likes talking to him, and now he's proving to be kind and thoughtful as well.

She looks into his brown eyes and realizes that he seems to actually adore her, just the way she is – warts and all. It's startling. She has cried off all her makeup and looks far from lovely. She takes a sip of her water.

"Did Beatrice tell you she came to see me the other day?" Peggy asks Bain, hoping to change the subject from herself.

He smiles. "She did indeed. I didn't know about it until afterwards, though. So now you know my secrets and I know yours.

I think that's the perfect way to start a relationship. Everything is on the table."

"After what I told you, you really still want to be with me?!" Peggy says, sounding tentative.

"The way I see it is this: you're not the Augusta matron any more. You're leaving that town behind. You're starting over here in Atlanta, right?"

"Well, I hope so? You still want me to learn the antiques business?"

"Sure. You should, just part-time, when you're not writing. Just let me help you re-make yourself. The person you were before will then be no more, Margaret," Bain says with a smile.

"Why do you insist on using that name? Everyone calls me Peggy."

"I think Margaret is more appropriate for this chapter of your life. Leave Peggy Harrington back there in Augusta."

"Hmm.. that's a little controlling but I'll give it some thought."

"I have something to ask you, and I want you to consider it carefully before answering," Bain says evenly.

Peggy sighs. "Okay."

"Leigh is your only daughter. Do you want to have a good relationship with her, or do you want to let her go?"

Peggy inhales sharply. The thought of letting Leigh go is a new and startling one. She has always sought to make Leigh into the perfect twentieth century southern belle, and Leigh has always resisted. However, Peggy has always loved her child.

"She's my daughter and I love her."

"Good. Then my suggestion is a simple one. Ask Leigh to go with you to counseling. Rebuild your relationship, but with a trained professional overseeing the process."

Peggy scowls. "I don't know…" Seeing a shrink is not part of her way of thinking. Her mother Matilda always sneered when talking about psychiatrists or psychologists, dismissing them as "crackpot head shrinkers with no balls."

Bain scrutinizes Peggy's uncertainty and knows instinctively she is resistant to seeing a psychologist because it's not something people talk about.

"I note that you're scowling. You need to let go of the old Augusta society ways of thinking and doing, if you want a good relationship with your daughter. . I know a terrific lady here in Atlanta, but who is from Augusta."

"Who?"

"You don't know her. Let's go back to my place and give her a call. I have her card there somewhere."

Peggy sits and thinks for a moment, staring down at a napkin and shredding it, then finally speaks.

"Well, I would probably be willing to try but I don't know about Leigh. She's awfully headstrong," Peggy remarks as they stand up and stretch.

"So are you, my dear. People can change," Bain says with a smile, leaning down to kiss her lightly on the lips.

CHAPTER 64 – THE NEW SOUTH

Two weeks later, Peggy is back in Augusta. She walks around the Fresh Market picking up salad makings, a good bottle of wine, and some fresh strawberries. She peruses the glass case filled with pre-made foods and selects some roasted turkey and a fruit salad.

She sees two women she knows, but they quickly avert their eyes from Peggy when she tries to make eye contact, and she knows they don't want to be seen talking to her.

Peggy smiles to herself and thinks, *Who gives a flying fuck?!*

What had once seemed unbearable now seems laughable. How had such a dramatic change occurred?

As she drives home, she thinks about her recent life and the changes. The recent two weeks spent with Bain in Atlanta have been the most significant weeks of Peggy's life.

They talked about antiques, and she agreed that she was fascinated, but she declined his offer of going into business with him. She pointed out, rightly, that she wasn't an expert, and she wasn't a saleswoman, and she didn't want to take the time to get up to speed in a new career. Her writing career was flourishing, and now that she wasn't running around crazily to all the clubs and organizations in Augusta, she was going to have a lot more time to write, and she loves writing. What had once been merely a way to make money had now become more therapeutic.

Before heading to Atlanta, Peggy had sent the first three chapters of her new book to her agent, who loved it, and pointed out that erotic thriller/mysteries would have more potential sales than short little "cozy" mysteries.

In Atlanta, Bain and Peggy went out to dinner at elegant restaurants. They strolled around the museums and antique stores. They played chess and watched movies on the VCR. Peggy met several people who were Bain's old friends and who accepted her easily. They didn't ask her for her mother's maiden name, or where her people were from. Peggy liked them, even though she knew nothing about their families.

This was the New South, not the Old South, and Peggy was fascinated to realize it was freeing to leave the Old South behind, with its hidebound customs and rituals.

Peggy and Bain also deepened their romantic relationship. Every night they made love, sometimes slowly and languorously, relishing each other's bodies, other times urgently, on the kitchen island or the stairs. Peggy knew there wouldn't be prying neighbors running by unexpectedly.

On the last night of Peggy's sojourn in Atlanta, Peggy confessed to Bain that she was falling in love with him.

"I cannot believe it, but I have to admit, I am falling in love with you," she said, snuggling into his arms. She had never previously been the first one to say that to any man because it felt like relinquishing power, but with Bain she didn't fear that. She knew he loved her from his tender looks to his consideration of her feelings, to his ability to make her laugh. Plus, he knew about her entire, messy life, and it had not driven him away. The wonder of that renewed her faith in a higher power, because she had always felt inadequate. However, he made her feel whole and perfect, not broken and battered by all she'd been through.

Bain pulled away from her in bed and looked at her face, free of makeup, showing the lines around her eyes but nonetheless beautiful.

"Well thanks for letting me know. I feel the same about you. I love you like a house afire, as my granny used to say. Now, you know that we can have a fine life here in Atlanta, right? I won you over? I just have to find a good manager for the River Tavern, and wind up a few business things in Augusta, and then we can move over here."

"I need a little time to wind up some things too," Peggy said.

"Take all the time you need. However, when you are ready, I want us to get married. That will stop the gossips in their tracks," Bain said casually.

Peggy pulled back and looked at him. "I've been married twice and both were disasters. You sure you want to marry me?"

Bain chuckles. "The Peggy who made those foolish marriages is not the woman I see before me. We all do stupid stuff when we're young. God knows I did some stupid stuff. Now we are older, and we see the world with different eyes."

Peggy snuggles back into his chest, her thoughts whirling for a few minutes, then says quietly, "Okay, but I don't care what anyone in Augusta thinks of my relationship with you. I don't give a damn any more."

"Good! That's the great thing about middle age isn't it? You realize all the stuff you thought was so important is really irrelevant. You can be happy regardless of anyone's opinion of you," Bain says, kissing her shoulder.

"True, but there are two people whose opinions I still value, very much. I want my children there at the wedding, and so I need to fix things with both of them."

"Agreed."

"I hope you like the idea of being an instant stepfather, even a step grandfather?"

"No worries. I won't try to bribe them with ice cream or ponies," Bain chuckles.

Back in Augusta, Peggy had quietly spoken to a real estate agent about listing her house. She didn't list it yet, however.

Peggy still nurses a tiny hope that the people in her circle of friends and acquaintances who know her well will rally to her side, despite the scandalous talk about her.

They don't.

After she returns from Atlanta, Peggy's phone doesn't ring. She goes to a meeting of the Flower Guild at St. Paul's and people politely say hello but don't include her in any conversations. She wears the flawless 3 carat emerald cut diamond engagement ring Bain bought her, but nobody even glances at it.

Her sociable neighbors fail to call her when they are in the back yards having drinks.

Even Susan, her tennis partner, calls to say she is going to try another sport; her tennis lesson days are over. She then says, "I have to go fix dinner. Take care," and hangs up. *Borderline rude*, thinks Peggy.

Even though she has lost 98% of the ability to care about old Augustans' opinions of her, the snubbing still is disconcerting. One night after four glasses of wine, Peggy decides that she wants to control things. The next morning, she takes three aspirins and drinks an iced tea glass full of filtered water and sits down with her address book and laptop and composes the following note, to every one of the organizations she belongs to:

Dear _____,

With regret, I must resign my membership of _____. I have so enjoyed the fellowship and fun of being a member, but now it's time to move on. I will soon be putting my house up for sale in preparation for moving to Atlanta. I am also preparing for my wedding to Bain McDonald.

She carefully tailors each letter to each organization, prints them out on beautiful monogrammed stationary, addresses the envelopes, stamps them, and drives over to the post office to personally mail them.

Peggy and Bain have dinner that night at Café Du Teau, and Peggy laughs and feels relaxed with Bain's friends, none of whom are "old Augusta."

Peggy heads over to Harry's house the next night, since Bain is out of town. Martha had decided to go out with a girlfriend, so it's just Peggy and Harry, eating steaks and salads.

"How are you doing?" Harry says as he greets her at the door, with a hug.

"I need a glass of wine, and then, I will tell you," Peggy replies with a smile.

They sit on the back patio with their drinks, and Harry scrutinizes Peggy. No makeup, old denim shorts and a tee shirt, flip flops, hair in a messy topknot. Peggy looks like what she is, a woman who has stopped caring what people think about her.

"You know, the past week has been a little sad since people are still shunning me, but I find I really don't care that much. I resigned from every organization I'm a member of, and I see Bain every day. I like that his friends are not old Augusta people, and they are nice to me. I can be myself around them. Atlanta is the same way. I don't feel perpetually judged. I can say SHIT or even the F word, and nobody cares."

Harry laughs. "I am glad to hear that. You have always been the most uptight person I've ever known, but now you're not. You've softened. You have obviously turned a corner, and I think that's great. How is Leigh?"

Peggy's smile fades, and she takes a long sip of her wine. "We had a big fight a few weeks ago. She hates me. She has met her aunt, and she told me she hates me for what I did. It was terrible. I cried for hours afterwards."

Harry sighs, and takes a sip of his Scotch. "Does Bain know about that?"

"Oh yes, we talk about everything. I told him my life story that very day and didn't leave out the ugly parts. He still loves me. It's a miracle, but he does."

Harry wrinkles his brow in puzzlement. The Bain he had heard about didn't seem like that type of enlightened man, but Peggy was clearly a woman happy and in love.

"You know Bain has skeletons in his closet, right?" Harry says casually.

Peggy regards Harry, puzzled. "What are you talking about?"

"Well, when I first heard the rumors about you two -- when that's all they were, rumors – I did some checking into his background. He was kicked out of McCallie for screwing a teacher's underage daughter. Good thing the guy didn't press charges. They say the money to open the River Tavern came from the mob. He screws around, a LOT. One rumor was that he had herpes from screwing so many women. He brought in a whole group of folks from Spain a few years ago and charged them outrageous prices for master's badges. Then there's Beatrice Arbuthnot; the rumor there is she isn't his aunt, but he is having some sick, weird affair with the old lady."

Peggy chuckles. "I will ask him about the rumors but I can tell you two things for sure: he doesn't have herpes and he's not having an affair with Beatrice. The rest of it I don't care about. I doubt it's true. Rumors are often not true, you know."

Harry nods. "I'm going to take up the steaks. Let's eat inside in the air conditioning."

"Good idea, and Harry?" Peggy says, getting up.

"Thanks for telling me the scuttlebutt on Bain. Thanks for checking up on him. You're a good brother."

Harry gives her a light hug. "Hey, if the guy isn't doing anything illegal, and he makes you happy, good for you both."

CHAPTER 65 – LIFE WITHOUT JACK

Leigh plods about her daily life with her head down after her emotional meltdown, literally and figuratively. For the rest of October and into early November she aggressively goes out and previews homes and takes all the clients she can get, showing houses and condos all over Atlanta for hours every day.

She sells four houses in as many weeks and for once has no concerns about money. There is even a healthy deposit into her savings account.

The day after her fight with Peggy, she leaves a phone message for Jack asking him to call her, but he doesn't.

Two weeks after the fight with Peggy, Leigh reluctantly accepts that Jack is most likely out of her life, thinking h*e should have at least called me. He is really being weird about it. Families fight. Good grief.*

She gives in to Jessica's entreaty to "go out drinkin" and gets wasted on 2 for 1 Margaritas at a local bar. After drinking and gossiping for two hours, they have to take a taxi home. The next day, horribly hungover and feeling like she has been run over and left for dead, Leigh vows to never ever drink anything alcoholic again. Ever.

The day after that, Leigh rearranges her dresser drawers and her closet and organizes everything by season and color. She also takes a load of old clothes to Goodwill.

Leigh starts swimming in the heated apartment pool most days, lap after lap of freestyle and breast stroke, alternating laps where she just jogs through the water. Her hair lightens in the sun, and she cuts out Diet Cokes and switches to all water, seeing good results with her clearer skin and lack of indigestion.

During the same time period, Leigh ignores a handwritten note from her mother and 11 phone messages asking her to get in touch.

She leaves three messages for Jack, but he doesn't return the calls. She thinks about just going to his house but decides it's too far to drive for no reason, especially since he is often gone for hours or out of town for work.

Instead, one night after crying for an hour and eating an entire pint of ice cream, Leigh sits and makes a list.

Why Jack Isn't Right for Me:

Obsessively neat, like Felix Unger neat. Ugh.

Mentioned once he didn't want a dog because they got hair all over the place and were too much trouble, but I love dogs!

Obsession with hamburgers is silly.

Too tight with a dollar – this is based on our discussion one night about buying a blender and his obsession with spending hours researching blenders.

She stares at the list for a while, wishing it were longer.

That night, much to her dismay, she has another anxiety dream.

She is back on a college campus that seems familiar and yet not familiar, at the same time. Walking and walking, she knows she needs to get to class because she has a test, but she can't find the building or the room. She wanders around campus looking into building after building, but nothing seems familiar.

Finally, she stops to rest, and up ahead she sees Jack wearing his black leather bomber jacket – but he is walking away from her. She starts running towards him, yelling his name, but the harder she runs, the further away he gets.

Then she hears someone calling her name, and she looks around. Her mother starts running towards her, yelling "Leigh I'm sorry – I'm sorry! Leigh!" – over and over. Leigh wants to get away from Peggy and find Jack, but she can't.

Finally, she wakes up, and her sheets and comforter are tangled in a big wad. Leigh rubs her eyes and feels as though she has run a long way.

She picks up her diary and sniffles as she writes.

I am finally rid of my mother, so why do I feel so miserable? Jack wasn't right for me. I have lost weight. I should be happy, but I am not.

CHAPTER 66 – THERAPY

Edmund and Greg get back to their apartment in New York after spending two weeks in Cancun. After putting the suitcases in the bedroom, Edmund sees there is a message on the answering machine from Peggy. He plays it.

"I know you don't think much of me, Edmund, but I need your help. This has to do with Leigh. Please call me."

Edmund looks at Greg, who shrugs. "So call her. Maybe Leigh is in trouble or ill or something. We need to know."

Edmund lights a Marlboro and sits on the sofa to dial Peggy. "Bring me a drink, please?"

"Yes, your highness…," Greg mutters, but he is smiling.

Peggy picks up on the first ring. "Well hello, Pegleg, how are you, honey? More importantly, what's up with Leigh?" Edmund drawls.

Peggy sighs and closes her laptop. "Thanks for returning my call, finally."

"I have been out of town. What's up?"

"Have you talked to Leigh lately? She and I had a big confrontation a few weeks ago."

"I have not spoken to her, actually. I was swamped with work before we left town, and we literally just got back an hour ago."

"I went to her apartment one morning a few weeks ago, got up early and drove over there, and her boyfriend answered the door. She said she had met her aunt and she hated me and threw me out of her apartment."

"Boyfriend named Jack Briggs? Kind of a short guy with thinning hair?"

"Yes. Seemed like a really sweet guy, but he wasn't happy about witnessing the fight. I have a feeling they aren't together any more which is such a shame. I want her to get married and have a family and she's running out of time, biologically."

Greg comes in the room and hands Edmund a short glass of Scotch.

"Well, Pegboard, you have to admit, you have been very demanding all of Leigh's life, and finding out you assaulted her aunt just nailed the lid on the coffin. You can't be surprised that she would resent you."

Edmund lights a Marlboro, ignoring Greg's frowning face. *He cannot seriously expect me to quit smoking in the middle of all this family drama?!* he thinks.

Peggy takes a deep breath and tries to stay calm. "I have regretted my actions for thirty years, Edmund. I had a terrible temper. I thought it was a blessing that Leigh didn't remember that day. I know you think I'm a racist and a snob and a bitch but I'm not! And listen, I love my daughter. I want only happiness for her, truly. It's killing me that she won't take my calls, wants to cut off all communication. I know I screwed up. I get it. But I still want a relationship. That's why I called you."

Edmund sips his drink and reluctantly stubs out his cigarette. "I'm listening."

"So, a little background. Bain and I are really dating, and we're serious. We are getting married, probably soon. He's a wonderful man. I love being with him. I know his reputation isn't great, but now mine isn't either and you know what? I don't give a damn. For the first time in my life, I could not care less what snobby elite Augustans think of me. I resigned from the DAR and all the stupid clubs and organizations. I am busy writing a new book, getting my house ready to sell, and spending time with Bain. I am going to move to Atlanta, and start a new life."

Edmunds eyebrows shoot to the top of his hairline, and he covers the phone and mouths to Greg "She's marrying Bain and moving to Atlanta!"

"Wow. Just wow. I'm truly glad to hear your life is changing and you are de-snobbing and re-inventing yourself. Truly. But what do you need from me?"

Peggy takes a sip of her wine and closes her eyes. "I am putting my house up for sale next week. Most of my furniture and things will be put in storage for when Leigh and Bubba are ready to inherit them. Movers are coming Wednesday. On Thursday, I am taking just my personal things and moving into Bain's townhouse in Atlanta."

"OK, that's great, but I fit in how?"

"Just give me a minute. When I move next week I will start seeing a psychologist in Atlanta, Dr. Amelia Lindsey. She is from Augusta, and Bain knows her. I met her recently and she seems like someone I can trust. I want Leigh to see her, too. After some time, I am hoping we can let Dr. Lindsey help us out, do therapy sessions with us both, so we can repair our relationship."

Peggy pauses, hoping her words are met with kindness. She listens to Edmund take a long draw off his cigarette.

Wow, she really is making radical changes. She sounds like an utterly different person, thinks Edmund..

"Peggy, I think that's a wonderful idea. I really do. So you want me to suggest that Leigh see this therapist? I have to tell you, she has been seeing therapists for a while now. She never sticks with them."

"What? Why?" Peggy blurts out, startled.

"I don't know. You'd have to ask her. I do know she's open to the idea of therapy, though. Perhaps if I offer to pay for her sessions and encourage her, she will go. I'll give it my best shot."

"If you can get her to go, that's all I ask. Thank you, Edmund." Peggy takes a deep breath. "I know I've been awful to you in the past. I'm sorry. I truly am. I've been doing a lot of thinking lately. I'm – well, I'm truly very glad you are in Leigh's life. I know she loves you a great deal."

Edmund feels tears well up in his eyes. "We are still family, Peggy, connected by your beautiful daughter. I accept your apology but it's not necessary. I've said and done a lot of things I regret, too. That's life. I want Leigh to have a good relationship with you, and to stay connected to you and Bubba. She needs all of her family around her. I will call you back and let you know what she says about a new therapist."

He writes down the phone number of the therapist, and they hang up.

Greg hands Edmund a Kleenex. "Well, damn. I need to know everything. You aren't a cryer. Spill it, honey."

Edmund tells him the conversation. As usual, Greg hones in on what he considers the most interesting detail.

"You need to call Leigh and find out what happened with Jack. He was a keeper. Maybe if you tell her a therapist will help her repair that relationship it will make her want to go."

"That's a great idea. I'm also going to call Jack and pretend I don't know about the breakup, see what I can find out."

CHAPTER 67 – A Death

Liz, wearing her bathrobe and slippers, has a bad feeling. She goes into her mother's room to check on Millie, who had gone to bed early saying she didn't feel well.

The moment Liz opens the door and looks at the bed, she knows Millie is gone. The older lady lies atop the bedspread wearing her best black church dress and holds her bible in her hands.

Liz stifles a sob, then walks over to the bed. Millie's face is calm and serene. Her eyes are closed. Liz puts her hand on her mother's cheek and closes her eyes to pray.

When she opens her eyes and looks up, Liz's eyes are drawn to two shimmering forms in the corner, a very young Millie, and Rose, smiling and holding hands.

Liz gasps. She can almost hear them. In her head she hears their voices as clearly as if they are speaking to her as living beings.

"Our sweet daughter! We love you so much."

The smiling faces fade from view.

Liz wipes the tears from her face with the back of her hand and walks back to the main room to call the funeral home and then her son.

CHAPTER 68 – NEGOTIATIONS

Edmund calls Leigh on Monday morning. He's freshly shaved, wearing his favorite cologne, his favorite purple Polo shirt and Ralph Lauren jeans. He has a large Dunkin Donuts coffee in front of him. He lights a Marlboro and inhales deeply.

Leigh picks up on the first ring. She has been eating cereal and watching *The Today Show*.

"Leigh baby! How are you Sweetheart?"

"Hi Uncle. I am okay, I guess."

"You don't sound okay. Tell me what's going on." He stares at the cigarettes in the pack, hoping not to have to buy more in the next hour.

"I had a big fight with Peggy a few weeks ago. Jack was here and saw the whole thing, and ran out of here. Haven't heard from him since."

"So Jack never actually said he was breaking up with you, he just stopped taking your calls?"

"Yep. I don't know what to do." Leigh holds the phone with one hand and rearranges the magazines on her coffee table with her other hand.

"Well, I have a suggestion. I want you to see a psychologist, both to talk about Jack and about your mother."

"I'm done with psychologists. They are useless," Leigh says, frowning as she takes a sip of her tea.

Well that was stupid. Should have chatted more before I blurted that out. Way to go, you old fool, thinks Edmund.

"Now hear me out, Leigh baby. This is a lady, Dr. Amelia Lindsey. She grew up in Augusta and she understands all about how Golftown operates."

Leigh considers this. Augusta is a unique little town, and if this lady understands it, maybe she will be helpful. Maybe.

"I don't know, uncle." She twists a bit of her shirt tail around in her fist.

"Look, kiddo, you're dealing with a lot of heavy emotional stuff. Give it a shot. She's not far from you. I already talked to her and she can see you Wednesday at 9 a.m. She is going to send me the bills for your treatment. I will pay for everything. Does that help?"

"I am not poor. I can afford to see therapists on my insurance."

"I understand, but whether or not she takes your insurance is not the point here. I am going to ask that you see her six times, once a week for six weeks. At the end of that time, call me and tell me how you feel, if you want to keep seeing her or not. If you don't feel like she is helping, I won't argue about it. You can quit going. Fair enough?"

Leigh thinks about this for a moment.

"All right, to please you I will give it a try, but I seriously doubt she will be able to help me."

"I just ask that you try, Sweetheart. I love you and I want you to be happy," Edmund says, lighting another cigarette off the first one.

Big tears form in Leigh's eyes. "I love you too, very much. You are my rock! Thank you for being there for me. Give Greg my love, too."

"Absolutely. Maybe soon you can come up and see us, take a little break?"

"Maybe. I will see."

Edmund next dials Jack's office, after mentally reminding himself not to let his emotions get the better of him. He now has a cup of coffee in front of him.

Jack picks up on the first ring, using his best baritone business voice. "Briggs Investigations. May I help you?"

"Jack, it's Edmund Harrington. How are you?

"Fine, Sir. How can I help you?" Jack winces, anticipating an awkward conversation. He sips his coffee and wishes he had some brandy in it.

"Well, I've been out of town and out of touch. I talked to Leigh a few minutes ago. She said she hasn't seen or heard from you in several weeks. I was very surprised to hear that," Edmund says, trying to keep his voice calm and neutral.

"Well, I know I should call her, but I'm sure she told you I witnessed her screaming at her mom. I hate drama. I hate raised voices and loud arguments and most of all I hate seeing women cry. They just do it to be manipulative," Jack replies evenly. "I thought Leigh was level-headed, more like a man. I was stunned to see how she treated her mother."

Deep breaths, Ed. Don't tell him off. Deep breaths.

"Jack, do you have a mother?"

"Yes, of course. I have a sister, too. I've never witnessed them fighting like Leigh and her mom."

Edmund stands up and paces, trying to calm down. He hopes the battery on his cordless phone won't die.

"Jack, I like you. I think you're a very smart young man. You're calm and steady and thoughtful and rational. You're neat and tidy. Those are all great things. You're also how old, thirty-five?"

"Yes, almost thirty-six. Why?" Jack stands up and paces, wishing the phone had a longer cord.

"Well, my situation is not so different from yours, even though I've never dated a woman. I lived for years thinking I would hold out until I found EXACTLY the right person. I had a long list of requirements, and I was damn determined not to settle. I was over 50 when it finally occurred to me that maybe that list was a mistake. Nobody is perfect. No guy would ever be perfect enough for me. I was lonely, and I hated it. No woman is going to meet all of your requirements. I suggest you sit down and make a list of all the pros and cons of dating Leigh. If you decide you really cannot live with the cons, at least go see her and have a conversation with her so she can have some closure."

Jack stares at the framed print of an 1895 map of Georgia that Leigh hung in his office.

"Well, I hear what you're saying. I've actually avoided calling her or seeing her because I couldn't quite bring myself to break up with her."

Edmund takes a deep breath and thinks, *okay, we can work with that. Steady, steady, bring the boat in gently...*

"Maybe that's good. Let me tell you what she's doing. She's seeing a psychologist, one who is actually from Augusta. Her mother is seeing the same psychologist. In a couple of weeks they are going to start getting counseling together. Leigh's mother has changed a lot recently and she wants a good relationship with Leigh. I think they are going to patch things up. So will you keep that in mind?"

"I guess. Okay," Jack says uncertainly.

"Good. I know I'm biased but I was really hoping you were the one for Leigh. I think you owe it to her to stick with her for a while. She's been through a lot lately, and she's still processing everything."

"Okay. I know you just want her to be happy."

"She's like a daughter to me. I love her," Edmund says, a little more forcefully than he meant.

Taken aback, Jack searches his mind for the appropriate response. "Leigh is very lucky to have you in her life. I will be in touch. Goodbye," Jack replies formally, before hanging up.

"Who was that?" Jack's brother William says, rubbing his eyes after a night on the guestroom futon.

"Former client. You headed back out today?" William was in town for a seminar on Y2K preparations. He was a computer genius.

"Yeah, I need to get home to Jeannie and the baby. Say, what happened with Leigh? Last time I came through you said she was awesome. Even said she might be The One."

"Well, I haven't seen her in a while. I witnessed a screaming fight she had with her mother and decided she's probably too much of a drama queen," Jack says with a sigh.

"Is that coffee?" William asks, pointing to the mug by Jack's side, on the desk.

"Yeah. There's more in the kitchen," Jack says.

William grabs the cup and drinks a big sip before putting it down and glaring at his brother.

"SHIT, that was hot. I needed the wakeup. Listen, I know I'm the younger brother and you don't think I have any sense, but I'm gonna say something you won't like so if you want to hit me, fine."

Jack, startled, furrows his brow and regards his "little" brother – who at 6'2 and 224 lbs. dwarfs him. William's hair is sticking up straight and he wears only a pair of boxer shorts and a wrinkled AC/DC tee shirt but that doesn't make him look less menacing.

William moves closer to Jack and looms over him, staring down at Jack, concern in his big brown eyes.

"You ALWAYS find some reason to break up with a woman after you sleep with her. Always. She's not a neat freak like you.

She has bad morning breath. She talks too much. She has weird friends. And on and on. I've watched you do this for YEARS. You need to seriously think about salvaging this relationship, Brother. Everything you said about Leigh was right on the money. She's beautiful, smart, clean, neat, has a good job, is a good cook, and she likes YOU."

"Why do you think that?" Jack says evenly, trying not to lose his temper.

"Why? Um, this photo?" William says, picking up a 5x7 of Jack and Leigh at the Atlanta Botanical Gardens that Jack keeps on his desk. "Or how about those?" he says, pointing to the hanging baskets of ferns on Jack's porch, clearly seen through the window. "Or how about the fact that you have a Pottery Barn catalog with pages turned down? That framed map she gave you? The stack of her business cards here on your desk?"

"Yeah, but the family drama…"

"Shit. Everybody has family drama sometimes. You holding out for an orphan?!"

"Well, her uncle did say she and her mom are going to see a psychologist, work things out."

"Well there you go. Problem being solved," William says. He goes into the guest room and returns a minute later with his wallet. He pulls out a hundred dollar bill and slaps it down on the desk in front of his brother.

"What's that for?"

"I'm going to teach you a life lesson here, Bro. You call all-out DEFCON 1 warfare and you put yourself back in the battle. You call up Leigh and tell her you're going to bring dinner over to her place tonight. You show up with some really good food, a nice bottle of wine, and maybe some flowers. You have two objectives here: one, repair your relationship, and two, get yourself laid, you sad sack of shit. Makeup sex will rock your world – which you would know if YOU EVER MADE UP with anyone. Take it from me, the old married guy."

"I don't need your money," Jack calls to William, who has padded into the adjacent kitchen.

"Yes, you DO, you cheap asshole. Don't go in there with McDonald's food and grocery store flowers," William calls back over his shoulder.

"Fuck you."

"Fuck you too. Where is your cereal? Jeez, you eat weird shit."

CHAPTER 69 – A FUNERAL

Leigh and Edmund sit in Millie's kitchen, making polite conversation with Liz's son TJ and his fiancée, Lily, around the big table, which is filled with food – deviled eggs, ham biscuits, fried chicken, green beans.

The small home was filled with friends right after the funeral, but now all the friends have left.

Leigh had never been to a black southern funeral. She didn't realize they are generally much more formal and yet more emotional.

The long day had started early. Edmund had arrived at her apartment early that morning wearing a beautiful black suit, starched white shirt, and sky blue tie. His black patent leather shoes gleamed.

"You can't wear that," he had said, studying Leigh with a critical eye after she opened the door. She looked down at her clothes, puzzled by his critical tone.

"What's wrong with this outfit? I don't have a black dress," Leigh answered. She wore black cotton slacks, an ivory silk blouse and leather flats.

"Darling, these folks dress up for funerals. You are family. You want to look appropriate. Elaine will be introducing us to folks," Edmund said, frowning.

"I have three nice churchy dresses but none are black or navy blue," Leigh argued.

"As always, Greg predicted this," Edmund said. He went out to his rental car and returned a moment later with a Macy's bag. He pulled out the garment and held it up for Leigh.

"Oh my God," Leigh said, awestruck. The sleeveless black linen dress with matching jacket was gorgeous, looking like something made by Chanel. "What size is it, though?"

It was a size 8 and it fit perfectly. At Edmund's urging, Leigh put her hair on top of her head in an elegant upswept coiffure, and added a short string of pearls. High-heeled black pumps completed the outfit.

"Much better!" Edmund said enthusiastically. "Hang on. I want to get a photo, to show Greg," he said, pulling a small camera out of his pocket.

"Do you ever go anywhere without a camera?!" Leigh said, smiling.

"Rarely."

Now Leigh smiles, thinking of the delight she felt when she looked at herself in the elegant suit. *I must remember to write dear Greg a thank you note.*

Edmund's camera comes out again, and he stands up and makes some snapshots of Leigh, TJ, and TJ's fiancé Lily.

"I swear, TJ, you look like you could be Leigh's brother. You have the same eyes as my mother. Just gorgeous," Edmund says, snapping another one.

"They are first cousins. They should look alike," Liz says as she comes into the room, smiling. Her feet are bare, although she still wears her funeral dress. She holds a sweating glass of iced tea in her hand.

"Can't believe it was only 70 out there, in November," TJ says. "A cool day, for sure." He finishes off the deviled egg on the plate he is holding, which had been filled with fried chicken, ham biscuits, and a large helping of peach cobbler.

"Well, that church was so packed you'd never hear me saying it was a cool day," Liz says with a chuckle.

The service had been longer than Liz had wanted. Her mother had left instructions, though. All Millie's favorite hymns were played.

Leigh, used to the quiet dignity of the Episcopal church, had found herself in tears when the soloist sang "There Will Be Peace in the Valley." By the time the last hymn was played, "Walk Around Heaven," she found herself humming along, and dabbing at her eyes with Edmund's handkerchief.

Edmund had wondered how Liz would explain the presence of him and Leigh but Liz had handled it. "This is my brother Edmund and my niece Leigh," she had said gracefully, introducing them after the service. "They drove over from Atlanta." Nobody had said a word, although one lady had grabbed Edmund and hugged him to her ample bosom. "Praise the holy name of Jesus!" she had exclaimed.

"Yes M'am," Edmund had replied, smiling.

At the graveside, Liz had asked for a few Bible verses to be read, but then, she addressed the crowd. "My mother is not in this world anymore, but she is with Jesus. So I want to sing the song she loved most in the world. I know she will hear us." She looked at the four older ladies who were from the choir and nodded. One of them, a strong alto, started singing "Oh Happy

Day." Liz, not a singer, but with a serviceable alto, sang along, holding Edmund's hand. Leigh sang along too, remembering happy times when Clarice would sing it around the house.

Now Liz looks around the small kitchen and smiles. "Edmund and Leigh, I want to thank you for coming over. It really meant a lot to me."

"We're your family. Of course we would be here," Edmund says. He has removed his suit coat and hung it up. His shirtsleeves are rolled up, and he is grateful the windows are open in the small house.

"I have never seen so much food in my life," Leigh said. "Come on, Lily, let's get it put up," she says, rising from her chair.

"I'll help too," TJ says. "Mom looks exhausted. Uncle, would you make her sit and rest for a bit, maybe on the porch?"

"Sure," Edmund says. "I like hearing you say uncle."

"I like saying it," TJ says with a smile. He is a tall, lanky man, very light-skinned. Edmund saw a photo of Liz's late husband in the family room, and noted that TJ looks very similar.

Leigh and Lily start cleaning.

378

Edmund and Liz open the door to the back porch.

"How are you holding up?" Edmund asks, as they settle into chairs. Edmund lights a Marlboro and inhales deeply.

Liz sits in a rocking chair and rocks slightly. "Well, it was a shock. A blessing too, though. She wasn't sick. She didn't have to go to a nursing home. She didn't break her hip or have a stroke. All in all, a good death, if there is such a thing."

"Yes, of course there is such a thing. Mother's death was the same. She didn't suffer. Of course, when Travis called to tell me about it, he couldn't stop sobbing. The shock is the worst part. Not getting to say goodbye."

Liz nods, sniffing and dabbing at her eyes with a tissue. "Yes, I wish I could have said goodbye, but I always told her I loved her right before she went to bed. You know, she always said to me, "One day, I will be in heaven with your fathers – both of them – and I can tell Nate what a wonderful blessing it was to be your mother.""

Edmund nods, his eyes filling.

"I know you are a psychic and a medium. Can you make contact with Millie, or Rose, or your dads?" he asks, curious.

Liz looks sad. "I usually cannot make contact with people close to me. I don't know why. However, when I found Mother last week I looked up and saw her, floating in the corner of the room with Rose, both smiling. I got this message, so clearly: Our sweet daughter! We love you so much."

"Really? Amazing," Edmund said softly.

"I heard their voices in my head, clear as day."

"That's wonderful," Edmund says, rocking.

"I also had a visit not long ago from the spirit of my grandmother Elizabeth. Rose's father was a white boy who raped Elizabeth. Terrible. At least now I know, though. I will tell Leigh about it one day."

"Wow," is all Edmund can think to say.

They sit and rock for a moment, watching the shadows lengthen across the back yard.

Edmund tells Liz about the big confrontation between Leigh and her mother. Liz just nods.

"I knew when I saw Leigh this morning that there was something wrong. She was twisting the fabric of her jacket in her fist again; that's what she does when she is anxious."

Edmund thinks for a moment. "You're right. I never thought about it, but you're absolutely right. She grabs the hem of her shirt or sweater or jacket and twists it around. Wow."

Liz stops rocking and looks at Edmund. "Did Leigh go see the psychologist yet?"

"How did you know?" he starts to say, then smiles. "She has been once, yes. I asked her in the car driving over here how it went and she just said fine. She didn't want to discuss it, but that's okay."

"You know, I have sensed all these years that Peggy Harrington was a very unhappy woman, constantly anxious about other people's opinions of her. She's not the terrible person Leigh thinks she hates, though. Peggy is now in love, and her life is changing radically. She and Leigh will be able to mend fences and have a great relationship. I know it. I'm glad about it."

Edmund rocks for a moment. "Are you saying that as wishful thinking or do you have some psychic information to go on?!"

Liz smiles. "I don't know how I know things, Ed, but I just know things sometimes. God has richly blessed me with the ability to know and understand things most people cannot."

Leigh comes out on the porch carrying a small glass of tea. "I am having such fun getting to know TJ and Lily. I am going to get us tickets to some Braves games, and Lily said she will teach me to crochet, too. I've always wanted to learn."

"That's wonderful," Elaine exclaims. "Sit down for a few minutes, Leigh. There's something important I want to explain to you."

Leigh sits down and takes a sip of tea. "Okay."

"Leigh, you are my niece and I love you. I already feel a closeness to you, like a mother/daughter closeness."

"I feel the same way!" Leigh says, her eyes shining.

"Well, I am happy about that, but I don't want you to think of me as a mother substitute, sweetheart. I am an aunt, not your mother. That's okay. You already have a mother. I know you're very upset with her, but you need to put the past behind you, and forge a new relationship with the new Peggy. She is changing a lot. She loves you very much. You will be able to love her back, once you let go of the past and forgive, like we talked about before."

Leigh casts her eyes down while Liz talks, and she shakes her head slightly. "You don't understand."

"No, not fully. I was blessed to have two wonderful mothers who loved me. However, I know this much. I know that if you will go to counseling with Peggy and really do the emotional work, you will have a terrific mother daughter relationship one day soon. She wants that very much. You have to forgive her, though."

"Forgive her? How?"

"Do you want Jack to forgive you?"

Puzzled, Leigh looks at Edmund, who just shrugs his shoulders.

"Well yes, of course. How do you know about Jack? Did Edmund tell you?"

"Not everything, but again, I just know things a lot of times."

"How can I forgive someone who did what Peggy did, who has always been so awful to me?" Leigh spits out the words, anger and anguish in her tone.

Liz shakes her head slightly, then gets up from her chair and goes to sit in the porch swing. She pats the empty space beside her, and Leigh gets up to go sit next to her aunt. Wordlessly, Liz puts her arms around Leigh's shoulders, and they rock for a moment. Then Liz turns slightly so she is looking Leigh in the eye.

"Leigh, I want to tell you something very, very important. This is something I know a lot about. Forgiveness is a gift you give yourself. It cleans out the darkness in your soul caused by holding onto grudges. It makes everything light and sunny and beautiful. It's a process, though. You need to ask God to help you and be honest with the therapist. She will help you. Forgiveness can heal you, make you new again."

You're a better person than I am, Leigh thinks, breaking eye contact to stare into her lap. *I can't let go of nearly thirty years of anger in the blink of an eye.*

Liz doesn't say a word, but she can hear Leigh's thoughts clearly.

Liz recalls something a wise teacher had said to her once about children. They learn to behave by watching how their parents behave.

"Leigh, do you remember your grandmother, not Rose, but the other one, Peggy's mother?"

Leigh looks up, puzzled. "She died when I was a kid, but yes, I remember her. She was not a nice person."

"Why do you say that?" Liz asks, although she knows the answer.

Leigh shifts uncomfortably in her seat and suddenly wishes she were home in her bathrobe in front of the TV.

"Well, she was always super critical of Mother. She was also a terrible racist."

"I see. So she was likely a big influence on your mother, don't you think?"

Leigh is silent for a while, studying on that. She vividly remembers how vicious and cutting Matilda had been to Peggy, and how she was always saying the maids were lazy and stole from her.

"I see your point. But Peggy was a big influence on me, yet I am not like her."

Edmund, who had been listening to this exchange with fascination, now spoke up. "Yes, but Leigh, you had Clarice, remember? She was like a mother to you."

Leigh looks out at the rain now falling on the green fields. Clarice was the one who wiped her tears away, who read stories to her, who went to school programs regularly, who

taught her how to cook, and how to love soul music. *Peggy probably didn't have a Clarice in her life, or she would have been nicer. Wow, I guess I should have seen that long before now,* she thinks.

Edmund gets up and stretches. "Well, I wish we could stay longer but I have to go back to Atlanta tonight to catch an early flight tomorrow."

"Thank you for making the trip," Liz says, standing up to hug him. "I should let you and Leigh know, I am leaving in January for a long trip with my friends Connie and Ann. We used to teach together. We are going to go to Rome, Paris, Athens, and London. We're just going to see everything we can, ride the train everywhere, and have fun. We will be back sometime in February. I've wanted to do this for a long time, but I didn't want to leave Mother."

Leigh hugs her tightly. "That sounds like a fantastic trip! I am so glad for you! You deserve a break!"

Liz smiles. "I will keep a journal, and you can read all about our adventures."

"Awesome! Can't wait," Leigh replies.

"I will send you a marvelous camera for the trip. I want to see all the photos!" Edmund says, beaming as he hugs her again.

CHAPTER 70 – JACK IS BACK

When Leigh gets home it is 7:34 p.m. Edmund drops her off and heads back to his hotel. Leigh goes inside and listens to the answering machine message from Jack.

"Um, hey, I was hoping you might be home tonight. I'd like to come over and talk."

Leigh plays two other messages from him, then picks up the phone.

An hour later, Leigh has changed into shorts and a tee shirt, washed her face, and is sipping a gingerale, when Jack knocks on the door. She has decided that his voice on the machine sounds cold so he is going to break up with her.

When she opens the door, though, she is shocked. Jack stands there holding a long white box from a florist, a bottle of wine, and a bag which clearly came from Godiva chocolates.

"Hey. Can I come in?" Jack says, grinning.

"Um, yeah, yes, of course," Leigh stammers, moving aside. Jack walks over to the table and puts everything down, then turns and looks at Leigh. He takes a deep breath.

"I'm sorry, Leigh. I've been an idiot. My brother William was in town a couple of days ago. I told him I, uh, hadn't seen you in a while, and he and I talked. He's happily married. He told me I should make amends with you. I realized he is a smart guy, and I am an idiot. I already said that. Sorry."

"It's okay. Uh -- I was at a funeral all day, at Liz's house. Her mother died. I didn't even think about checking messages," Leigh responds, noting that Jack has shadows under his eyes and fine worry wrinkles she has not noticed before.

Not knowing what else to do, Leigh walks over to him and puts her arms around his waist, then leans in to rest her head on his shoulder. His arms come around her and he gently lifts her chin away from his chest and kisses her deeply.

Thank you, God, Leigh thinks.

CHAPTER 71 – NEW BEGINNINGS

Weeks later and it's mid December in Atlanta. The temperatures have calmed down to the 50's most afternoons, and Christmas is a breath away.

Peggy rushes around the handsome three story brick townhouse, anxiously checking the flowers and making sure everything looks perfect. Her antiques are displayed beautifully and the decorator helped her with the muted color scheme of neutrals with pops of blue.

The house is filled with the light pouring in from the windows.

Bain smiles at her.

"Hey, quit doing that. Calm down. They will be here any minute. Everything is FINE," he says, grabbing her from behind and kissing her lightly on the neck.

"Do you really think this is a good idea, doing it this way?" Peggy asks, turning and looking into his eyes.

"You wanted a no-fuss wedding with just close family around, and that's what we're doing."

They had gotten married very quietly that morning at the Fulton County Courthouse, with just Bain's brother and sister-in-law in attendance. All afternoon, Peggy has fussed over the party details, even though there are only ten people invited.

Now, Peggy takes a deep breath, and flicks an imaginary piece of lint off of Bain's beautiful dark blue suit. She wears a tea length ivory organza gown with cap sleeves and an illusion neck. Her hair is arranged in a simple chignon and the only jewelry besides her engagement ring set is a pair of tiny diamond studs in her ears.

The invitations said simply, *Housewarming Party*, but Peggy called each of her children to make sure they would be there, and Bain's family is represented by his brother and wife. His parents are in an assisted living home and can't make the journey, and Beatrice sent her regrets.

Leigh had been hesitant about attending, but after several therapy sessions with Peggy, their relationship is on a new footing, and she doesn't dread them. Leigh and Peggy even have cordial phone conversations. Peggy is happy, in love, and willing to talk about everything, even the painful events of the past.

Bubba and his wife and daughters arrive first, parking the minivan and unbuckling both toddlers.

Leigh and Jack arrive next, in Jack's truck. Leigh introduces Jack and her brother and they talk about the military, their heads together, beers in hand. Leigh is very pleased they like each other.

Leigh and Missy corral the twins and admire the elegant townhouse and its furnishings, and make polite small talk with Bain's brother Simon and his wife Brenda.

The toddlers keep everyone following along behind so they don't break anything.

After everyone is assembled in the living room, the twins safely in their parents' arms, Bain makes sure the champagne is ready and calls Peggy to his side.

"I am very, very fortunate to have this beautiful lady by my side, and I wanted to let everyone know we got married this morning. The real reason for this little party is to celebrate that."

Bubba and Leigh exchange looks and smiles. They suspected this was coming but had not let on.

"Congratulations Mom!" they say simultaneously.

After everyone hugs and exclaims over Peggy's ring, Bain passes around glasses and offers a toast. "To the most beautiful woman in the world, and her exceptional offspring. Proud to be joining the family!"

Everyone sips their champagne.

Peggy nods. "We are delaying the honeymoon until after Christmas, but I wanted to keep one tradition going, and toss the bouquet."

Peggy takes the small bouquet of roses from the side table and looks at Leigh and Jack. Leigh's eyebrows are raised but she is smiling. Peggy turns around but looks over her shoulder.

"My darling daughter, CATCH!" Peggy says, and tosses the bouquet to a surprised Leigh, who easily catches it.

Everyone laughs.

It is the new beginning of everything Leigh has always wanted.

THE END

AFTERWORD

I have been a writer for a long time but **Ghosts in the Garden City** came about because I kept writing novels that didn't quite work, and yet I didn't give up. I knew there was a novel in me that would come out one day and be entertaining and a page turner. I am not trying to write great literature, just a good story.

I am blessed to have friends and family members who believe in me and were willing to help me.

Joanne Jones Cheng, my lifelong friend, read the manuscript and offered excellent critical advice early on. She has read all my writings, bless her, and been willing to take the time to give very detailed and helpful feedback.

My mother Elva Hasty Thompson read the manuscript and said it was as good as anything on Amazon. That's high praise from someone who has read 2-4 books a week for more than seventy years.

I like to think the book will appeal to men as well as women. Jack Wheeler is a retired attorney from Knoxville and an old family friend. I had almost decided to just shelve the manuscript of **Ghosts in the Garden City**, but Jack read it and offered encouragement at a time when I badly needed it.

My old friend Jeff Joslin has been a constant supporter for years, and his advice and encouragement are always welcome. We have known each other since elementary school. Jeff put me in touch with Stephanie Wolfe, a freelance editor in Los Angeles who didn't know me at all. Stephanie readily and helpfully took a deep dive into the manuscript and offered advice and feedback which really trimmed the excess and pulled the story out and put it front and center. She is a writer herself and understands the process and the way to help authors. I am very grateful to her.

Linda Harris is my first cousin but has also become a real friend in recent years. She read the entire manuscript and was very encouraging. Her top-notch photography skills came in very handy when I was designing the covers, and the beautiful Cedar Plantation in Acworth Georgia was the perfect choice for the cover images. (Cedar Plantation is a great wedding and event venue, just fyi.)

My mother and my son Michael Thompson live with me and they are always my staunchest supporters, while also paying a steep price for their love and loyalty. My mother and my son put up with me writing for long stretches of time and ignoring them. My dog Lola puts up with postponed or hurried walks. While I was writing this, countless pots of food on the stove got burned. Beds went un-made. Groceries went un-bought. Writing is a solitary process and there is always a price to be paid.

Finally, I should explain a few things about the city of my birth, Augusta Georgia. It's far more than a setting for the beautiful and storied golf tournament you see on TV every April. It's known as The Garden City, hence the title of this book.

I was born in the old University Hospital on July 4th – I always say I wanted to make a big entrance, and I did. The doctor who delivered me, Dr. Walter "Curly" Watson, unwrapped the cord from around my neck and gave me life, and some might say he set me loose on the world. Dr. Watson also delivered my brother and many of my cousins. I am proud to be one of more than 15,000 "Watson Babies." He delivered babies well into his 90's and lived to be 102.

Augusta is a gracious southern city with a rich history, filled with wonderful people from all backgrounds and walks of life. It's the birthplace and home of the late singer James Brown. It was the childhood home of Woodrow Wilson. Augusta boasts a renowned medical college. It's far more than just the home of The Master's Tournament.

I hope this book didn't give outsiders the impression that all Augustans are snobby and intolerant. Nothing could be further from the truth. (I suspect that only a few Augustans are snobby and intolerant, and to be fair, all small towns everywhere have some of those folks.)

My dad grew up in Hephzibah, Georgia, just down the road from Augusta. I have cousins who still live in Augusta.

We left Augusta when I was 8 and moved to Knoxville, Tennessee. My parents moved back to Augusta in 1991. My father, Anthony Thompson, died there in 1996 after being diagnosed with cancer.

My mother left Augusta and moved here to Atlanta in 2005 to help me with my children.

I last visited Augusta in 2005, for a family wedding. Augusta may have changed a lot since then, which is part of why I set Ghosts in the Garden City in 1996.

Full disclosure: my mother is a member of the DAR (Daughters of the American Revolution). I am also eligible to be in the Huguenot Society (Dad's side), Colonial Dames, and the First Families of Virginia. My ancestors are truly interesting to me, but like Leigh I am not the debutante or Junior League type. I recently did one of those DNA tests and found out I am .6% African, which is one of the things that inspired me to write Ghosts in the Garden City.

I am proud to be a genetic mutt, and proud that the south I love is evolving into a far more diverse place than ever before. My great-grandparents would likely be astonished to know I have close friends who are of different races and a son who is mixed race. My south is far different than the place they knew.

If you liked **Ghosts in the Garden City**, please leave a positive review on Amazon.

Thanks for reading this far. You can email me at dethompson62@yahoo.com and/or check out my blog The Crab Chronicles. I will announce on there when my next book is ready to go.

Happy reading!

Dee Thompson

July 2019

Made in the USA
Columbia, SC
21 August 2019